立正大学文学部学術叢書 10

LITERATURE AS SCIENCE:
A Statistical Analysis of the Structures of the Works of Elizabeth Gaskell in Quest of the Absolute Interpretations 1848-59

科学としての文学:
統計的構造分析によるエリザベス・ギャスケル作品の絶対解釈探求 1848-59

Tatsuhiro OHNO　大野 龍浩

KADOKAWA

LITERATURE AS SCIENCE:
A Statistical Analysis of the Structures of
the Works of Elizabeth Gaskell in Quest of
the Absolute Interpretations 1848-59

Tatsuhiro OHNO

TABLE OF CONTENTS

TABLE OF CONTENTS 3

PREFACE 7

LIST OF TABLES 9

LIST OF FIGURES 10

LIST OF ABBREVIATIONS 12

INTRODUCTION 14

CHAPTER 1 Chronology and Statistics: Objective Understanding of
    Authorial Meaning 21
  1.1. Introduction 21
  1.2. The Norm of Criticism: Authorial Meaning 22
    1.2.1. Hirsch and Eagleton 22
    1.2.2. Meaning and Significance 22
    1.2.3. Interpretation and Criticism 24
    1.2.4. Husserlian Phenomenology 25
    1.2.5. Language and Meaning 27
    1.2.6. Historicism 28
    1.2.7. Author and Text: Is the Text the Reflection of the Author's Meaning? 30
    1.2.8. Hermeneutical Circle 32
    1.2.9. Creative Reading 33
    1.2.10. Urauthor, Meaning, and Urinterpretation 34
    1.2.11. Suitability of Hirschian Theory 38
  1.3. The Sanger-Kroeber Method 40
    1.3.1. Sanger's Approach 40
    1.3.2. Kroeber's Approach 42
    1.3.3. Merits and Demerits 43
    1.3.4. Summary 46
  1.4. Conclusion 48

CHAPTER 2 *Mary Barton*: Who Is the Central Protagonist? 51
  2.1. Introduction 51
  2.2. Construction of Chronology 53
  2.3. Comprehensive Chronology 58
    2.3.1. Characters' Appearance Rate 59
    2.3.2. Ternary Structure 63
    2.3.3. Mary's Constant Appearance 64
    2.3.4. Interaction of Plots: Jem's Role 68
    2.3.5. Time Sequence 70

    2.3.6. Narratorial Intervention 72
    2.3.7. Place of Action 76
  2.4. Historical Author's Confession 79
  2.5. Concluding Remarks: John or Mary? 82

CHAPTER 3 *Ruth*: Is the Heroine's Martyrdom Inconsistent with the Plot? 89
  3.1. Introduction 89
  3.2. Comprehensive Chronology 92
  3.3. Ruth's Interaction with Three Families 97
  3.4. Dramatic Irony 105
  3.5. Conclusion 110

CHAPTER 4 *North and South*: The Novel of Two Themes 113
  4.1. Introduction 113
  4.2. Comprehensive Chronology 114
  4.3. Characters' Frequency of Appearance 116
  4.4. Shift of Location 120
    4.4.1. Location Shift in the Narrative 121
    4.4.2. Location Shift in Milton 125
  4.5. Plot Interaction 135
  4.6. Conclusion 143

CHAPTER 5 A Topic-Modelling Analysis of Christianity in *The Life of Charlotte Brontë* 145
  5.1. Introduction: Structure and Religion 145
  5.2. Topic Models 147
  5.3. Top 19 Keywords 150
    5.3.1. Topic Modelling Analysis 150
    5.3.2. AntConc Analysis 158
    5.3.3. Unique Discoveries 162
  5.4. Results of Contextual Categorisation 162
    5.4.1. Overview 162
    5.4.2. Previous Studies 169
    5.4.3. Religion/Morals 173
  5.5. Conclusion: Gaskell as a Christian Missionary 184

CHAPTER 6 *Lois the Witch*: The Story of Christian Fortitude 187
  6.1. Introduction 187
  6.2. Chronology and Statistical Comparison 188
    6.2.1. Chronology for *Lois the Witch* 188
    6.2.2. Statistical Comparison between Upham's Text and Gaskell's 189
  6.3. Comparison with the Source 191
    6.3.1. The Atmosphere of New England 192
    6.3.2. Witch Trials 195
    6.3.3. Victims with Christian Fortitude 200

  6.3.4. The Penitent 201
  6.3.5. The Rationalist Interpretation of the Witch Panic 205
  6.3.6. Summary 208
 6.4. The Structure of the Story 210
 6.5. Conclusion 219

CONCLUSION 221

APPENDIX 1 Comprehensive Chronologies 225
 The Comprehensive Chronology for *Mary Barton* (1848) 226
 The Comprehensive Chronology for *Ruth* (1853) 235
 The Comprehensive Chronology for *North and South* (1854-55) 243
 The Comprehensive Chronology for *Lois the Witch* (1859) 257

APPENDIX 2 Characters' Correlation Diagrams for in Gaskell's Fiction 261
 Characters' Correlation Diagram for *Mary Barton* 262
 Characters' Correlation Diagram for *Ruth* 263
 Characters' Correlation Diagram for *North and South* 264
 Characters' Correlation Diagram for *Lois the Witch* 265

APPENDIX 3 Gaskell's Manipulation of Upham's *First Lecture on Witchcraft* 267

WORKS CITED 319
INDEX 336

PREFACE

This study is Part 1 of an effort to detect Elizabeth Gaskell's intended meanings for her major works, including *Mary Barton*, *Ruth*, *North and South*, *The Life of Charlotte Brontë*, and *Lois the Witch*, through statistical analysis of the structure of each text. Its purport is to explore a singular, definitive interpretation of each work, attributed not to the historical author but rather to the author construct, or the urauthor who emerges through meticulous analysis of the text's structure. A similar analysis of her other major works, including *Cranford*, *Sylvia's Lovers*, *Cousin Phillis*, and *Wives and Daughters*, shall be conducted in Part 2, which is planned for publication in the near future.

The theoretical basis for this approach stems from the intentionalist hermeneutists' claim that a literary work requires a standard interpretation; otherwise, it invites critical anarchy, or predomination of subjectivism. They distinguish "textual meaning" which is immutable once a text is produced from "textual significance" which is changeable depending on readers or eras. They also differentiate the author construct, or a functional figure the reader creates in interpreting a text, from the historical author as person, or the real author, who may not always be reliable. The goal of a standard interpretation, therefore, is to uncover the textual meaning ascribed to the author construct.

The methods selected to achieve this objective fulfilment of this purpose are twofold: (a) a detailed chronology for each work of fiction and (b) the quantification of key structural elements, such as characters' frequency of appearance, the sequence of time, shifts in setting, and the author's choice of words. These techniques help us take a comprehensive, bird's-eye view of each text's structural framework.

The statistical investigation discloses the meaning of the Gaskell construct for *Mary Barton* is to draw a love story rather than a Condition-of-England novel; for *Ruth*, to describe the eponymous heroine's Christian integrity through her interactions with the three families, each representing "shallowness," "conscience," and "hypocrisy"; for *North and South*, to advance the political and love plots in parallel; for *The Life of Charlotte Brontë*, to focus on Charlotte's piety through the depiction of her life in Haworth; and for *Lois the Witch*, to depict Lois's Christian fortitude rather than the public fear of the witchcraft delusion.

While subjective readings may inevitably be replaced by others over time, an interpretation grounded in objective evidence will endure. The findings disclosed here are expected to stand the test of time for the benefit of future readers, since they are based on a thorough and rigorous inspection of Gaskell's works to ensure an accurate interpretation of her intended meanings.

This research is an expanded edition of my MLitt dissertation submitted to the University of Bristol in 2007. I would like to express my sincere gratitude to my supervisors Dr Rowena Fowler and Dr Tom Mason for their invaluable guidance and support; to my external examiner Dr Jane Spencer of the University of Exeter and my internal examiner Dr Myra Stokes for their thorough reading of my dissertation and their generous feedback; and also to Dr John Lee of the Bristol English Department, who has been sympathetic to my situation since our first meeting in Fukuoka, Japan, on 11 October 1999. Last but not least, my gratitude goes to my current institution, the Faculty of Letters at Rissho University, for agreeing to publish this study as the 10th volume of their academic research series.

This book is dedicated to my late father, whose reticent encouragement and financial support were invaluable throughout my solitary study at the University of Bristol.

28 January 2025

Tatsuhiro OHNO

LIST OF TABLES

Table 1.1. Distinction between Criticism and Interpretation 34

Table 2.1. Characters Focused in *Mary Barton* 61
Table 2.2. Top Twenty Dates in Order of Allocated Page Percentage in *Mary Barton* ... 71
Table 2.3. The Narrators' Appearance Rates in Gaskell's Novels 73
Table 2.4. The Narrator's Direct Remarks on John and Mary 74
Table 2.5. Places of Action in Order of Allocated Page Percentage 77
Table 2.6. Occurrences in Barton's House in *Mary Barton* 78
Table 2.7. Appearance Rates of Top Three Characters in Gaskell's Novels 87

Table 3.1. Families Focused in *Ruth* 98
Table 3.2. Protagonists Focused in *Ruth* 98

Table 4.1. Top Ten Rates of Characters' Appearance in *North and South* 117
Table 4.2. Scene Allocation in *Mary Barton* 126
Table 4.3. Characters' Movement in Milton in *North and South* 130
Table 4.4. Five Characters' Frequency of Visits in *North and South* 130

Table 5.1. A Sample of "Keys" Generated by MALLET (Extract) 150
Table 5.2. A Sample of "Composition Table" Generated by MALLET (Extract) 151
Table 5.3. Top Five Topics in Each of Ten MALLET Operations 154
Table 5.4. Prominent Topics and Their Most Frequently Used Words in *LCB* 156
Table 5.5. Probability of Distribution of Top 2 Topics of Each of 10 MALLET Operations for *LCB* 158
Table 5.6. Frequency of Appearance of the Brontë Family Names in *LCB* 159
Table 5.7. Frequency of Occurrence of Geographical Place Names in *LCB* 160
Table 5.8. Top 11 Topic-Modelling Keywords and Their Numbers of Examples in *LCB* 163
Table 5.9. Top-Ranked Topic-Model Keywords Appearing in the Bible in *LCB* 164
Table 5.10. Summary of the Categorisation of the 2,795 Examples of the 11 Topic-Modelling Keywords in *LCB* 165
Table 5.11. Contextual Categorisation of the Total 2,795 Examples of the Top 11 Topic-Modelling Keywords in *LCB* 176
Table 5.12. Categorisation of the 271 Examples of the "Religion/Morals" group in the Topic-Modelling Analysis of *LCB* 178
Table 5.13. Characters Associated with Sub-Categories of the "Religion/Morals" Group in the Topic-Modelling Analysis of *LCB* 182

Table 6.1. Comparison between the Two Texts in *Lois the Witch* A 198
Table 6.2. Comparison between the Two Texts in *Lois the Witch* B 199
Table 6.3. Page Allocation in *Lois the Witch* 210
Table 6.4. Protagonists Focused in *Lois the Witch* 211

LIST OF FIGURES

Fig. 0.1. Intentionalist vs Anti-Intentionalist 15
Fig. 0.2. Critical Anarchy 17

Fig. 2.1. Characters' Frequency of Appearance in *Mary Barton* (Percent) 62
Fig. 2.2. Characters' Frequency of Appearance in *Mary Barton* (Times) 62
Fig. 2.3. Scene Percentage in *Mary Barton* 64
Fig. 2.4. Trade Union members drawing lots for the murder of Harry Carson (Web) 65
Fig. 2.5. Image of Plot Flow in *Mary Barton* 67
Fig. 2.6. Monthly Sequence in *Mary Barton* 70
Fig. 2.7. Daily Sequence in *Mary Barton* 71

Fig. 3.1. Characters' Frequency of Appearance in *Ruth* 97
Fig. 3.2. Image of Plots' Flow in *Ruth* 103

Fig. 4.1. Characters' Frequency of Appearance in *North and South* 117
Fig. 4.2. Frequency of Appearance of Top Three Characters and Nicholas Higgins in *North and South* 118
Fig. 4.3. Shift of Location in *North and South* A 121
Fig. 4.4. Shift of Location in *North and South* B 122
Fig. 4.5. Margaret's Geographical Movement in *North and South* 123
Fig. 4.6. Shift of Location in Milton in *North and South* 126
Fig. 4.7. Modified Shift of Location in Milton in *North and South* A 127
Fig. 4.8. Modified Shift of Location in Milton in *North and South* B 127
Fig. 4.9. Plot Interaction in *North and South* 136
Fig. 4.10. "Oh, do not use violence! He is one man, and you are many" (*NS* 178). (Web) 137

Fig. 5.1. Blei's Image of Topic Model ("Probabilistic" 78) 148
Fig. 5.2. Basic Idea of a Topic-Model Document 149
Fig. 5.3. The Frequency of Occurrence of the Brontë Family Members in *LCB* 161
Fig. 5.4. The Frequency of Occurrence of Geographical Place Names in *LCB* 161
Fig. 5.5. Categorisation of the 2,795 Examples of the 11 Topic-Modelling Keywords in *LCB* 166
Fig. 5.6. Categorisation of the 271 Examples of the "Religion/Morals" group in the Topic-Modelling Analysis of *LCB* 179
Fig. 5.7. Characters Associated with Sub-Categories of the "Religion/Morals" Group in the Topic-Modelling Analysis of *LCB* 181
Fig. 5.8. Characters' Belief in the Next World Depicted in the "Faith" Sub-Category in the Contextual Analysis of the Top Topic-Modelling Keywords of *LCB* 182

Fig. 6.1. Gaskell's Quotation from Upham's First Lecture in *Lois the Witch* (Page) ······ 189
Fig. 6.2. Gaskell's Quotation from Upham's First Lecture in *Lois the Witch* (Segment) ·· 190
Fig. 6.3. Characters' Frequency of Appearance in *Lois the Witch* ······································ 212
Fig. 6.4. Lois's Christian Fortitude in *Lois the Witch* ·· 213

LIST OF ABBREVIATIONS

Brontë Letters	Smith, Margaret, editor. *The Letters of Charlotte Brontë: with a Selection of Letters by Family and Friends*. Vols. 1–3. Clarendon, 1995–2004.
CB	Charlotte Brontë
CJEBH?	Sutherland, John. *Can Jane Eyre Be Happy?: More Puzzles in Classic Fiction*. Oxford UP, 1997.
CP	*Cousin Phillis and Other Tales*
Dickens's Letters	Storey, Graham, et al., editors. *The Letters of Charles Dickens*. Vol. 6–10, The Pilgrim Edition, Clarendon, 1988–98.
EG	Elizabeth Gaskell
Further Letters	Chapple, John, and Alan Shelston, editors. *Further Letters of Mrs Gaskell*. Manchester UP, 2000.
IHAM	Sutherland, John. *Is Heathcliff a Murderer?: Puzzles in 19th-Century Fiction*. Oxford UP, 1996.
LCB	*The Life of Charlotte Brontë*
Letters	Chapple, J. A. V. and Arthur Pollard, editors. *The Letters of Mrs. Gaskell*. Manchester UP, 1966.
LW	Upham, Charles W. *Lectures on Witchcraft: Comprising a History of the Delusion in Salem in 1692*. Carter, Hendee and Babcock, 1831.
MB	*Mary Barton*
NS	*North and South*
Observation	Sharps, John Geoffrey. *Mrs. Gaskell's Observation and Invention: A Study of Her Non-Biographic Works*. Linden, 1970.
RU	*Ruth*
Salem Witchcraft	Upham, Charles W. *Salem Witchcraft: With an Account of Salem Village and a History of Opinions on Witchcraft and Kindred Subjects*. 1867. New York: Dover, 2000.

sc(s).	Scene(s)
Themes	Duthie, Enid L. *The Themes of Elizabeth Gaskell*. London: Macmillan, 1980.
WD	*Wives and Daughters*

INTRODUCTION

This dissertation is Part 1 of an attempt to detect Elizabeth Gaskell's authorial meanings for her major works, including *Mary Barton*, *Ruth*, *North and South*, *The Life of Charlotte Brontë*, and *Lois the Witch*, through statistical analyses of the structure of each text, the best objective means. The same attempt on her other major works, such as *Cranford*, *Sylvia's Lovers*, *Cousin Phillis*, and *Wives and Daughters*, shall be carried out in Part 2 of my study to be published in the near future.

Is there any absolute interpretation for Gaskell's works? This dissertation started from this simple question. Many people believe that there is no correct interpretation in literature, which intrinsically demands a variety of readings. If our interpretation is only one of such readings, however, do not our time, energy, and effort spent to seek it out look vain? I myself would like to produce "one and only one correct interpretation" (Juhl, *Interpretation* 238) if possible.

This view is shared by some hermeneutists, such as E. D. Hirsch, Jr., P. D. Juhl, and William Irwin, called "Intentionalist." They insist literature requires standard interpretation, without which it invites critical confusion. They point out two constituents of a text: "significance," which may change once it is produced, and "meaning," which does not (Hirsch, *Validity* 8). Textual significance allows a plurality of readings; textual meaning represents what the author intends to communicate. In addition, intentionalists draw our attention to the two types of authors: "an actual historical agent who produces a text" and "a figure we construct in interpreting that text" (Irwin, *Intentionalist Interpretation* 28). Irwin insists, "it is not the author as person with whom we are concerned but the author as a particular mental construct, the urauthor, and it is through our conception of the urauthor that we seek meaning" (*Intentionalist Interpretation* 112). Some factors unconsciously incorporated into a text by "the historical author as person" are, in fact, of conscious insertion by "the author construct." Accordingly, standard interpretation is the interpretation intended by the author construct, and its target is the "meaning" of his/her text.

Irwin emphasizes the possibility of absolute interpretation by observing,

The correct interpretation is, of course, the one that reproduces the meaning of the text, i.e., the author's intended communication. [. . .] Any interpretation that exactly and completely captures the author's intended communication would be a definitive interpretation. (*Intentionalist Interpretation* 62)

If there is one definitive, or absolute, interpretation, then the next question is how it can be searched for. The process must be carried out by as objective a method

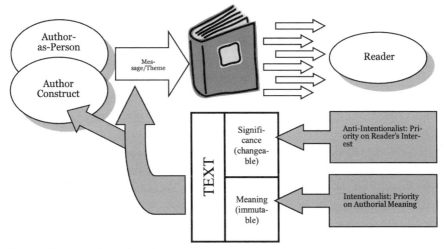

Fig. 0.1. Intentionalist vs Anti-Intentionalist

as possible; otherwise, the interpretation discovered falls into one of many possible readings. "Criticism" can be subjective since its primary concern is to read a text out of critics' interest. "Whereas interpretation is rigorously objective and can be judged by objective standards," Irwin states, "criticism is less rigorously objective and can, to some extent, be judged by subjective standards" (*Intentionalist Interpretation* 118).

The most objective method for the detection of authorial meaning should be statistical investigation into the key structural elements of fiction along with chronological inspection of the plot. The meaning of an author construct is fundamentally conveyed through structural devices within a text, as Irwin observes, "Texts act as indicators of meanings" (*Intentionalist Interpretation* 64); "the meaning of a text is the author's intended communication" (*Intentionalist Interpretation* 112). Therefore, if the values of such essential formal elements as frequency of characters' appearance, passage of time, and shift of places could be clarified through statistical quantification, the outcome should offer one of the most objective hints for identifying the author's design for creation. If its validity could be proved by careful examination of the text, the authorial meaning should be detected at the highest level of accuracy.

Modelled after C. P. Sanger's chronological analysis of the structure of *Wuthering Heights* and Karl Kroeber's statistical investigation into styles in fiction,[1] a com-

---

[1] "Statistical data is often the key to innovative and authentic research" (Murase 110). The statistical analyses by Brian Vickers, J. F. Burrows, Franco Moretti, and Michaela Mahlberg also provide their insightful examples. Burrows observes that "statistical analysis of the peculiarities of incidence makes it possible to approach the whole penumbra of 'meaning' in a new and fruitful way" (4). Fundamentally,

prehensive chronology is prepared for Gaskell's fiction. It is composed first by dividing the narrative into scenes principally by time indicators, such as "this morning," "two weeks later," or "in 1850," and then by surveying main characters' frequency of appearance and the change of locations scene by scene. A character is judged "active" when he/she appears in a scene, and "referred to" when he/she does not appear but is only referred to by some other characters including the narrator. The length of each scene is denoted in percentages which are worked out after dividing its page numbers by the total page numbers of the story. The appearance rate of a character is determined by counting up the percentage of each scene where he/she is active or referred to. Hence, a comprehensive chronology provides statistical data concerning Gaskell's use of time, characters, and places—three pivotal elements of the structure of realist fiction—, and a bird's-eye view of the plot as well. The quest for authorial meaning pursued in this dissertation is principally based on this device.[2]

All critical methodologies can be divided into two categories depending on critics' stance towards authorial intention—namely whether priority is given to the readers' strategy for understanding a text or to the authors' for conveying their themes. Critics of the former position, or anti-intentionalists, regard a text as "a multi-dimensional space in which a variety of writings, none of them original, blend and clash," and not as "a line of words releasing a single 'theological' meaning (the 'message' of the Author-God)" (Roland Barthes 146). Inevitably, their criticism invites innumerable readings of a text, or "critical anarchy" (Eagleton, *Literary Theory* 60) in which diversity is welcomed as evidence of textual richness. By contrast, for critics of the latter position, sometimes called intentionalists, "a text means what its author meant" (Hirsch, *Validity* 1), and the chaotic state of critical heterogeneity is just the outcome of moral and ethical impertinence for authors: "If we are to be compelled to recover authorial intent it must be on ethical grounds" (Irwin, *Intentionalist Interpretation* 69). These critics stress two aspects of a text: its significance and meaning. Textual significance to the author may vary whenever and wherever, and therefore could be the target of anti-intentionalists' criticism. Textual meaning, on the other hand, remains constant once a text is produced, and this is the object of intentionalists' interpretation. Taking intentionalist hermeneutics as its theoretical

---

however, their concern lies rather with linguistic styles than with authorial meaning.
2 Chapter 1 surveys the assertions of Terry Eagleton and E. D. Hirsch, Jr., perhaps the most formidable advocates of anti-intentionalism and intentionalism, and proposes, taking Hirsch's hermeneutics as its theoretical backbone, that chronologies and statistics, as have been demonstrated by C. P. Sanger and Karl Kroeber in their structural analyses, are probably the most effective means for the objective identification of authorial meaning.

backbone, this study proposes that chronologies and statistics are probably one of the most effective means for the objective identification of authorial meaning.

Reservations will probably be expressed by anti-intentionalists and liberal humanists[3] as to the effectiveness of our methodology. The following are summaries of some of their contentions, and our responses.

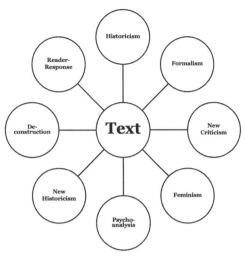

Fig. 0.2. Critical Anarchy

(a) **"The structural elements that you are measuring are not 'consciously' registered by the author—indeed, the more detailed the objective measurements that you undertake become, the less likely an author is to be aware of such factors"; "Statistical results do not necessarily reflect authorial meaning."** The object of our analysis is the meaning of the Gaskell construct, not of the historical Gaskell as person. Historical authors "often misunderstand their own work and are [...] confused about it"; they "truly exists outside their texts" and "have no interpretive authority over them" (Nehamas 686). Author constructs, in contrast, "are not individuals but characters manifested or exemplified, though not depicted or described, in texts" (Nehamas 686). In other words, "an intentionalist needs an author construct because we can never even hope to 'have' the real historical author. All we ever have is a more or less accurate version of him as related to his text, an author construct" (Irwin, *Intentionalist Interpretation* 29). Characters' appearance rates discovered through the statistical analysis are probably unnoticed by the real Gaskell, but fabricated by the Gaskell construct with the intention of conveying her meaning as effectively as possible.

(b) **"It is normally not particularly difficult to work out who is the protagonist of a novel. If it is, this difficulty is itself part of the structure of the novel and part of the experience of reading"; "Careful readers can detect who among characters appears most, without quantifying it."** Which assertion is more convincing, the

---

3 Liberal humanists dislike methodologies, prefer to read by intuitions and intelligent sensibility, and aim at nurturing spiritual wholeness in the world (Eagleton, *Literary Theory* 173-74). See Section 1.3.3. of this chapter.

INTRODUCTION 17

one based on critics' insight only or the one supported by structural evidence?

(c) "An 'objective' measure of the character that appears most often misses the point of the novel: when critics disagree, it is often not because one is wrong and the other right, but because the text itself offers—indeed demands—more than one interpretation." Our measurement of characters' appearance rates does not necessarily afford the conclusion of a dispute concerning the chief protagonist, but just offers a hint for its solution. The result of measurement must be scrutinized and supported by some other pieces of evidence. If the text demands multiple interpretations, the authorial meaning for that device should be reflected on its structure.

(d) "There are serious problems with your claims about 'objectivity': in particular, it is not clear that what you are doing is, in your sense, itself objective—since in fact 'subjective' decisions have to be made on, for example, what to focus on, the kinds of questions that one asks about a novel, how one discerns a character to be present in a scene, how one divides a novel into scenes, questions of narratorial 'focalization,' and so on. All these are questions of reading, which is precisely what you want to eliminate. In other words, the objectivity that you are seeking is something of an illusion, pervaded as it inevitably is by your own 'subjective' judgements." Subjective judgement is unavoidable in any scientific method of any discipline. It is rather natural that researchers choose the best effective means to achieve their goals. We choose, as the main target of our statistical analysis, characters' frequency of appearance, time sequence within the story, and shift of places, because they are fundamental structural elements without which almost all realist fiction is impossible to be produced. If the investigation into the three elements gives few hints for authorial meaning, then we try the method on some other formal devices which we think should best reflect authorial meaning. The point is whether the result of the investigation is reproducible or not. We must confess that there may be some small counting errors in quantifying the elements, and that there are several scenes in which it is difficult to judge whether a character is active or not.[4] Notwithstanding, such a case is so rare as to hardly affect the result of statistical inquiry. As long as our calculation standards are applied, almost the same results will certainly be reproduced.

---

4 For example, such a case occurs for the character who is undoubtedly in the scene but is silent. After careful consideration, they are counted as "active." So it does for narrators. After all, the narrator is counted as "active" when her comment is made in the first person; so is she if she inserts a direct address to the reader in the second person or a comment with exclamation marks, such as "Alas! Poor Mary! bitter woe did thy weakness work thee" (*MB* 46); "Poor Jem! it is not an auspicious moment for thee!" (*MB* 149).

Therefore, statistics is probably one of the best tools to spotlight authorial intention as objectively as possible. Since the validity of the outcome is carefully examined through analysis of the text, reading is not eliminated. Finally, it is highly probable in Gaskell's fiction that characters' frequency of appearance goes up in proportion to the degree of importance of their roles, as demonstrated in the subsequent discussion. This principle would hardly be discovered without statistical measurement of structural devices.

Chapter 1 begins by elucidating the significance of authorial meaning as a cornerstone of literary criticism, focusing on intentionalist hermeneutics as its theoretical backbone. The chapter then delves into C. P. Sanger's chronological manifestation of textual events and Karl Kroeber's stylometric analysis of four structural elements—location, characters, their actions, and temporal ordering—within a text. The critics' use of statistics for the interpretation of literary texts, or the statistical analysis of the structures of a text provided by its comprehensive chronology, is presented as one of the most effective means for the objective detection of authorial meaning.

Chapter 2 challenges the classical reading of *Mary Barton* as an industrial novel. Our statistical analysis reveals the intriguing fact that industrial factors are not a constant concern of the Gaskell construct. For instance, John Barton, the leading trade unionist, appears in 51.7% of the text, while his daughter Mary appears in 85.5% and her lover Jem in 63.0%. These figures imply that the narrative is more concerned with Mary's romantic journey than John's fight for workers' rights.

The soundness of Ruth Hilton's martyrdom has long been debated by critics, who often argue that her death diminished the narrative credibility despite her moral triumph over her seducer, as Pollard observes, the "price of sin has to be paid in death, at the cost of narrative credibility" (*Mrs Gaskell* 102). Chapter 3 seeks to resolve this abiding issue by analysing the formal devices in this Mary Magdalene novel, demonstrating Ruth's death is not an error, but the logical culmination of the Gaskell construct's narrative intent.

One of the enduring debates surrounding *North and South* is which of its two major plots—the industrial plot (conflict and reconciliation between the mill-owner John Thornton and the trade unionist Nicholas Higgins) or the love plot (the proud Margaret Hale's prejudice against and understanding of Thornton)—dominates the novel's theme. Chapter 4 seeks to settle this question by examining the interaction between these plots, revealing how both industrial and romantic elements are intertwined to advance the story's thematic concerns.

Chapter 5 employs topic modelling, a prominent text-mining technique in Digital Humanities, to discover the most frequently used keywords in *The Life of Charlotte Brontë* to find the hidden authorial meaning. This chapter also focuses on the Gaskell construct's use of the religious language to argue her Christianity which has been regarded as one of the typical features of the real Gaskell's thought.

Chapter 6 scrutinizes the validity of common critical reading that *Lois the Witch* is intended to draw the appalling horror of the Salem witchcraft delusion. First by comparing the text with its source material, and then by visualizing the eponymous heroine's evolving relationships with the other five key characters, the chapter argues that the Gaskell construct's meaning lies more in stressing Lois's Christian fortitude than the external terror of her circumstances.

The Conclusion summarizes the statistical analyses of the structures of various texts undertaken in this research to discover the meanings of the author constructs, and affirms the importance of blending subjective and objective approaches in literary criticism to identify a more comprehensive and absolute interpretation of a text. Through these analyses, this study reasserts the significance of authorial meaning, offering a model for future literary inquiry.

CHAPTER 1 Chronology and Statistics: Objective Understanding of Authorial Meaning

1.1. Introduction[5]

Is the quest for authorial meaning an appropriate aim of literary analysis? The history of literary theories, in a sense, has been the history of critics' attempts to look for an answer to this long-standing issue. In his legendary essay "The Death of the Author" (1968), Barthes laments that classical criticism has wrongly believed a text is "the 'message' of the Author-God" although it is actually "a multi-dimensional space in which a variety of writings, none of them original, blend and clash" (146). In *Validity in Interpretation* (1967), "perhaps the most formidable theoretical defence of the principles and methods of traditional literary scholarship and cognitive criticism to have been written in English" (Lodge 253), E. D. Hirsch, Jr. remarks "there has been in the past four decades a heavy and largely victorious assault on the sensible belief that a text means what its author meant" (1). Although published almost at the same time in the late 1960s, both writings offer completely different recognition of the critical trend at that time. Barthes considers classical criticism "has never paid any attention to the reader" (171), while Hirsch finds it is the author that has been neglected.

Considering literary texts as the faithful reflection of authors' meanings, Hirsch proclaims that the aim of literary analysis is to find them out. For Eagleton, by contrast, the belief in authorial intention is an objectivist illusion. The two literary theorists' views on this subject will be surveyed in the following Section 1.2, where our own standpoint will also be made explicit.

If the search for authors' meanings could be a target of critical reading, how can we know them, and, above all, in the most objective way? The novelist writes fiction because he/she "has an idea of what he[/she] wants to convey" (Hirsch 101), that is, its theme in the broadest sense. It may be one, two, or three in number, but should hardly be hundreds (especially in the case of realist writers), as often presented by the current subjectivist critics (in truth, they offer criticism on textual "significance," not interpretation of textual "meaning," of which the difference will be explicated in Section 1.2). In Section 1.3, we shall introduce the structuralist approaches of C. P. Sanger and Karl Kroeber as sensible methods for achieving the objective interpretation of authorial meanings, and discuss their merits and demerits. Finally, Section 1.4 concludes that the Sanger-Kroeber method is one of the most illuminating

---

5 This chapter is a revised version of my paper of the same title published in *English Studies*, vol. 87, no. 3.

means for objective interpretation of realist fiction.[6]

1.2. The Norm of Criticism: Authorial Meaning

1.2.1. Hirsch and Eagleton

The essential divergence between Hirsch and Eagleton lies in their views on the norm of literary criticism. The former considers it vital in the analysis of literature and insists the only criterion that could be the norm is authorial meaning: "If [a critic's] claim to validity is to hold, he must be willing to measure his interpretation against a genuinely discriminating norm, and the only compelling normative principle that has ever been brought forward is the old-fashioned ideal of rightly understanding what the author meant" (*Validity* 26). The latter, on the other hand, expresses doubts about the American hermeneutist's theory by quoting some anti-intentionalist literary theories in his own defence. Some basic conceptual grounds of each critic will be focused in this section.

First, Hirsch's distinction between meaning and significance will be explained (Section 1.2.2); then, that between interpretation and criticism (Section 1.2.3)—the two central principles in hermeneutics. Next, the discrepancies between Eagleton and Hirsch will be examined under the headings of Husserlian Phenomenology (Section 1.2.4), Language and Meaning (Section 1.2.5), Historicism (Section 1.2.6), Author and Text (Section 1.2.7), Hermeneutical Circle (Section 1.2.8), and Creative Reading (Section 1.2.9). Section 1.2.10 inspects William Irwin's argument of authorship, a useful supplement to Hirschian intentionalist theory. Finally, after the summary of the discussion above, our standpoint will be made clear in Section 1.2.11.

1.2.2. Meaning and Significance

Hirsch distinguishes the meaning of a text from its significance: "*Meaning* is that which is represented by a text; it is what the author meant by his use of a particular sign sequence; it is what the signs represent. *Significance*, on the other hand, names a relationship between that meaning and a person, or a conception, or a situation, or indeed anything imaginable" (*Validity* 8). Meaning is "determined once and for all by the character of the speaker's intention" (Husserl, qtd. in Hirsch, *Validity* 219), or permanent, while significance is variable.

---

6 Since the effectiveness of the Sanger-Kroeber method has been examined chiefly through the analysis of Elizabeth Gaskell's novels, the target of this research is set on realist fiction. In contrast to modernist and postmodernist texts, which "subvert the basic conventions of earlier prose fiction" (M. H. Abrams 167), realist texts presuppose that signified is the faithful representation of signifiers. Therefore, they are more fitting a target for the SK method. See also Section 1.3.3 of this chapter.

There is a difference between the meaning of a text (which does not change) and the meaning of a text to us today (which changes). The meaning of a text is that which the author meant by his use of particular linguistic symbols. Being linguistic, this meaning is communal, that is, self-identical and reproducible in more than one consciousness. Being reproducible, it is the same whenever and wherever it is understood by another. However, each time this meaning is construed, its meaning to the construer (its significance) is different. Since his situation is different, so is the character of his relationship to the construed meaning. It is precisely because the meaning of the text is always the same that its relationship to a different situation is a different relationship. (Hirsch, *Validity* 255)

Hirsch's purport is, as succinctly summarized by Eagleton, that "a literary work may 'mean' different things to different people at different times. But this [...] is more properly a matter of the work's 'significance' rather than its 'meaning.' [...] Significances vary throughout history, whereas meanings remain constant; authors put in meanings, whereas readers assign significances" (*Literary Theory* 58). Hirsch's answer to the post-structuralist argument that the meaning of a text changes even for its author,[7] therefore, would be that "the *significance* of the work to the author" may change, but that its *meaning* does not (*Validity* 8).

In support of Hirsch's distinction between meaning and significance, Irwin insists in his *Intentionalist Interpretation* that the meaning of a text, i.e. "what the author wanted to communicate" (48), is "a principle of stability provided by the author" (42) and "ever the same" (48), while the significance of a text, i.e. "meaning-as-related-to some context" (48), is "a principle of change—it is meaning-as-related-to (to me, to us, to our time, etc)" (42) and "ever in flux" (48). In short, it is "only the significance of a text that changes and not its meaning" (42).

Irwin's support of the dual role of the text is repeatedly inserted in his *Intentionalist Interpretation*. For instance, "Suffice it to say that by 'meaning' we are to understand the author's intended communication, regardless of what the text may seem to say in accord with the convention of language. By 'significance' we are to understand meaning-as-related-to anything other than the text itself. Significance is the product of non-urinterpretation (i.e., criticism), which under certain circumstances may

---

7 For instance, "a text is not a line of words releasing a single 'theological' meaning (the 'message' of the Author-God) but a multi-dimensional space in which a variety of writings, none of them original, blend and clash" (Barthes, "The Death of the Author" 146).

be an acceptable and quite desirable product" (61); "If we use and understand the terms 'meaning' and 'significance' with the precision Hirsch's account makes possible, then we will conclude that the meaning of a text cannot change. It is given once and for all by the author. Beardsley can make only the obvious claim that the significance of a text can and does change" (48).

1.2.3. Interpretation and Criticism

Hirsch's principle of direct correspondence between authorial and textual meaning and his differentiation of meaning from significance are contested by Eagleton:

> To secure the meaning of a work for all time, rescuing it from the ravages of history, criticism has to police its potentially anarchic details, hemming them back with the compound of 'typical' meaning. Its stance towards the text is authoritarian and juridical: anything which cannot be herded inside the enclosure of 'probable authorial meaning' is brusquely expelled, and everything remaining within that enclosure is strictly subordinated to this single governing intention. The unalterable meaning of the sacred scripture has been preserved; what one does with it, how one uses it, becomes merely a secondary matter of 'significance.' (*Literary Theory* 59)

Eagleton's disingenuous exposition of Hirschian theory is probably produced from his disregard of the central principle of hermeneutics—the distinction between interpretation and criticism:

> Interpretation is the construction of textual meaning as such: it explicates [...] those meanings, and only those meanings, which the text explicitly or implicitly represents. Criticism, on the other hand, builds on the results of interpretation; it confronts textual meaning not as such but as a component within a larger context. [...] The object of interpretation is textual meaning in and for itself and may be called the *meaning* of the text. The object of criticism, on the other hand, is that meaning in its bearing on something else (standards of value, present concerns, etc.), and this object may therefore be called the *significance* of the text. (*Validity* 210-11)

Calling all critical writing on texts by the name of the neutral term "commentary," Hirsch proposes to reserve the familiar term "criticism" for commentary about significance and "interpretation" for commentary about meaning (*Validity* 143). The cardinal function of "interpretation" is to understand the author's meaning; that of "criticism" to judge the significance of that meaning, i.e. "its relation to ourselves, to history, to the author's personality, even to the author's other works" (*Validity* 143). Irwin elucidates Hirsch's contrast by observing "For Hirsch, interpretation aims at discovering meaning, as opposed to criticism, which aims at articulating significance" (48). In a nutshell, the goal of interpretation is the accurate understanding of authorial meaning, that of criticism the sensible judgement on the text's significance; or, "understanding" is to interpret textual meaning, "judgement" to criticize textual significance (*Validity* 143-44).[8] After all, as a result of disregarding the differences of goals between criticism and interpretation, Eagleton complains that his aim of textual criticism cannot be achieved by Hirsch's theory whose real aim is textual interpretation.

In response to Eagleton's doubt about the dual function of a text, Hirsch argues that "To say that verbal meaning is determinate is not to exclude complexities of meaning but only to insist that a text's meaning is what it is and not a hundred other things" (*Validity* 230).[9] "The interpreter's job," therefore, "is to reconstruct a determinate actual meaning, not a mere system of possibilities" (Hirsch, *Validity* 231). In the Hirschian thesis, "significance is the proper object of criticism, not of interpretation, whose exclusive object is verbal meaning" (Hirsch, *Validity* 57).

1.2.4. Husserlian Phenomenology

The purpose of Hirsch's *Validity in Interpretation* is to awaken us to the need of a permanent standard for literary criticism:

> [I argue] against certain modern theories which hamper the establishment of normative principles in interpretation and which thereby encourage the subjectivism and individualism which have for many students discredited the analytical movement. By normative principles I mean those notions which concern the nature of a correct interpretation. When the critic clearly conceives what a

---

8 In this study, these terms are used principally in the senses of the Hirschian definitions. Hirschian "interpretation" is the same as what Irwin calls "urinterpretation": "we can speak of interpretation as the activity concerned with seeking the meaning rather than the significance of a text. The normative approach of urinterpretation is, as we have argued, the correct way of seeking meaning. Criticism is the activity that seeks the significance rather than the meaning of a text; it is a very broad and encompassing term" (*Intentionalist Interpretation* 112).

9 "Verbal meaning" is authorial and sharable meaning: it is "whatever someone has willed to convey by a particular sequence of linguistic signs and which can be conveyed (shared) by means of those linguistic signs" (Hirsch, *Validity* 31), or "*that aspect of a speaker's 'intention' which, under linguistic conventions, may be shared by others*" (Hirsch, *Validity* 218).

correct interpretation is in principle, he possesses a guiding idea against which he can measure his construction. Without such a guiding idea, self-critical or objective interpretation is hardly possible. Current theory, however, fails to provide such a principle. (212)

Deploring "wilful arbitrariness and extravagance in academic criticism" (*Validity* 2) brought about by the prevalence of the theory of authorial irrelevance, the American hermeneutist asserts that "To banish the original author as the determiner of meaning" is "to reject the only compelling normative principle that could lend validity to an interpretation" (*Validity* 5).

As he himself acknowledges (*Validity* 242), Hirsch somewhat owes his idea to the German philosopher Edmund Husserl, who considers "all realities must be treated as pure 'phenomena,' in terms of their appearances in our mind, and this is the only absolute data from which we can begin" (*Literary Theory* 48). Hence, in the Husserlian phenomenological analysis,

> The text itself is reduced to a pure embodiment of the author's consciousness: all of its stylistic and semantic aspects are grasped as organic parts of a complex totality, of which the unifying essence is the author's mind. To know this mind, we must not refer to anything we actually know of the author—biographical criticism is banned—but only to those aspects of his or her consciousness which manifest themselves in the work itself. Moreover, we are concerned with the 'deep structures' of this mind, which can be found in recurrent themes and patterns of imagery. (*Literary Theory* 51)

To "penetrate to the very interior of a writer's consciousness," Eagleton's explanation continues, "phenomenological criticism tries to achieve complete objectivity and disinterestedness. It must purge itself of its own predilections, plunge itself empathetically into the 'world' of the work, and reproduce as exactly and unbiasedly as possible what it finds there" (*Literary Theory* 51-52).

This Husserlian phenomenological methodology is derided by Eagleton as "a wholly uncritical, non-evaluative mode of analysis" and "an idealist, essentialist, anti-historical, formalist and organicist type of criticism, a kind of pure distillation of the blind spots, prejudices and limitations of modern literary theory as a whole": "Criticism is not seen as a construction, an active interpretation of the work which will inevitably engage the critic's own interests and biases; it is a mere passive reception of the text, a pure transcription of its mental essences" (*Literary Theory* 52).

For Husserlian criticism, "the language of a literary work is little more than an 'expression' of its inner meanings" (*Literary Theory* 52); meaning is "identical with whatever 'mental object' the author had in mind, or 'intended,' at the time of writing" (*Literary Theory* 58). Accordingly, for Hirsch, who is sympathetic to Husserlian phenomenology,[10] the insistence of the German philosopher Martin Heidegger,[11] his successor Hans-Georg Gadamer, and Eagleton "that meaning is always historical," is only what "opens the door to complete relativism" (*Literary Theory* 61). For Hirsch, meaning accords with language and remains unchangeable; for Eagleton, it cannot be the reflection of language which is social, historical, and unstable.

1.2.5. Language and Meaning

The two conflicting standpoints as to the correlation between language and meaning are plainly expressed in Eagleton's recapitulation:

> [L]anguage is a much less stable affair than the classical structuralists had considered. Instead of being a well-defined, clearly demarcated structure containing symmetrical units of signifiers and signifieds, it now begins to look much more like a sprawling limitless web where there is a constant interchange and circulation of elements, where none of the elements is absolutely definable and where everything is caught up and traced through by everything else. If this is so, then it strikes a serious blow at certain traditional theories of meaning. For such theories, it was the function of signs to reflect inward experiences or objects in the real world, to 'make present' one's thoughts and feelings or to describe how reality was. (*Literary Theory* 112)

The Post-Structuralist view in the first half of this quotation is repeatedly inserted in Eagleton's book because it is his own view: "All language, as de Man rightly perceives, is ineradicably metaphorical, working by tropes and figures; it is a mistake to believe that any language is *literally* literal" (*Literary Theory* 126). He defends his

---

10 For Husserl, "the author alone is the determiner of a text's meaning" (Hirsch, *Validity* 248). Husserlian intentionality and bracketing are explained by Irwin as this: "Bracketing is the process by which, Husserl argued, we could eliminate what did not belong to the object of awareness and so 'get back to the things themselves.' Such phenomenological bracketing is a very useful way of conceiving the project of removing our own perspective in order to get to the thing itself, which for Hirsch is the author's meaning" (*Intentionalist Interpretation* 48). This study argues that chronology and statistics are the most useful tools for bracketing.

11 Summarizing Heidegger's historicism, Irwin observes: "For Heidegger, understanding has intimate connections to both *Dasein* [human existence] and time; understanding is said to be part of the ontological structure of *Dasein*, and, inasmuch as being itself is time, understanding has an important temporal dimension" (*Intentionalist Interpretation* 74).

assertion also by introducing William Empson's view that "the meanings of a literary text are always in some measure promiscuous, never reducible to a final interpretation" (*Literary Theory* 46). Consequently, meanings are unsteady and indeterminate, since "they are the products of language, which always has something slippery about it"; "An author's intention," Eagleton continues, "is itself a complex 'text,' which can be debated, translated and variously interpreted just like any other" (*Literary Theory* 60).

In contrast, in Hirschian theory, language is a stable vehicle through which the author's meaning is conveyed; accordingly, if a text is unreadable, literature is unlikely to survive. Eagleton's distrust in language stability may be applicable to modernist fiction in which "what we are seeing might always have happened differently, or not happened at all" (*Literary Theory* 161). Empirical evidence shows that texts may become figurative in some cases, but not always; for otherwise communication is impossible. To dispute a principle by quoting a few atypical instances and ignoring the textual genre is unwise as a tactic of debate, especially when the principle reasonably explains almost all internal phenomena as in realist fiction.

1.2.6. Historicism

Historicism is Eagleton's ideological stance: "all readers are socially and historically positioned, and how they interpret literary works will be deeply shaped by this fact" (*Literary Theory* 72). In support of Gadamer's historicism, he states:

All understanding is *productive*: it is always 'understanding otherwise,' realizing new potential in the text, making a difference to it. The present is only ever understandable through the past, with which it forms a living continuity; and the past is always grasped from our own partial viewpoint within the present. The event of understanding comes about when our own 'horizon'[12] of historical meanings and assumptions 'fuses' with the 'horizon' within which the work itself is placed. At such a moment we enter the alien world of the artefact, but at the same time gather it into our own realm, reaching a more complete understanding of ourselves. (*Literary Theory* 62)

"It is hard to see," Eagleton continues, "why Hirsch should find all this so unnerving. On the contrary, it all seems considerably too smooth" (*Literary Theory* 62).

On the other hand, for Hirsch, historicism is "the very target of his polemic"

[12] "The term 'horizon' [...] is meant to suggest our situatedness and contextuality. Gadamer defines a horizon as, 'the range of vision that includes everything that can be seen from a particular vantage point'" (Irwin, *Intentionalist Interpretation* 84).

(*Literary Theory* 61). Past meaning is irreproducible in the present "because the past is ontologically alien to the present"—such historicity is "ultimately an argument against written communication in general and not just against communication between historical eras. For it is merely arbitrary, on this argument, to hold that a meaning fifty years old is ontologically alien while one three years or three minutes old is not" (Hirsch, *Validity* 256). He feels historicism unnerving because it "cannot provide any satisfactory norm of validity" (153). If there is no norm of interpretation, literary commentary only invites critical anarchy; the only criterion that could be the norm is authorial meaning; meaning is unchangeable as it is permanently fixed at the time of textual production—this is his fundamental standpoint. In addition, he distinguishes textual meaning from textual significance which is variable in accordance with cultural and historical backgrounds. Hirsch's notion of the textual independence from social influences has a strong affinity with Kroeber's: "No one doubts that the arts, especially fiction, reflect the course of social and cultural history. Yet all the arts (as historians of the fine arts have been quickest to recognize) possess a history of their own, a system of continuity and innovation which is to some degree independent of, often surprisingly resistive to, the influence of social transformations" (4).

Irwin's explanation (and his criticism) of Gadamer's historicism is detailed in his book *Intentionalist Interpretation* (84-92). Gadamer is critical of historical reproduction of authorial meaning:

> Every age has to understand a transmitted text in its own way, for the text belongs to the whole tradition whose content interests the age and in which it seeks to understand itself. The real meaning of a text, as it speaks to the interpreter, does not depend on the contingencies of the author and his original audience. It certainly is not identical with them, for it is always co-determined also by the historical situation of the interpreter and hence by the totality of the objective course of history. [. . .] Not just occasionally but always, the meaning of a text goes beyond its author. That is why understanding is not merely a reproductive but always a productive activity as well. (*Truth and Method* 296)

His argument is summarized by Irwin as follows:

> The projects of historically reproducing the author's intention or understanding [. . .] would actually be impossible. We are still historically situated even when we make our concern the past intention or understanding of an author. Our

account of authorial intention or understanding, then, will inevitably be no more than one historical perspective on them. (*Intentionalist Interpretation* 85) He argues that because our present horizon is laden with presuppositions and prejudices that are different from those of a given historical past, we cannot recreate the understanding of the past. Rather than attempt such a futile project, we are to bring about new and productive understanding through a fusion of past and present horizons. (*Intentionalist Interpretation* 88).

Irwin, then, counterargues Gadamer's view: "there is no logical impossibility precluding the reproduction of a past meaning or understanding," referring to the phenomenon that the lights of stars we see at present are actually the ones in the past (*Intentionalist Interpretation* 88). Irwin's standpoint is Hirsch's differentiation of meaning from significance of the text:

> In contrast, there is something permanent about a text; once produced by the author, it truly remains the same (barring any textual corruption). It is only our interpretation of it that can change. The normative question that Gadamer broaches here is: *Should* our interpretations of a text always change? [. . .] What is far more important, however, is that the essence of our understanding remains the same as previous correct understanding if we can be said to understand at all. [. . .] If we do not preserve the essence of our understanding, we open the door to interpretive relativism, a fate Gadamer wishes to avoid. (*Intentionalist Interpretation* 91)

This study estimates that Gadamer's disbelief in textual reflection of authorial meaning comes from his doubt about the intentionalist target of interpretation, i.e. the meaning of the author construct, not of the historical author.

1.2.7. Author and Text: Is the Text the Reflection of the Author's Meaning?

Another common objection to the Hirschian theory is that the text often fails to reflect authorial meaning: "The author's desire to communicate a particular meaning is not necessarily the same as his success in doing so" (Hirsch, *Validity* 11). This argument corresponds to Pierre Macherey's doubt about the author's dependability as a witness to the meaning of their text: "We know that a writer never reflects mechanically or rigorously the ideology which he represents, even if his sole intention is to represent it: perhaps because no ideology is sufficiently consistent to survive the test of figuration" (218). Macherey's view is shared by another anti-intentionalist, W. W. Robson: "A writer probably intended his work to have a certain emotional effect, but there is no way in which he can ensure that it actually has that effect. In this sense, then, liberty of interpreting is our prerogative as readers. It means freedom of judgment, of personal decision whether or not the writer has actually performed what he seemed to promise" (39). The distinction of authorial meaning from textual meaning is the position shared by Eagleton as well: "There are obvious problems with trying to determine what is going on in somebody's head and then claiming that this is the meaning of a piece of writing. For one thing, a great many things are likely to be going on in an author's head at the time of writing" (*Literary Theory* 59). He then concludes that we "can never [. . .] come to know in some absolutely objective way" what an author has actually in mind, and that any "such notion of absolute objectivity is an illusion" (*Literary Theory* 60).

Hirsch makes little defence against the anti-intentionalists' assertion, but rather accepts it, because he acknowledges the difficulty of attaining outright certainty in understanding authorial meaning: "Since genuine certainty in interpretation is impossible, the aim of the discipline must be to reach a consensus, on the basis of what is known, that correct understanding has *probably* been achieved" (*Validity* 17). The detection of authorial meaning may be too tricky to be done with definite conviction, but can be, or rather should be, achieved with relative probability.

Against the psychoanalysts' statement that "what it [the text] does not say, and *how* it does not say it, may be as important as what it articulates; what seems absent, marginal or ambivalent about it may provide a central clue to its meanings" (*Literary Theory* 155), Hirsch asserts, "by claiming to perceive implications of which the author was not conscious, we may sometimes distort and falsify the meaning of which he was conscious, which is not 'better understanding' but simply misunderstanding of the author's meaning" (*Validity* 21). In connection with the Freudian concern with lies, he observes, "When I wish to deceive, my secret awareness that I am lying is irrelevant to the verbal meaning of my utterance. The only correct interpretation of my lie is, paradoxically, to view it as being a true statement, since this is the only correct construction of my verbal intention. Indeed, it is only when my listener has *understood* my meaning (presented as true) that he can *judge* it to be a lie" (*Validity* 243). Hirsch, in short, insists that whether unconsciousness or deception affects the textual meaning depends entirely on the correct detection of authorial meaning. The unconscious would reveal itself only when the conscious is revealed. The psychoanalysts' "'symptomatic' places in the text—distortions, ambiguities, absence and elisions which may provide a specially valuable mode of access to the 'latent content,' or unconscious drives" (*Literary Theory* 158) would become meaningful if their import were proved in an objective way, not by personal insight. One of the most effective methods for this purpose, for instance, would be to analyse the frequency and context of their appearance by statistical quantification of such spots: if they appeared in accordance with a rule, they could be the reflection of some authorial stratagem; if not, they would only be the discovery by the critic's subjectivism. Thus, the outcome of a statistical survey should be a reliable criterion for adjudicating whether "symptomatic" spots represent any authorial intention.

To the Formalist, New Critical, Structuralist, and Post-Structuralist view of semantic autonomy that, because "textual meaning has nothing to do with the author's mind," "the object of interpretation is not the author but his text" (Hirsch, *Validity* 224), Hirsch expresses opposition in terms of its failure to supply a normative standard of validity in interpretation: "the task of finding out what a text says has no determinate object, since the text can say different things to different readers" (*Validity* 11). What a text says must be "the saying of the author or a reader," for it "does not exist even as a sequence of words until it is construed; until then, it is merely a sequence of signs" (Hirsch, *Validity* 13). This Hirschian view of the author as the determiner of textual meaning is championed by Irwin, who insists "a text cannot necessarily tell us whether it is indeed a text; we must refer to an author to confirm this" (*Intentionalist Interpretation* 43):

> The text alone allows for a plurality of possible meanings, often notoriously including conflicting and contradictory meanings. Fortunately, we rarely, if ever, have simply the text alone. In reading a text we instinctively form an author construct (urauthor in my terms), usually making the defeasible assumption that the author was a rational person making conventional use of the language. The criterion of 'the text alone' appears rather arbitrary in its application, not limiting the meanings of the text in any final way. (*Intentionalist Interpretation* 44)

1.2.8. Hermeneutical Circle

Presuming "works of literature form an 'organic' unity," the Hirschian approach "seeks to fit each element of a text into a complete whole, in a process commonly known as the 'hermeneutical circle'" (Eagleton, *Literary Theory* 64): "the whole can be understood only through its parts, but the parts can be understood only through the whole" (Hirsch, *Validity* 76). The hermeneutical circle is elucidated by Irwin also: "we must understand the whole in terms of its parts, but to understand the parts we must understand the whole" (*Intentionalist Interpretation* 76). This hermeneutical unity is condemned by Eagleton: "Hermeneutics does not generally consider the possibility that literary works may be diffuse, incomplete and internally contradictory, though there are many reasons to assume that they are" (*Literary Theory* 64); "There is absolutely no need to suppose that works of literature either do or should constitute harmonious wholes" (*Literary Theory* 70). The disparity between Hirsch and Eagleton has arisen again from their different stances towards literary commentary: one is intentionalist, the other anti-intentionalist. The former considers a text as the reflection of authorial meanings, while the latter regards it as independent of the author. The "interdependence of part and whole" (Hirsch, *Validity* 76) has something in common with Kroeber's hypothesis that the form of any fictional element is affected by the entire scheme of the novel (8).

1.2.9. Creative Reading

Wolfgang Iser, "of the so-called Constance school of reception aesthetics" (Eagleton, *Literary Theory* 67), "permits the reader a fair degree of freedom, but we are not free simply to interpret as we wish. For an interpretation to be an interpretation of *this* text and not of some other, it must be in some sense logically constrained by the text itself. The work, in other words, exercises a degree of determinacy over readers' responses to it, otherwise criticism would seem to fall into total anarchy" (Eagleton, *Literary Theory* 73). As a receptionist theorist, Stanley Fish is more aggressive than Iser: "The true writer is the reader: dissatisfied with mere Iserian co-partnership in the literary enterprise, the readers have now overthrown the bosses and installed themselves in power. For Fish, reading is not a matter of discovering what the text means, but a process of experiencing what it *does* to you" (Eagleton, *Literary Theory* 74).

In Deconstruction also, the reader's power is much stronger than the author's. Roland Barthes, who doubts the straightforward correspondence between signifiers and signifieds,[13] regards the "realist or representational sign" as "unhealthy," since it "denies the *productive* character of language" (Eagleton, *Literary Theory* 118); for him, the text is "less a 'structure' than an open-ended process of 'structuration'" (Eagleton, *Literary Theory* 120) to be radically revised and reshuffled. Indeed there are some textual contradictions in Gaskell's fiction which will be welcomed by Deconstructionists as opportunities for their criticism. For example, her time sequence is distorted between Chapters 5 and 6, Volume 2, of *North and South* where the event of August 1848 suddenly becomes that of October. Whether investigation into such aporias is fruitful or not depends upon the frequency of their occurrence. The high-

---

13 In his legendary essay "The Death of the Author," Barthes laments that classical criticism has wrongly believed that a text is "the 'message' of the Author-God" although it is actually "a multi-dimensional space in which a variety of writings, none of them original, blend and clash" (146).

er the rate is, the more meaningful they become. If there is only one aporia in a novel of 500 pages long, it is probably safer to consider it only as an example of authorial carelessness than to develop a subjective investigation into the meaning of inconsistency. Deconstructionists may disagree, but statistics is an effective tool even for their approach.

The reader-response theorists' and Deconstructionists' notion that the text is open parallels with Eagleton's: "The claim that we can make a literary text mean whatever we like is in one sense quite justified. What after all is there to stop us? There is literally no end to the number of contexts we might invent for its words in order to make them signify differently" (*Literary Theory* 76). Hirsch's counter-argument to their position would be: textual meaning allows only one interpretation, but textual significance as many potential readings of the text as critics wish.

1.2.10. Urauthor, Meaning, and Urinterpretation

Before delving into the practical methods for uncovering authorial meaning, it should be useful to examine the authorship of Irwin, a fervent advocate of Hirschian theory. His distinction between the author construct (urauthor) from "the historical-author-as-person" (*Intentionalist Interpretation* 21) provides a foundation for identifying the absolute interpretation of a text.

	Non-Urinterpretation, or Criticism	Urinterpretation, or Interpretation
Author's Name	historical-author-as-person, or real author, writer	urauthor, author construct, author function, implied author, author's second self, author
Research Target	the significance of the text, or the intention of a historical-author-as-person	the meaning of the urauthor

Table 1.1. Distinction between Criticism and Interpretation

One of Irwin's quintessential contributions is the distinction between the author construct (the urauthor) and the historical author (the real-author-as-person): "The urauthor is not the historical producer of the text, but a mental construct resembling the historical producer as closely as possible in all relevant ways" (Irwin, *Intentionalist Interpretation* 61). The goal of absolute interpretation, or urinterpretation, is to identify the textual meaning intended by the urauthor. Any literary text can offer countless interpretations as it embodies numerous significances.

The author construct, or urauthor, "is not the historical producer of the text, but a mental construct resembling the historical producer as closely as possible in all relevant ways. [. . .] The urauthor is our vehicle for gaining access to the meaning, the intended communication, of the author himself" (Irwin 61-62). In other words, the author construct—a term coined by intentionalist hermeneutists to distinguish a historical or living author from the functional author who constructed a text—, emerges only through careful reading of the structures of a text. Irwin's "author construct" is another name of Wayne C. Booth's "implied author" (*Rhetoric* 74) or Katherine Tillotson's "author's 'second self'" (qtd. in Booth, *Rhetoric* 71).

Hirsch emphasizes two key attributes of a text: significance and meaning. While the significance of a text may change depending on the reader, its meaning remains constant (it is this stability of the latter that actuates the reader's accurate understanding of the author's intended message): "The meaning of the text is a principle of stability provided by the author, while the significance of a text is a principle of change—it is meaning-as-related-to (to me, to us, to our time, etc.). It is, as we shall see, only the significance of a text that changes and not its meaning" (Irwin, *Intentionalist Interpretation* 42). For the renowned hermeneutist Hirsch, the only solution to the chaos of contemporary literary criticism is to establish the standard interpretation of a text, i.e. the interpretation intended by the author: 'To banish the original author as the determiner of meaning was to reject the only compelling normative principle that could lend validity to an interpretation' (*Validity* 5). Hirsch's theory is refined by Irwin's distinction of the author construct from the historical author. The clue to achieving absolute interpretation, therefore, lies in uncovering the meaning of the author construct.

The distinction between the urauthor and the historical author, as well as the difference between meaning and significance, forms the basis of Irwin's differentiation between urinterpretation and non-urinterpretation:

> An urinterpretation is not necessarily the original interpretation of the text, but rather the interpretation made in accord with the original meaning of the author, as he intended to communicate it. An author may not fully understand his text, and neither may his contemporaries, and so recapturing his or their understandings is not always worthwhile. Inasmuch as the author's text is an intentional effort to communicate, however, his intention is indeed worth recapturing. [. . .] A non-urinterpretation is one that does not seek to capture the intention of the author, but rather points to, what we will call with Hirsch, some significance of the text. [. . .] [U]rinterpretation has a certain primacy over non-urinterpretation. A non-urinterpretation that is not acknowledged as such is unethical; it misrepresents the author of the text and it deceives the audience. [. . .] Non-urinterpretations relate some significance of the text to the reader. Such interpretations can actually bring a text to life in a new way, sowing the seeds of progress and inspiration. A world of only urinterpretations would be a

dull and stagnant world indeed. (*Intentionalist Interpretation* 12)

Why is authorial meaning so important in interpretation? Irwin considers it as the interpreter's moral duty to respect the author's intended meaning. Citing Hirsch's "fundamental ethical maxim for interpretation"—*Unless there is a powerful overriding value in disregarding an author's intention (i.e. original meaning), we who interpret as a vocation should not disregard it.* Mere individual preference would not be such an overriding value, nor would the mere preferences of many persons (*Aims* 90)—, Irwin emphasizes, "The author's attempt to communicate meaning generates an attendant obligation on the part of the interpreter to seek that meaning. To do otherwise is, potentially, to be morally at blame" (*Intentionalist Interpretation* 50).

Another important contribution of Irwin to Hirschian intentionalism is his clarification that the author construct, not the text, is the determiner of textual meaning: "The text, a product in language, is only a better or worse indicator of the meaning in the mind of the author. [...] The text itself is of restricted value in interpretation, because an interpreter can seemingly make a text say whatever she wants" (*Intentionalist Interpretation* 57). In short, "texts apart from the meaning an author indicates by them mean nothing [...]. Texts are simply convenient indicators of meaning but truly speaking cannot possess meaning themselves" (*Intentionalist Interpretation* 60). Irwin further explains, "the author did have a meaning, his text serves to indicate that meaning, and it is the task of the urinterpreter to find and articulate that meaning" (*Intentionalist Interpretation* 64). Urinterpretation is therefore the process that keeps "the author's intended communication at the center of concern" while providing "an appropriate interpretive mechanism" (Irwin, *Intentionalist Interpretation* 64).

To establish the only correct interpretation, or the one intended by the author construct, we must first and foremost uncover the authorial meaning, or "the intended communication" of the urauthor (Irwin, *Intentionalist Interpretation* 62). How can we discover the meaning of the author construct? Irwin suggests that we should rely on as much available evidence as possible, including "relevant available biographical information, likely intentions, use of language in the text itself, information concerning the author's context and audience, and other texts of the author inasmuch as they inform the other elements of the urauthor" (*Intentionalist Interpretation* 30). Then we undertake the process of validation, or "probability judgement," in the Hirschian term (*Validity* 174): first, genre guess; second, process of validation;[14] third, choice of false hypotheses; fourth, use of common sense; and fifth, no correct method (Irwin, *Intentionalist Interpretation* 48-49). According to Hirsch,

"The aim of validation [...] is not necessarily to denominate an individual victor, but rather to reach an objective conclusion about relative probabilities" (*Validity* 172). Stressing the importance of validation, Irwin observes,

> Validation is the process of narrowing the field of competitors until we reach only one. Because we cannot have certainty that knowledge of meaning has been achieved, that we have the truth, the only possible method of choosing between two hypotheses is to prove that one of them is false. [...] In judging among competing interpretations, we must weigh the relevant and available evidence and eliminate false interpretations. All evidence is relevant that aids us in deciding what the author could have meant. (*Intentionalist Interpretation* 49)

Irwin's process of validity closely resembles Hirsch's method for discerning authorial meaning (*Validity* 180-98).

The methods proposed by the two leading theorists of intentionalism are helpful in theory, but a more practical approach may be more effective in practice. This study adopts the Sanger-Kroeber method, or the application of chronology and statistics to the structural analysis of a literary text. This method is not merely one of the most effective tools for seeking out authorial meaning but also represents an invaluable contribution to hermeneutic intentionalism. Irwin observes that "Even an urinterpretation that appears highly valid is always subject to being completely wrong," because we are "always open to new evidence, and so the process of validation becomes, as Hirsch calls it, a 'survival of the fittest'" (*Intentionalist Interpretation* 62). Nonetheless, the use of chronology and statistics in this study is less likely to encounter contradictory evidence that would undermine the validity of interpretation, since these methods centre on key structural elements with data collected on the basis of objectivity. Although Irwin concedes the difficulty of finding the definitive interpretation when he states that "the meaning indicated by the text of the interpretation can certainly be definitive; it can be an exact match for the author's meaning—though [...] we can never be certain of when this occurs" (*Intentionalist Interpretation* 62-63), the statistical quantification of structural elements should lead us closer to an interpretation that is "an exact match for the author's meaning."

Irwin distinguishes between the urauthor (the author construct) and the author (the historical-author-as-person), as well as between meaning and significance, and

14 "Many interpretive hypotheses are possible on the basis of the immediately available evidence and genre guess. Validation is the process of narrowing the field of competitors until we reach only one" (Irwin, *Intentionalist Interpretation* 49).

interpretation and criticism. The interpreter's task is to find the urauthor's meaning of a text, and the process is called interpretation. The central claim of urinterpretation is that "the meaning of a text is the author's intended communication. Importantly, it is not the author as person with whom we are concerned but the author as a particular mental construct, the urauthor, and it is through our conception of the urauthor that we seek meaning" (Irwin, *Intentionalist Interpretation* 112). In contrast, the critic's task is to discern the real author's significance of a text, and the procedure is known as criticism. To note, however, even Irwin, a staunch defender of Hirschian hermeneutics,[15] acknowledges the value of criticism: "Non-urinterpretation, or criticism, that activity that aims at significance, must have its place as well. A world of only urinterpretation would be a dull and sterile one indeed" (*Intentionalist Interpretation* 64), as "Criticism is what keeps a text 'alive' and spurs the further progress of ideas" (*Intentionalist Interpretation* 114).

1.2.11. Suitability of Hirschian Theory

We have examined the theoretical difference between Eagleton and Hirsch under several headings. Eagleton doubts the language (signifier) is the faithful reflection of meaning (signified), because of his support for historicism in which meaning is unstable. "What had been narrow-minded about previous theories of meaning," he asserts, "was their dogmatic insistence that the intention of the speaker or writer was always paramount for interpretation. In countering this dogmatism, there was no need to pretend that intentions did not exist at all; it was simply necessary to point out the arbitrariness of claiming that they were always the ruling structure of discourse" (*Literary Theory* 100-01). For Hirsch, on the other hand, language is trustworthy as the mirror of meaning; otherwise, communication is unattainable, and no norm for interpretation can be established. Depending on the German philosopher Wilhelm Dilthey's hermeneutic principles,[16] Hirsch asserts: "to verify a text is simply to establish that the author probably meant what we construe his text to mean. The interpreter's primary task is to reproduce in himself the author's 'logic,' his attitudes, his cultural givens, in short, his world" (*Validity* 242). For Hirsch, "the thesis that an author's verbal meaning is inaccessible" is "an empirical generalization which neither theory nor experience can decisively confirm or deny" (*Validity* 19).

"Most authors," actually, "believe in the accessibility of their verbal meaning, for otherwise most of them would not write" (Hirsch, *Validity* 18). In spite of the

---

15 "Hirsch's defense of the author's meaning as the only acceptable normative criterion for interpretation stands unshaken" (Irwin, *Intentionalist Interpretation* 54).

16 For Dilthey, understanding is "the imaginative reconstruction of the speaking subject" (Hirsch, *Validity* 242).

long-standing dispute among critics as to whether language can be the obedient reflection of authorial meaning, "this universal faith" (Hirsch, *Validity* 18), after all, represents the fundamental premise for the interpretation of literature: no literary work exists without authorial meaning. To find it out, therefore, can be one of the crucial aims of literary interpretation.

Because our interest lies in presenting a valid and permanent interpretation of Gaskell's fiction, not a short-lived criticism arising from personal insight, we cannot but consider Hirsch's theory as more suitable to our purpose. It furnishes the soundest solution to the perennial problem that "if we do not choose to respect the author's meaning then we have no 'norm' of interpretation, and risk opening the floodgates to critical anarchy" (Eagleton, *Literary Theory* 60). Besides, our standpoint is strengthened by the following two facts. First, despite his radical rejection of the Hirschian principle of close correspondence between language and meaning, Eagleton admits that in some cases language reflects intentions: "though language may not be best understood as individual expression, it certainly in some way involves human subjects and their intentions" (*Literary Theory* 98). Second, "critical anarchy" has been considered as undesirable even by some fervent supporters of "intentional fallacy," or the idea of "what an author intended is irrelevant to the meaning of his text" (Hirsch, *Validity* 12).

For instance, Paul de Man observes that, despite Post-Structuralist scepticism about Hirsch's principle, authorial meaning has "always played a prominent part" in the history of literary theories, "although it was mostly a negative one" (24); moreover, the Belgian Deconstructionist's disapproval of New Criticism is based on its rejection of authorial intention as a fallacy: "The partial failure of American formalism [. . .] is due to its lack of awareness of the intentional structure of literary form" (27). Macherey and Robson, quoted in Section 1.2.7, have paid respect to the author's intention in their concessions. French Post-Structuralist Jacques Derrida, Eagleton remarks, "is not seeking, <u>absurdly</u>, to deny the existence of relatively determinate truths, meanings, identities, intentions, historical continuities; he is seeking rather to see such things as the effects of a wider and deeper history—of language, of the unconscious, of social institutions and practices" (*Literary Theory* 128; emphasis added). Although insisting "[t]he true writer is the reader" and that "the object of critical attention is the structure of the reader's experience, not any 'objective' structure to be found in the work itself," American Receptionist Stanley Fish is also "careful to guard against the hermeneutical anarchy to which his theory appears to lead. To avoid dissolving the text into a thousand competing readings, he appeals to certain 'interpretative strategies' which readers have in common, and which will govern their personal responses" (Eagleton, *Literary Theory* 74). Eagleton himself confesses transcendental meaning is a necessary criterion for the prevention of literary criticism from falling into chaos: "That any such transcendental meaning is a fiction—though <u>perhaps a necessary fiction</u>—is one consequence of the theory of language I have outlined" (*Literary Theory* 114; emphasis added).

The detractors of Hirschian theory recognize the necessity of authorial meaning, the direct correspondence between language and meaning, and the danger of critical anarchy; in other words, they express sympathy to his theory. Modern critical theories, in a sense, have developed in parallel with critics' shift from support for authorial meaning to its denial. Therefore, even for its most polemical denigrators, it should be difficult to make a flat denial of its existence. In *The Life of Charlotte Brontë*, Gaskell quotes Brontë as appreciating a French reviewer of *Shirley* for his "just comprehension of the author's meaning" (Angus Easson ed. 324). This is one of the clear pieces of evidence to indicate that Gaskell and Brontë believe authorial meaning does exist. Another piece of evidence that structures echo authorial meaning is found in Gaskell's notes concerning the republication of the *Household Words* text of *North and South* in two volumes which denote her attempt to design her novel to best reflect her meaning: "I can not insert small pieces here & there—I feel as if I must throw myself back a certain distance in the story, & re-write it from there; retaining the present incidents, but filling up intervals of time &c &c" (*Letters* 329).

1.3. The Sanger-Kroeber Method
1.3.1. Sanger's Approach

If both language mirrors meaning and seeking for authorial intention could be the aim of interpretation, one of the most efficient means to achieve it in an objective way should be to focus on the structure of a literary work. Like language, structure not only mirrors authorial theme, but also remains stable in the sense that key structural elements—such as "time," "location," and "characters"—remain "the *same* throughout the ages" (Hirsch, *Validity* 214).

The pioneering study of the fictional time sequence is Charles Percy Sanger's now-classic analysis of the structure of *Wuthering Heights*, where he demonstrated its careful time schemes and symmetrical family trees. His argument was reinforced by Charles Travis Clay's genealogical table (100-05)[17] and J. F. Goodridge's inge-

---

[17] A. Power assumes Clay's chronology was composed independently because he made no reference to Sanger (139).

nious graph of the novel's time structure (47-50). Power pointed out the errors in Sanger's chronology and Clay's, and even Emily Brontë's miscalculations (139-43). Notable corrections were offered to Sanger's timings by A. Stuart Daley when he solved inconsistencies by disclosing the concurrence of the three harvest moons in the novel with the almanacs of 1826 and 1827 ("Moons and Almanacs" 337-53). The discoveries made by Sanger and Daley were synthesized by Inga-Stina Ewbank (487-96). Having argued against Sanger and Power as to the date of Heathcliff's death ("Heathcliff's Death" 15-19), Daley incorporated his conclusion into a revised chronology ("Revised Chronology" 169-73). The object of their structural analysis, after all, was "to give a detailed proof of the consummate care" the author "devoted to the construction of" her work (Clay 104).

For nearly eighty years since chronology was spotlighted as one of the most effective methods for understanding authorial meaning, a considerable numbers of literary analyses have been written from this angle.[18] In his exploration of the "implied and ambiguous world which lies on the other side of the words on the page" (*IHAM?* ix), John Sutherland unconsciously expresses his concern with Sanger's perspective in solving the puzzles about *Mansfield Park* (*IHAM?* 5-7), *Pride and Prejudice* (*CJEBH?* xi-xii), *Shirley* (*CJEBH?* 91-92), and *Barchester Towers* (*CJEBH?* 109-16). Not merely does he refer to three letters from his readers who investigated the chronologies of Jane Austen's and Anthony Trollope's fiction (*CJEBH?* xi-xii), but also infers Rose Yorke's afterlife beyond the text of *Shirley* by comparing the fictional time with the chronological data of Mary Taylor, her model. Notwithstanding, chronology has attracted little attention from Gaskell scholars.[19] Although having clarified the diversity of critical approaches, the succinct surveys of criticism by Patsy Stoneman (*EG* 1-20) and Kate Flint (*EG* 60-68) record no research of this type.

There is no lack of evidence to show that time plays a crucial role in Gaskell's works: distinctly or indistinctly, her narrator never fails to date her events. "Although not obtrusive—complete dates do not occur," Daley observes in his formal review of *Wuthering Heights*, "the dates and time are deducible, sometimes even to the hour of a specified day, sometimes within the span of a few days or weeks" ("Moons and

18 For instance, W. A. Bie 9-13; E. L. Davidson 48-56; J. F. Kobler 517-21; J. Meckier 157-94; G. M. Moore 195-204; B. Richardson 283-94; Spear 217-18; J. E. Tanner 369-80; D. Taylor 65-58; S. Towheed 217-18; F. L. Walze 408-15.

19 Exceptions are, to the best of my knowledge, five: (a) Nancy Henry, introduction, *Ruth* xxiii-xxxvii; (b) P. J. Yarrow, "The Chronology of *Cranford*" 27-29; (c) Graham Handley, "The Chronology of *Sylvia's Lovers*" 302-03; (d) Andrew Sanders, "A Revised Chronology for *Sylvia's Lovers*" 508-09; and (e) Angus Easson, "Explanatory Notes," *Wives and Daughters* 689-90.

Almanacs" 343). The same is true of Gaskell's fiction.

1.3.2. Kroeber's Approach

Whereas Sanger and his followers spotlighted only chronology as a means for clarifying authorial meaning, Karl Kroeber highlights "location or setting," "action (narrative and dialogue)," and "characters," in addition to "time or temporal ordering." In order to analyse "the underlying structures of novels," he distinguishes the "four basic elements sure to be present in any work of fiction," displays "something of each element's function on each page of every novel studied" (*Styles* 141), and tabulates the results of his analysis. His hope is to "define more-or-less objectively some generic characteristics of one author's larger structural patterns relative to another's" by "identifying, even if only by pages, different novelists' treatment of time, setting, action, and characters" (*Styles* 141).

"Of the four elements studied," observes Kroeber, "the most objective is indubitably that of 'character'" (*Styles* 145). He makes a list of characters who appear "on at least five percent of total pages of their novel"—i.e. Jane Austen's six novels, Charlotte Brontë's four, and George Eliot's seven—, and "the percent of total pages of novel on which the character appears" (*Styles* 231). One of the intriguing outcomes of his investigation is that the protagonist who appears most often in the novel corresponds to the eponymous hero or heroine, or the character who is generally estimated as hero or heroine, at the rate of 82 percent. Exceptions are three: in *Shirley*, Shirley Keeldar appears 40 percent of the total pages, but Caroline Helstone 53; in *Felix Holt*, Felix 26 percent, but Esther Lyon 35; in *Romola*, Romola 52, Tito Melema 68 (*Styles* 231-34). In the other fourteen novels, the chief or eponymous protagonist shows the highest percentage of appearance. Apart from the inaccuracy Kroeber's calculation may inevitably entail—data were collected by the unit of the page (*Styles* 141) and the instructions given to his students leave room for subjective judgement (*Styles* 216)—, this result suggests the possibility of establishing the hypothesis that the chief protagonist is the character who appears most often. Indeed, in the case of Austen, this criterion applies to all her novels without exception (*Styles* 234). Could the chief protagonist be pinpointed by this rule, the whereabouts of authorial meaning should also be, because the protagonist is normally the character into whom authorial meaning is condensed, or because, in Kroeber's phrase, "the form of any segment of a novel is to a significant degree determined by the total design of the novel as a whole" (*Styles* 8). Another intriguing outcome of his formal scrutiny is that it confirms readers' familiar impression about the difference of appearance ratios among the chief protagonist, secondary characters, and minor characters. Stressing the importance of this seemingly commonplace result, Kroeber states that "The worth of such analyses lies in their depiction of familiar arrangements freed from the details of the stories of the novels. Formal analyses should articulate formal patterns" (*Styles* 148). Kroeber's analyses of characters "support the traditional attitude of regarding characters as the essential element in novels," and "suggest that 'characters' are as vital a feature of form as of subject matter" (*Styles* 145).

Pointing out some problems in the current critical arena, he enunciates the aim of his methodology:

> The principal objections to modern literary criticism [. . .] are that it is separatist, egocentric, and committed to perfection. The work of even the best critics is of very little use to subsequent critics. Too often our criticism is either a gathering of personal insights unorganised by a methodology which would enable someone else interested in the same topic to build upon those insights, or a thinly veiled philosophical, religious, or political polemic. Very little of our criticism is honestly exploratory. (*Styles* 181-82)

His complaint about modern criticism as "a gathering of personal insights" and his trust in exploratory criticism correspond to Hirsch's lamentation over modern theories' favouring of subjectivism and individualism (*Validity* 212) and his regarding of "literary study as a corporate enterprise and a progressive discipline" (*Validity* 209). One subjective reading will be replaced by another sooner or later, but an objective interpretation should survive.

1.3.3. Merits and Demerits

One of the defects of this type of objective measure is, as Kroeber himself acknowledges, that it tends "to miss or to obscure nuances of representation which over the course of a long novel are probably decisive for establishing its predominant aesthetic" (*Styles* 141-42); even if "the total time span of fictional action" is clarified, it is "only rarely [. . .] of much aesthetic significance" (*Styles* 142). Kroeber's concession, however, is made on a false premise. Chronology and statistics are fundamentally intended to detect the authorial focus in an objective way. It is still the investigator's task to scrutinize "nuances of representation" and "predominant aesthetic" before reaching the final conclusion. The same is true with the total time span of fictional action. Its detection is aimed at drawing an unbiased inference about authorial meaning; the hypothesis has to be reinforced by other internal and external components of the target fiction. In addition, it depends entirely on the fiction whether the discovery is of aesthetic importance: while the symmetrical pedigrees of two families in *Wuthering Heights* and the intermixture of the double plots in *Mary Barton* may be the keys to understanding the aesthetic achievement of both novels, the chronology for *Cranford*, a collection of daily events of ordinary people, simply enhances the reality of their ordinary life. Furthermore, the disadvantage of Kroeber's methodology is probably caused by his stylistic concern: he examined page by page whether the amount of time covered by an action was minutes, hours, days, months, or years, since his aim was to clarify which authors among the three preferred a longer time span (*Styles* 217-18). If the duration of action were calculated for the purpose of pinpointing the centre of authorial concern, a novel's "predominant aesthetic" should be brought to light.

About structuralist techniques, Eagleton expresses an apprehension similar to Kroeber's: "The structuralist confidence in rigorous analysis and universal laws was appropriate to a technological age, lifting that scientific logic into the protected enclave of the human spirit itself [. . .]. But in doing so it offered, contradictorily, to undermine one of the ruling belief systems of that society, which could be roughly characterized as liberal humanist, and so was radical and technocratic together" (*Literary Theory* 192). The liberal humanists, who believe that "in reading we should be flexible and open-minded, prepared to put our beliefs into question and allow them to be transformed" (*Literary Theory* 69), dislike methodologies; prefer to read by intuitions and intelligent sensibility; and aim at nurturing spiritual wholeness in the world (*Literary Theory* 173-74). Their "distaste for the technocratic" (*Literary Theory* 174) is in constant disagreement with Sanger and Kroeber's concern with formalism; the former prefers arbitrary subjectivism, the latter rational objectivism.

The problem of this approach lies rather with the difficulty in detecting authorial meaning, for normally the structure of fiction is highly elaborate. For example, the investigator often encounters seeming chronological discrepancies. In fact, the periods of Mary's convalescence and her father's disappearance conflict with the linear progression of *Mary Barton*'s chronology. These may be created by Gaskell's formal stratagems—such as "plurality of times" (different time schemes may be set for her narrator and characters) or "interrelation of chronological paradox with characters" (confused time may be a reflection of characters' perplexity). Or, it may be an error unamended, for "the author did not believe it was wrong" (Sutherland, *IHAM?* 18). In *North and South*, indeed, chronological inconsistency is found even in the text which originally appeared as a serial and was later revised by the author herself (Whether this is Gaskell's intentional device or unintentional, this distortion could hardly be found without analysis of the novel's internal chronology).

The most valuable means for clearing up this difficulty is to pay attention to (a) the text's genre, (b) other evidence, and (c) structural emphasis. In a realist narrative, where "words are felt to link up with their thoughts or objects in essentially right and uncontrovertible ways" (Eagleton, *Literary Theory* 118), the possibility of plural times or chronological paradox being used is less likely than in modernist fiction; hence, chronological incongruity may be simply the result of authorial carelessness. In a modernist narrative, on the other hand, where the text "has no determinate meaning, no settled signifieds, but is plural and diffuse, an inexhaustible tissue or galaxy of signifiers, a seamless weave of codes and fragments of codes" (Eagleton, *Literary Theory* 119), seeming errors in the time scheme may probably be the spots where authorial devices are concealed. "To be concerned with the precise genre of a text," Hirsch claims, "is to give every text its due and to avoid the external imposition of merely mechanical methods and canons of interpretation" (*Validity* 263); "the genre concept is so important in textual study. By classifying the text as belonging to a particular genre, the interpreter automatically posits a general horizon for its meaning. The genre provides a sense of the whole, a notion of typical meaning components" (*Validity* 222).

Other information, intrinsic or extrinsic, is also precious in determining authorial meaning. Two ideas have been conflicting about Gaskell's intention for *Lois the Witch*, the short fiction about the innocent 18-year-old English girl Lois Barclay being executed as a witch in 17th century Salem. Some view it as a study of "the devastating consequences of prejudice and mass hysteria on the lives of innocent people" (Ganz 217); others in terms of Lois's Christian perseverance in the face of her surrounding threats. The Sanger-Kroeber analysis endorses the second reading. The investigation into Gaskell's source, Charles Upham's *Lectures on Witchcraft*—extrinsic information—, also champions it. Consequently, it should be most appropriate to conclude that the second interpretation represents authorial meaning.[20] Hirsch is never weary of emphasizing that the outcome of statistical analysis must be examined by other data for its verification: "there always exists relevant evidence beyond such internal evidence, and failure to use it simply makes our guesses unreliable and all attempts at adjudication well-nigh impossible" (193); "it is unsound to insist on deriving all inferences from the text itself. [. . .] The extrinsic data is not, however, read into the text. On the contrary, it is used to verify that which we read out of it. The extrinsic information has ultimately a purely verificative function" (241).

---

20 Detailed discussion is conducted in Chapter 6 of this dissertation: "*Lois the Witch*: The Story of Christian Fortitude."

The third clue for pinpointing authorial meaning is to discover structural elements on which the author placed special emphasis. In disparaging inclusivist tolerance of variety in interpretations, Hirsch observes: "The fundamental flaw in the 'theory of the most inclusive interpretation' is that it overlooks the problem of emphasis. Since different patterns of emphasis exclude one another, inclusivism is neither a genuine norm nor an adequate guiding principle for establishing an interpretation" (*Validity* 230). Because authorial meaning is "a *structure* of component meanings," he asserts, "interpretation has not done its job when it simply enumerates what the component meanings are. The interpreter must also determine their probable structure and particularly their structure of emphases" (*Validity* 230).

We thus guess the most "probable" authorial meaning. Absolute certainty may be unattainable—"a limitation which interpretation shares with many other disciplines" (Hirsch, *Validity* 164)—, but we still aim at reaching "an objective conclusion about relative probabilities" (Hirsch, *Validity* 172). "The interpreter's goal," Hirsch stresses, "is simply this—to show that a given reading is more probable than others. In hermeneutics, verification is a process of establishing relative probabilities" (*Validity* 236).

Despite his frank criticism of literary theories other than Marxism and Feminism, Eagleton is tolerant of the diversity of critical methodologies: "These forms of criticism differ from others because they define the object of analysis differently, have different values, beliefs and goals, and thus offer different kinds of strategy for the realizing of these goals. [. . .] There are many goals to be achieved, and many ways to achieving them" (*Literary Theory* 184-85); "Perhaps we should celebrate the plurality of critical methods, adopt a tolerantly ecumenical posture and rejoice in our freedom from the tyranny of any single procedure" (*Literary Theory* 172). In admitting methodological multifariousness, Hirsch shares Eagleton's view: "There are no correct 'methods' of interpretation" (*Validity* 139).

Old or new, contentual or formal (The contentual method focuses on what is said in the text, while the formal analysis how it is said), literary or scientific, the methodology should be chosen that is most suitable for the critic's purpose, for, as Hirsch states—"No one has ever brought forward a concrete and practical canon of interpretation which applies to all texts, and it is my firm belief that practical canons are not consistently applicable even to the small range of texts for which they were formulated" (*Validity* 200)—, probably, there is no literary methodology which is universally applicable.

1.3.4. Summary

"Literary criticism," remarks Eagleton, "does not usually dictate any particular reading as long as it is 'literary critical'" (*Literary Theory* 77). If the Sanger-Kroeber method appears to lack "critical analysis," it is probably because it centres on the elucidation of the structure of fiction, not on its evaluation, as is Structuralism's "analytical, not evaluative" method (*Literary Theory* 83). "When we analyse literature we are speaking of literature," but "when we evaluate it we are speaking of ourselves" (*Literary Theory* 80). Eagleton would criticize statistical quantification as preserving "the *formalist* bent of New Criticism, its dogged attention to literature as aesthetic object rather than social practice" (*Literary Theory* 79), and question the significance of "the search for a purely objective reading of literary works" (*Literary Theory* 106). For, it "seems impossible to eradicate some element of interpretation, and so of subjectivity, from even the most rigorously objective analysis" (*Literary Theory* 106). We may have to admit that subjective judgement is required in interpreting the data in literary studies, but it is the same even in scientific research. As we have seen above, chronological inquiry and statistical quantification produce almost the same and reproducible result at any time as long as attempted on the equal calculation principle, as scientific analysis does. Another objection to the SK method is that the emotion produced in the readers' mind by literary works cannot be measured by statistical data. We may have to accept this concern also, but have to address the following vital points simultaneously. Twists in the plot such as a climactic moment and a flashback which generate tension in readers, are reflected faithfully on the data. Besides, emotional upheavals are a factor of subjective value-judgement, and differ depending on individuals.

"[T]ime-consuming, as well as messy and frustrating" (Kroeber, *Styles* 4) as it may, the SK method unearths some pivotal forms of a novel. Their techniques help the reader infer its focal points, take a bird's-eye view of the entire narrative, and thus provide hints for detecting authorial meaning more expressly than ever. Statistical quantification of the textual elements offers no superficial apprehension of the text's form and content, but rather a comprehensive and objective understanding of its key structures. It overlooks no fundamental conflicts of the text, but rather spots them. In truth, statistics is employed by Hirsch himself as a means for examining the legitimacy of the interpreter's probability judgement (*Validity* 184-85). To note, nonetheless, the validity of reading must be tested by every possible evidence, external or internal. To this point Hirsch calls our special attention: "The interpreter needs all the clues he can muster with regard not only to the text's *language* and genre, but also to the cultural and personal attitudes the author might be expected to bring to bear in specifying his verbal meanings" (*Validity* 240).

Many conservative scholars are "hostile to, or at least suspicious of" (Anthony

Kenny 116) this statistical approach. However, this is employed as "means of refining our subjective impressions" (Kroeber, *Styles* 239). In defence of stylometry, Kenny asserts,

> If we are to compare the stylometrist's procedure to a piece of scientific apparatus, the appropriate comparison is with the camera of an aerial photographer. <u>Photography from the sky can enable patterns to be detected which are obscured when one is too close to the ground: it enables us to see the wood despite the trees.</u> So the statistical study of a text can reveal broad patterns, macroscopic uniformities in a writer's work which escape notice as one reads word by word and sentence by sentence. (116; qtd. in Vickers 99; emphasis added)

If an analysis of viewing the textual wood as well as the textual trees could be conducted, the interpretation closest to the authorial meaning should be achieved. Statistics, which has been employed by such stylometric critics as Kroeber, Kenny, and Vickers, is one of the most effective methods to detect the author construct's meaning.

1.4. Conclusion

We "always interpret literary works to some extent in the light of our own concerns"; without them, we are incapable of making criticism (Eagleton, *Literary Theory* 10). Psychoanalysts spotlight ambiguities in dialogues to detect the protagonist's unconsciousness. Marxists centre on the class struggle to explain it from the historical or political perspective. Feminists focus on the heroine's sufferings or strength to study gender and sexuality. Critics are free to undertake their own reading, disregarding authorial meanings, since, as Barthes states, "the birth of the reader must be at the cost of the death of the Author" (148). This trend in literary criticism, nonetheless, is the very cause that has invited "critical anarchy." A typical example of this situation is the difference of interpretation as to the theme of *Mary Barton* between Marxists and Feminists: the former regard it as the "social-problem" novel, the latter the heroine's Bildungsroman. This chaos may be agreeable for a receptionist critic like Wolfgang Iser, for "different readers are free to actualise the work in different ways, and there is no single correct interpretation which will exhaust its semantic potential" as long as the reader rewrites the text "to render it internally *consistent*" (Eagleton, *Literary Theory* 70). It is a deplorable situation, nevertheless, for the hermeneutist Hirsch and the structuralists Sanger and Kroeber. Hirsch advocates authorial meaning as the only norm of literary criticism. For its objective understanding, Sanger and Kroeber resort to chronology and statistics in examining "time, location, and characters," three pivotal structural elements in all literary works. Chronologies of novels bring to light which hour, day, or year is most emphasized and described in fullest details. Statistical investigation into topographical movement demonstrates the central and marginal locations of fiction. Statistical quantification of the frequency of characters' appearance reveals who are central protagonists or sub-characters. In short, the Sanger-Kroeber method affords a bird's-eye view of the text, and hence clarifies in the most objective way the spots where authors, consciously or unconsciously, have condensed their intentions.

Scientific analysis of fiction may be embarrassing since literature is traditionally believed to be "identical with the opposite of analytical thought and conceptual enquiry," in other words, with "feeling and experience" (Eagleton, *Literary Theory* 22). Although approaches are different, however, the linguistic analyses by Russian Formalists, Structuralists, and New Critics were also "scientific."[21] It was his "scientific" impulse which led Northrop Frye to "a formalism even more full-blooded than that of New Criticism" (Eagleton, *Literary Theory* 80). Psychoanalysts may criticize statistical quantification for its overlooking of textual evasion and omission. On the contrary, it helps us find the spot where their method is most useful, and also whether it is worth attempting or not. Eagleton concludes his survey of literary theories by observing "What you choose and reject theoretically [. . .] depends upon what you are practically trying to do. This has always been the case with literary criticism. [. . .] In any academic study we select the objects and methods of procedure which we believe the most important, and our assessment of their importance is governed by frames of interest deeply rooted in our practical forms of social life" (*Literary Theory* 184). Hirsch expresses his idea of the purpose of literary criticism in his Preface: "The theoretical aim of a genuine discipline, scientific or humanistic, is the attainment of truth, and its practical aim is agreement that truth has probably been achieved. Thus the practical goal of every genuine discipline is consensus—the winning of firmly grounded agreement that one set of conclusions is more probable than others—and this is precisely the goal of valid interpretation" (*Validity* viii-ix). The Sanger-Kroeber method is the most sensible technique for "the attainment of truth," i.e. the objective realization of authorial meaning.

Sanger employed chronology, and Kroeber statistics, as "means of refining our subjective impressions" (Kroeber, *Styles* 239). The scientific application of their

---

21 Liberal humanists' embarrassment at structuralist confidence in scientific and technological approach is brought to light by Eagleton (*Literary Theory* 191-92).

methods to literary interpretation—hypothetical deduction of authorial meaning from statistical quantification and tabulation of structural components—may provoke uneasiness in more literary-minded critics who consider "arid abstractions are out of place when it comes to art" (Eagleton, *Literary Theory* 207). On the other hand, the authors of *The Craft of Research*, express their support for visual devices, which help us "communicate complex data," "discover patterns and relationships," stimulate thinking, and organize ideas: "What would a graph look like that contrasted Macbeth's moral development with Lady Macbeth's? [. . .] Like other formal devices, visuals encourage you to discover ideas and relationships that you might not have seen otherwise" (Booth 197-98). "[N]ew conceptions, new analyses, new results [. . .] give more knowledge, more understanding, more insight, more control" (Booth 126) (although the Sanger-Kroeber method is actually not new). In truth, as Hirsch emphasizes, there is no methodological distinction between the sciences and the humanities:

> Our self-confirming pre-understanding needs to be tested against all the relevant data we can find, for our idea of genre is ultimately a hypothesis like any other, and the best hypothesis is the one that best explains all the relevant data. This identity of genre, pre-understanding, and hypothesis suggests that the much-advertised cleavage between thinking in the sciences and the humanities does not exist. The hypothetico-deductive process is fundamental in both of them, as it is in all thinking that aspires to knowledge. (*Validity* 263-64)

Subjective readings will be superseded by new ones someday. But, readings based on objective data will not.

CHAPTER 2 *Mary Barton*: Who Is the Central Protagonist?

2.1. Introduction[22]

To determine the central protagonist is crucial to the detection of Gaskell's meaning, especially in *Mary Barton*, since the statistical investigation into the form of fiction produces the outcome which is at variance with the authorial avowal. That is, the structure indicates the centrality of Mary Barton, the eponymous heroine, while the author emphasizes that of her father John Barton. The solution of this contradiction is the main concern of this chapter. If Gaskell's declaration expresses her textual meaning, the result of our statistical analysis will be fallacious. If our result reflects her author construct's meaning, conversely, the author's avowal will be misleading.

"'John Barton' was the original title," confesses Gaskell to Mary Greg, the sister-in-law of W. R. Greg, the most eminent detractor of *Mary Barton*,[23] "Round the character of John Barton all the others formed themselves; he was my hero, *the* person with whom all my sympathies went, with whom I tried to identify myself at the time [of writing]" (*Letters* 74).[24] A confession of a similar intention is made in a letter to Julia Lamont, her friend: "'John Barton' was the original name, as being the central figure to my mind; indeed I had so long felt that the bewildered life of an ignorant thoughtful man of strong power of sympathy, dwelling in a town so full of striking contrasts as this is, was a tragic poem, that in writing he was [. . .] my 'hero'" (*Letters* 70). In her Preface to this novel, moreover, Gaskell declares that her compassion towards Manchester labourers motivated her writing it: "The more I reflected on this unhappy state of things between those so bound to each other by common interests, as the employers and the employed must ever be, the more anxious I became to give some utterance to the agony which, from time to time, convulses this dumb people; the agony of suffering without the sympathy of the happy, or of erroneously believing that such is the case."[25]

Critics' opinions about its protagonist differ depending on their responses to

---

22 Section 2.1, 2.3, 2.4, and 2.5 of this chapter is the original version of my article "Is *Mary Barton* an Industrial Novel?" (*The Gaskell Society Journal*, vol. 15); Section 2.2 is that of my paper "*Mary Barton*'s Chronology" (*Gaskell Studies*, vol. 9).
23 Handley mistakenly regards Mrs Greg as the "wife of W. R. Greg" (*Chronology* 57), actually, of his brother Samuel (Jenny Uglow, *EG* 160). See also Angus Easson, *Critical Heritage* 163; A. W. Ward, introduction, *MB* lxv.
24 At the beginning of this often-quoted letter, Gaskell mistakenly conjectures that the writer of the critical remarks is Samuel Greg, her correspondent's husband and W. R. Greg's brother (Easson, *Critical Heritage* 163; Uglow, *EG* 160; Ward, introduction, *MB* lxv).

these authorial avowals. Some favour John Barton, the epitome of Manchester's poverty-stricken workers; others Mary Barton, his daughter.[26] These interpretations, advanced through their own approaches, are all sound and enlightening. Regrettably, however, none of the critics I have consulted take a formal approach to determining the novel's protagonist. The understanding of a novel will be greatly promoted should its structure be seen clearly alongside its theme, because theme and structure are usually intricately interwoven, as themes are conveyed only through structural elements, and as structure invariably mirrors the urauthor's meanings. Accordingly, if her meanings regarding her protagonist, hidden in the structure of the novel, were explained, we might be able to end the debate as to who her central character is.

  Section 2.2 explains the process of composing as most accurate a chronology as possible for the novel; the composed table will serve as the source of statistical analysis. Based on the data provided by the Comprehensive Chronology, the array of quantified formal aspects, Section 2.3 analyses some of its essential structures, such as characters' appearance rate, shifts of scenes, plot interaction, the transition of time, narratorial intervention, and places of action, to examine the reliability of Gaskell's insistence on John Barton's centrality. This section also seeks to demonstrate that equal emphasis is placed on both plots by highlighting Jem Wilson's involvement in Mary's love plot and John's industrial plot. In contrast to the centrality of Mary Barton revealed by our structural analysis, Section 2.4 examines the historical author's confessions to highlight that her intention was always to establish John Barton's centrality. Finally, in Section 2.5, the summary of our analysis is presented as a challenge to the conventional reading of *Mary Barton* as an industrial novel.

---

25 *Mary Barton: A Tale of Manchester Life*, edited by Edgar Wright, Oxford UP, 1998, pp. xxxv-xxxvi. Subsequent page references are to this edition and hereafter given parenthetically in the text with the abbreviation *MB*.

26 Comments in favour of John are found in W. A. Craik (*EG* 35), Brian Crick ("Implications" 517-18), Macdonald Daly ("Essentially, the narrative is a drama of working-class radicalisation and its consequences, both personal and social" [xxiii]), Monica Correa Fryckstedt (98, 102), Margaret Ganz (63), Winifred Gérin (*EG* 87-88), A. B. Hopkins (*EG* 76-77), Margaret Lane (introduction, *MB* vii), Laurence Lerner (Gaskell wrote *Mary Barton* "to take the side of the workers, and her hero is a Chartist" [introduction, *WD* 13]), Arthur Pollard (*Mrs Gaskell* 109-10), Thomas Edward Recchio ("The Problem of Form" 30), Aina Rubenius (230), J. G. Sharps (*Observation* 57, 59, 67-68), Kathleen Tillotson (211), Anna Unsworth (*EG* 42-43), and Edgar Wright (*Mrs Gaskell* 31, 35, 233; introduction, *MB* xv). Meanwhile, those for Mary are found in Tessa Brodetsky (16), Robin B. Colby ("*Appointed*" 36, 40, 44-45), Deirdre d'Albertis (*Dissembling* 50), Easson (*EG* 73, 78; introduction, *MB* 15-16), Coral Lansbury (*EG* 17), Hilary M. Schor (*Scheherezade* 18, 38), Alan Shelston (introduction, *MB* xxiv), Uglow (*EG* 200), and Ward (introduction, *MB* lxxiv).

2.2. Construction of Chronology

The story opens with an excursion made by the Bartons and the Wilsons to Green Heys Fields (The subsequent explanation would be better understood if "The Comprehensive Chronology for *Mary Barton*" [Appendix 1] and "Characters' Correlation Diagram for *Mary Barton*" [Appendix 2] were referred to whenever necessary). It takes place on "an early May evening [. . .] ten or a dozen years ago" (*MB* 2). Gaskell started on this novel soon after she lost her son on 10 August 1845 (Ellis H. Chadwick 156; Gérin, *EG* 73; G. D. Sanders 17; and Uglow, *EG* 152); therefore, the year of the narrative's opening would be about 1834.[27]

The events of one day are traced until two fifths of the way through Chapter 3 of the novel. At midnight on the same day her mother dies in childbirth (*MB* 19), when Mary is nearly "thirteen" years old (*MB* 10, 383). Hence, it can be surmised that she was born in the summer of 1821. The narrator tells us in Chapters 1 and 2 that Jem Wilson, a worker and her future husband, will be "eighteen" years old "in two months" (*MB* 10, 17), which means the date of his birth falls on a July day in 1816.

"Three years" (*MB* 26) have passed since Mrs Barton's death; Mary, "a girl of sixteen" (*MB* 27), becomes apprenticed to Miss Simmonds, milliner and dressmaker. The story moves on to 1837 by the end of Chapter 3. "Another year passed on" (*MB* 28), observes the narrator at the start of Chapter 4. Mary's first encounter with Margaret Jennings, a kind-hearted neighbour, and her grandfather Job Legh, during "the early winter" (*MB* 30) described in Chapters 4 and 5, therefore, is the event of 1838. The two young girls become close friends "ere the end of that winter" (*MB* 45), when the story enters 1839. The fire at the Carsons' mill breaks out "towards the end of February" (*MB* 48) of the same year. Chapter 6, portraying the vivid contrast between the poor labourers' kindness and the mill-owner's indifference to the dying Ben Davenport, covers several days in "March" (*MB* 64) 1839.

Mrs Davenport regains her strength in "a week or two" (*MB* 83) after her husband's demise. The death of Wilson's twin boys (*MB* 85-86) appears to take place in March or April because it happens soon after her recovery. This calculation accords with the chronological data in Chapter 8: Jem's Sunday-afternoon visit to Mary is

27 Easson states the story "opens about 1835/37 and the main action can be dated about 1840, perhaps coloured also by the serious depression of 1841" (*EG* 74); his opening year must have been inferred from counting backwards from 1847, when, according to the author's observation in her Preface, this tale was complete (*MB* xxxvi). Daly estimates it as 1835 (xxiv); an anonymous reviewer 1836 (Easson, *Critical Heritage* 128); Craik 1838 (*EG* 6); Hopkins (*EG* 71) and K. Tillotson (205) 1839; Lucas (52) and Stone (146) in the late 1830s; Uglow in the mid-1830s (*EG* 194); Michael Wheeler 1838-39 (*Art of Allusion* 45); and Whitfield 1839-41 (11).

paid "about three weeks after" (*MB* 93) his brothers' death, and in "early spring" (*MB* 94) of "1839" (*MB* 97).

Calendar facts and figures are scattered throughout the novel. The chronology slightly changes depending on which information the researcher counts on. One of the most reliable pieces of information with which the time sequence of the novel may be determined is found on pages 97 and 98, where the narrator relates how John Barton was appointed as one of the delegates to the Chartist petition of "spring" in "1839." Historically, this petition was submitted to Parliament in May (or, 14 June [Ward, introduction, *MB* lvii]) 1839, and rejected on 12 July of the same year (Edgar Wright, introduction, *MB* x; Koga 120; Ward, introduction, *MB* lvii). It can reasonably be supposed, therefore, that Chapters 8 and 9, sketching Barton's departure for London and his miserable return, depict events that happened between May and July 1839.[28]

That Mary can secure two meals and tea a day at Miss Simmonds's (*MB* 131) is one of the strongest pieces of evidence that the opening two-fifths (*MB* 130-36) of Chapter 10 are dealing with events of the later months of 1839. She was apprenticed to the dressmaker in 1837, three years after her mother's death (*MB* 26), with the promise that she could dine and take tea there after "two years" (*MB* 28).

Chastised by her father "one evening" for neglecting to see Jane Wilson, his late friend's wife, Mary calls on her the following afternoon (*MB* 136). In order to pin down the time of this visit, the date of John Barton's meeting with his sister-in-law, Esther, on 10 February 1840, is of great help, because it occurs "[s]ome weeks after" (*MB* 142) Mary's visit to Mrs Wilson. Hence, it is most likely paid on a day in January 1840.

For the clarification of the reason why the date of Barton's encounter with Esther can be dated as above, the date of his murdering Harry Carson, John Carson's son and Mary Barton's wealthy lover, provides a valuable clue. The narrator observes that the crime was committed "early on Thursday night" (*MB* 273, 300), or 18 March (*MB* 449); the year is no doubt 1840, insofar as the encounter is described immediately after the events of "summer" (*MB* 132, 134, 136), 1839. She also notes that it is on "Wednesday [. . .] St Patrick's day [17 March]"[29] that John Barton calls on Jem to borrow the murder weapon (*MB* 450).[30] The rendezvous between masters and workers, and the latter's drawing of lots to decide the assassin of Harry Carson,

---

28 Craik refers to this 1839 petition as an important example of Gaskell's adroitness in incorporating history into fiction (*EG* 18). Her view is supported by Brodetsky (18), Hopkins (*EG* 75), Ward (introduction, *MB* lvii), and E. Wright (introduction, *MB* x).

29 The perpetual calendar shows that 17 March 1840 was actually a Tuesday ("Perpetual Calendar").

take place "on a Tuesday" (*MB* 224), that is, 16 March 1840. Jem fights with Harry "some days" (*MB* 247) before the fatal day, 18 March. If we presumed that the day of this scuffle is 15 March, Jem's meeting with Esther would fall on 10 March, because it happens on "the fifth" day (*MB* 206) since the day on which he began to look for Harry—which is the day following his interview with her. Esther speaks with Jem on the very day when her one month's imprisonment (*MB* 145, 184) is over. It can be deduced, accordingly, that John Barton's encounter with Esther occurs on the night of 10 February 1840, and that on the "next morning" (*MB* 145), 11 February, she is taken up to the gaol.

This inference accords with other chronological details. If we assume that the "evening" (*MB* 164) when Mary acknowledges to Margaret her love for Jem—"some weeks" (*MB* 167) after her January visit to Mrs Wilson—is that of 4 March 1840, the unexpected call of Will Wilson, the sailor, on Alice, his aunt and foster-mother, is supposed to be made on 5 March; for, it is "the next day" (*MB* 169) that Mary welcomes her old playmate with Alice and Jane Wilson at Mrs Wilson's home. Mary comes to notice Will's love for Margaret by the time of "ten days or so" (*MB* 204) after his arrival in Manchester—that is, by around 14 March. He leaves the city on "Thursday" (*MB* 224) evening, 18 March, the day of John Barton's shooting of Harry Carson (*MB* 449); this dating is supported by Mary's words of regret to the departing Will: "But it's not a fortnight since you came" (*MB* 225).

Esther walks to the scene of the murder at "dawn" (*MB* 273) on a "Friday" (*MB* 250, 273-74) to find a scrap of paper used as wadding for the gun on which Mary's name is inscribed in Jem's handwriting; she spends the day collecting details relevant to the homicide, and calls on Mary to give her the piece of paper "after midnight" (*MB* 272), on Saturday, 20 March.

After Mary discovers that her father is the real murderer, the focus of the story shifts to her determined efforts to prove Jem's alibi. On Saturday "morning" (*MB* 291), she calls on Job Legh to seek his advice; around "Saturday at noon" (*MB* 300), she recalls the name of Will's ship; on "Sunday morning" (*MB* 317), she tells Jane Wilson her plan to rescue her son; and, all the necessary arrangements being worked out in two days, she takes a train to Liverpool "on Monday morning" (*MB* 332), 22 March. Her breathtaking adventure in pursuit of Will, the only witness who can prove Jem's innocence, is undertaken that afternoon (*MB* 342, 351, 354); her mis-

---

30 The narrator writes on page 395 that it is "only two days before" the day of murder, or on 16 March, that John Barton borrows the gun from Jem; this statement contradicts the date specified on page 450, 17 March. I shall follow the latter date because it is one of the few concrete dates given in the text and because the chronology will then run more smoothly.

sion is to bring Will to Jem's trial which is to be conducted on "Tuesday" (*MB* 311), 23 March. Hardly has his safety been assured than she falls into delirium resulting from her excessive physical and emotional strains, and is taken care of at the house of Ben Sturgis, a considerate boatman, "that night" (*MB* 395). Early on Wednesday morning (*MB* 395, 397, 398), 24 March, Job Legh comes to his abode to tell Jem to go home with Mrs Wilson and Will to bid farewell to dying old Alice. They presumably arrive in Manchester that afternoon, only to see Alice meet a peaceful death "the day after their return" (*MB* 399), on Thursday, 25 March. Her funeral is held on "Sunday afternoon" (*MB* 400), 28 March, and shortly after "eleven" (*MB* 406) o'clock that night, Jem happens to glimpse John Barton enter his house. Jem goes back to Liverpool by the first train on 29 March (*MB* 400) to find Mary still hovering between life and death in Sturgis's house.

The text gives no chronological details of the period of her convalescence except for two vague hints. The first is found on page 429 when John Barton tells John Carson that he has been suffering from an acute agony of repentance "this fortnight past" "since that night [18 March]." His words taken literally, the date of his talk with the mill-owner would fall on 31 March. Furthermore, it is made explicit on page 421 that it takes place on the "fourth" day "from Mary's return home." From these two details, it can be deduced that Mary comes back home from Liverpool on 28 March. This deduction conflicts with our previous argument which suggests that she is still being nursed at Sturgis's home on that day. In consequence, we can only take John Barton's "fortnight" as a statement which provides an approximate, rather than a definite, period of Mary's recuperation—that is, as meaning a period of about a few weeks. The following two extracts from Chapter 34 serve as the second clue for determining the term of her convalescence: "There came a fine, bright, balmy day. And Mary tottered once more out into the open air" (*MB* 412); "At last a day, fine enough for Mary to travel on, arrived" (*MB* 413). They imply that her sickness is not so slight as to be cured in a few days but serious enough to require more than a few weeks of recovery. Because these two hints suggest "a few weeks" to be Mary's most likely period of convalescence, let us advance the hypothesis, for the sake of convenience, that her recovery takes two weeks—from 23 March, the day of her being seized with convulsions at the court, to 5 April, that of her returning home. According to this hypothesis, Jem is to spend one week from 29 March, the day of his return to Liverpool, before taking Mary home on 5 April. They take a train which departs around "two" (*MB* 414) o'clock in the afternoon, and reach Manchester on the same day. This time sequence looks appropriate, but involves the controversial problem as to the acceptability of John Barton's miscalculation of "seven days."

As has been explained above, John Barton disappears from his home on the night of 18 March, and reappears on the moonlit evening (*MB* 407) of 28 March. He lives alone for some "days" (*MB* 417), receives his daughter on 5 April who comes back from Liverpool, and divulges his crime to John Carson at around "eight o'clock" (*MB* 424) on the "fourth" (*MB* 421) night after her return, i.e. 8 April. In other words, there is a time span of twenty-one days between his act of violence (18 March) and his initial confession (8 April) which he reckons as only fourteen days (*MB* 429) himself. It is debatable whether his miscalculation of "seven days" could be regarded as the understandable error of a character who has suffered three weeks of agonising conscience, or merely as an authorial anachronism. To argue this point would carry us so far away from our present purpose that this contradiction shall be left unsolved.

John Barton breathes his last in John Carson's arms in the early "morning" (*MB* 438) of 9 April. On the following "morning" (*MB* 442, 446, 449), John Carson's note to summon Job Legh and Jem to his home arrives. His interview with the two labourers, which Chapter 37 centres on, is held in the afternoon of the same day, 10 April, when he asks about the details of the murder and John Barton's motive for killing his son. The narrator relates on page 449 that this interrogation is carried out a "few weeks" after his son's death (18 March), or, according to our calculation, on the twenty-fourth day since the bloodshed day. This almost exact correspondence between these two timelines is one of the strong pieces of evidence to prove the accuracy of our chronology. The same is true of the narrator's statement at the end of Chapter 36 in which she declares that the events she has related took place "six or seven years ago" (*MB* 447). As the main events of the story are set in 1840, the date of this narrative is supposed to be 1846 or 1847. This precisely coincides with the years when Gaskell actually engaged herself in the novel's composition (*MB* xxxv-xxxvi).

In all probability, Esther's burial (*MB* 463) takes place during April 1840, because Jem's emigration, arranged not "many days after" (*MB* 458) John Barton's funeral, has to be carried out "almost immediately" (*MB* 458), and because she is laid to rest before Jem starts his voyage.

The novel closes with the idyllic scene of a cheerful home in Canada. The "imperfect" (*MB* 464) pronunciation of Johnnie, Mary and Jem's baby boy, suggests that he is little more than two years old. Hence, the year is presumably 1842 or 1843.

Critics' opinions differ as to the years in which the novel is mainly set.[31] Be that as it may, our detailed chronology shows that the story begins in May 1834, chiefly describes the events of March and April 1840, and ends in 1842 or 1843; thus, it deals with approximately eight and a half years.

2.3. Comprehensive Chronology

To clarify the authorial meaning through the formal scheme of the novel, we have constructed as precise a chronology as possible by checking calendar facts and figures scattered over the text. Based on this is created "The Comprehensive Chronology for *Mary Barton*" (See Appendix 1), a collection of statistical data on three fundamental structural elements—time, place, and characters. The story is divided into scenes according to the shift of time or place, to which Scene Numbers are allocated. The length of each scene is specified by page numbers and scene percentages. In addition, the place of action is examined scene by scene. The cells corresponding to Mary's adventurous six-days are coloured grey, since the conspicuous length of pages allocated to this period affords a key to an understanding of the authorial meaning for this novel.

Main characters' appearance rate is also provided in the Comprehensive Chronology. If a character appears in a certain scene, his or her cell is painted deep grey. If not, it is blank. If he or she is only referred to by others including the narrator, it is coloured light grey. In a scene where a character dies, the relevant cell is crossed. For example, Chapter 1 of the novel, which relates the afternoon excursion of the Bartons and the Wilsons to Green Heys Fields, features all members of both families, so that their cells are shaded deep grey. Esther and Alice Wilson are only spoken of in the conversation between John Barton and George Wilson (*MB* 4-8, 10); thus, their cells are coloured light grey (scs. 2-4). No mention is made of other characters in this chapter; therefore, their cells are blank. Because the first one and a half pages (*MB* 83-84) of Chapter 7, or Scenes 46 and 47, give only the narrator's explanation of Mrs Davenport's recovery, and her brief allusions to the Wilsons, Alice, Margaret, Mr and Mrs Barton, and Mary's flirtation with Harry Carson, these characters' cells are all tinted light grey. The light grey cells which sometimes appear in Mrs Barton's column after Scene 12 show that she is still mentioned even after her death.

---

31 For example, 1836 and after (G. D. Sanders 20); 1837-42 (E. Wright, introduction, *MB* vii); 1838 or 1840 (Easson, *EG* 48, 74); 1839 (Henry, introduction, *RU* xxiii); 1839-41 (Charles Kingsley qtd. in Easson, *Critical Heritage* 153); 1839-42 (Ganz 49); around 1840 (Brodetsky 16); 1841-43 (early reviewers qtd. in Easson, *Critical Heritage* 74, 108); about 1842 (W. R. Greg qtd. in Easson, *Critical Heritage* 164, 172); 1842-43 (Ward, introduction, *MB* lv); 1840s (E. H. Chadwick 208; Stephen Gill 21; Lane, introduction, *MB* v; Rubenius 22; Williams, *Culture and Society* 99).

The progress of an action can be monitored by the Chronology as well. For instance, it is eight months afterwards when Mary's copy of Samuel Bamford's poem[32] functions as a clue for making her notice the true assassin of Harry Carson, as it is duplicated in July 1839 (*MB* 129) and brought by Esther to her on 30 March 1840 (*MB* 286). There is only an interval of one month or so between Mary's rejection of Jem's proposal and her seeing him again at the Liverpool assizes, inasmuch as the former is the event on a February evening of 1840 (sc. 84; *MB* 150), the latter on 23 March 1840 (scs. 202-08; *MB* 373-93), and Scene 202 is the first scene after Scene 84 for which their cells are both imbued with deep grey. Likewise, Mary's reunion with her father on 5 April (sc. 223; *MB* 416) takes place about 18 days after his disappearance on 18 March (sc. 125; *MB* 232-33).[33]

2.3.1. Characters' Appearance Rate

(a) The most intriguing result demonstrated in the Comprehensive Chronology is that it is not *John* Barton but *Mary* Barton who is most active throughout the novel.[34] It presents one of the strong pieces of evidence for our scepticism about the traditional reading of *Mary Barton* as a Condition-of-England novel. Mary's centrality will be examined in the subsequent discussion in this Chapter. (b) The second striking result will be that the character who comes after Mary in the appearance-rate table is Jem Wilson, not John Barton.[35] The reason for Jem's second-highest prominence lies in his involvement in Mary's plot and John's. A detailed analysis of Jem's role will be conducted in the following Section 2.3.4. (c) The third eye-catching outcome will be that references to God (including such an icon of Christianity as Christ, the Bible, and church) are found in 86 scenes out of the total 257, or at the rate of 33.5%.[36] This outcome implies Gaskell's fundamental principle of solving the

---

32 Samuel Bamford (1788-1872), "formerly hand-loom weaver" (*Letters* 84) and humanitarian reformer, writes a letter on 9 March 1849 to Gaskell to praise her novel (qtd. in Easson, *Critical Heritage* 150-51, and Waller 7-8).

33 In the process of constructing the chronology, an error about the John Cropper was discovered. In her attempt to save Jem, Mary recollects the name of Will's ship: "He had named it, she had been sure, all along. He had named it in his conversation with her that last, that fatal Thursday evening" (*MB* 300). The ship name appears for the first time on page 178 in Will's tale of adventure, and it does not until recollected by Mary on page 300. Therefore, as far as the description in the text is concerned, Will makes no mention of "John Cropper" to Mary at his Thursday farewell visit (*MB* 224-29).

34 This aspect is also noted by Bodenheimer: "It is surprising [. . .] to discover how rarely John Barton appears as an actor in dramatized scenes" ("Private Grief" 197), and by Craik: "the novel as it stands spends less time on him [John] than on Mary" (*EG* 32).

35 Thus, Stone's assertion that Alice Wilson is the third significant character (149) contradicts the result of our examination. Jem is regarded by some critics as the novel's hero (J. G. Sharps, *Observation* 57; Uglow, *EG* 163).

36 In case of God, the appearance rate by times (Fig. 2.2) would be more reliable than that by percent (Fig.

Appearance	Pt.I active	Pt.I referred	Pt.I subtotal	Pt.II active	Pt.II referred	Pt.II subtotal	Pt.III active	Pt.III referred	Pt.III subtotal	Total active	Total referred	Grand Total	Pt.I active %	Pt.I referred %	Pt.I subtotal %	Pt.II active %	Pt.II referred %	Pt.II subtotal %
narrator	30	0	30	23	0	23	11	0	11	64	0	64	15.3	0	15.3	12.5	0	12.5
John Barton	39	35	74	5	17	22	10	20	30	54	72	126	15.8	15.1	30.9	0.8	9.1	9.9
John Carson	2	14	16	12	5	17	8	4	12	22	23	45	0.5	9.7	10.2	5.8	1.3	7.1
Harry	10	30	40	0	31	31	0	8	8	10	69	79	3.9	15.7	19.6	0	15.7	15.7
Sally Leadbitter	6	6	12	4	1	5	2	1	3	12	8	20	2.1	2.4	4.5	1.4	0.1	1.5
Mrs Davenport	6	3	9	4	7	11	0	1	1	10	11	21	3.5	0.4	3.9	1.8	2.9	4.7
Job Legh	7	12	19	28	9	37	11	13	24	46	34	80	6.5	3.7	10.2	11.3	4.5	15.8
Margaret	22	9	31	7	10	17	6	10	16	35	29	64	13	2.1	15.1	3.5	3.5	7
Will	4	4	8	5	26	31	2	2	4	11	32	43	2.2	1.8	4	3.8	12.8	16.6
Alice	18	10	28	7	24	31	2	4	6	27	38	65	7.7	4.5	12.2	2.7	9	11.7
Jem	19	32	51	9	48	57	30	10	40	58	90	148	8.4	14.3	22.7	4.7	22.2	26.9
Jane Wilson	11	24	35	21	20	41	11	6	17	43	50	93	4.5	13.3	17.8	9.9	8.3	18.2
George Wilson	16	21	37	0	3	3	0	2	2	16	26	42	8.5	10.1	18.6	0	1.1	1.1
Esther	4	15	19	2	2	4	2	4	6	8	21	29	1.9	6.3	8.2	1.5	2	3.5
Mrs Barton	8	18	26	0	6	6	0	1	1	8	25	33	2.7	7.3	10	0	3.8	3.8
Mary Barton	66	27	93	64	13	77	30	10	40	160	50	210	28.6	11	39.6	27.9	4.9	32.8
God	0	39	39	0	28	28	0	19	19	0	86	86	0	25.7	25.7	0	16.3	16.3

Pt. III	active	0	8.4	0	0.3	0	3.2	10.9	0.3	0.6	1.5	4.7	0	0.6	0	4.4	3.1	5.1
	referred	8.7	4.7	0.4	2.4	2.4	2.6	2.5	1.7	0.9	3.2	3.4	0.5	0.1	4.8	1.1	7.8	0
	subtotal	8.7	13.1	0.4	2.7	2.4	5.8	13.4	2	1.5	4.7	8.1	0.5	0.7	4.8	5.5	10.9	5.1
Total	active	0	64.9	2.7	3.7	8.5	17.6	24	10.7	6.6	18	22.5	5.3	4.1	3.9	10.7	19.7	32.9
	referred	50.7	20.6	11.5	10.7	13.6	24.2	39	15.2	15.5	8.8	11.6	3.8	2.6	36.2	12.1	32	0
	Grand Total	50.7	85.5	14.2	14.4	22.1	41.8	63	25.9	22.1	26.8	34.1	9.1	6.7	40.1	22.8	51.7	32.9

Top three in each Part are coloured grey. Data in the Times division correspond almost accurately with those in the Percent division except in the God column. The discrepancy takes place since a character is counted "active/referred" irrespective of the length of a scene if he/she appears there even once; appearance percentage is calculated by adding up the percentage of scene length.

Table 2.1. Characters Focused in *Mary Barton*

industrial conflict by letting masters and workers apply themselves to the teachings of God, or her essential quality as a Christian writer.[37]

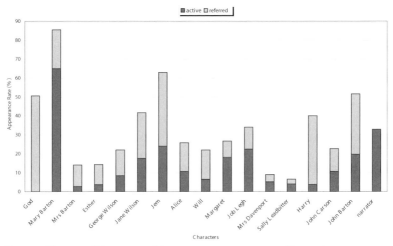

Fig. 2.1. Characters' Frequency of Appearance in *Mary Barton* (Percent)

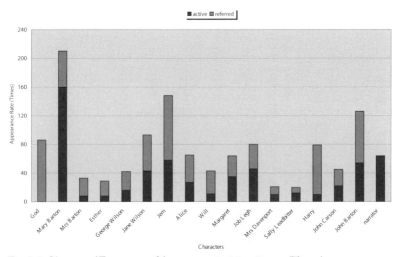

Fig. 2.2. Characters' Frequency of Appearance in *Mary Barton* (Times)

2.1), since God is referred to once or twice in one scene in most cases, not throughout the scene as other characters.

[37] J. E. Bradford states in the *Christian Examiner* that *Mary Barton* "is written in the dominating spirit of Christianity throughout" (qtd. in Handley, *Chronology* 59). See Conclusion of this dissertation also.

These three features are distinctly shown in "Table 2.1. Characters Focused in *Mary Barton*," created from data in the Comprehensive Chronology, and in "Fig. 2.1." and "Fig. 2.2," both featuring Characters' Frequency of Appearance in *Mary Barton*, constructed on the basis of the figures in the total percentage and times boxes of Table 2.1.

2.3.2. Ternary Structure

As much as 37.2% of the total pages is given to Mary's escapade of only six days while 48.0% to about six years and 14.9% to roughly three years—this bizarre page-allocation ratio makes us suspect some authorial meaning might be hidden in the six-day escapade. Accordingly, the narrative is divided into three Parts with Mary's adventure put in the central Part. To visualize this ternary structure is composed "Fig. 2.3. Scene Percentage in *Mary Barton*." Data are taken from the scene-percentage column in "The Comprehensive Chronology for *Mary Barton*."

This 3-D pie chart throws light on two significant features of the structure of the novel. First, more than one third of the total number of pages is assigned to Chapters 17-33 (scs. 120-210), which portray John Barton's murder of Harry Carson, Mary's frantic efforts to prove Jem's innocence, his trial, and her collapse.[38] The fact that 37.2% of the story is spent narrating Mary's six days from 18 to 23 March 1840—although the book as it stands covers eight or nine years in total—is curious enough to make us wonder if it conceals an important key to the understanding of the author's purpose.[39] This speculation is fuelled by Gaskell's remark that the "tale was originally complete without the part which intervenes between John Barton's death and Esther's; about 3 pages, I fancy, including that conversation between Job Legh, and Mr Carson, and Jem Wilson" (*Letters* 75), as it confirms Part II was initially incorporated into the novel. Secondly, Fig. 2.3 suggests that the novel has two peaks—John's assassination of Harry Carson and the confirmation of Jem's innocence—where the plot displays crucial shifts from Part I (chs. 1-16; scs. 1-119) to Part II (chs. 17-33; scs. 120-210) and from Part II to Part III (chs. 33-38; scs. 211-257). The percentage of the text assigned to each part is roughly 48.0%, 37.2%, and

---

38 That the death of Harry Carson marks the beginning of the second part is agreed by Easson (*EG* 79; introduction, *MB* 11), Catherine Gallagher (67), K. Tillotson (213), and E. Wright (introduction, *MB* xvii).
39 The second part's baffling length is also noted by Colby ("This section is given a significant amount of space in the novel, spanning several chapters. It is clear that Gaskell viewed these events as a crucial expression of Mary's identity" ["*Appointed*" 41]), and by E. Wright (*Mrs Gaskell* 233).

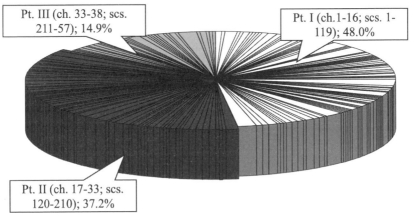

Fig. 2.3. Scene Percentage in *Mary Barton*

14.9%.

2.3.3. Mary's Constant Appearance

It has long been highlighted that *Mary Barton* has two main plots: John Barton's murder plot and Mary Barton's romance plot.[40] A brief summary of each would be as follows:

> John's plot: rich people's lack of sympathy for the poor—John Barton's murder of Harry Carson—Jem Wilson's trial—John Barton's confession—John Carson's forgiveness—John Barton's death;
> Mary's plot: Jem's love for Mary—her association with Harry—her recognition of her love for Jem—the murder of Harry—her efforts to prove Jem's innocence—his trial—her marriage to him.

The first plot's sudden disappearance after John Barton's act of violence has been criticized especially by those who favour John Barton as the novel's central character.[41] Conversely, this duality is eulogized by other critics, particularly feminists, who

---

40 Particularly by Chris Baldick (*Frankenstein's* 84), Craik (*EG* 5, 31), d'Albertis (*Dissembling* 50), Flint (15, 17), C. Gallagher (67, 75-78, 81-82, 280), Ganz (69, 73), Gill (introduction, *MB* 21-22), Hopkins (*EG* 76), Lansbury (*EG* 10, 17), Recchio ("The Problem of Form" 20, 29), Schor (*Scheherezade* 14-15, 17, 20, 33, 37-38), Shelston (introduction, *MB* xxvi), Stoneman (*EG* 84), K. Tillotson (213-14), Uglow (*EG* 206), Wheeler (*Art of Allusion* 46, 59-60; *English Fiction* 40), Williams (*Culture and Society* 100-01), and E. Wright (introduction, *MB* xiv, xvii-xviii).

41 Craik (*EG* 5) and Ganz (69) assert that two plots are too much for a single work, while Ganz (73), Gill (introduction, *MB* 20-21), Hopkins (*EG* 76-77), K. Tillotson (213), and Williams (*Culture and Society*

acknowledge Mary's establishment of identity in the double-plot framework.[42]

The opinions of both groups are insightful enough to aid our comprehension of the novel. The only drawback, however, is that they pay little attention to the two points Table 2.1, Fig. 2.1, Fig. 2.2, Fig. 2.3, and "Fig. 2.5. Image of Plot Flow in *Mary Barton*" (See below) advance: Mary's constant appearance in the first half (or, as we put it, Part I) as well as in the second (Parts II and III), and the novel's construction in three parts, not two.

As the "subtotal, Pt. I" box in Table 2.1 shows, Mary is involved in the story (93 scenes or 39.6%) as constantly as her father (74 scenes or 30.9%); furthermore, the "active, Pt. I" box reveals

Fig. 2.4. Trade Union members drawing lots for the murder of Harry Carson (Web)

that she is more active (66 scenes or 28.6%) than he (39 scenes or 15.8%) in Part I. These facts remind us that, however ardently critics may underline the graphic representation of John Barton's increasing indignation against the industrial masters in Part I, Mary's love for two young men is also depicted as one of its two main streams—Jem appears in 51 scenes (22.7%) and Harry does in 40 scenes (19.6%). Critics are ambiguous about the existence of the third part and its length.[43] As Tables and Figures nonetheless display, there is a definite distinction between the contents of Part II and Part III. Mary's six-day ordeal ends when Part III begins, as her

---

100-02, 114-15) lament that the change of emphasis halfway through the novel represents a flaw in its theme and shape.

42 Lansbury argues that John Barton's decline offers a vivid contrast to his daughter's rise (*EG* 17); Schor (15) and Stoneman (*EG* 79) observe that Mary's whole story unfolds the process of her acquiring the ability to speak for her own self.

43 For instance, Bodenheimer (Barton's "story appears in only ten of the first eighteen chapters, after which he disappears from the narrative until the end" ["Private Grief" 204]), Fryckstedt ("John Barton is absent from the moment he murders Henry Carson until he returns at the end" [98]), C. Gallagher ("The concluding chapters of *Mary Barton* return us to the story of John" [83]), and Schor (The workers' plot is "revealed again at the novel's end" [*Scheherezade* 16]).

CHAPTER 2 *Mary Barton: Who Is the Central Protagonist?* 65

father reappears to complete his own plot.

Table 2.1 demonstrates John Barton's virtual disappearance from the drama and his daughter's monopolization of the narrative in Part II: as represented in the "active" box, he is active only in five scenes (0.8%) while Mary in 64 (27.9%). This is why Mary, "a decidedly minor figure, a rather negligible personality" (Hopkins, *EG* 77) in the first part, appears suddenly to emerge from the book "with increased stature" (Lane, introduction, *MB* viii) in the second.[44]

To visualize storylines' interweaving, "Fig. 2.5" has been created from data on the three leading characters' appearance in the Comprehensive Chronology: two points are given to a character if he/she is active, one if referred to, and none if the character makes no appearance. In the first part, the two plots are introduced in parallel. In the middle, Mary's effort to save Jem becomes the focus of the narrative; hence, John's industrial plot sinks under the surface. In the final part, the love between Mary and Jem ripens into marriage, whereas John Barton's confession and death bring about John Carson's understanding of the workers; thus end both plots.

The plots' interactions are prompted by the killing of Harry Carson, because the enemy of the weavers is also Jem Wilson's rival for Mary's heart. The suspicion of murder is cast upon Jem, who had his scuffle with Harry witnessed by a constable three days before the latter's death. The wadding paper Esther brings from the crime scene serves to convince Mary of the true criminal, and thus begins her tough task of proving Jem's innocence without sacrificing her father, a "situation fit for the highest Greek tragedy" (Maria Edgeworth qtd. in Easson, *Critical Heritage* 90, and in Ross D. Waller 10).[45] The close interlacing of the two strands weakens after the trial scene, "a great showpiece in the novel" (Easson, introduction, *MB* 16), in which she fulfils her mission with complete success.[46]

John Barton's assassination of the mill-owner's son lies at the heart of Mary's endeavour to save her lover's life which simultaneously involves her attempt to keep her father's guilt secret; in other words, his industrial plot helps his daughter's romance plot flow, and vice versa. This arrangement is pivotal to the effective advance-

---

44 Or in Bodenheimer's phrase, "Mary is released into an active, responsible, and independent role" ("Private Grief" 211).

45 Unmitigated praise is bestowed upon the author's portrayal of Mary's breathtaking expedition especially by E. H. Chadwick (166) and E. Wright (*Mrs Gaskell* 268).

46 The plot interrelation in Part II is discussed by Craik (*EG* 31, 35), C. Gallagher (83), Ganz (69), Hopkins (*EG* 76), E. Holly Pike (41), Schor (40), and Wheeler (*English Fiction* 40). Besides, its occurrence even in Parts I and III is implied by Craik (*EG* 35), C. Gallagher (82), Shelston (introduction, *MB* xxvi), Uglow (*EG* 206), Wheeler (*Art of Allusion* 59), and E. Wright (introduction, *MB* xiv).

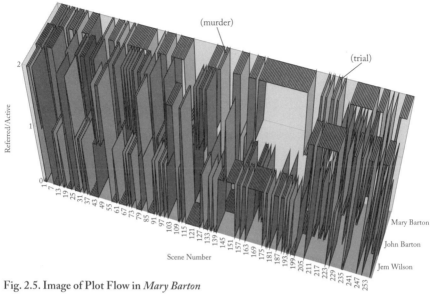

Fig. 2.5. Image of Plot Flow in *Mary Barton*

ment of both plots: to end hers in marriage, his in death. This principal design underlies the author's interlinking of the two plots.[47] It is for this reason that she allocated 37.2% of the total page count to the narration of "Mary's great test and the novel's climax" (Craik, *EG* 35).

Some critics evaluate Mary's plot as "less arresting, less strikingly original" (Craik, *EG* 35), "[dealing] with secondary characters" (G. D. Sanders 28), and "of secondary importance" (J. G. Sharps, *Observation* 68). Hopkins disparages it: "Although the title directs that Mary should bear the responsibility of the central figure, she does not step forward in this role until the latter part of the story" (*EG* 76). Sharing "most critics' sense of the inadequacy and tiresomeness of the murder plot and the subsequent legal melodrama," Daly concludes that Mary is "never meant to be the protagonist" (xx-xxi). In contrast, Shelston finds a positive and deeper meaning in her storyline: "Mary's story is integral from the start" (introduction, *MB* xxiv). So does Colby: "Throughout the novel Mary is portrayed as *acting*" ("*Appointed*" 36); his remark is upheld by Fryckstedt (98) and Uglow (*EG* 200). Deborah Epstein Nord attempts to explain Mary's centrality from her feminist perspective: "the novel concerns itself from the very first with the public role of women, especially but not

---

47 Although her approach is different from ours, Nord has noticed this authorial design in stating: "Gaskell's rewriting of the sexual plot is at all points inseparable from the plot of class antagonism and is in a real sense both the starting point and the dominant preoccupation of her text" (*Walking* 149-50).

exclusively Mary's role" (*Walking* 154).

Mary's sudden ascendancy (in other words, John's disappearance, or the change of emphasis from him to her) in Part II has been pointed out by some critics.[48] Our scrutiny of the movement of the two storylines, however, reveals that Mary is present throughout the novel, and that, even if the focus appears to shift in the middle from John's conflict to Mary's romance, it is because he temporarily hides himself from the reader's eyes, not because she makes a sudden appearance in the limelight.

2.3.4. Interaction of Plots: Jem's Role

The supposed reason for Jem's second highest frequency of appearance is his close involvement in both plots, which is distinctly shown in Gaskell's three manoeuvres for intermixing the industrial and love plots.[49]

(a) First, the valentine sheet Jem gives Mary which carries Samuel Bamford's poem of the poor people's belief in God's help is used as a wadding paper for the gun Barton uses to shoot Harry, the archetype of the rich people's ignorance.

(b) Second, Mary wavers between the rich mill-owner Harry and the poor labourer Jem, and chooses the latter after all.[50] This authorial technique is hinted at when Mary feels guilty conscience towards "the strange contrast" between Margaret's woeful news about Jem's twin brothers who are "seriously ill" and "the gay and loving words" Mary has "been hearing on her walk home" (*MB* 85). It is also intimated in the episode where Mary never notices a narcissus Jem has brought for her while Jem never knows her jug has been "filled with a luxuriant bunch of early spring roses, [. . .] the gift of her richer lover" (*MB* 94). Even in Mary's love plot, there is the element of "the seeming injustice of the inequalities of fortune" (*Letters* 74): a working-class girl's longing for marriage to a wealthy master, her awakening to her true affection for a diligent mechanic, and her marriage to the latter. Esther is used as a warning to Mary against marrying Harry Carson, a fickle rich lover.

(c) Third, Harry is disliked by Jem as his rival and loathed by John as the workers' enemy. Gaskell sets Jem as Harry's rival, heightening the artisan's hatred against

---

48 For example, Bodenheimer ("Private Grief" 196), C. Gallagher (67), Nord (*Walking* 154), and Williams (*Culture and Society* 100-01).

49 Bodenheimer explains that the plots intertwine in two ways: (a) by Jem's involvement into the industrial plot, that is, Barton's knowledge of Harry's sexual sin against his daughter and "its attendant anger" are "left for Jem Wilson [. . .]. Thus Barton and the falsely accused Jem become split doubles in the murder plot"; (b) by the secret and shared attempt of Mary and Jem to keep the true murderer from suspicion ("Private Grief" 207).

50 J. J. Taylor delivers a sharp attack on Gaskell's unnatural characterization of her heroine: the genuine, simple-hearted, and faithful Mary's flirtations with her rich lover (qtd. in Easson, *Critical Heritage* 143). On the other hand, the *Sun*, London daily paper, admires it "for its comprehension of the complex feelings which are present in women's motivation" (qtd. in Handley, *Chronology* 55).

the young master towards the end of Part I to make it natural for him to be misunderstood as the assassin of the industrial master. Jem, who has quarrelled with Harry concerning Mary, is suspected of being the murderer (*MB* 259). Harry is assassinated by Barton because of his merciless behaviour towards workers, but believed by people to be killed by Jem, who felt jealousy towards Mary's lover (*MB* 267). Hence, Harry's assassination is a pivot of the intermingling of the two plots.

Harry's murder is given another important function, that is, the emphasis of Jem's moral integrity. The daughter of the operative John Barton is loved by Harry, the mill-owner John Carson's son, and by Jem, his employee George Wilson's son. After knowing that Harry's murderer is Mary's father, Jem determines to bear Barton's guilt as a sign of his selfless devotion for Mary. Truthfulness of his "deep love" (*MB* 46) towards the girl is intensified by his resolution to be hanged to save her father, the true assassin, which is concealed in his letter to Job Legh (*MB* 373-75), because his resolution is an echo of Jesus Christ's discourse on the perfect love: "Greater love hath no man than this, that a man lay down his life for his friends" (John 15.13). Jem's innocence being confirmed, the story's focus shifts to the search for the Trade Unionist John Barton, and thus returns to the industrial story.

Jem's love for Mary is endorsed by Barton, who "now and then admitted the thought, that Mary might do worse when her time came, than marry Jem Wilson, a steady workman at a good trade, a good son to his parents, and a fine manly spirited chap" (*MB* 47), and wonders "If Jem Wilson would but marry her! With his character for steadiness and talent!" (*MB* 148). Barton's favour for Jem, which is acknowledged by the young mechanic himself—"he's told me more than once how much he should like to see us two married!" (*MB* 151)—denotes the narrator's support for labourers, not capitalists.

Jem is "the victim" (*MB* 271), for he is suspected of being Harry's murderer as the result of Mary's ambition to be a wealthy lady or of her flirtation with the young employer. "If her father was guilty," observes the narrator, "Jem was innocent. If innocent, there was a possibility of saving him. He must be saved. And she must do it; for, was not she the sole depositary of the terrible secret? Her father was not suspected; and never should be, if by any foresight or any exertions of her own she could prevent it" (*MB* 289). It is here that Part II starts. Mary's determination to save Jem is explicit in following quotations: "She longed to do all herself; to be his liberator, his deliverer; to win him life though she might never regain his lost love by her own exertions" (*MB* 300) and "Will can prove this [Jem's innocence]. I must find Will. [...] When I know I'm doing right, I will have no fear, but put my trust in Him; for I'm acting for the innocent and good, and not for my own self, who have done so wrong. I have no fear when I think of Jem, who is so good" (*MB* 306). Her trust in God, which is an echo of the Apostle Peter's teaching that "And who *is* he that will harm you, if ye be followers of that which is good? / But and if ye suffer for righteousness' sake, happy *are* ye: and be not afraid of their terror, neither be troubled; / But sanctify the Lord God in your hearts" (1 Pet. 13-15), signifies the improvement of her moral sense. Mary's testimony in the Liverpool assizes that she loves Jem better than Harry (*MB* 383) symbolizes not merely Jem's winning of her, but also workmen's victory over employers.

After all, Jem is created to involve himself positively in the two plots, and this tactic causes the rate of his appearance frequency to be second highest. In other words, Gaskell construct's strategy for Jem activates her scheme for treating the two plots with equal emphasis.

2.3.5. Time Sequence

The investigation into the time sequence of the story also indicates Mary's prominence. "Fig. 2.6. Monthly Sequence in *Mary Barton*," where scene percentages in the novel are arranged by the monthly unit, demonstrates that the narrative of March 1840 occupies 53.1% of the total page numbers. To examine the events of the month, "Fig. 2.7. Daily Sequence in *Mary Barton*" was created by adding up scene percentages according to the daily unit. In "Table 2.2. Top Twenty Dates in Order of Allocated Page Percentage in *Mary Barton*," the top twenty dates are arranged according to the percentages of pages assigned to each day. Fig. 2.7 and Table 2.2

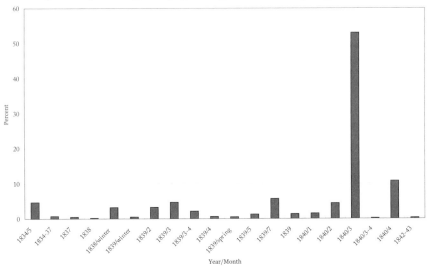

Fig. 2.6. Monthly Sequence in *Mary Barton*

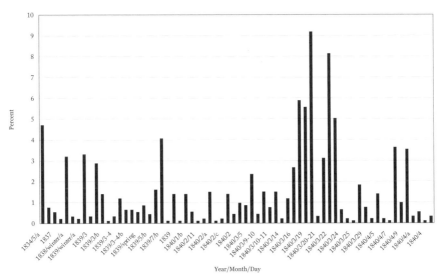

Fig. 2.7. Daily Sequence in *Mary Barton*

Order	Date	Scene Percentage According to Length
1	1840/3/20	9.17
2	1840/3/22	8.12
3	1840/3/18	5.88
4	1840/3/19	5.55
5	1840/3/23	5.01
6	1834/5/a	4.7
7	1839/7/b	4.06
8	1840/4/8	3.63
9	1840/4/10	3.53
10	1839/2/a	3.3
11	1838/winter/a	3.2
12	1840/3/21	3.11
13	1839/3/a	2.87
14	1840/3/16	2.66
15	1840/3/9	2.34
16	1840/3/28	1.82
17	1839/7/a	1.6
18	1840/3/10	1.5
19	1840/2/a	1.49
19	1840/3	1.49

Table 2.2. Top Twenty Dates in Order of Allocated Page Percentage in *Mary Barton*

show that the day to which the largest number of pages is assigned is 20 March (9.2%), when Mary, having realized from her aunt Esther's information that the true assassin of Harry Carson is her father, starts to act for rescuing her lover Jem Wilson, who has been arrested as the murder suspect. The second largest space is offered to 22 March (8.1%), which delineates Mary's adventure of catching Will Wilson in Liverpool. The third is allocated to 18 March (5.9%), the day recording Will's farewell to Mary, John Barton's departure from Manchester, Alice Rose's fatal stroke of paralysis, and the Carsons' agony for the death of their son. 19 March (5.6%), when Mary realizes Jem has been arrested as the suspected murderer of Harry, comes fourth, followed by 23 March, the day of Jem's trial (5.0%). In short, the main subject of six days from 18 March is Mary's efforts to save Jem.

Sixthly comes the scene other than that of Mary's adventure for the first time: the excursion of the Bartons and the Wilsons at Green Heys Fields, John Barton and George Wilson's talk about missing Esther, tea at the Bartons, and the sudden death of Mrs Barton in labour, which all happen on a day in May of 1834 (4.7%). The seventh scene dealing with a July day in 1839 depicts Barton's disappointments in his London mission, Job Legh's recollection of his London experiences, and his quotation from Samuel Bamford's poem which later provides a clue to Mary's identification of Harry Carson's true murderer (4.1%). In the eighth and ninth scenes, treating 8 and 10 April 1840, are mainly described Barton's confession of his crime, Carson's melting, and the mill-owner's demonstration of Christian forgiveness (3.6% and 3.5%). The tenth scene centres on Jem's rescue of his father from fire at the Carson mill (3.3%).

Accordingly, the structural analysis of the time sequence—in addition to the analyses of characters' frequency of appearance, allocated scene percentages, and plots' interaction—also hints at the centrality of Mary Barton.

2.3.6. Narratorial Intervention

As the fifth means for the objective detection of the authorial meaning, narratorial remarks are surveyed by categorizing them into three groups, depending on the treated subject, that is, the industrial plot, the romance plot, or neither of them. The narrator's appearance rate in *Mary Barton* (32.9%; 64 out of 257 scenes) is conspicuously higher than in Gaskell's other novels (See "Table 2.3. The Narrators' Appearance Rates in Gaskell's Major Novels" created from the data in the Comprehensive Chronologies for Gaskell's novels), which implies that she is given the role of the author construct's spokesperson.

The survey shows that the narratorial comments on the industrial plot can be categorized into three depending on their objective: (a) to underline the conflict

Narrator	Mary Barton	Ruth	North and South	Sylvia's Lovers	Wives and Daughters
Appearance Rate (%)	32.9	12.9	0.7	3.2	4.9
Scenes of Appearance (times)	64	32	3	13	15
Total Scenes (times)	257	241	451	434	463

NOTE: The division of appearance scenes by total scenes does not necessarily accord with the appearance rate, which is the sum of the rough percentage of each scene.

Table 2.3. The Narrators' Appearance Rates in Gaskell's Novels

between masters and workers, (b) to draw the reader's attention to the latter's plight, and (c) to describe the agony of John Carson, the industrial master whose son is murdered by John Barton. The narrator's resolute stance of the sympathizer towards the suffering, expressed in the quotations below, is probably one of the main factors which affects the reading of *Mary Barton* as the Condition-of-England novel.

Her first objective is intimated at the very beginning of the novel where the reader's attention is drawn to the contrast between the two classes: "I do not know whether it was on a holiday granted by the masters, or a holiday seized in right of Nature and her beautiful spring time by the workmen, but one afternoon [. . .] these fields were much thronged" (*MB* 2). It is reiterated by the narrator in the following quotation: "The most deplorable and enduring evil that arose out of the period of commercial depression to which I refer, was this feeling of alienation between the different classes of society" (*MB* 96).[51]

Her second aim is hinted at in the early part of the novel as well: after describing too great a contrast in the life style "between the employers and the employed" (*MB* 23), the sympathizer of the latter clarifies her position by stating "I know that this is not really the case [. . .] but what I wish to impress is what the workman feels and thinks" (*MB* 24). In the scene where Barton, being out of work and having lost his little son due to his failure to give good nourishment, sees his former employer's wife come out of a shop "followed by a shopman loaded with purchases for a party," the narrator appeals to readers for their sympathy with Barton's bitter resentment: "You can fancy, now, the hoards of vengeance in his heart against the employers" (*MB* 25). She defends workmen by stressing their secret virtues: "The vices of the poor sometimes astound us *here*; but when the secrets of all hearts shall be made known, their virtues will astound us in far greater degree. Of this I am certain" (*MB*

---

51 Her first objective is echoed in her narration of Barton's lamentation as well: "John Barton's overpowering thought [. . .] was rich and poor; why are they so separate, so distinct, when God has made them all? It is not His will that their interests are so far apart. Whose doing is it?" (*MB* 198-99).

64). The staunch supporter of the poor praises their angelic patience and expresses an understanding of their rudeness: "when I hear, as I have heard, of the sufferings and privations of the poor, [...] can I wonder that many of them, in such times of misery and destitution, spoke and acted with ferocious precipitation?" (*MB* 96-97). Her deep compassion for Barton, who takes opium "to forget life, and its burdens," is articulated in the citation: "before you blame too harshly this use, or rather abuse, try a hopeless life, with daily cravings of the body for food" (*MB* 198). Immediately after quoting John Carson's remark about workers' cruelty against knob-sticks, "I for one won't yield one farthing to the cruel brutes; they're more like wild beasts than human beings," the narrator inserts the accusation of mill-owners: "Well, who might have made them different?" (*MB* 213).

Her third purpose for industrial concern, i.e. to stress John Carson's paternal affection and pain, is explicit when she observes "how shall I describe the vehemence of passion which possessed the mind of poor Mr Carson, as he saw the effect of the young sailor's statement?" (*MB* 389) in the court scene where he witnesses the jury's bewilderment after hearing Will's testimony of Jem's innocence. In response to Barton's claim for forgiveness and Job Legh's subsequent prayer for it, the master takes "his hands away from his face" before swearing his vengeance on his son's murderer. Here, the storyteller addresses the reader, "I would rather see death than the ghastly gloom which darkened that countenance" (*MB* 432). The remark connotes the depth of Carson's agony caused by the futile hostility between masters and workers.

Few critics have noted, however, that the storyteller's references to Mary's romance plot appear as frequently as those to John's industrial plot. "Table 2.4. The Narrator's Direct Remarks on John and Mary," the result of categorizing all narratorial interventions, illuminates that there is only a slight difference in number and percentage between the two plots (14 scenes [21.9%] and 16 scenes [25.0%] respectively). For instance, her first direct comment on Mary is inserted to defend her from the reader's criticism of her silly fancy for becoming a lady: "Before my telling

Narrator's Direct Remarks on	Times (Scenes)	Percent
John Barton's industrial plot	16	25.0
Mary Barton's romance plot	14	21.9
Others	34	53.1
Total	64	100.0

Table 2.4. The Narrator's Direct Remarks on John and Mary

you so truly what folly Mary felt or thought, injures her without redemption in your opinion, think what are the silly fancies of sixteen years of age in every class, and under all circumstances" (*MB* 27). Her next remark—"Alas! poor Mary! Bitter woe did thy weakness work thee" (*MB* 46)—depicts her disapproval of Mary's association with Harry Carson.[52]

From the start of the novel, the storyteller, setting Jem as Mary's preferable lover, is always sympathetic towards him.[53] In the scene of the fire at Carsons' mill, for example, she emphasizes Jem's bravery: "In far less time than even that in which I have endeavoured briefly to describe the pause of events, the same bold hero stepped again upon the ladder, with evident purpose to rescue the man yet remaining in the burning mill" (*MB* 59). The narrator laments Jem's untimely confession of love in Mary's home: "Poor Jem! It is not an auspicious moment for thee!" (*MB* 149). She praises Mary for awakening to her mistaken vanity, i.e. for her conviction that the man she truly loves is Jem Wilson, not Harry Carson: "That was some comfort: I mean her clear perception of what she ought not to do; of what no luring temptation should ever again induce her to hearken to" (*MB* 153). Comparing the actions of Mary's two rejected lovers—Harry's effeminately tenacious attachment and Jem's manly lofty detachment—, the storyteller addresses an encouraging remark to the mechanic: "Oh, Jem, Jem, why did you not come to receive some of the modest looks and words of love which Mary longed to give you, to try and make up for the hasty rejection which you as hastily took to be final, though both mourned over it with many tears" (*MB* 183). In contrast, she hurls disparagement on Harry for his too shallow morality to understand Jem's rectitude in demanding his seriousness in love for Mary: "So little faith in goodness have the mean and selfish!" (*MB* 209).

The narrator's direct intervention underlines her heroine's integrity as well. In the scene where Mary enters the Wilsons' house to inquire after Alice Rose, her face flushes an instant in anticipation of meeting Jem. "But I do assure you, she had not thought of it before" (*MB* 252)—the comment is inserted to stress that Mary's motive for visit is her genuine solicitude towards the old invalid. Even though in des-

---

52 Although excluded from our result of calculating the narrator's frequency of appearance since it is indeterminate whether they are of direct narratorial intervention or just of narratorial description, the quotations below convey her disapproval of Mary also: "we all, in our old-Adam state, fancy things forbidden sweetest" (*MB* 92); "Such were the castles in air, the Alnaschar-visions in which Mary indulged, and which she was doomed in after days to expiate with many tears" (*MB* 92); "Her love for him was a bubble, blown out of vanity; but it looked very real and very bright" (*MB* 134).

53 The narrator's support for Jem is explicit in her following statement: "Surely, in time, such deep love [of Jem] would beget love" (*MB* 46). This example is excluded from our counting of the narratorial intervention because of the same reason as above.

perate need for the intelligence concerning Will Wilson's whereabouts, Mary refrains from asking the suspected murderer Jem for help; their interview would be painful because of their shared knowledge of the true assassin. The narrator here draws the reader's attention to Mary's discretion: "And even if she could have gone to him, I believe she would not" (*MB* 300). In contrast to Jane Wilson, who openly bemoans her miserable powerlessness in saving her son, Mary determines to bear it secretly although her pain and stress might be greater than his mother's: "But think of Mary and what she was enduring," observes the storyteller, "Picture to yourself (for I cannot tell you) the armies of thoughts that met and clashed in her brain; and then imagine the effort it cost her to be calm, and quiet, and even in a faint way, cheerful and smiling at times" (*MB* 319). Mary's goodness is emphasized here again.

After the trial scene, the focus of narratorial insertion shifts to the young couple's mutual love. Persuaded by Job Legh to return to Manchester to see his dying aunt Alice, Jem leaves delirious Mary in Liverpool with heartrending grief: "Jem felt how right Job was, and could not resist what he knew to be his duty, but I cannot tell you how heavy and sick at heart he was as he stood at the door to take a last fond, lingering look at Mary" (*MB* 397-98). Even seeing John Barton enter his house after ten days' absence, Jem hesitates to approach him because the father would certainly wish to see his daughter should he know her condition, and wonders what would be the consequences if she met the blood-shedder with the tender filial affection for him: "Jem could not, and would not, expose her to any such fearful chance: and to tell the truth, I believe he looked upon her as more his own, to guard from all shadow of injury with most loving care, than as belonging to any one else in this world" (*MB* 408). The tête-à-tête the lovers have after Jem asks Mary to meet his mother as his fiancée includes the narrator's emphasis on their happiness: "Yet a little more lovers' loitering; a few more words, in themselves nothing—to you nothing—but to those two, what tender passionate language can I use to express the feelings which thrilled through that young man and maiden, as they listened to the syllables made dear and lovely through life by that hour's low whispered talk" (*MB* 426).

2.3.7. Place of Action

The place of action was inspected as the seventh formal element to discover Gaskell's authorial meaning, and arranged in the order of the page percentage assigned to each place (See "Table 2.5. Places of Action in Order of Allocated Page Percentage"). Besides, as Table 2.5. indicates that Barton's house is the centre of action, occurrences in his house were classified into the three groups according to the plot they are connected to: the social conflict and reconciliation, the development of Mary's love, and those difficult to classify into either of them.

Occurrences relevant to the social-problem plot which take place in Barton's house are, for instance, (a) his neighbour workers' assembly to voice their political demands to be conveyed to the Parliament (sc. 59; *MB* 98-101), (b) Barton's talk about the unsuccessful petition (sc. 65, *MB* 111-13; sc. 67, *MB* 114-17), (c) Job's reading of Samuel Bamford's poem whose subject is the poor people's wretched lives and their expectation of God's help (sc. 69; *MB* 127-29), (d) "desperate members of trades' unions" frequenting the house of opium-chewing Barton (sc. 73; *MB* 135-36), (e) the entrance of restless Barton, the appointed murderer (sc. 122; *MB* 229-30), (f) Job Legh's interest in his Glasgow mission, the old worker's criticism of the Trade Union (scs. 123-24; *MB* 230-32), (g) Barton's request for Mary to tell Jem to come to his house (sc. 231; *MB* 423-24), (h) his confession of guilt to John Carson (sc. 234; *MB* 427-33),[54] (i) the dying Barton's acknowledgement of the importance of the teachings of the Bible (sc. 237; *MB* 436-38), and (j) his death in Carson's arms (scs. 238-40; *MB* 438-39).[55]

Incidents connected to the romance plot which happen in Barton's house are, for example, (a) Barton's awareness of Jem's affection for his daughter (sc. 26; *MB* 47-48), (b) his swearing to give Mary to the brave Jem (sc. 33; *MB* 62), (c) Mary's

Order	Places	Percentage of Allocated Pages
1	Barton's house	28.7
2	Liverpool	15.1
3	Wilson's house	11.0
4	Carson's house	7.5
5	Legh's house	6.9
6	Davenport's house	2.9
7	Alice's house	1.9
8	Others	26.2
Total		100.2

Table 2.5. Places of Action in Order of Allocated Page Percentage

---

54 Although there is a brief reference to Mary's romance—Barton's appreciation to Jem for loving the assassin's daughter (*MB* 430)—in this confession scene, its chief subject is no doubt the first face-to-face encounter between the industrial enemies, so it is classified into the first group.

55 In the scene of Barton's death, the characters presented are Barton, Mary, and Carson only: prompted by Mary, the mill-owner prays to God for mercy and forgiveness, listening to which the blood-shedder dies in his arms (*MB* 438). Gaskell makes Jem and Job leave Barton's house just before the operative's death (*MB* 438), only to highlight the reconciliation between employer and employed.

CHAPTER 2 *Mary Barton: Who Is the Central Protagonist?*

Events	Percentage of Allocated Pages
Related to Barton's industrial plot	4.9
Related to Mary's love plot	5.9
Others	17.8

Table 2.6. Occurrences in Barton's House in *Mary Barton*

guilty conscience about enjoying Harry's loving words and "the golden future" without doing her duty towards Jem's family (sc. 48; *MB* 84-85), (d) her midnight meditation about why she prefers the rich lover to the poor labourer and how her ambition to become a lady is related to her wish to "surround her father with every comfort" (sc. 52; *MB* 90-92),[56] (e) Jem's narcissus ignored by Mary, who has already had "a luxuriant bunch of early spring roses" from Harry (sc. 55; *MB* 93-94), (f) Sally's bringing Harry's letter to Mary (sc. 62; *MB* 104-07), (g) Barton's upbraiding of Mary for "the loss of Jem" (sc. 82; *MB* 147-48), (h) Mary's refusal of Jem's proposal and her ensuing regret (scs. 84-85; *MB* 149-54), (i) Mary's request for Sally to tell Harry that she does not love him (sc. 88; *MB* 155-56), (j) her confiding her affection for Jem to Margaret (sc. 94; *MB* 164-67), (k) Mary's fear of Harry's persevering pursuit, and regret of her "giddy flirting" (sc. 103; *MB* 182-83), (l) Mary's self-reproach of her longing for a rich lover and her anxious sympathy for Jem, the jealous murder suspect (sc. 152; *MB* 270-72), (m) Sally's teasing of Mary about Jem, and Mary's belief in his innocence (sc. 180; *MB* 325-26), (n) Jem's goodness in keeping his dismissal secret from Mary (sc. 230; *MB* 423), (o) Jane Wilson's innate generosity towards Mary shown at her condolatory visit to her future daughter-in-law's house (scs. 246-47; *MB* 444-47),[57] and (p) Mary's inquiry to Jem about how he comes to know about her association with Harry, and his reply (sc. 252; *MB* 459-60).

The scenes to be classified into the third group, as treating both subjects or some other, are as follows: (a) the Bartons' preparation of tea for the Wilsons (sc. 6; *MB* 12-15),[58] (b) a tea at the Bartons (sc. 8; *MB* 16-18), (c) the death of Mrs Barton (sc.

---

56 A short reference to the industrial conflict—"her father's aversion to the rich and the gentle" (*MB* 92)—is inserted in Mary's contemplation, but its central topic is her holiest plan of surrounding him "with every comfort" by marrying the wealthy gentleman Harry Carson "till he should acknowledge riches to be very pleasant things" (*MB* 92). Viewed in this light, her meditation could be interpreted as representing the mixture of industrial and romantic plots.

57 Although a short mention of Barton's murder of Harry Carson (*MB* 447) is included here, this scene mainly deals with Jane Wilson's condolatory visit to her son's fiancée, so categorized into the second group.

58 It may be possible to sort this scene into the second group in consideration of Barton's amusing suggestion that "Jem and Mary can drink out of one" teacup and of her inward rejection of it, as they

12; *MB* 19-22), (d) Mary's report to her father about her new acquaintance with Margaret and Job (sc. 24; *MB* 45), (e) Mary and Margaret's chat over stitching, the latter's confession of her growing blind, and their leaving for Carson's mill (scs. 29-30; *MB* 49-54), (f) Jem's pondering over Mary's conduct while hearing Barton's talk of the approaching strike and danger (sc. 56; *MB* 94-96), (g) Barton's talk about Jane Wilson's accident as a young girl (sc. 60; *MB* 101-02), (h) Margaret's gift of a sovereign to Mary (sc. 95; *MB* 167-68),[59] (i) Mary's solitary meditation at home about her father's mysterious departure for Glasgow, Harry's continuing threats, and her pain for Jem's heart (sc. 129; *MB* 236), (j) her midnight interview with Esther (sc. 156; *MB* 279-85),[60] (k) Mary's discovery of the true assassin, and her resolution to save Jem (scs. 157-58; *MB* 285-90), (l) Mary's planning as to how to prove Jem's innocence without sacrificing her father (sc. 164; *MB* 298-301), (m) her selfless nursing of her agonized father and her missing "Jem's tender love" (sc. 227; *MB* 419-20), (n) Mary's pondering over Barton's guilty conscience, the narrator's confirmation of Jem's tenderness, and Job and Margaret's consideration for Mary (sc. 241; *MB* 439-40), and (o) finally Esther's return to Barton's house to die (scs. 254-55; *MB* 461-63).

That Barton's house has been the main place of Gaskell's story is hinted at in her heroine's reflection in the closing chapter of the novel: Mary "thought over the scenes which had passed in that home she was so soon to leave for ever" (*MB* 462). The outcome of the above investigations is displayed in "Table 2.6. Occurrences in Barton's House in *Mary Barton*," which shows how events dealing with the love plot appear almost equally to or slightly more frequently than those with the industrial plot.

2.4. Historical Author's Confession

The objective scrutiny of the novel's seven key structures—characters' appearance frequency, scene allocation, plots' interaction, Jem's role, time sequence, narratorial intervention, and action places—champions Mary Barton's centrality. A distinct disadvantage of this reading, notwithstanding, would be authorial avowals to

---

foreshadow the development of the couple's relation as one of the story's focal points. However, we chose the present classification to avoid subjectivism since the main topic of the scene is no doubt the Bartons' preparation of tea for the Wilsons.

59   Although containing some remarks concerning the social problem, this scene is categorized into the third group since its gist is Margaret's sympathy for the Bartons, whose breadwinner is out of work.

60   Esther's bringing Mary the scrap of Jem's valentine paper used for the fatal gun accelerates the interaction of the industrial and romance plots. The following two examples are sorted into the third group, because the depicted events relate to both plots.

the opposite effect.

The survey of Gaskell's letters written before and after the publication of *Mary Barton* indicates that her intention lay on the industrial plot. In her four letters of inquiry to Edward Chapman, her publisher, as to the date of publication, she wonders if delay might negate the present topical relevance of her industrial matter.[61]

On 5 December 1848, about seven weeks after the publication of *Mary Barton* in 18 October 1848, Gaskell writes to Chapman about her unbounded gratitude for Thomas Carlyle's letter (*Letters* 64), in which the eminent novelist and historian praises her "real contribution (almost the first real one) towards developing a huge subject, which has lain *dumb* too long, and really ought to speak for itself, and tell us its meaning a little, if there be any voice in it at all" (qtd. in Easson, *Critical Heritage* 72, and in Haldane 48), that is, the Condition-of-England question. On 23 December 1848, Gaskell writes to Catherine Winkworth, her husband's student and her friend, about "the master and workman part" of the novel: "Some say the masters are very sore, but I'm sure I *believe* I wrote truth" (*Letters* 66). Moreover, in her letter to Mary Ewart, her friend (*Further Letters* 76), written in late 1848, Gaskell makes a clear statement on her intention for the novel:

> I wanted to represent the subject in the light in which some of the workmen certainly consider to be *true*, not that I dare to say it is the abstract absolute truth. / That some of the men do view the subject in the way I have tried to represent, I have personal evidence; and I think somewhere in the first volume you may find a sentence stating that <u>my intention was simply to represent the view many of the workpeople take</u>. But independently of any explicit statement of my intention, I do think that we must all acknowledge that there are duties connected with the manufacturing system not fully understood as yet, and evils existing in relation to it which may be remedied in some degree, although we as yet do not see how; but surely there is no harm in directing the attention to the existence of such evils. No one can feel more deeply than I how *wicked* it is to do anything to excite class against class; and the sin has been most unconscious

---

61 "I can not help fancying that the tenor of my tale is such as to excite attention at the present time of struggle on the part of work people to obtain what they esteem their rights" (21 March 1848, *Letters* 54); "I think the present state of public events [i.e. Chartist movement, which] may be not unfavourable to a tale, founded in some measure on the present relations between Masters and work people" (2 April 1848, *Letters* 55); "my own belief that the tale would bear directly upon the present circumstances" (12 April 1848, *Letters* 56); *Mary Barton* "is not catchpenny run up since the events on the Continent have directed public attention to the consideration of the state of affairs between the Employers, & their work-people" (10 July 1848, *Letters* 58).

if I have done so. (*Letters* 67; emphasis added)

In her 1 January 1849 letter to Edward Chapman, Gaskell, lamenting masters' superficiality in understanding her intention for treating class distinction, observes "no one seems to see my idea of a tragic poem" (*Letters* 68). Her 5 January 1849 letter to Julia Lamont discloses that *John Barton* is her first-choice title: "it was a London thought coming through the publisher that it must be called *Mary* B. So many people overlook John B or see him merely to misunderstand him, that if you were a stranger and had only said that one thing (that the book shd have been called *John* B) I should have had pleasure in feeling that my own idea was recognized" (*Letters* 70; emphasis added). Furthermore, in her early 1849 letter to Mrs Greg, she writes about the origin of her novel:

[T]he prevailing thought in my mind at the time when the tale was silently forming itself and impressing me with the force of a reality, was the seeming injustice of the inequalities of fortune. Now, if they occasionally appeared unjust to the more fortunate, they must bewilder an ignorant man full of rude, illogical thought, and full also of sympathy for suffering which appealed to him through his senses. I fancied I saw <u>how all this might lead to a course of action which might appear right for a time to the bewildered mind of such a one, but that this course of action, violating the eternal laws of God, would bring with it its own punishment of an avenging conscience far more difficult to bear than any worldly privation</u>. Such thoughts I now believe, on looking back, to have been the origin of the book. (*Letters* 74, emphasis added)

In her 29 May 1849 letter to Eliza Fox, her artist friend, Gaskell discloses the existence of a model for John Barton: "Nobody and nothing was real [...] in M. Barton, but the character of John Barton; the circumstances are different, but the character and some of the speeches, are exactly a poor man I know" (*Letters* 82).[62]

Her April 1849 letter to Mary Greg, written six months after the publication of the book (Daly xxxi; Walter E. Smith, *Catalogue* 6), acknowledges that the whole story grew up in the author's mind "as imperceptibly as a seed germinates in the earth," so that she "cannot trace back now why or how such a thing was written, or such a character or circumstance introduced" except for John Barton (*Letters* 74).

---

62 In the same letter, the author makes a short mention of Mary: "I am glad you like Mary, I do: but people are angry with her just because she is not perfect" (*Letters* 82). Its brevity in contrast to her extended observation of John also suggests that her chief concern lies in him.

Gaskell's strategic arbitrariness expressed in this extract, in addition to Barton's centrality, is repeated in her 29 May 1849 letter: "I told the story according to a fancy of my own" (*Letters* 82). These confessions pose a hypothesis that Gaskell as a historical person constructed the story with John Barton as its core, thus making other characters develop themselves.

This reading matches the authorial confession in the preface to *Mary Barton*: "I bethought me how deep might be the romance of those who elbowed me daily in the busy streets of the town where I resided" (xxxv).[63] The subsequent citation reveals that the historical Gaskell's intention for the novel is focused on industrial concern: "I believe what I have said in Mary Barton to be perfectly true, but by no means the whole truth. [. . .] the utmost I hope from Mary Barton has been that it would give a spur to inactive thought, and languid conscience in this direction" (*Letters* 119-20).

The historical author's remarks quoted above explicitly demonstrate that the central character who had been occupying her consciousness was not Mary Barton but always her father.

2.5. Concluding Remarks: John or Mary?

Since the date of its publication, *Mary Barton* has been considered as one of those so-called "industrial," "social," or "Condition-of-England" novels. The most feasible reasons for this interpretation would be the following six: (a) Gaskell's "sympathy with the people of Manchester" (Uglow, *EG* 153) and repeated emphasis on John Barton's centrality in her letters, (b) her announcement in the Preface that she wrote her book to give some utterance to the Manchester factory-workers' agony of suffering for which the rich have shown little sympathy (*MB* xxxvi), (c) the early reviewers' condemnations of her account of capitalists' lack of compassion for their labourers, and her naïve response to these reviews, especially the essayist and industrialist W. R. Greg's, (d) critics' categorization of this fiction into the "social-problem" novels,[64] (e) the narrator's intervention to draw the reader's attention to the social problem, as examined in Section 2.3.6, and (f) the dramatic impacts of the climax scenes describing reconciliation between two Johns, especially in Chapters 35 and 37.[65] It would not be unfair to say that these authorial confessions, early

---

63 "Romance" here means tribulations or difficulties, not love affairs, as is specified in the narrator's account of working-class people in *Mary Barton*: "How do you know the wild romances of their lives; the trials, the temptations they are even now enduring, resisting, sinking under?" (*MB* 70).

64 For example, Louis Cazamian discussed the novel in his 1903 study of the English social novels, and Raymond Williams categorized it into the industrial novels in his 1958 book of *Culture and Society*.

65 For instance, (a) the conscious-stricken John Barton's confession to revengeful John Carson (*MB* 428-

judgements, and the novel's content determined the direction of *Mary Barton*'s reception as industrial fiction.

For the objective detection of Gaskell construct's meaning, we first established "The Comprehensive Chronology" by focusing on internal time data, scene development, topographical movement, and main characters' appearance. Based on this Chronology, we scrutinized seven fundamental structural elements: main characters' appearance rate (Section 2.3.1), scene development (Section 2.3.2), interaction of the two plots (Section 2.3.3, 2.3.4), the sequence of time (Section 2.3.5), the narrator's intervention (Section 2.3.6), and the place of action (Section 2.3.7).

Section 2.3.1 revealed that Mary Barton was the most frequently appearing character, followed by Jem Wilson and John Barton. Section 2.3.2 centred on the disproportionate length of the description of Mary's six-days of desperate efforts to prove Jem's alibi (Part II). In Section 2.3.3 it was disclosed that Mary and John were top two frequent appearers in the introductory part; in the middle part, Mary was most active, while Jem referred to most often; Jem's appearance rate was almost equal to the heroine's in the final part. Section 2.3.4 pointed out that Jem's positive involvement into the two plots was caused by the Gaskell construct's meaning to manipulate them equally. Section 2.3.5 clarified that the year and the date to which the longest number of pages was allocated were those which treat Mary's selfless effort to save Jem. Investigation into the narrator's direct remarks on John's plot and Mary's in Section 2.3.6 denoted that there was no wide gap between their appearance rates. Finally, the examination of the place of action in Section 2.3.7 indicated that the events relating to Mary's plot were depicted more often than those to her father's.

From the formal perspective, therefore, it is open to question whether the true purpose of the novel is to spotlight the plight of John Barton in order to stress the industrial masters' mercilessness. Rather, the form demonstrates the novel's aim is to tell a love story, against the background of the everyday life of Manchester's poverty-stricken people, with John and Mary as their representatives.[66] The form and content suggest Mary's centrality, while the authorial avowal and the emotional impact do John's prominence.

33), (b) Barton's awakening to the mistake of his belief (*MB* 431-32), (c) the author's summary of Barton's motive for violence through her proxy Job Legh that what hurts Barton severely is the rich people's merciless indifference to the poor people's plight (*MB* 453), (d) the author's Christian message through Job that "when God gives a blessing to be enjoyed, He gives it with a duty to be done; and the duty of the happy is to help the suffering to bear their woe" (*MB* 454), and (e) the industrial master's deepening sympathy towards workers and his subsequent improvement of employment system (*MB* 455-58).

The possible stances on the contradiction between the authorial avowal and the statistical outcome concerning the central protagonist of the novel would be the following three.

(a) First, to stick to the subjectivist (anti-intentionalist, traditionalist, or "liberal-humanist") reading which ignores the result of statistical investigation as nonsense. Despite the outcome of statistical analysis, subjectivists would still regard John Barton as the central protagonist. Some would insist, for instance, that Mary's desperate efforts to save her lover during 18-23 March 1840, the occurrence occupying 37.2% of the whole pages, is drawn as a prerequisite for heightening tension towards the climactic scenes of John Barton's confession of his guilt on 8 April, of his death in his enemy John Carson's arms on 9 April, and of the mill-owner's subsequent learning of Christian charity on 10 April. Some would consider the unnatural length of Mary's six days only as the natural outcome of Gaskell's power of the pen. Others may view Mary's seeming centrality as caused by Gaskell's careless planning of the story, as is suggested in her letter of 29 May 1849: "I told the story according to a fancy of my own" (*Letters* 82). The impact of the operative's tragedy is so great that its quality can hardly be quantified by statistics.

(b) Second, to advocate the objectivist (or intentionalist) reading which pays little attention to the historical Gaskell's protestation as misleading. Objectivists who regard the result of statistical measurement as a faithful reflection of the author construct's meaning to depict Mary's love as her novel's core would take caution in accepting the historical author's observations as they are. Their assertion is tantamount to Abrams's: "If the author's stated intentions do not accord with the text, they should be qualified or rejected in favour of an alternative interpretation that conforms more closely to the shared, or 'public,' linguistic and literary conventions that the text itself incorporates" (126-27). Gaskell's confession that John Barton was her hero, quoted at the beginning of this chapter, was only made in response to W. R. Greg's biased reading of *Mary Barton*—he could not but be a bitter critic especially because of the bankruptcy of his brother Samuel, cotton-spinner and philanthropist: this adversity befell him months before the appearance of this fiction, and due to his workers' strike (Valentine Cunningham 135; *Letters* 120).[67] Therefore, it

---

66 Tillotson's assertion that Manchester life is the keystone which gives the novel the unity (210, 214) accords with the structure of the novel; so do Williams's and E. Wright's: "The really impressive thing about the book is the intensity of the effort to record, in its own terms, the feel of everyday life in the working-class homes" (*Culture and Society* 99); "[C]onstantly present as an essential setting for the characters and the complicated plot is Manchester" (*Mrs Gaskell* 32). Opinions which support these are found in Easson (*Critical Heritage* 14; introduction, *MB* 12), Hopkins (*EG* 71, 73), Lansbury (*EG* 12), Shelston (introduction, *MB* xxii), Sheila M. Smith (84), Jane Spencer (*EG* 34, 40), and E. Wright (introduction, *MB* xvii).

is very likely that the social problem alone was consequently selected as the target of her vindication. The author's Preface to the novel was unwillingly "concocted" (*Letters* 58) at her publisher's request a few weeks before its publication (Gérin, *EG* 74; Uglow, *EG* 191).[68] The narrator's insertion of direct comments on Mary's love is almost equal in number to that on Barton's struggle, as examined in Section 2.3.6 above. The historical author's stress on John's centrality, therefore, is misleading.

"Despite Gaskell's claim after publication that 'John Barton' was the original title," claims Easson, "the original names ["A Manchester Love Story" and "A Tale of Manchester Life"] suggest that Mary's love was, along with Manchester life, always central to her design" (*EG* 73). Presumably, John Barton's tragedy should be interpreted as only one of the two main plots in this pageant of Manchester's poor people. Otherwise, *Mary Barton* would turn out to be a failure, because we should have to admit that the author's intention to write about John Barton was not properly reflected in its structure. Mary Barton's romance is as crucial as her father's fight against employers; Gaskell's meaning is to call the public attention to the plight of Manchester workers with Mary, Jem, and John as the three leading characters of the two main plots. Consequently, the title "Mary Barton: A Tale of Manchester Life" is the faithful reflection of the novel's content and structure.

The "author's subjective stance," as Hirsch emphasizes, "is not part of his verbal meaning even when he explicitly discusses his feelings and attitudes" (*Validity* 241). Extrinsic knowledge should be employed only to authenticate what we read out of the text; for, if we read it into the text, it hampers us from detecting authorial meaning, which "must be represented by and limited by the text alone" (Hirsch, *Validity* 241-42).

(c) Third, to try a reconciliatory reading to seek an appropriate explanation of the inconsistency. Paying respect to the authorial avowal as well as to the statistical outcome to the opposite effect, reconcilers would judge that Gaskell's meaning is to draw both John Barton's tragedy and his daughter's love. Bodenheimer gives a suc-

67 W. R. Greg, the most prominent critic among the early reviewers who vented the Manchester magnates' refutations of the charges which Gaskell's industrial plot levelled against them (Item Nos. 16, 17, 19, and 23 in Easson's *Critical Heritage*), allocated most of his essay to the defence of the employers rather than to any literary appreciation of the work (Easson, *Critical Heritage* 163-87). For example, he says "The author of 'Mary Barton' has also, in our judgment, done very great injustice to the employers" (Easson, *Critical Heritage* 107). He is deprecated by J. G. Sharps: "Greg is guilty of misreading in regarding John Barton's attitude as that of the average workman" (*Observation* 65). Gaskell's bewilderment caused by masters' anger against *Mary Barton* is expressed especially in her 1 January 1849 letter to her publisher Edward Chapman (*Letters* 68).
68 "If you think the book requires such a preface I will try to concoct it; but at present, I have no idea what to say" (Gaskell's 10 July 1848 letter to her publisher Edward Chapman [*Letters* 58]).

cinct summary of this reading: "the important contribution of the novel is the portrait of John Barton, and [. . .] the story of Mary [. . .] is designed to entertain the reading public" ("Private Grief" 196). Namely, Gaskell's meaning is to depict John Barton's conflict, and his daughter's seeming centrality is only an outcome of the author's plan to incorporate her plot for the reader's amusement.

Some other reconcilers might argue that it is highly probable for Gaskell herself to be uncertain about the theme of her fiction. This uncertainty is typically implied in the alteration of proposed titles. Originally she gave the title *John Barton* to her book (*Letters* 70, 74), then, agreeing to the publisher's request, changed it to *Mary Barton: A Manchester Love Story* six months before the publication (*Letters* 56). Finally, however, her book was published as *Mary Barton: A Tale of Manchester Life* on 18 October 1848 (W. E. Smith, *Catalogue* 6). These alterations of the title imply that Gaskell as a historical author sensed the existence of the two focal points in her novel, and finally chose the title which reflected the everyday life of ordinary Mancunians as John and Mary as their representatives.

Which of the three stances to be taken entirely depends upon readers' discretion.

In concluding the discussion of *Mary Barton*'s structure, let us remind supporters of the first and third stances that, in Gaskell's other novels, the chief protagonist is always the one who appears most frequently in the text (See Table 2.7). In *Ruth*, Ruth Hilton's appearance occupies the highest rate (active=66.4%, referred=19.1%, total=85.5%), followed by the kind dissenting minister Thurstan Benson's (active=41.9%, referred=12.4%, total=54.3%) and her son Leonard's (active=22.0%, referred=22.4%, total=44.4%). In *North and South*, Margaret Hale ranks first (active=80.3%, referred=14.8%, total=95.1%), her father Richard Hale second (active=32.1%, referred=23.4%, total=55.5%), and the industrial master John Thornton third (active=22.5%, referred=27.1%, total=49.6%).[69] In *Sylvia's Lovers* comes Sylvia Robson first (active=61.6%, referred=19.2%, total=80.8%), her cousin Philip Hepburn second (active=49.8%, referred=23.7%, total=73.5%), and Sylvia's mother Bell Robson third (active=25.3%, referred=25.2%, total=50.5%). In *Wives and Daughters* Molly Gibson is ranked first (active=61.9%, referred=22.8%, total=84.7%),

---

69 This outcome might lead the reader to doubt the validity of viewing *North and South* as a social problem novel which deals with the process of the capitalist's understanding of his labourers' plight. Inquiry into the heroine's topographical movement discloses the close interrelation between the industrial and love plots, and the author's intention to incorporate the two themes into one book. Its detailed analysis is attempted in Chapter 4 of this dissertation.

	Mary Barton	*Ruth*	*North and South*	*Sylvia's Lovers*	*Wives and Daughters*
1	Mary Barton 85.5 (64.9+20.6)	Ruth Hilton 85.5 (66.4+19.1)	Margaret Hale 95.1 (80.3+14.8)	Sylvia Robson 80.8 (61.6+19.2)	Molly Gibson 84.7 (61.9+22.8)
2	Jem Wilson 63.0 (24.0+39.0)	Thurstan Benson 54.3 (41.9+12.4)	Richard Hale 55.5 (32.1+23.4)	Philip Hepburn 73.5 (49.8+23.7)	Bob Gibson 66.1 (25.4+40.7)
3	John Barton 51.7 (19.7+32.0)	Leonard 44.4 (22.0+22.4)	John Thornton 49.6 (22.5+27.1)	Bell Robson 50.5 (25.3+25.2)	Clare Kirkpatrick 59.4 (33.4+26.0)

Figures: Total (active + referred) %

Table 2.7. Appearance Rates of Top Three Characters in Gaskell's Novels

followed by her father Bob Gibson (active=25.4%, referred=40.7%, total=66.1%) and her step-mother Clare (active=33.4%, referred=26.0%, total=59.4%). Consequently, it is highly probable that, in Gaskell's fiction, the chief protagonist is equivalent to the most active character who appears in the text most frequently, i.e. the epitome of authorial meaning. If the central character were John Barton, *Mary Barton* would turn out to be an exception.

"Whatever Gaskell's later feelings about the centrality of John Barton," Easson writes, "she did accept the title *Mary Barton* and Mary's is the dominant consciousness, through which much of the action is mediated" (*EG* 78).[70] Our structural analysis endorses his assertion. In other words, the purpose of the historical Gaskell may have been to depict the industrial conflict, but the meaning of the Gaskell construct is probably to dramatize Mary's love more constantly than her father's struggle.

---

[70] He is championed by Brodetsky: "[T]he change of title was reasonable, and it was obviously considered a more attractive one" (16).

CHAPTER 3 *Ruth*: Is the Heroine's Martyrdom Inconsistent with the Plot?

3.1. Introduction[71]

"Why should she die?"—Charlotte Brontë, in response to Gaskell's sketch of her new work *Ruth*, protested against the heroine's death in her often quoted letter to our author dated 26 April 1852 (Gérin, *EG* 131; *Brontë Letters* 3: 43; Thomas James Wise 3: 332). As is expressed in Jill L. Matus's succinct summary—"the novel's ending has raised objections from many readers, including Charlotte Brontë and Elizabeth Barrett Browning,[72] who didn't see why the woman had to die" (*Unstable* 130)—,[73] for example, the validity of Ruth Hilton's martyrdom has been one of the key topics of discussion in analysing this Mary Magdalene novel since its publication on "10 January 1853" (Easson, introduction, *RU* xxix; W. E. Smith, *Catalogue* 58).

Including Schor, who observes "the evident fictionality of the end (Pasley, after all, sailed cheerfully off to Australia[74] [...]) is [...] a suggestion of the failure of even this novel to step outside the fallen woman's plot" (*Scheherezade* 74), many critics state that Gaskell has succumbed to the Victorian convention that "sexual notoriety can be dispelled only through death or emigration" (d'Albertis, *Dissembling* 79).[75] Some view Ruth's death as the triumph over her seducer (Jenkins 112; Terrence Wright 93, 94), while others the author's strategy for evoking the reader's compassion: "it is a mark of Gaskell's success in convincing her readers of Ruth's worth that

---

71 This chapter contains the original version of my articles "The Structure of *Ruth*: Is the Heroine's Martyrdom Inconsistent with the Plot?" (*The Gaskell Society Journal*, vol. 18) and "Dramatic Irony in *Ruth*" (*The Gaskell Society Journal*, vol. 21).
72 "Was it quite impossible but that your Ruth should *die*? I had that thought of regret in closing the book—Oh, I must confess to it—Pardon me for the tears' sake!" (her letter to Gaskell on 16 July 1853 qtd. in Waller 42).
73 See also Hopkins (*EG* 123, "[H]er death is purely gratuitous" [*EG* 130]); Ruth Y. Jenkins 175; Deborah A. Logan, *Fallenness* 38; and Stoneman, *EG* 114-15.
74 Jeannette Eve's painstaking investigation on the correct order of the references to the 16-year-old prostitute Pasley, the supposed model of Ruth, in Gaskell's four letters (Nos. 55, 61, 62, and 63) is particularly helpful in clarifying her scheme for Pasley's emigration and her production of "Lizzie Leigh." "A number of writers on Mrs Gaskell quote from these letters, either in connection with her philanthropy or with *Ruth*," remarks Eve, "and several of them have been misled by the mistaken chronology" ("Misdated" 38). The letter dated 26 November 1849 on *Letters* 89 is probably misdated; it should be 19 February 1850. See *Further Letters* 44 and *Dickens's Letters* 4: 29 also. She has proved on the same page that Pasley's destination is the Cape, not Australia. Ruth's parallels with her are discussed by Bodenheimer (*Politics* 151), d'Albertis (*Dissembling* 99), Gérin (*EG* 128), Lansbury (*EG* 26), Nord (*Walking* 164-65), Schor (*Scheherezade* 49), J. G. Sharps (*Observation* 149), Shelston (introduction, *RU*, vii), and Uglow (*EG* 247).
75 See also Françoise Basch 250; Ganz 112; Fryckstedt 165; and Pollard (the "price of sin has to be paid in death, at the cost of narrative credibility" [*Mrs Gaskell*] 102]).

she should have aroused protest by killing her off." (Flint, *EG* 27; see also Easson, introduction, *RU* xiii). Some ascribe a positive meaning to the ending;[76] others negative.[77] One of the sternest attackers of Ruth's death is Schor:

> *Ruth* in many ways turns against its own plot: as Gaskell's contemporaries and subsequent critics have noted, it martyrs its own heroine, sacrificing her to a plot of Christian forgiveness; indeed, it turns on some of its own assumptions, and in its jumpiness, its contradictions, its shifts in discourse, its inability to reach a satisfying ending, suggests some of its author's own dissatisfaction with the form of the novel. (*Scheherezade* 47)

Each opinion is convincing in its own way so that it seems almost impossible to settle this dispute by furnishing conclusive evidence. What we are trying to do in this chapter, however, is to make this attempt, especially by paying attention to the novel's form. If the meaning of the heroine's death could be explained not by subjective (but insightful) criticism as most critics have attempted,[78] but with support of objective evidence, i.e. the formal devices within the text, a reading faithfully representing the authorial meaning (not the authorial intention) should be achieved. Authors normally select such structural elements as characters, time, places, and words, which best fit their purpose; hence, their meanings are principally conveyed through these elements. Authorial meanings are transmitted fundamentally through the text; the text forms internal structures; therefore, authorial meanings should be mirrored on structures. Against this standpoint, Schor defends her subjective (in the sense of championing intentional fallacy) reading by quoting Macherey: we "know that a writer never reflects mechanically or rigorously the ideology which he represents, even if his sole intention is to represent it: perhaps because no ideology is

---

[76] "Ruth dies, gloriously crucified, in order to demonstrate the purity of her soul, the disinterestedness of her deeds" (d'Albertis, *Dissembling* 99); "Ruth's death reflects the author's insight that her fallen heroine would be required to continue proving herself for the rest of her life" (Logan, *Fallenness* 46); "a heroic expression of woman's most noble trait" (Sally Mitchell 38); "Ruth had to die, if only to wring a final tear of sympathy from readers and hardened critics" (Uglow, *EG* 337).

[77] "[E]ven the most generous criticism is bound to feel that the ultimate irony of her death as a consequence of nursing her erstwhile seducer is ill judged" (Shelston, introduction, *Ruth* xix).

[78] For example, "Gaskell uses the idea of typhus, in fact, beyond this cancelling out of the idea of Ruth's danger to the innocent, to *reverse* the standard paradigm of sexual and moral contamination—the paradigm offered by Mrs Bellingham, Mrs Pearson, and Mr Bradshaw. It is Ruth who heals, and it is Bellingham who infects and kills" (Nord, *Walking* 164). Although not about Ruth's death, "[Benson's] literal fall [...] identifies him with the fallen Ruth, and signals Gaskell's theme that all mankind is fallen and in need of succor" (Morse 59) is another example of subjective and perceptive criticism.

sufficiently consistent to survive the test of figuration" (218, qtd. in Schor 77). Macherey's assertion is correct in one sense, for Gaskell fails to be meticulously precise in designing her formal schemes, as is shown in her miscalculation of the novel's chronology and the narrator's arbitrary, therefore, incoherent intervention, or, in Shelston's words, "her direct—and frequent—authorial interpolations" (introduction, *RU* xi). Ward goes so far as to state, "Construction was at no time her *forte*" (introduction, *RU* xxi). Nevertheless, it is also correct that she employs some fundamental formal devices to exhibit her theme which appear if a bird's-eye view of the whole is taken. One of these most crucial internal structures is the one we depend upon in the following argument. Doubting "certain modern theories which hamper the establishment of normative principles in interpretation and which thereby encourage [. . .] subjectivism and individualism" (*Validity* 212), E. D. Hirsch, Jr. asserts that "The interpreter's primary task is to reproduce in himself the author's 'logic,' his attitudes, his cultural givens, in short, his world" (*Validity* 242). Our position is close to his.

In addition, Gaskell's remarks on her formal designs can hardly be ignored:

"I have spoken out my mind in the best way I can" (*Letters* 221); "I tried to make both the story and the writing as quiet as I could, in order that 'people' (my great bugbear) might not say that they could not see what the writer felt to be a very plain and earnest truth, for romantic incidents or exaggerated writing." (*Letters* 225)

These remarks signify the author's prearrangement of her novel's construction. Moreover, in the aforementioned letter addressed to R. M. Milnes, her friend who said her "presence in Manchester alone made that town possible as a residence for people of literary taste" (Waller 57), she stresses that the novel is the manifestation of her truth: "I only knew how very close to my heart it [*Ruth*] had come from."[79] Such being the case, the usefulness of ignoring the authorial meaning in analysing Gaskell's "novel with a purpose" (Easson, introduction, *RU* xi; J. G. Sharps, *Observation* 148, 158) or "moral problem worked out in fiction" (G. H. Lewes qtd. in Easson, *Critical Heritage* 215) is still open to discussion.

To solve the question from the structural viewpoint whether Ruth's demise is consistent with the plot or not, we shall first establish the novel's chronology. Its composition procedure and the discoveries made will be explained in Section 3.2.

---

79   *Letters* 225; see also J. G. Sharps, *Observation* 160.

Section 3.3 centres on the four salient families our statistical analysis has revealed, and investigates how their stories are interwoven. Section 3.4 pays attention to the dramatic irony the author has used to express her theme with. Based on the result of the scrutiny of the novel's form, we shall consider the author's meaning of the heroine's martyrdom in the concluding Section 3.5.

3.2. Comprehensive Chronology

Creating the strict chronology of *Ruth* is the key to the understanding of this fiction especially because calendar data are deliberately incorporated into the text as if they were expected to be linked in proper order.

Gaskell's date for the action is vague (*Letters* 225; see also J. G. Sharps, *Observation* 160). Nonetheless, some historical references within the narrative give us a hint as to the period of its setting. First, the coexistence of stagecoach and railway systems[80] implies that the action takes place from the 1830s through the early 1840s. For, "the golden age of coaching [...] lasted until the 1830s" (Asa Briggs 245), and during "1842 and 1843 famous coaches [...] and many others, ceased running" (G. M. Young 2: 294); furthermore, "it was in 1836 and 1837 [...] that there was the first sense of a railway 'boom'" (Briggs 248; see also David Thomson 42), and the "rapid growth of railways in the inland" took place "during the forties" (G. M. Trevelyan 546). The Eccleston election (*RU* 250) provides us with the second hint for establishing the novel's chronology. It was conducted seemingly under the provision in the 1832 Reform Bill ("An Act to Amend the Representation of the People in *England* and *Wales*" [7 June 1832] qtd. in N. Simons, vol. 12, 728), for "factory hands" (*RU* 250) are included among voters (Easson, notes, *RU* 376; Henry, introduction, *Ruth* xxxiii; Shelston, notes, *RU* 459, 468; E. P. Thompson 900; and David Thomson 73-76). The third clue is the typhus epidemic (*RU* 422-23), "rife in 1836 and again in 1842" (Uglow, *EG* 141). Frederich Engels reports its fury spread across the British Isles in 1817-18, 1837, and 1842-43 (130-31). The plague year is important not only because of the narrator's deliberate insertion of the comment "it was this year to which I come in the progress of my story" (*RU* 423), but also because of the pestilence giving Ruth an opportunity "for glorious public redemption and a credible cause of death" (Basch 250). The fourth and final hint is the "national triumph of arms" which took place in the same year as the typhus fever (*RU* 423), for "the only year in which a war victory, notable for increasing trade, coincided with a

---

80   Elizabeth Gaskell, *Ruth*, Oxford UP, 1985, p. 131, p. 289. Subsequent page references to this work are included parenthetically in the text with the abbreviation *RU*.

typhus epidemic" is 1842, when the Treaty of Nanking was concluded on 29 August to end the Opium War (Henry, introduction, *RU* xxxiii; see also Chris Cook & Brenda Keith 177-78). To prove her hypothesis, Henry points out that the two general elections referred to in Chapter 21 (*RU* 249-51) and Chapter 33 (*RU* 423) as well as Richard Bradshaw's coach accident in Chapter 31 (*RU* 414) almost match historical facts, and concludes "*Ruth*'s action is set between the winters of 1830 and 1843" (introduction, *RU* xxxiii).

The novel's outset was assumed as "the late 1830s" (introduction, *RU* xii; notes, *RU* 459) by Shelston in 1985. The co-existence of stagecoach and railway systems, and the 1832 Reform Act, were the main bases of his assumption. Easson slightly revised it as "about 1840" (introduction, *RU* xiv; notes, *RU* 376) in 1997; he used the narrator's brief reference to the 1840 birth of Queen Victoria's first child (*RU* 124) as his additional ground (notes, *RU* 376; Cook & Keith 106). In 2001, focusing on the concurrent occurrence of the "typhus fever" (*RU* 422) and "the national triumph of arms" (*RU* 423), Henry advanced the above-mentioned proposition in which she paid more attention to the role of chronology than the other two. Nevertheless, there is a crucial miscalculation in their chronologies. Trusting Faith Benson's remark too much that Leonard will "be twelve next February" (*RU* 437), they have failed to notice that the internal time has in fact progressed two more years than the one estimated by Miss Benson.

There is a time span of seven years, not five years, between 1835 when Leonard is six years old (*RU* 201, 207) and 1842 when Faith makes the aforesaid comment. Ruth is dismissed from the post of Bradshaw's governess on a Wednesday (*RU* 335) in August (*RU* 334) 1837. Jemima engages herself to Farquhar "about a year after Ruth's dismissal" (*RU* 376), i.e. August 1838. Her wedding day is fixed on 14 August (*RU* 384), probably of 1839, as "[t]wo years" have passed away (*RU* 384) since Ruth's dismissal from her job.[81] One "November evening" (*RU* 387) of that year, Ruth tells her friend of her intention to be a nurse. On 14 (*RU* 438) "October" (*RU* 432) 1842, "three years" after her marriage (*RU* 431), Jemima pays her last visit to Ruth, who

---

81 The narrative of some small events taking place in the Bensons' household in the year of Jemima's engagement (*RU* 376-77) is presumably over by the end of the first paragraph on page 381. For it is hinted in the next paragraph that Jemima's wedding is approaching (*RU* 382). This should be connected with the phrase "Jemima was going to be married this August" in the second paragraph of page 384. In short, Farquhar's announcement of his engagement (*RU* 382) should probably be made in 1839, the year of his marriage, not in 1838, that of his engagement. In consequence, it is Ruth's dismissal, not Jemima's engagement, that takes place "[t]wo years" (*RU* 384) before Jemima's wedding. This calculation accords with the narrator's statement in the autumn of 1839 that Leonard's illness occurred "three years ago" (*RU* 387), as it happened in October 1836 (*RU* 310-12).

dies in the following month (*RU* 432, 449). Therefore, when Faith utters the problematic words on 14 October 1842, Leonard is actually thirteen, not eleven. Thus, the action of *Ruth* turns out to be set between January 1828 and November 1842.

The chronology thus composed is shown in "The Comprehensive Chronology for *Ruth*" in Appendix 1. With the help of these data and the narrator's statements on their ages, some primary characters' dates of birth can be identified. This process is explained below, and the result displayed in "Characters' Correlation Diagram for *Ruth*" in Appendix 2.

Sally, the Bensons' servant, tells Ruth in a February night of 1829 that she will be "sixty-one next Martinmas" (*RU* 169). Accordingly, her birthday falls on 11 November 1768. Her September 1828 comment that she has lived with the Bensons for "forty-nine" years come Michaelmas, or 29 September (*RU* 145), reveals that she became their servant in September 1779. Thurstan Benson was a lad of "three year old and better" (*RU* 138) then. Hence, his year of birth can be conjectured as 1776.

In the conversation Faith has with Sally some time in or before autumn (*RU* 208) of 1835, she confesses she will be "fifty-seven next May" (*RU* 206). Her birthday, therefore, can be surmised as a day in May 1779. This surmise corroborates our calculation of Sally's, for Faith is "better than ten years younger than" her (*RU* 206). Though the relative ages of the Bensons are made deliberately ambiguous by the narrator—"I do not know whether she was older than her brother" (*RU* 111)—, our chronology reveals that Faith is approximately three years younger than Thurstan.

The narrator implies that Ruth was born in "February" (*RU* 40), while Jemima says her birthday is in "autumn" (*RU* 331). Ruth is "fifteen" (*RU* 38) at the beginning of the story where events of January 1828 are related, and "sixteen" (*RU* 51, 198) in May of the same year when she accompanies Bellingham to London (*RU* 123). Accordingly, the narrator is more reliable than Jemima. In addition, setting Ruth's birthday in February better reflects the author's intention of emphasizing the indestructible ties between her child and her, for Leonard's also is in February (*RU* 437). Consequently, the most appropriate date of her birth is a day in February 1812. This agrees with the authorial calculation that she is "five-and-twenty" (*RU* 331) in 1837.

Since Jemima is twenty-three in March 1836 (*RU* 331), her birthday falls on a day in March 1813. As Farquhar is "nearly forty" in April 1836 (*RU* 215) and "forty, if he is a day" in the summer of 1837 (*RU* 331), he was born, presumably, in 1797. This almost matches his thought of April 1836 that it is preposterous for a man of "nearly forty years of age" to be in love with "a girl of twenty" (*RU* 215), when he is thirty nine, and his fiancée twenty-two. The supposed birthdays of Ruth and Jemima accord with the account that the former is "not many months older in years" than the latter (*RU* 241). Mary Bradshaw, Jemima's younger sister, is "twelve years" old in April 1836 (*RU* 218); her birthday, therefore, can be inferred as a day from May to December 1823 or from January to April 1824. The first option seems more suitable for minimizing the discrepancy between our calculation and the author's: Mary is "nearly eight years younger than Jemima" (*RU* 214). Henry Bellingham's year of birth is probably 1805, since he is "hardly three-and-twenty" in January 1828 (*RU* 31).

Although Gaskell's calculation is generally accurate, there are some instances which show it is not. On a Monday in February 1830, Faith reproaches her brother for his distrust of Ruth's character even after living "a twelvemonth" with her (*RU* 198); to be precise, it should be eighteen months, for it is in September 1828 that he brought Ruth to his Chapel-House. Jemima bursts out in front of her father in August 1837 that she learnt of Ruth's past "weeks and weeks ago—a year it may be" (*RU* 338), which she actually did in a "June afternoon" (*RU* 324) of the same year. In recounting the events of 1838, the narrator refers to Benson as "only sixty" (*RU* 378); his birth year, 1776, however, implies that he is sixty one or two then.

There are two particularly problematic data in determining the novel's time sequence. One is the date "29th" (*RU* 400) written in Bradshaw's letter for the insurance company. Farquhar's observation of "nearly twelve months" having passed since Watson, Bradshaw's clerk, paid Benson his dividend in "June" 1839 (*RU* 396, 397) makes us presume that it falls on 29 June 1840. After "two" sleepless nights (*RU* 401) since the dispatch of this letter, Bradshaw pays a night visit to Benson to confirm his son's forgery. This day is 1 October 1840 because it is specified as "an October morning" (*RU* 406). Thus, the "29th" turns out to be 29 September 1840. The other misleading information is found in Faith's remark on 14 October (*RU* 432, 438) as to Leonard's age: "He'll be twelve next February" (*RU* 437). Should we rely on her, the year treated would become 1840, since his month of birth is February 1829. On the same day, the narrator tells us that happiness has "called out beauty" in Jemima which she lacked "three years ago" (*RU* 431). Should we trust this observation, the year would be 1842, as it presumably alludes to her wedding on 14 August 1839. In both cases, our chronology verifies that the correct answer is the second option.

Our chronology also discloses critics' careless counting of internal dates. Relying on Faith's reference to Leonard's age (*RU* 437), Easson thinks the novel's action "occupies not much over twelve years" (notes, *RU* 376); so does Henry (introduction, *RU* xxiii); Craik thinks it is "about thirteen years" (*EG* 67). In fact, it covers fourteen years and ten months. Counting backwards from the year of publication, 1853, Easson surmises Ruth's story begins "less than fifty years ago" (*EG* 115); our calculation shows twenty-five. Gérin writes that Leonard is "nine or ten" when he is informed of his illegitimacy by his mother (*EG* 130) on a Wednesday, August 1837; to be more precise, he is eight. Hopkins regards Bellingham as "some ten years" Ruth's senior (*EG* 120); actually, he is only seven years older. Joseph Kestner considers the national triumph as the victory at Waterloo in 1815, and the typhus outbreak as that of 1817 (163), disregarding the fact that the two events are described as happening in the same year (*RU* 423). Deborah Denenholz Morse thinks that Bellingham and Ruth appear in a Wales village "a year after" he swept her away to London (58); in truth, it is two months after. Uglow understands there is an interval of "five years" between Ruth's acceptance of the job of governess and the reappearance of Bellingham (*EG* 323); strictly speaking, it is six years and seven months. Wheeler remarks that Ruth hurries back to Eccleston on the day succeeding her interview with Bellingham/Donne in Abermouth ("Sinner as Heroine" 156-57); actually, she does so a "few days" after (*RU* 305-06).

Furthermore, our chronology illuminates some long-neglected facts: (a) Ruth's encounter with Bellingham/Donne at Abermouth takes place eight years after their separation in Wales; (b) Ruth's disguise as a widow has been kept secret nine years; (c) Bradshaw returns to Benson's chapel four years after the declaration of his intention never to enter it again; (d) he comes to respect Ruth again five years after his dismissal of her; (e) Bellingham is thirty seven at the close of the story; and (f) Leonard is thirteen when Ruth dies at thirty.

It is almost inevitable that chronologies in fiction become relative to some extent, since writers' dating may differ according to the information they use as the basis for their calculation, especially when actual events have to be referred to in establishing the dates of fictional ones. In our chronology, which has been constructed to reflect as many internal data as possible, Ruth's coach journey with the Bensons from Llan-dhu to Eccleston in September 1828 (*RU* 131), Bradshaw's railway journey with Bellingham/Donne to Abermouth (*RU* 266) and return to Eccleston (*RU* 289) in September 1836, and the overturn of Richard Bradshaw's coach in October 1840 (*RU* 414), for instance, accurately concur with the historical backgrounds. On the other hand, the general elections Henry used to support her assertion no longer do so: historically, they were held in 1835, 1837, and 1841 (Cook & Keith 138-39), while, by our calculation, the text has them occurring in 1836 and 1842. Notwithstanding, these contradictions, intentional or unintentional, are minor in comparison with what has been clarified by the time sequence and primary characters' ages—Gaskell's art of plotting and the intensity of her imagination. Indeed, there should be few variations in chronologies as long as investigators pay due attention to data.

3.3. Ruth's Interaction with Three Families

"Fig. 3.1. Characters' Frequency of Appearance in *Ruth*," constructed on the basis of the results shown at the bottom of the "Main Characters" column in "The Comprehensive Chronology for *Ruth*," demonstrates how often a character is active and referred to by other characters including the narrator. This bar chart manifests two essential aspects—(a) the main forces promoting the plot are four families: the Bellinghams (Margaret and Henry), the Hiltons (Ruth's parents, Ruth, and Leonard), the Bensons (Thurstan, Faith, and Sally), and the Bradshaws (Mr and Mrs Bradshaw, Richard, Jemima, Mary, Elizabeth, and Walter Farquhar); (b) the most active member of each family is, Henry Bellingham, Ruth Hilton, Thurstan Benson, and Richard Bradshaw, Sr., respectively. Hence, Fig. 3.1 indicates that the key to the novel's theme lies in the functions of four dominant families, especially of the four leading protagonists. "Table 3.1. Families Focused in *Ruth*" and "Table 3.2. Protagonists Focused in *Ruth*" are the contrivances composed to review its storyline from their perspectives. Table 3.1 demonstrates in percentages each family's frequency of appearance (activity plus reference) in relation to the other three families in ten

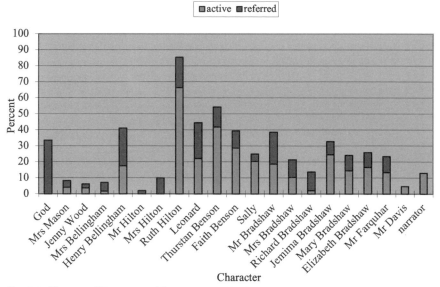

Fig. 3.1. Characters' Frequency of Appearance in *Ruth*

phases into which the total 241 scenes are divided at the pivotal points of the story. Table 3.2 does the same for each protagonist. They reveal not merely the novel's fundamental structure but also the author construct's purpose in writing Ruth's martyrdom.

Phase 1 chiefly depicts Ruth's past and her dreary hours as a seamstress. Her association with Bellingham is treated in Phase 2. The focus moves on to Benson's rescue and protection of her in Phase 3. Her seemingly peaceful life and commitment to the Bradshaw family as a supposed widow are the main topics of Phase 4; the subplots of Jemima's jealousy against Ruth and Richard's forgery are introduced in this phase. Phase 5 prepares and depicts our heroine's reunion with her seducer

phase	scene	outline	the Hiltons	the Bellinghams	the Bensons	the Bradshaws	page allocation
1	1-5	seamstress	100	0	0	0	2.5
2	6-48	seduction	50	46.4	3.6	0	18.4
3	49-88	rescue	33.9	10.4	46.4	9.3	17.6
4	89-120	peaceful life	23.2	0.5	20.7	55.7	15.2
5	121-50	meeting again	26	16.9	11	46.1	12.1
6	151-71	secret disclosed	24.1	5	12.8	58.2	8.0
7	172-98	aftermath	29.5	0.6	33.1	36.7	11.8
8	199-215	forgery	7.5	0	21.5	71	6.5
9	216-27	redemption	41.9	4.7	37.2	16.3	3.4
10	228-41	death	32.1	11.5	37.2	19.2	5.0
		Average	36.8	9.6	22.4	31.3	

NOTE: Figures except in the phase and scene columns are percentages, and highlighted if conspicuous.
Table 3.1. Families Focused in *Ruth*

phase	scene	outline	Ruth Hilton	Henry Bellingham	Thurstan Benson	Mr Bradshaw	page allocation
1	1-5	seamstress	100	0	0	0	2.5
2	6-48	seduction	49.4	45.9	4.7	0	18.4
3	49-88	rescue	41.5	16	36.2	6.4	17.6
4	89-120	peaceful life	38.8	1.5	23.9	35.8	15.2
5	121-50	meeting again	30.4	32.9	12.7	24.1	12.1
6	151-71	secret disclosed	42.2	13.3	20	24.4	8.0
7	172-98	aftermath	38.5	1.5	35.4	24.6	11.8
8	199-215	forgery	9.1	0	48.5	42.4	6.5
9	216-27	redemption	50	10	35	5	3.4
10	228-41	death	37.8	24.3	32.4	5.4	5.0
		Average	43.8	14.5	24.9	16.8	

NOTE: Figures except in the phase and scene columns are percentages, and highlighted if conspicuous.
Table 3.2. Protagonists Focused in *Ruth*

on the Abermouth sands. The central subjects of Phase 6 are Jemima's discovery of her friend's secret and Ruth's dismissal from her post as the Bradshaw daughters' governess. Delineated in Phase 7 are the ordeals Ruth and Benson are obliged to endure, including her confession of sin to her son and the minister's interview with his old church member who terminates their friendship; Jemima's marriage to Farquhar as the conclusion of her subplot and Ruth's gaining a reputation as a nurse are also recounted in this phase. The focal point shifts to the other subplot, Richard's fraud and its consequence, in Phase 8, which closes with Bradshaw's attendance at Benson's service, the sign of a renewal of their severed tie. Phase 9 relates Ruth's selfless nursing in the typhus-fever ward and people's approbation of her noble conduct. Finally, in the contentious Phase 10, the narrator describes her heroine's devoted care for the dying Bellingham/Donne, her demise, his visit to Benson, the minister's condemnation of his irresponsibility, and Bradshaw's comforting Leonard, whom he once insulted as "bastard" (*RU* 339) and "heir of shame" (*RU* 340).

This outline unearths the novel's essential framework: the plot is constructed around the Hiltons' mingling with the Bellinghams, the Bensons, and the Bradshaws,[82] who symbolize "shallowness," "conscience," and "Pharisaism" respectively. Gaskell's intention to mix Ruth with three emblematic protagonists is hinted at by her alliterative naming of their families with "B" as their initial letter.

The cornerstone of the storyline is Ruth Hilton: she appears most often (see Figure 3.1). As her columns in "The Comprehensive Chronology for *Ruth*" and Table 3.2 imply, attention is focused throughout on her "specifically Christian growth from ignorant, youthful sinfulness to a saintlike devotion to the care of others" (Wheeler, "Sinner as Heroine" 151). "One simple way to describe the plot of *Ruth*," observes Susan Morgan, "is that the fallen woman becomes the angel in the house who then becomes the angel in the town" (50).

Henry Bellingham is described as a man of shallow soul. He has been accused of various misdeeds since his childhood (*RU* 32). He shows little compunction about acquiescing to his mother's suggestion that he should discard the girl he seduced (*RU* 90). His speeches are "of a low standard, of impatient self-indulgence, of no acknowledgment of things spiritual and heavenly" (*RU* 163). He remembers Ruth for the first time in eight years in perceiving Mrs Denbigh's resemblance to the innocent orphan he deserted (*RU* 278). Only after realizing she has no intention of

---

82 Craik notices this work's fundamental structure in observing that "Ruth is always central and passive, and (with a few important exceptions) others actively support, contrast with, or illuminate her, contribute to her development, or influence her fate" (*EG* 64).

going back to her former state as his mistress, does he offer her a formal proposal of marriage as "a higher price" (*RU* 302) as if she were an object he could purchase.[83] His shallowness is contrasted with her integrity in her summary of their eight-year separation: "We are very far apart. The time that has pressed down my life like brands of hot iron, and scarred me for ever, has been nothing to you. You have talked of it with no sound of moaning in your voice—no shadow over the brightness of your face; it has left no sense of sin on your conscience, while me it haunts and haunts" (*RU* 302-03).

Thurstan Benson, "Ruth's main source of spiritual guidance and support" (Wheeler, "Sinner as Heroine" 152), and his family are an epitome of Victorian conscience, or, to borrow other critics' phrases, "the sanctified moral center of the novel" (d'Albertis, *Dissembling* 85) and "models of Christian charity" (Jenkins 109). They all shield the guilty heroine from the outside world of strict morality, of which Mr Bradshaw is the prototype. "It is not just Ruth's endeavours that are seen to be important," Kate Flint asserts, "but the fact that she is helped by people round her: Benson, his sister Faith, and their practical servant Sally, provide necessary exempla of compassion and Christian charity" (23-24). Benson's kindliness is intimated also in such minor but touching episodes as his picking up an Irish tramp's baby left at his door (*RU* 148) and his quiet tending to typhus-infected people (*RU* 425).[84] His goodness is most fully portrayed in his defence of his protégée in front of the Pharisaic manufacturer: "to every woman, who, like Ruth, has sinned, should be given a chance of self-redemption [...] in the spirit of the holy Christ" (*RU* 351). Brodetsky detects the author's Christian faith in her drawing of Thurstan Benson: "We see Elizabeth Gaskell courageously incorporating her own deeply held views and high moral standards into her writing" (48).

Richard Bradshaw, Sr. has long been estimated as an "evil" character (Schor, *Scheherezade* 70). Fryckstedt calls him "the foremost mouthpiece of the hypocrisy of society" (155-56); W. R. Greg "the very distilled essence of a disagreeable Pharisee" (qtd. in Easson, *Critical Heritage* 327); Patricia Thomson "the real sinner of the novel" (134); Lansbury an "indecent" fraud (*EG* 30). Sally Mitchell explains "Mrs. Gaskell intends the reader to see Mr. Bradshaw in an unpleasant light" (34). T. Wright, one of his most harsh detractors, attacks him as "a monster of oppressiveness,

---

83 Bellingham's superficial view of human relations is pointed out also by d'Albertis, *Dissembling* 85; Lansbury, *EG* 28; Logan, *Fallenness* 43; and Schor 70.
84 His model is thought to be the Reverend William Turner of Newcastle (Arbuckle 127; E. H. Chadwick 71, 104; Gérin, *EG* 132,133; Uglow, *EG* 58; Ward, introduction, *RU* xxi). Meta, Gaskell's second daughter, denies their resemblance (Uglow, *EG* 629).

self-righteousness and inward corruption, to be seen not only as the patriarch condemned, but as a contrast with Ruth's truly spiritual absoluteness" (88). Indeed, Mr Bradshaw is "so severe, so inflexible" (*RU* 125), tacitly permits bribery in the election (*RU* 307), and spares his daughters' governess no ruthless censure after her history is disclosed (*RU* 339-40). At the same time, however, he is "a keen, far-seeing man of business" (*RU* 210), and "essentially no hypocrite" (Easson, introduction, *RU* xxii; ---, *EG* 123) since he judges his corrupt son and others by the same standard (*RU* 212, 404). Above all, he admits his lack of compassion later and becomes humble, while Bellingham does not. Therefore, it is questionable whether the author really intends him as a wicked character.[85] It would rather be reasonable to suppose that she has emphasized his human weakness to make his subsequent repentance intensely striking. In addition, the Bradshaws—a patriarchal father, his submissive wife, depraved son, rebellious daughter, and innocent younger daughters full of curiosity—are the quintessence of fictional Victorian middle-class families.[86] In this sense, Richard Bradshaw, Sr., and his family are designed to embody the mentality of ordinary Victorians. This view on Bradshaw is echoed by a few critics: "a symbol of society's attitude to sex offenders" (Hopkins, *EG* 130), "Mr Bradshaw embodies society's punishment of the sinner" (Craik, *EG* 50), and "Bradshaw himself is primarily the representative of the public opinion" (Craik, *EG* 73).

The two Tables show that the Bradshaws are one of Gaskell's indispensable tools to convey her theme. (a) The average boxes of Table 3.1 show that they appear more often than the Bensons and the Bellinghams. The reason is not so simple as to be explained by the difference in the number of family members—the Hiltons, the family of virtually two (Ruth and Leonard), are described more often than the Bensons, that of three; the Bellinghams appear far less frequently than the Hiltons although the numbers of their family members are practically the same (Bellingham's father is mentioned only once [*RU* 32]). (b) The average boxes of Table 3.2 indicate Bradshaw is in focus as frequently as Bellingham, the very cause of our heroine's tribulation. (c) The "page allocation" columns of both Tables demonstrate that 35.0% of the total pages is given to Phases 4, 6, and 7 featuring her involvement with the Bradshaws, while 30.5% belongs to Phases 2 and 5 describing Ruth's experiences with the upper-class gentleman. That is, the former occupy as high a percentage as the latter, the pivotal stages of the plot (The significance of the wealthy manufactur-

---

85 This view is shared by G. D. Sanders: Gaskell "does not treat him with harshness" (54).
86 Lansbury observes they represent "the conventional family" (*Social Crisis* 65). "Mr Bradshaw," asserts J. G. Sharps, "is the most prominent figure [. . .] Mrs Gaskell must have met almost daily in the course of her 'ministerial' life" (*Observation* 152).

er's family is stressed especially in Phase 5: Ruth's crucial interview with her erstwhile lover is set in the spot where she stays with them). These three analyses disclose that her interweaving with the Bradshaws is almost equal in importance to or occasionally greater than that with the other two families.[87] Gaskell's concern about how to awaken compassion for seduced women in the Pharisaic Victorians is reflected in this result. It is mirrored also in her choice of two Bradshaw children as the main characters of her subplots: Jemima as the witness to Ruth's uprightness, and Richard as his father's guide to acknowledging his own weakness and mercilessness.[88] Simultaneously, Gaskell's careful treatment of the Bradshaw family echoes the intensity of prejudice of the "great bugbear" (*Letters* 225) against fallen women, since it implies that Victorian Pharisaism requires so meticulous handling from the author.

As Benson's remark "Mr Bradshaw has frequently opposed me" (*RU* 157) and the narrator's "their parallel existences running side by side" (*RU* 383) typically imply, they are drawn in contrast.[89] Gaskell's purpose behind this tactic is manifested in the scene of the compassionate Dissenting minister's defence of Ruth from Bradshaw's accusation where he appeals to the spokesperson of the relentless public for mercy (*RU* 351). Through "the Benson-Bradshaw debate as a clash between Unitarianism and Calvinism," or on "humane Unitarianism versus punitive Calvinism" (Stoneman, *EG* 111), the author makes "the Calvinistic Bradshaw finally see the error of his ways" (Wheeler, "Sinner as Heroine" 160). Gaskell's scrupulous tackling of her "great bugbear" is revealed again in this contrastive delineation of the two protagonists.

In spite of some critics' disparagement of the novel's formal imperfection,[90] the

---

87 The Bradshaw family's significance is stressed by an anonymous reviewer: in the second and third volumes, "Ruth, though the centre of interest and the leading person, is subordinate as regards space to sketches in the town of Eccleston. [. . .] Various other persons, especially of the Bradshaw family, might be particularized, but Mr Bradshaw himself is [. . .] the chef d'oeuvre of the book" (Easson, *Critical Heritage* 213-14). Although inaccurate as to "space," he/she notices the fundamental structure of the novel. Craik remarks the Bradshaw story and Ruth's "run concurrently, and mutually illuminate" (*EG* 54).
88 It is suggested in John Forster's letter to the novelist dated 12 November 1852 that she was thinking of Richard's forgery only as an episode (qtd. in Rubenius 35; J. G. Sharps, *Observation* 166), not an essential strand as Forster considers. This is further evidence to show that her chief interest lies in her heroine's interaction with Bellingham, Benson, and Bradshaw.
89 This authorial device is noticed by Bodenheimer (*Politics* 162), Easson (introduction, *RU* xii-xiii), Ganz (127), Jenkins (95), Lansbury (*EG* 33; *Social Crisis* 65), Morse (60), Pollard ("As Bradshaw represents the severity of the world's judgment, so Benson shows forth the charity of God's judgment" [*Mrs Gaskell* 104]), Stoneman (*EG* 104), G. D. Sanders (47), Shelston (introduction, *RU* xvii-xviii), and T. Wright (86).
90 For example, Gaskell "could ruin her works herself, being sometimes apparently not able to see clearly what she was doing or what her real intentions were. *Ruth* shows her weakness in planning with its

investigation on Ruth's intermingling with the three households uncovers its principal form. Gaskell's objectives for this fiction are three: to criticize selfish seducers,[91] to give seduced women opportunities for compensation under the protection of compassionate people,[92] and to awaken the public to their ignorance of their own unfairness.[93] As the central protagonist for each objective, Bellingham, Benson, and Bradshaw are created. Her story is arranged so that all purposes are accomplished in Phase 10, whose core events are Benson's condemnation of Bellingham as the instigator of Ruth's ordeals, the seduced woman's redemption and salvation, and repentant Bradshaw's respect for her and compassion for her son. This structure is sketched out in "Fig. 3.2. Image of Plots' Flow in *Ruth*."

The author's first aim is carried out by Benson, "the author's mouthpiece" (d'Albertis, *Dissembling* 92),[94] who rebuffs the seducer's offer of financial assistance for Leonard in front of his dead mother: "He shall never touch a penny of your money. Every offer of service you have made, I reject in his name,—and in her presence. [. . .] Men may call such actions as yours, youthful follies! There is another name for them with God" (*RU* 454). This aim of condemning the double standard has been noted by some critics.[95] As a means of censuring

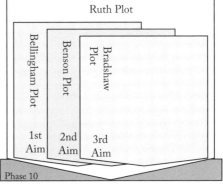

Fig. 3.2. Image of Plots' Flow in *Ruth*

thematic contradictions" (John McVeagh, "Narrative Technique" 463); all Gaskell's "earlier novels bear evidence of faulty construction, and in *Ruth* she is at her worst" (G. D. Sanders 50); "Taken as a whole, the structure of *Ruth* is very weak; the work fails as an artistic unity" (J. G. Sharps, *Observation* 161).

91 Catherine Winkworth has noticed this object in stating about Bellingham: "One of Mrs. Gaskell's objects was to make her readers feel how much worse he was in every way than Ruth" (qtd. in Hopkins, *EG* 126-27).

92 This second object is noted by Brodetsky: "Thurstan Benson is clearly expressing Mrs Gaskell's own conviction that the unmarried mother should be given the opportunity to rehabilitate herself" (48).

93 The orthodox summary of the novel's purpose is given by J. G. Sharps: "both to protest against the double standard of Victorian sexual morality and at the same time to plead for a more charitable, a more truly Christian, attitude toward the 'betrayed' mother, whose child the novelist saw as a possible means of redemption rather than as a badge of shame" (*Observation* 148). His view is shared by Shelston (introduction, *RU* xvi) and T. Wright ("Gaskell's indictment of her society's hypocrisy" [73]).

94 Benson is regarded as such also by Ganz ("the central spokesman of the author" [124]) and Jenkins ("Through this dissenting minister's compassion and pronouncements, Gaskell 'speak[s] [her] mind out,' challenging society" [93]).

CHAPTER 3 *Ruth: Is the Heroine's Martyrdom Inconsistent with the Plot?* 103

Bellingham "with uncharacteristic severity" (Kucich 138), Gaskell uses dramatic irony, which is discussed in f. of Section 3.4.

She unfolds her second objective, the fulfilment of Ruth's redemption, in two ways: earthly and heavenly. Her earthly absolution is illustrated in Phase 9, which centres on her nursing at the typhus-fever ward and its outcome. Moved by her selfless care, a social outcast utters, "Such a one as her has never been a great sinner; nor does she do her work as a penance, but for the love of God, and of the blessed Jesus" (*RU* 429). To this old man, Leonard utters with proud heart, "Sir, I am her son!" (*RU* 430). Schor considers Ruth's beatification is completed here (*Scheherezade* 72). Mr Grey, the Eccleston rector, brings her the Infirmary Secretary's formal letter of gratitude for her nursing, and tells Leonard that he may read the testimony to his mother's noble conduct with pride and pleasure in the future (*RU* 433). In answer to Ruth's question whether Mr Grey knows her past, Jemima proclaims "he knew—everybody in Eccleston did know—but the remembrance of those days is swept away" (*RU* 434). These extracts have moved many critics to believe that the heroine's absolution is complete here (e.g. Basch 250; Ganz 130), and that the later scenes are surplus (one example is Schor's criticism quoted in Section 3.1 of this chapter). Uglow also considers the plot's development into Ruth's nursing her former lover as unnatural: "In the eyes of all who know her, including Bradshaw, Ruth has completed her penance; there is no practical or moral need for her to nurse Bellingham, lying sick at the inn. [. . .] Ruth's guilt and self-torment appear ludicrously out of proportion to her offence, particularly since she has recreated her life through her love for her Leonard and self-sacrificing work" (*EG* 336). Nevertheless, Gaskell has her reason for inserting the episode, and it is probably to depict her heroine's double redemption. Careful reading reminds us that there are some allusions to Ruth's heavenly salvation in Phase 10, particularly in her last words on her death bed: "I see the Light coming" (*RU* 448),[96] and in the biblical phrases Benson quotes in her funeral sermon: "These are they which came out of great tribulation, and have washed their robes, and made them white in the blood of the Lamb. [. . .] God shall wipe

---

95 For example, Bonaparte 78; Easson, *EG* 110; ---, *Critical Heritage* 292; Flint ("The circumstances of her death provide a means of dramatizing the irredeemably contaminating effects of men like Bellingham" [26]); Matus ("the ending is effective as a way of refocusing the issue of male responsibility" [*Unstable* 130]); G. D. Sanders ("*Ruth* is a plea for the single standard of morality for men and women" [47]); and Catherine Winkworth (qtd. in Easson, *Critical Heritage* 246). Rubenius observes "the purpose of the book is summed up" in these words of Benson's to Bradshaw (205).
96 The light is a common allusion to Christ or God ("I am the light of the world" [John 8.12]; "The Lord is my light and my salvation" [Psalm 27.1]).

away all tears from their eyes" (Rev. 7.14, 17 qtd. on 457). As regards Ruth's compensation, Easson observes "the importance of Ruth lies not in any sin, for which a punishment might be exacted, but rather in the value of what she can achieve after the world would cast her out as worthless" (introduction, *RU* xiii). On the other hand, Flint states that death takes her into "a happier world than that which she has known," and functions as "a celebration [. . .] of Ruth's life" (26); Jenkins senses Ruth's affinity with "a Christ or prophet figure" in her death (112). Easson refers to the seduced girl's earthly redemption; Flint and Jenkins, to her heavenly one.

That the author's third purpose of letting Bradshaw acknowledge his mistakes is being fulfilled is hinted at in Jemima's words to Ruth in Phase 9: "papa has been quite anxious to show his respect for you" (*RU* 432). Its complete fulfilment is achieved on the very last page of the book: having "been anxious to do something to testify his respect for the woman, who, if all had entertained his opinions, would have been driven into hopeless sin," he orders the first stone-mason of the town to make a tombstone for her (*RU* 458). He comforts the weeping Leonard, touches him on the shoulder for the first time (*RU* 458), and takes him to Benson's Chapel-House, which he enters for the first time in two years and one month. The story concludes with the narration: "for a moment, he could not speak to his old friend, for the sympathy which choked up his voice, and filled his eyes with tears" (*RU* 458). Therefore, there is no doubt that Phase 10 is intended to illustrate Bradshaw's remorse, compassion for Ruth and her son,[97] and reconciliation with Benson. Here, as Jenkins correctly remarks, Gaskell "presents a radical vision of her culture's need to replace Old Testament values and religion with New Testament charity by her representation of Ruth's death" (112).

As our analyses of the three families' raison d'être and of the function of Phase 10 illuminate, this novel would come to an end with the author's three purposes unfulfilled if closed without Ruth's martyrdom.

3.4. Dramatic Irony[98]

Gaskell employs some other formal devices: for instance, nature as the reflection of the protagonist's states of mind;[99] biblical references as a narrative strategy;[100]

---

97 Jenkins is correct in stating that Bradshaw "achieves his greatest salvation through this son of a fallen woman" (115).
98 This section is the original version of my paper published in *The Gaskell Society Journal*, vol. 21.
99 "In the first nine chapters, which tell the story of the seduction and abandonment, Ruth's emotional life is charted almost entirely through her responses to natural scenes" (Bodenheimer, *Politics* 157-58); Craik (*EG* 60); Easson (introduction, *RU* ix); Morse (57); Pike (55-59); Pollard (*Mrs Gaskell* 94-95); Shelston (introduction, *RU* xi); "Ruth's inner struggles are powerfully conveyed by the untamed aspects of the

dreams as a subtext of Ruth's consciousness;[101] and the "lack of maternal care" (*RU* 54) as an essential ideology in the novel.[102] The most noteworthy technique would be dramatic irony that, although used consistently, has attracted little attention of critics. The following six instances are all planned to direct the reader's sympathy towards our heroine or to emphasize the shallowness of hypocrites.

a. The first instance is Margaret Bellingham's complaint about Ruth's rudeness to her convalescent son at Mrs Morgan's inn: "this girl pushed herself before me, and insisted upon speaking to me. I really had to send Mrs Morgan to her before I could return to your room" (*RU* 89). The reader has known that the actual situation is different from what she describes. Ruth stands "right before Mrs Bellingham," not pushes herself before her (*RU* 85). She makes an inquiry after her lover's condition twice since she has been unable to obtain his mother's answer to her first question (*RU* 85). Ruth neither forces herself into his room nor obstructs his mother's returning to it, for "though it would have been an infinite delight to her to hover and brood around him, yet it was of him she thought and not of herself" (*RU* 86). Mrs Bellingham's biased interpretation, therefore, only contributes to deepening the reader's sympathy towards Ruth.

b. The second case of dramatic irony appears in Margaret Bellingham's note she leaves for Ruth with a solatium bank-note of fifty pounds (*RU* 92). Having explained her son's realization of the sinful nature of his life with Ruth, she adds that they will leave the inn by his "earnest desire" and to avoid seeing her. "I wish to exhort you to repentance," she continues, "and to remind you that you will not have your own guilt alone upon your head, but that of any young man whom you may succeed in entrapping into vice" (*RU* 92). That this message is concocted by the mother to save her son from his plight is obvious for the two reasons. First, it is doubtful that his desire of separation from Ruth is "earnest"; for, he feels as if he were "not behaving as he should do, to Ruth" (*RU* 91). Second, Mrs Bellingham's explanation that the fault lies with Ruth not with her son is hardly acceptable as it stands.[103] For, as Ganz asserts that "Bellingham alone is given the full responsibility

---

natural world, wild mountains, storm and water" (Uglow, *EG* 331).
100 "Gaskell, throughout the novel, has characterized Ruth with biblical allusions" (Jenkins 174); "The most important scenes in the novel are underpinned with biblical quotations, which help to shape the text and thus also the reader's response to it" (Wheeler, "Sinner as Heroine" 148).
101 Easson, introduction, *RU* xiv; Henry, introduction, *RU* xxv; Pollard, *Mrs Gaskell* 95-97; Stoneman, *EG* 100-09; Uglow, *EG* 333.
102 Bodenheimer, *Politics* 157; Henry, introduction, *RU* xxv; Jenkins 104-05; Logan, *Fallenness* 39; "All her life, Ruth will long to recreate this mother-daughter relation" (Morse 54); Stoneman, *EG* 105; Trudgill 290-91.

for her fall" (117), the initiative has been taken always by him as he says to Ruth, "Ruth, would you go with me to London?" (*RU* 56), and then to his mother, "No, mother, but I led her wrong" (*RU* 88). In the latter half of her note, Mrs Bellingham writes, "I shall pray that you may turn to an honest life, and I strongly recommend you [. . .] to enter some penitentiary" (*RU* 92). Her prayer is hypocritical, and her recommendation self-interested, because her true motive for them is to save the honour of herself, not of Ruth, as is implied in her reproach to her son: "I suppose you are not so lost to all sense of propriety as to imagine it fit or desirable that your mother and this degraded girl should remain under the same roof, liable to meet at any hour of the day?" (*RU* 90). Accordingly, her note only awakens the reader's compassion for the deserted girl and indignation against Mrs Bellingham.

c. The third example is found in the hearsay of Mrs Bellingham's maid. Simpson relates to her employer what she has heard about Ruth from Mrs Mason, the Fordham dressmaker:

> "[Ruth's] guardian [. . .] washed his hands of her when she ran off; [. . .] the girl was always a forward creature, boasting of her beauty, and saying how pretty she was, and striving to get where her good looks could be seen and admired,—one night in particular, [. . .] at a country ball; [. . .] she used to meet Mr Bellingham at an old woman's house, who was a regular old witch, [. . .] and lives in the lowest part of the town, where all the bad characters haunt." (*RU* 107)

Ruth never runs off from her guardian, but was apprenticed to the milliner peremptorily by him (*RU* 38). Ruth does say, "I know I am pretty," evoking other seamstresses' displeasure, but only from her simplicity rather than her forwardness, as is indicated by her artless explanation: "for many people have told me so" (*RU* 12). Mrs Mason's account of Ruth's motive for going to a ball is false. Ruth only followed her employer's directions, and, indeed, on one occasion, rejected her offer: "I ought not to go" (*RU* 10-11). Old Nelly Brownson's "mean little cottage" (*RU* 23) here referred to as frequented by "all the bad characters" is not the place of the young couple's regular meeting. They visit her only once in carrying her drenched grandson Tom into her house. Its filthiness is purposely exaggerated because of Bellingham's scorn: "It is more fit for pigs than human beings" (*RU* 26). Thus Simpson's talk is intended to stress Ruth's wickedness. However, having already noticed her innocent sincerity,

---

103   Reading her account sincerely rather than ironically, Henry states, "Mrs Bellingham's twisted view of the situation turns her son into the victim, and she assures him that Ruth 'led you wrong with her artifices'" (introduction, *RU* xxviii).

the reader perceives that the author's intent here is to ridicule the superficiality and hypocrisy of three women: Mrs Mason, who pays "an extreme regard to appearances" (*RU* 8); Simpson, too priggish to nurse the sinful girl (*RU* 106); and Mrs Bellingham, who regards the Dissenting minister Benson's request for a nurse maid for her son's sick concubine as a "delicate hint that some provision ought to have been made" (*RU* 107).

d. The fourth dramatic irony takes place when Jemima misunderstands Ruth's true reason for her seeming intrigue with her father Mr Bradshaw. Ruth tacitly complies with his request to advise his daughter to improve her behaviour towards Walter Farquhar, his favoured candidate for his son-in-law. One evening in April 1836, owing to Ruth's ingenuity, Jemima is led to talk cheerfully with her father's business collaborate (*RU* 234); on the following morning, she hears Bradshaw's secret plan from her mother, and begins to suspect her friend's machination. Jemima's misjudgement is obvious to the reader who knows the actual situation: Ruth, having rejected Bradshaw's request once by stating she would tell Jemima of her faults in private should she perceive them (*RU* 227), sets aside the resolution later, because she feels really sorry for Jemima's serious change of mood. Here, dramatic irony is employed to emphasize Ruth's integrity and tenderness.[104]

e. Mrs Pearson offers the fifth example in giving a deceptive account of Ruth. On a Saturday in June 1837, this Eccleston dressmaker talks to Jemima about the beautiful but vicious woman called Ruth Hilton who was once apprenticed to her sister-in-law:

> "[This] young creature was very artful and bold, and thought sadly too much of her beauty; and, somehow, she beguiled a young gentleman, who took her into keeping. [. . .] His mother followed him into Wales. She was a lady of a great deal of religion, and of a very old family, and was much shocked at her son's misfortune in being captivated by such a person. [. . .] I hear that she had gone off with another gentleman that she met with in Wales." (*RU* 320-21)

As was discussed in the third example c, Ruth is innocent in referring to her own beauty rather than bold; it is Bellingham who was active in approaching her, not Ruth in meeting him (*RU* 25, 30). Besides, Pearson's description of Margaret Bellingham's piety reminds us that her religion is somewhat of Old Testament

---

[104] Matus explains Jemima's misinterpretation as an example of her maiden pride, not dramatic irony (*Unstable* 28).

strictness, not of New Testament mercy, although she herself believes that hers is of genuine moralist. In the last sentence, the dressmaker falsely insinuates Ruth's promiscuity: the gentleman mentioned is Thurstan Benson, her rescuer minister. Hence, this dramatic irony is inserted to draw the reader's sympathy towards Ruth, whose truth has been spread thus in a distorted form.

f. The final instance of dramatic irony is found in the self-conceited utterance Bellingham gives in visiting Benson's Chapel-House after Ruth's death: "I cannot tell how I regret that she should have died in consequence of her love of me" (*RU* 453).[105] Ruth's true motive for nursing him is made vague on purpose: in answer to the question of Mr Davis, his surgeon, if she loves him, she remarks, "I have been thinking—but I do not know—I cannot tell—I don't think I should love him, if he were well and happy—but you said he was ill—and alone—how can I help caring for him? [. . .] He is Leonard's father" (*RU* 441). The careful reader, however, would sense the heavenly motive, not earthly, in her resolution. Her affection for her lover is depicted as pure from the outset of the novel to "the very end" (Lansbury, *EG* 31);[106] her inner struggle before and after the crucial interview with him on the Abermouth sands intimates "despite what she says, she loves him still" (Easson, *Critical Heritage* 210).[107] Notwithstanding, she refuses his marriage proposal, only to protect Leonard from contamination.[108] Her eight-year life of repentance under the care of the Bensons has deepened her spiritual growth to notice his lack of sincerity. She tries to save the life of such a despicable man. Here, her love has been elevated to Godly, which Bellingham misunderstands as earthly. This irony brings his shallowness into sharp relief: from the beginning to the end, money is his standard of judgement, even in making a marriage proposal (*RU* 302) and expressing sympathy (*RU* 24, 453).[109] Gaskell's harsh attack of Victorian seducers is hinted at in this technique.

---

105 Jenkins quotes this utterance to explain Ruth's death being a victory over Bellingham, not its ironical meaning (*RU* 113-14).
106 The genuineness of the heroine's love is characteristically demonstrated in the narrator's observation: "her own love was too faithful" (*RU* 92).
107 Ruth's faithfulness to Bellingham is pointed out also by Craik (*EG* 53), Easson (*Critical Heritage* 235), and Hopkins (*EG* 122). Lansbury states it is not "love" that takes her to his side, but "a sense of duty" (*Social Crisis* 79).
108 "She knows," Lansbury correctly observes, "he is not a good man and would not make a good father to their son" (*EG* 28). The similar view is expressed by Mews (86).
109 Basch justly points out, "he is singularly lacking in substance and complexity" (249).

3.5. Conclusion

Was Ruth's death really necessary for the plot? To this long-disputed subject, our structural analysis offers the following answer. First, Gaskell had three principal purposes for this "revolutionary model to reform her culture" (Jenkins 115): (a) to accuse seducers of their cruel irresponsibility; (b) to give the seduced chances to expiate their sin; (c) to appeal to the Victorian public for reconsideration of their strict morality, or, to borrow Gérin's phrase, to awaken "the conscience of the virtuous to their duty of Samaritan charity" (*EG* 131).[110] She then created three central households as the embodiment of "shallowness," "conscience," and "Pharisaism," intending to achieve her goals by letting the seduced heroine interact with them. This is why their frequency of appearance has become high, or rather why the plot unfolds substantially around them. While emphasizing Ruth's virtue[111] and the superficiality of the hypocrites through the technique of dramatic irony, Gaskell accomplishes her aims in the final three chapters. Chapter 34 describes Ruth's earthly redemption, or "social rehabilitation" (Ganz 120); Chapter 35 her heavenly or "spiritual" salvation (Ganz 120); and Chapter 36 treats Benson's condemnation of Bellingham's shallowness, God's promise of Ruth's deliverance, and Bradshaw's conversion from strict moralist to compassionate Christian (thus, Gaskell presents her three purposes in the final chapter). If the novel ended with Chapter 34, the author's second purpose only would be achieved and that only partially. In terms of the novel's structure, consequently, Ruth's martyrdom is a logical conclusion, not an authorial error.[112]

In contrast to Schor's criticism of Ruth's death being inconsistent with the plot, quoted in Section 3.1 of this chapter, Flint regards it as "the logical fulfilment of certain narrative strands within the novel" (26). "This ending," she continues, "uses

---

110 E. H. Chadwick considers *Ruth*'s primary purpose is the third one, "mercy for the erring" (112); so does Unsworth (*EG* 88). Ganz calls Gaskell's third and second aims "her double goal in challenging social prejudice against the fallen woman: to ask greater indulgence for her original error and to suggest her ultimate rehabilitation" (110).

111 Ruth's goodness is noted by Brodetsky 44; d'Albertis (*Dissembling* 95); Gérin ("that there was no vice in Ruth is the whole argument of the book," *EG* 132); Pollard ("too good," *Mrs Gaskell* 102); Shelston (Gaskell gives us "a heroine to whom no one could conceivably object," introduction, *RU* xv); Stoneman (*EG* 111); and T. Wright 87.

112 The letter of Gaskell's friend Catherine Winkworth to her sister Emily Shaen dated 22 November 1852 implies that the author has paid thorough attention to the construction of the ending: *Ruth* is "not finished yet. Lily is not satisfied with the last 100 pages, and we are going over it very carefully to take out superfluous epithets and sentences, of which there were certainly enough here and there to give it a slightly sentimental twang" (Emily Shaen, editor, *Letters and Memorials of Catherine Winkworth*, vol. 1, privately printed, 1883, p. 369, qtd. in Easson, introduction, *RU* viii; Uglow, *EG* 308).

the reader's response of feeling cheated or bereft," or his/her regret about Ruth's sacrifice, "to challenge the assumptions which lie behind" the Victorian convention that fallen women should have to die (28). Her observation is shared by Easson: our heroine's significance lies "in the world's realization, confronted by the death that crowns Ruth's life, of what has been lost" (introduction, *RU* xiii). The result of our structural analysis supports their interpretation. However harshly the heroine's martyrdom may be condemned, the novel's form indicates that it is consistent with the development of the story.

CHAPTER 4 *North and South*: The Novel of Two Themes

4.1. Introduction[113]

It has long been one of critics' main concerns in discussing *North and South* which of its two major plots represents its theme more appropriately: the industrial, social, political, or public one (the naming differs depending on critics, but its chief purport is conflict and reconciliation between the mill-owner John Thornton and the trade unionist Nicholas Higgins),[114] or the love, romance, marriage, or private one (the proud Margaret Hale's prejudice against and understanding of Thornton).[115] Few readers will disagree that *North and South* is a story of Margaret Hale, but it does not necessarily mean that more focus is placed on the development of her romance than on the growth of Thornton's industrial understanding. For, she is involved in both plots almost in the equal ratio.

In which plot is the theme of this novel (or its authorial meaning) more explicitly expressed? To find the answer to this question mainly through scrutiny of plots' interaction is the primary aim of this statistical study. Should its actual situation be brought to light, the Gaskell construct's scheme for structure will be unveiled, and consequently her meaning for writing this fiction as well. Formal analysis should be effective in identifying its theme, not merely because form is "so important to her as a writer" (Uglow, *EG* 368), but also because Gaskell had "the plot and characters" in her head long before embarking on this fiction (*Letters* 328).

After explaining a sample process of constructing "The Comprehensive Chronology for *North and South*" in the next section 4.2, we shall investigate chief characters' frequency of appearance in Section 4.3 to spotlight the raison d'être of Richard Hale, Margaret's father. Stage alterations both in the whole novel and in Milton, its major place of action, are examined in Section 4.4, where the Gaskell

---

113 This chapter is the original version of my paper published in *The Gaskell Society Journal*, vol. 22.
114 Nicholas is a fervent supporter of the trade Union: "I'm a member o' the Union; and I think it's the only thing to do the workman any good" (*NS* 292); "It's a great power: it's our only power" (*NS* 293).
115 For instance, Colby ("*Appointed*" 47), David (38-39), G. D. Sanders (74-75), Spencer (*EG* 87-88), Wheeler ("Sinner as Heroine" 149), Williams (*Culture and Society* 103-04), and especially early reviewers of the novel (Easson, *Critical Heritage* 337, 340) regard the social conditions of England as its central topic. Margaret's love and growth are supported by Brodetsky (53, 57), Chapple ("A Reassessment" 464, 470), Martin Dodsworth (introduction 16-18), Mews (92), Schor (150), Pollard (*Mrs Gaskell* 110), and Larry K. Uffelman (76, 83). Craik (*EG* 95), Kuhlman ("Education" 24), Mary Lenard (132), and Uglow (*EG* 369-70) consider that both are essential (For instance, "*North and South* links the themes of love and class war in a quite different way from [*Mary Barton*]" [Uglow, *EG* 370]). The reason for this diversity in interpretation lies chiefly in the complexity of the plots' mingling, as is suggested by Lansbury (*EG* 35-36) and E. Wright (*Mrs Gaskell* 132-34).

construct's meaning for topographical change will be brought to light. Section 4.5 explores the interaction between the industrial and love plots to illuminate the Gaskell construct's structural design. Despite its engagement with the textual significance and critical subjectivism, the argument in this section is developed to ensure that all available evidence is thoroughly examined for the best accurate inference of the author construct's intended meaning. The concluding section 4.6 presents the urinterpretation intended by the Gaskell construct.

4.2. Comprehensive Chronology[116]

The purpose of this section is to call critics' attention to the effectiveness of a chronology as a means for objective understanding of Gaskell's meaning in *North and South*. Its comprehensive chronology is composed first by dividing the narrative into scenes in accordance with the shift of time, and then by examining main characters' frequency of appearance and the change of locations scene by scene. Elucidating its construction procedure together with some contradictions that have been uncovered during the process, this section eventually aims at displaying "The Comprehensive Chronology for *North and South*" (See Appendix 1). It is a device to pinpoint the Gaskell construct's meaning for her novel as well as to take a bird's-eye view of its structure.

There is no mention of a specific calendar year in this novel. One of the rare historical references is the 1844 act of smoke prevention John Thornton briefly speaks of in Chapter 10.[117] From the mill-owner's remark that no Milton chimney has been informed against "for five years past" (*NS* 82), it can be assumed that this chapter deals with the events of 1849. As time data across the novel show that the story covers four years, and that Chapter 10 illustrates an event in the second year, the period treated turns out to range from 1848 to 1851.[118] Thus, it is brought to

---

[116] This section is a revised edition of my article "The Chronology of *North and South*," *Kumamoto Journal of Culture and Humanities*, vol. 87.

[117] Elizabeth Gaskell, *North and South*, edited by Angus Easson, Oxford UP, 1982, p. 82. Subsequent references are to this edition and inserted parenthetically in the text with the abbreviation *NS*. Editors differ in identifying this law. Easson (notes, *NS* 439) and Patricia Ingham (introduction 430) regard it as the 1847 Act of "the Prevention of Smoke" (10 & 11 Victoria, c. 34), but Dorothy Collin (*NS* 532) does as the 1844 "Act for the Good Government and Police Regulation of the Borough of Manchester" which includes the regulation of smoke prevention (7 & 8 Victoria, c. 40). We follow the latter's suggestion because the 1844 law was intended particularly for the borough of Manchester (Simons, vol. 17, 485), the 1847 for the whole British Isles (Simons, vol. 18, 537). If we take the suggestion of Easson and Ingham, however, the years covered in this fiction will range from 1851 to 1854. Some critics consider the novel is set in the 1850s (Bonaparte 167; E. H. Chadwick 208; Kestner 164; G. D. Sanders 64).

[118] Henry states that the temporal context of the story is "set firmly after 1847" (introduction, *RU* xxiii).

light that one of the most crucial events in the novel—the heroine Margaret Hale's protection of Thornton in front of the mob (ch. 22, vol. 1; "Oh, do not use violence! He is one man, and you are many" [*NS* 178])—occurs on Saturday, 23 August 1849, as is disclosed in the explanation below.

The following explanation demonstrates a process of arranging internal events chronologically and a couple of instances of Gaskell's careless dating. It is "the latter part of July" (*NS* 17) when the story begins, because it is only "three days" (*NS* 9) after the farewell party for Edith that Margaret leaves Aunt Shaw's house in Harley Street, London, for her home in Helstone, the event of "the latter part of July" (*NS* 17). This calculation is confirmed by the anniversary of Edith's marriage being in "July."[119] Chapter 19 of Volume 1 depicts Margaret's visit to Bessy Higgins. From the factory girl's remark "The twenty-first—that's Thursday week" (*NS* 151), the reader realizes that the Thorntons' dinner party is being held on Thursday the 21st, and that the heroine's visit to Bessy occurs between Friday the 8th and Tuesday the 12th. On "the very day before Mrs Thornton's dinner-party" (*NS* 153), that is, Wednesday the 20th, Margaret comes upon the scene of John Boucher's argument with Nicholas Higgins where the neighbouring workman accuses the Union leader of his false prediction on a Wednesday that the strike should end in a fortnight, adding "it's now Tuesday i' th' second week" (*NS* 154; emphasis added). This inconsistency is recorded as it is in our chronology. As the source of subsequent dating, however, the narrator's date should be appropriate rather than Boucher's since the party is held on the next day (*NS* 158-60), not two days after the argument.

By the day of the dinner party at the Thorntons, 21 August 1849, the mill-owner has arranged to employ Irish workers (*NS* 165), as the strike shows no sign of ending. Since he determined at the end of Chapter 18 of the novel that he would give strikers "a fortnight,—no more" (*NS* 146), the day Chapter 18 deals with should be 7 August. On the party night, Mrs Hale's health declines (*NS* 167-68). On "the third day" from then (*NS* 171), Saturday, 23 "August" (*NS* 171), Margaret goes to Marlborough Street to borrow a waterbed for her mother from Mrs Thornton,

---

There is another historical reference in the text (ch. 15, vol. 1): "Very lately," Margaret says to Thornton, "I heard a story of what happened in Nuremberg only three or four years ago" (sc. 110; *NS* 121). The case of the mysterious boy Kaspar Hauser was brought into public view in May 1828 (Easson, "Explanatory Notes" *NS* 442; "Kaspar Hauser"; Martin Kitchen 25); Margaret's calculation suggests that the year treated in this chapter is 1831 or 1832, which controverts our year 1849. After careful consideration of the whole plot, we choose the first historical reference (to the 1844 Smoke Prevention Act) as more appropriate to the chronology for *North and South*.

119 "It was now drawing near to the anniversary of Edith's marriage" (*NS* 103); "It's nearly a year since Edith was married!" (*NS* 147).

where she dares to shield John Thornton from the violence of frenzied labourers. At the earnest request of her weakening mother, Margaret writes a letter to Frederick, her brother, and posts it on the following day (*NS* 192, 199), Sunday the 24th; Mrs Hale expects her exiled son to come home "in twenty-two days" (*NS* 204). In the afternoon of Monday the 25th (*NS* 212, 213, 215), Thornton pays a brief visit to Crampton Crescent to give Mrs Hale a fruit basket. In "the next morning" (*NS* 234, 236), Tuesday the 26th, he brings her another gift of fruit. His mother comes to see the valetudinarian "the next morning" (*NS* 238, 240), Wednesday the 27th; in the afternoon, Frederick appears (*NS* 243-44). According to our calculation, therefore, he arrives in England three days after the letter was dispatched, not "twenty-two days." His return may seem unnaturally quick, but Mrs Hale's dating cannot but be judged as incorrect to minimize the inconsistency of the chronology. She becomes unconscious next day and dies before the Friday morning comes (*NS* 250), 29 August, which the narrator calls "the October morning" (*NS* 251). Frederick leaves Milton from the Outwood railway station Friday evening (*NS* 260), when he causes George Leonards, his former subordinate in his navy days, to stumble at the moment when he jumps into the train. Because it is understood from the calendar data on the subsequent pages (*NS* 272, 278, 283, 316) that this incident takes place on Thursday, 26 October, our date of Mrs Hale's death (Friday, 29 August 1849) turns out to conflict with the narrator's (Wednesday, 25 October 1849). This contradiction is left unsolved in our chronology.

One of the examples which show the accuracy of our chronology would be that Margaret's period of staying in Milton, "eighteen months" (*NS* 357), exactly matches our calculation: the Hales' settlement in the manufacturing town is the event of November 1848 while Margaret's departure from there takes place on April 1850.

Margaret's birthday could be surmised from the Chronology. On 25 October 1849, Frederick tells his sister that Dolores Barbour is "not eighteen" (*NS* 258). His fiancée's birthday, therefore, falls on one day between 26 October 1831 and 25 October 1832, depending on whether 25 October 1849 is her last 17-year-old day or first. A few days later, on 1 November 1849, Margaret observes, 17-year-old Dolores is "younger by fourteen months than" (*NS* 287) she is. Accordingly, Margaret's birthday turns out to occur probably between August 1830 and August 1831, when it is counted backwards from Dolores's deduced birthday. At the time of autumn 1849, therefore, Margaret is eighteen or nineteen.

4.3. Characters' Frequency of Appearance

Fig. 4.1 illustrates the result of investigation into characters' appearance rate (composed of data provided by "The Comprehensive Chronology for *North and South*"). The bar chart shows how often each character is active and referred to within the total pages. Fig. 4.2 visualizes the result from another angle. The most conspicuous feature exhibited by both would be the following two. First, Margaret Hale's total appearance amounting to 95.1% of the whole pages (active=80.3%, referred=14.8%) signifies that *North and South* is her story. Second, the second most physically present character in the book is neither the industrial master John Thornton nor the trade unionist Nicholas Higgins, but Richard Hale, her father. As for the centrality of Margaret, much discussion has already been conducted by other critics;[120] therefore, the following examination shall centre on the raison d'être of Richard Hale.

As demonstrated in the "Main Characters" column in the Comprehensive

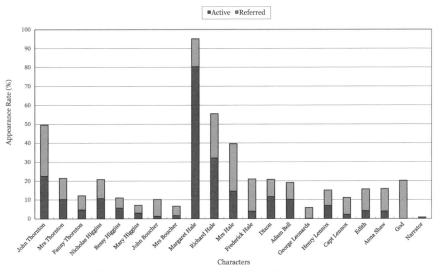

Fig. 4.1. Characters' Frequency of Appearance in *North and South*

Ranking	Characters	%	Ranking	Characters	%
1	Margaret	95.1	6	Frederick Hale	21.0
2	Mr Hale	55.6	7	Nicholas Higgins	20.9
3	John Thornton	49.6	8	Dixon	20.8
4	Mrs Hale	39.8	9	God	20.2
5	Mrs Thornton	21.5	10	Adam Bell	19.1

Table 4.1. Top Ten Rates of Characters' Appearance in *North and South*

CHAPTER 4 North and South: *The Novel of Two Themes* 117

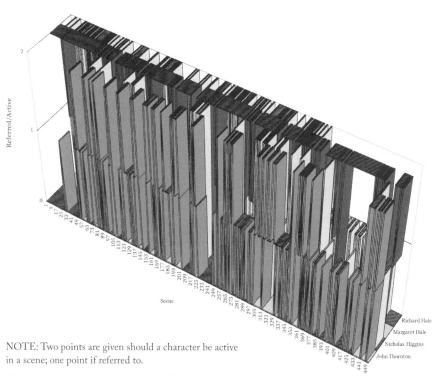

NOTE: Two points are given should a character be active in a scene; one point if referred to.

Fig. 4.2. Frequency of Appearance of Top Three Characters and Nicholas Higgins in *North and South*

Chronology and "Table 4.3. Characters' Movement in Milton in *North and South*" (See Section 4.4.2 for the details of its function), Hale appears even after his death in Chapter 16 of Volume 2 until Chapter 25 of the same volume, the third chapter from the last. This is chiefly because the two roles of mediation are assigned to him: (a) between Thornton and his daughter, and (b) between the mill-owner and

---

120 As has often been quoted, the novel's original title was *Margaret Hale* (E. H. Chadwick 146-47; David 10; Dodsworth, introduction 18; Easson, *EG* 90; ---, introduction xii; Constance D. Harsh 23; "North and South appears to me to be a better name than Margaret Hale" (*Dickens's Letters*, 7: 378); Schor 120; E. Wright, *Mrs Gaskell* 131; Ward, introduction, 4: xvi). Margaret as the core of the novel has been discussed by Craik (*EG* 94), C. Gallagher ("Margaret's mental processes are the primary subject of the book" [171]), Gérin ("[Plot-building is] based firmly on a central feminine character" [152]), Harsh ("her personality and development constitute one of Gaskell's concerns from its opening" [23]), Pollard (*Mrs Gaskell* 110), Spencer (*EG* 90-91), and Uffelman (73, 76). Fig. 4.1 verifies the correctness of their arguments. In addition, Margaret's dignity is emphasized in the text (*NS* 61, 62, 76, 77); so is her masculine strength (*NS* 51, 53, 56, 248, 250, 251-52, 297, 317). Throughout the novel, Margaret has been depicted as a strong woman. In her deep misery, notwithstanding, she confesses her weakness: "I am weary of this continual call upon me for strength" (*NS* 322); see also *NS* 271.

Higgins.

His first part is acted unconsciously: he involuntarily assists the young couple to foster mutual affection. For instance, as Thornton's tutor, Hale gives him opportunities to visit his home. Hale's most favourite student often becomes Crampton's domestic topic (*NS* 69). His invitation of Thornton to tea affords Margaret a chance to be familiar with his character (*NS* 80-86). Even after having his love rejected by Margaret, Thornton still has an excuse to see her at Crampton although his sole purpose of visit is to receive private lessons from her father (*NS* 342). In addition, Hale plays unintentional Cupid to the young couple. On their way home from the Thorntons' dinner party, he asks his daughter to "do justice to Mr. Thornton" (*NS* 166); two and a half months later, he praises her for doing so (*NS* 309). His compliment chokes Margaret, as she notices that she has begun to feel Thornton's value acutely when it is too late (*NS* 309). Hale's imprudent question about whether she has any reason for thinking Thornton cares for her reminds Margaret of her bitter remorse (*NS* 340). Hale's inadvertent actions, thus, help his daughter deepen her affection for the young master.

Hale's second role is played voluntarily: having heard workers' grounds for the strike as well as masters' justification for unyieldingness, he attempts to bridge the two (Pollard, *Mrs Gaskell* 127). For instance, he lays "antagonism between the employer and the employed" and workmen's grievances before Thornton to ask for his explanation about them (*NS* 119, 152). By asking Higgins about the strike, Hale, along with his daughter, prompts him to disclose the Union's thoughtless action, namely, that the "workmen's calculations were based (like too many of the masters') on false premises" (*NS* 228), and reminds him that masters and labourers are on the same boat (*NS* 230). Nicholas admits the tyranny of the Union, but still supports it: "It's th' masters as has made us sin, if th' Union is a sin" (*NS* 232). Hale recommends Thornton to Higgins as an ideal master who may have a talk with his fellows about their difficulties (*NS* 230). Furthermore, the resigned Anglican minister accompanies his daughter to Frances Street to meet and console Higgins (*NS* 289, 338-39). Hale proposes to write a reference for the jobless operative when Margaret urges him to speak to Thornton (*NS* 308). It is verified in Higgins's utterance to Hale and his daughter—"Meddling 'twixt master and man is like meddling 'twixt husband and wife than aught else: it takes a deal o' wisdom for to do only good" (*NS* 308)— that they are performing the role of mediator between employers and employees. After all, the former minister's kindness leads the weaver to humble himself enough to read the Bible that Margaret gives him as her father's memento before she leaves Milton (*NS* 371).

Because his religious doubts seem improbable, Richard Hale has often been criticized only as a temporary tool for bringing his daughter to the industrial city where she meets her future husband.[121] Perhaps Ward's criticism represents most readers' honest impression on him: "in the eyes of most readers, good Mr Hale's religious difficulties are likely to occupy a less prominent place in the story than they perhaps did in the design of Mrs. Gaskell" (*North and South* xxii-xxiii).[122] The defect of the novel's introductory section is acknowledged by the author herself: "I feel it to be flat & grey with no bright clear foreground as yet" (*Letters* 280); "It is dull; & I have never had time to prune it. I have got the people well on,—but I think in too lengthy a way" (*Letters* 290). Immediately after the second citation, however, she declares "But I can still make it good I am sure." Richard Hale's frequent appearances in the later stages, accordingly, are the outcome of her embodiment of this conviction.[123] In directing the seemingly religious story to her originally intended one of class conflict and romance, Gaskell allocates two roles to the apostate to save him from being condemned as implausible; to put it another way, this authorial contrivance throws into relief her construct's meaning of progressing the political and romance plots in parallel. This is why Hale's appearance is the second most frequent. In spite of Gaskell's remark that he only fills up an unimportant place in the story (*Letters* 353), our statistical analysis shows that he is one of her construct's important structural devices for blending the two plots.

4.4. Shift of Location

This section inspects the Gaskell construct's meaning for the change of loca-

---

121 His lack of strength is also severely attacked by Lansbury ("A man who can accept neither the reality of suffering nor the inevitability of death cannot minister to others" [*Social Crisis* 103]; *EG* 42-43). In the narrative, frequent reference is made to his weakness or effeminacy. For instance, he is "always tender and gentle" (*NS* 21), acutely sensitive (*NS* 35), "cowardly" (*NS* 45), "almost feminine" (*NS* 80, *NS* 206, *NS* 244), "I am too weak" (*NS* 245, *NS* 249, *NS* 252), "I cannot go alone. I should break down utterly" (*NS* 267), "I have not strength left in me" (*NS* 268), "He was trembling from head to foot" (*NS* 295), and Mrs Shaw's criticism of him as "a weak man" (*NS* 355).

122 See also Ganz (84, 85), Gérin (*EG* 151), Rubenius (248), and E. Wright (*Mrs Gaskell* 142). Gaskell defends her scheme by stating that seemingly unnecessary and unrealistic characters, including Mr Hale, "were wanted to fill up unimportant places in the story, when otherwise there would have been unsightly gaps" (*Letters* 353; J. G. Sharps, *Observation* 570). Gaskell's father William Stevenson and her friend J. A. Froude are considered as the prototype of Richard Hale (*Letters* 353; Yvonne Ffrench 62; Lansbury, *Social Crisis* 101; Rubenius 246-47; Whitfield 125). A. Sanders is sympathetic with Hale's religious scruples ("A Crisis of Liberalism" 46); so is Whitfield (125).

123 Later in the text, Gaskell lets Hale defend himself about his abandonment of his priesthood (*NS* 349), and Mr Bell support his decision (*NS* 349, 380). Gaskell herself defends the apostate, and confesses the existence of a model for him (*Letters* 353).

tions.

4.4.1. Location Shift in the Narrative

"Fig. 4.3. Shift of Location in *North and South* A" illustrates how the main setting changes in line with the development of the story and what percentage each location occupies in the total pages. "Fig. 4.4. Shift of Location in *North and South* B" aims at expressing both objectives with one bar: the shifting order of location and the percentage of each location are combined in the bar chart. The diagrams demonstrate two key features.

First, the principal stage of action, occupying 74.3% of the whole, is Milton.[124] The manufacturing town's leading role has been a topic of critics' concern. Bodenheimer asserts that "the intense activity at the center of the Milton section offers the possibility of active women's lives" (*Politics* 63); "Milton," Craik observes, "is probably the greatest character in *North and South*" (*EG* 120).[125] Milton provides Margaret with opportunities to meet the Thorntons and the Higgins; without them, nei-

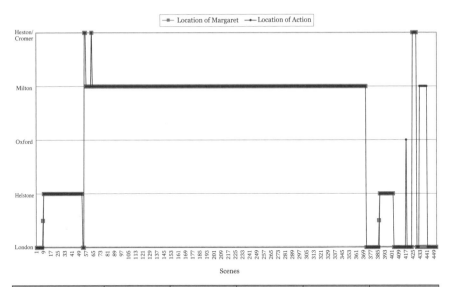

Place	London	Helstone	Oxford	Milton	Heston/Cromer
Scene Percentage	10.4	12.8	0.1	74.3	0.4/0.7

Fig. 4.3. Shift of Location in *North and South* A

124   Milton's centrality is pointed out also by Craik: "Manchester (here disguised as Milton Northern), the setting for thirty-nine of the novel's fifty-two chapters" (*EG* 93).
125   See also Bonaparte, *Politics* 188; Bonnie Gerard 22; Lansbury, *Social Crisis* 98; ---, *EG* 35-36; Nord, *Walking* 173, 177; G. D. Sanders 68; E. Wright, *Mrs Gaskell* 135.

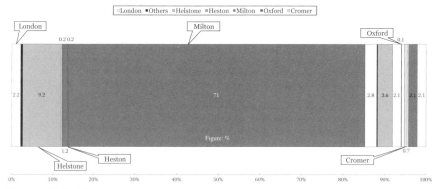

Fig. 4.4. Shift of Location in *North and South* B

ther her involvement with industrial conflicts nor her understanding of the mill-owner would take place.

Second, this narrative shift of place/location including Margaret's locations forms a symmetry within the story/novel.[126] The story returns to the starting places, London and Helstone, in the end. The opening and closing scenes are set in the same drawing room (Brodetsky 56; G. D. Sanders 68). As shown in Fig. 4. 3, the shift of narrative locations almost perfectly corresponds to Margaret's geographical movement; the only exceptions are Scene 417 depicting her father's fatal trip to Oxford while she remains in Milton (ch. 23, vol. 2) and Scenes 432-40 focusing on Thornton's struggle in Milton when she stays at the London house (ch. 25, vol. 2). If all but the three major locations—London, Helstone, and Milton—are omitted from the analysis, there appears irrefutable narrative symmetry in the novel (See Fig. 4.5). Margaret moves from London, Helstone, London, Milton, London, Helstone back to London.

The Gaskell construct's strategy of making her heroine return to the places where she lived earlier[127] is most effective to give her an opportunity to compare the present and the past, and to awaken to the reality that everything in life—including herself—is in the state of flux. In the second London phase where the Hales stay at a hotel one night on their way to Heston (scs. 53-54; *NS* 56-57), the family "in a complicated trouble" feel that "London life is too whirling and full to admit of even

---

126 Collin calls this shift "the balance of the novel": "In the new chapters it is possible to discern an attempt to restore the balance of the novel by dwelling upon its southern aspects" ("Composition" 92-93).
127 This structural device has been pointed out by Bodenheimer (*Politics* 56), Dodsworth (introduction 26), Flint (36), Kuhlman ("Education" 14), Lansbury (*EG* 46; *Social Crisis* 125), Uffelman (77), Schor (149), Pollard (*Mrs Gaskell* 111), and E. Wright (*Mrs Gaskell* 136).

Fig. 4.5. Margaret's Geographical Movement in *North and South*

an hour of [...] deep silence of feeling" (*NS* 57). Even in this brief phase, the vicissitudes of life are underlined by the exclamation of Mrs Hale, for whom a visit to London is the chance given for the first time in many years: "how altered!" (*NS* 57). In contrast, in the third London phase, the counterpart of the second in the symmetrical arrangement of locations, Margaret, now an orphan, feels "a strange unsatisfied vacuum" in her heart and mode of life (*NS* 373), and afraid lest she may be lulled into passivity (Nord, *Walking* 168).

The authorial meaning hidden in this symmetry is hinted at especially in the scene of Margaret's return to Helstone for the first time in one year and eight months (She leaves the village in November 1848 and makes an overnight trip there in June 1850) where her gradual acceptance of "mutability in life" is depicted. Margaret walks the Helstone road alone now which she passed with her parents twenty months ago (*NS* 385); she informs the proprietor of the inn, who knows her parents, of their death (*NS* 386); Margaret's former pupils have "grown out of children into great girls, passing out of her recollection in their rapid development, as she, by her three years' absence," is "vanishing from theirs" (*NS* 392); the parsonage has been "so altered, both inside and out" by the new vicar and his wife (*NS* 392-93). Mutability in life is emphasized by characters also: for instance, Mrs Purkis says to Margaret, "times is changed, miss" (*NS* 387); Mr Bell, "I take changes in all I see as a matter of course. The instability of all human things is familiar to me, to you it is new and oppressive" (*NS* 388); and Margaret herself ponders, "There was change everywhere;

slight, yet pervading all" (*NS* 394). On the first night at Helstone revisited, a "sense of change, of individual nothingness, of perplexity and disappointment, [. . .] and this slight, all-pervading instability" overwhelm Margaret (*NS* 400). Margaret then thinks, "love for my species could never fill my heart to the utter exclusion of love for individuals" (*NS* 400). In this thought, Uglow sees Gaskell's difference from Florence Nightingale, who "does not care for *individuals* [. . .], but for the whole race as being God's creatures" (*EG* 364; *Letters* 317). As the morning comes, however, she begins to accept the reality as it is: "After all it is right. [. . .] [T]he progress all around me is right and necessary" (*NS* 400). Before her departure, she finally acknowledges that she herself changes perpetually, and discovers the beauty of such transition (*NS* 401). To quote Wendy Parkins, "Margaret is able to accept change by positioning herself within the flux of modern life" (512). David finds that her visit to Helstone is "to be one of discovery and acceptance of change in herself and in her society" (47).

What is the Gaskell construct's purpose of making her chief protagonist "lose some of her remaining nostalgic idealization of the place" (Easson, "Notes on the Text," *NS* xxxv)? The most plausible would be her need for letting Margaret prepare for her final reunion with Thornton and making the fulfilment of their love feasible. This hypothesis is corroborated by the fact that the second Helstone episode was inserted by the author herself into the book edition.[128] In Gaskell's view, it should take time for such characters of totally different backgrounds as Thornton and Margaret to surmount obstacles to marriage.[129] Hence, she revises the original text of *Household Words* to insert Margaret's revisit to Helstone (ch. 21) between her waiting for Dixon's return from Milton (*NS* 374, ch. 19) and the old servant's settling in Harley Street as her maid (*NS* 402, ch. 22), both the events of summer 1850. The Gaskell construct thus gives Margaret spiritual education before her affection is reciprocated by Thornton in the last chapter. The scene of Margaret's meditation at Cromer beach was prepared out of the same necessity. At Cromer, she learns that she must one day answer for her life and what she has done with it (*NS* 416). The therapeutic value of the seaside, Cromer, is examined by Parkins: "Her solitary med-

---

128 This authorial interpolation is mentioned by Collin ("Composition" 27), Easson ("Notes on the Text," *NS* xxxv), Ingham (xxvii), J. G. Sharps (*Observation* 569), and Uffelman ("This return to her childhood home resolves certain of her feelings left unresolved in the *Household Words* text" [81]). Comparison between the World's Classics edition (*NS* 372-412; ch 19-23) and the serial publication (*HW*, vol. 10, 547-50) brings to light traces of authorial corrections.

129 Gaskell, uncertain about the suitability of the ending of the *Household Words* version, hints at need for revision in her letter to Anna Jameson in January 1855: "when the barrier gives way between 2 such characters as Mr Thornton and Margaret it would not go all smash in a moment" (*Letters* 329).

itations on the shore are presented as a time for assessing her past experiences and planning her future; the contemplation of temporality and human mortality was particularly evoked by the ocean" (515). The critic views the Hales' first trip to the seaside, Heston, in the same light (514). Lessons Margaret learns at Helstone and Cromer make her "independent, self-reliant, and fully realized" (Uffelman 83), and finally her ultimate determination to live as the industrial master's wife in Milton convincing. Collin reads the last few chapters as "a measured and relentless process of stripping from Margaret all her attachments in preparation for her solitary encounter with Mr Thornton in which she recognizes and acknowledges to the reader's satisfaction her only remaining support" ("Composition" 93). Her reading is similar to ours in viewing that the Gaskell construct's meaning in these chapters is to make her heroine prepare herself for her final encounter with Thornton.

The protagonist who has innocently enjoyed the middle-class comfort in the busy capital and a peaceful life in her home village, goes through new experiences in the manufacturing town, and eventually becomes aware of the meaning of life in her former beloved places.[130] The Gaskell construct's symmetrical setting of Margaret's geographical movement is planned according to her artistic demand for making her heroine experience spiritual growth as a prerequisite for the fulfilment of her love.

4.4.2. Location Shift in Milton

Even within Milton, the location of action moves from place to place. How it shifts in the Milton phase (scs. 57-371) is illustrated in "Fig. 4.6. Shift of Location in Milton in *North and South*," together with the percentage of pages allocated to each scene. Fig. 4.7, a modified graph of Fig. 4.6, was created to present a clearer image of location shifts in Milton, in which, in order to spotlight the three major locations—the homes/houses of the Hales, the Thorntons, and the Higginses—, other places, including streets, stations, and trains, were excluded, and the original scene percentages of the three adjusted to make their total 100%. Fig. 4.8 is a bar chart of the same purport, with scene percentage, instead of scene numbers, incorporated.

These diagrams bring three structural devices of the author into relief. First, the focus of the story is placed on "the three worlds of Milton-Northern" (J. G. Sharps, *Observation* 216)—Crampton Crescent (the location of the Hales' house), Marlborough Street (the Thorntons'), and Frances Street (the Higgins'). Second, the number

---

[130] This summary of the key plot is shared by Colby ("*Appointed*" 47), Kuhlman ("Education" 14), Lansbury (*EG* 41), G. D. Sanders (65), Uglow (*EG* 369), Ward (introduction, *NS* xxi), and T. Wright (99-100, 115).

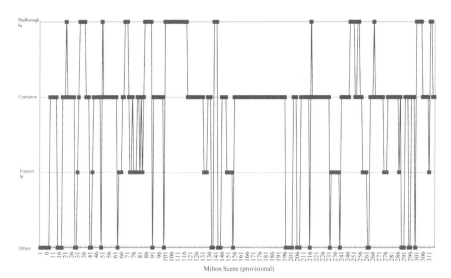

Milton Places	Others	Frances St	Crampton	Marlborough St	Total
Scene Percentage (Raw)	8.8	9.9	39.2	13.3	71.2
Scene Percentage (Converted)	12.3	13.9	55.1	18.7	100

Fig. 4.6. Shift of Location in Milton in *North and South*

Location	Carson's	Barton's	Wilson's	Legh's	Alice's	Davenport's	Liverpool	Others	Total
Scene Percentage	7.5	28.8	11.0	6.8	1.9	2.9	15.1	26.5	100.5
				51.4					

Table 4.2. Scene Allocation in *Mary Barton*

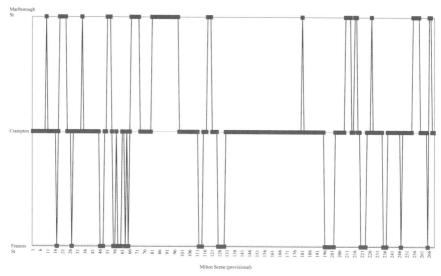

Milton Places	Frances St	Crampton	Marlborough St
Adjusted Percentage	16.0	63.1	21.4

Fig. 4.7. Modified Shift of Location in Milton in *North and South* A

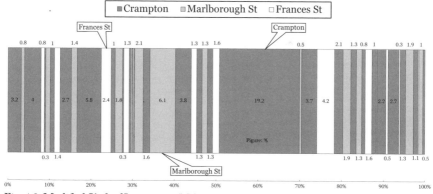

Fig. 4.8. Modified Shift of Location in Milton in *North and South* B

of pages allocated to the scenes at the labourer's house in Frances Street (9.9%) is similar to that at the mill-owner's in Marlborough Street (13.3%). Their closeness is obvious when they are compared with the rates in *Mary Barton*, where 28.8% is given to the scenes at the trade unionist Barton's house and 22.6% at the houses of other working-class characters, including George Wilson and Job Legh, but only 7.5% at the capitalist Carson's (See Table 4.2). This tactic is a reflection of the Gaskell construct's meaning to give Higgins and Thornton equal treatment. Third, as indicated especially in Fig. 4.8, the scenes at Frances Street and Marlborough Street almost always come after Crampton scenes. This arrangement illuminates the Gaskell construct's scheme for creating the plot through the Hales' interaction with the Higgins and the Thorntons.

To investigate the Gaskell construct's meaning for the third structural device concerning location shifts, composed was Table 4.3, which displays five major characters' geographical movement in the Milton phase (scs. 57-371; *NS* 59-371), along with the main topic of each occasion. The table displays three significant features.

a. First, as highlighted by the bold-lined boxes, Margaret's visit to the Higgins takes place soon after Thornton's to the Hales with the probability of 75.0% (nine out of 12 occasions). This formal scheme signifies that the novel's concern lies in their interaction. The Gaskell construct's meaning to place Thornton and Higgins in the spotlight is hinted at also in her strategy of introducing "a poorly-dressed, middle-aged workman" and his unhealthy daughter (*NS* 72) within a few pages after the description of Hale's starting tutorials for Thornton (*NS* 68-69). In addition, this structural scheme mirrors the author construct's objective to make Margaret a mediator between the mill-owner and the mill-hand. It is unveiled also in her tactics of Thornton's visits to Crampton and Margaret's to Frances Street recording the highest and the second highest frequency among the five characters' geographical movement (See Table 4.4).

Higgins's visit to Marlborough Street is recorded only once in the text, and so is Thornton's to Frances Street. After their exchange of visit, their mutual understanding deepens, as implied in Higgins's utterance: "Yon Thornton's good enough for to fight wi', but too good for to be cheated" (*NS* 347). In the scene of their reconciliation where the master makes his apology to the artisan for his mercilessness at his mill and offers him a place of working there, it is acknowledged by both that Higgins was advised to ask Thornton for help by Margaret (*NS* 325, 347). Thus, they find that Margaret has acted as a bridge to their reconciliation. The Gaskell construct's meaning to make her their mediator is concealed in this manoeuvre also.

Margaret performs the act of mediation with Christian morality as her guide-

| M: Margaret Hale | R: Richard Hale | J: John Thornton | H: Hannah Thornton | N: Nicholas Higgins |

Vol	Chapter	Scene	Date	Frances St	Crampton	Marlborough St	Events
1	8	68	winter 1848-49		J		Hale's starting tutoring for Thornton
	9	76	spring 1849		J		Hale invites Thornton.
	10	80-82		one day		J①	Thornton's first visit to the Hales; his criticism of self-indulgence and his respect for self-denial.
	11	87	late spring/ early summer 1849	one day	M		Bessy's escapist view of life; Higgins's materialist. "I believe what I see, and no more" (91).
	12	94-96			H		Mrs and Miss Thornton pay the Hales a visit.
	13	99		one day	M		Margaret sees after Bessy.
	15	103	1849	one day		R	M	Hale and Margaret's return call
		108-10				J②	Thornton's despotism versus Margaret's mutual dependence
	17	120-22		next day	M		Higgins's view of a strike; Margaret's consolation for Bessy.
		129-30	14		M		Bessy: "Some's pre-elected; others toil and moil" (150).
	19	131				J③	Hale's attempt at mediation; Thornton shows little sympathy with workmen (152).
		132-34	20		M		Discussion between Higgins and Boucher; Margaret gives Bessy some money for Boucher.
	20	141-46	21			R	M	The dinner party at the Thornton's
	22	158-70	24			M	Margaret protects Thornton from the angry mob.
	24	182-84				J④	Thornton's confession of love to Margaret
	25	188-90	25		M		Higgins's agony about the failure of the strike
2	2	202				J⑤	Thornton offers Mrs Hale a fruit basket.
	3	206-10	26		M		Margaret comforts bereaved Nicholas.
		215-19				N	Hale's attempt at mediation; Higgins joins family prayer.
	4	222	27			J⑥	Thornton brings another offering of fruit to Mrs Hale.
	5	225-26	28			H	Mrs Thornton visits Mrs Hale at her request.
	6	248	25	10		J⑦	Frederick's prejudice against Thornton
	9	266	31			J⑧	Thornton's words make Margaret's eyes filled with tears.
	10	285-86	1			J⑨	Thornton brings a requested book for Hale.
	11	289	2		R	M		Higgins out of work; Boucher's body carried in.
	12	298-302	1849 3	11		N	Margaret advises Higgins to go to Thornton for work.
	13	308-09 311	one day			H	N	Mrs Thornton remonstrates with Margaret. The first meeting between Thornton and Higgins
	14	315			M		Margaret's talk with Higgins about his application

CHAPTER 4 *North and South: The Novel of Two Themes* 129

2	14	316	1849	11	one day	J		Thornton offers Higgins a job at his mill.
	15	324-27			one day		J[10]	Margaret has become a Miltonian. Mr Bell's suspect: Margaret and Thornton in love?
		332	winter		one day	R	M	Higgins tells Mr Hale and Margaret his view of Thornton.
	16	338	1850	2			J[11]	Thornton's occasional visit to Mr Hale
		343			one day		M	Higgins takes an interest in the sacred things he formerly scouted.
	17	354		4	one day		J[12]	Mr Bell is glad to hear Thornton's voice at the door.
	18	367				M		Margaret's farewell visit to Higgins
		368-69			Thurs		M	Handshake on the memorable doorstep
		371					N	Higgins's promise to read Hale's Bible

Table 4.3. Characters' Movement in Milton in *North and South*

(Unit: Times)	Frances Street	Crampton	Marlborough Street
Margaret Hale	12		4
Richard Hale	2		2
John Thornton	1	14	
Hannah Thornton	0	3	
Nicholas Higgins		3	1

Table 4.4. Five Characters' Frequency of Visits in *North and South*

line, as is explicitly expressed in her insistence to Thornton that capitalists and labourers are fundamentally equal—"God has made us so that we must be mutually dependent" (*NS* 122)—and in her defence of her public protection of the master: "[T]here should be fair play on each side; and I could see what fair play was. [. . .] Let them insult my maiden pride as they will—I walk pure before God!" (*NS* 190-91). It is this moral integrity of her that makes Thornton hold the image of "the truthful Margaret" (NS 279). She is rewarded for her effort. Higgins, once a materialist (*NS* 91, 226) and "a drunken infidel weaver" (*NS* 223), gradually takes "an interest in the sacred things" (*NS* 347), and, on the day of her departure from his town, promises her that he will study her father's Bible she has kept especially for him (*NS* 371). "But Nicholas was neither an habitual drunkard nor a thorough infidel," the narrator insists, "He drank to drown care, as he would have himself expressed it: and he was infidel so far as he had never yet found any form of faith to which he could attach himself, heart and soul" (*NS* 225). In helping Boucher's orphans, Higgins shows "a sober judgement, and regulated method of thinking, which were at variance with his former more eccentric jerks of action" (*NS* 338). Nicholas wins Margaret's reliance after all: "You only do me justice. And you'll not forget me, I'm sure. If no one else in Milton remembers me, I'm certain you will; and papa too"

(*NS* 371). His return to the Bible is similar to John Barton's in his deathbed (*MB* 437-38); this similarity implies Higgins is created as Barton's successor. Thornton finally accepts her Christian belief of mutual dependence (*NS* 419, 420-21). At Edith's party, he expresses his newly-acquired conviction about ideal relations between masters and workers:

"The advantages were mutual: we were both unconsciously and consciously teaching each other. [. . .] My only wish is to have the opportunity of cultivating some intercourse with the hands beyond the mere 'cash nexus.' [. . .] We should understand each other better, and I'll venture to say we should like each other better." (*NS* 431-32)

This remark is summary of the conclusion of the industrial plot. Thornton's inward piety is referred to by the narrator: "Man of action as he was, busy in the world's great battle, there was a deeper religion binding him to God in his heart, in spite of his strong wilfulness, through all his mistakes, than Mr Hale had ever dreamed" (*NS* 276).

b. Secondly, as displayed in the "Events" column of Table 4.3 (and the "Brief Summary" column of the Comprehensive Chronology), the first three pairs of scenes (scs. 80-82/87, 108-10/120-22, 131/132-34) are designed to provide Margaret with the opportunities to learn about the deep-seated antagonism between the industrial enemies. She calls on the Higgins soon after having received Thornton's calls at her house; accordingly, she is acquainted with workers' plights as well as masters', and involuntarily becomes "the medium of reconciliation between men of widely divergent belief" (Lansbury, *Social Crisis* 105).[131] In talking to Thornton, she expresses Higgins's view, while in speaking with Higgins, she observes Thornton's idea.

(a) **Scenes 80-82/87** For instance, to Margaret, who condemns Milton work-

---

131 Margaret's function as an observer of class differences is pointed out by Flint (40), Ganz ("mainly through the heroine's successive visits to the households of Nicholas Higgins and Mr Thornton, we are introduced to the problems which the incipient strike presents for both workmen and masters" [96]), Josephine M. Guy (165), Harsh (37), Kestner (122, 164), Lansbury (*Social Crisis* 117), and Nord (*Walking* 169); her role as a mediator by Bodenheimer ("Margaret's linking role in the triangle [Margaret, Thornton, and Higgins] is evident" [*Politics* 62]), Colby ("*Appointed*" 47, 55, 59), C. Gallagher (172), Harsh (21), Lansbury (*EG* 44), Spencer (*EG* 88, 91), Stoneman (*EG* 126, 128), and E. Wright (The relationship between the three [Margaret, Thornton, and Higgins] is "the heart of the book" [*Mrs Gaskell* 143]); Margaret as a spiritual guide for Thornton and Higgins by Lansbury (*EG* 44), Pike (93-94), and Whitfield (123).

ers—"I see men here going about in the streets who look ground down by some pinching sorrow or care—who are not only sufferers but haters. Now, in the South we have our poor, but there is not that terrible expression in their countenances of a sullen sense of injustice which I see here" (sc. 80; *NS* 81)—, Thornton praises the Miltonian social system in which "a working-man may raise himself into the power and position of a master by his own exertions and behaviour." She criticizes him for his unkindness towards hapless workers: "You consider all who are unsuccessful in raising themselves in the world, from whatever cause, as your enemies, then" (sc. 80; *NS* 84). Several days later, she has a chance to catch a glimpse of poverty-stricken labourers' agony when she listens to Bessy's pessimist view of the present life ("Do you think such life as this is worth caring for?") and Higgins's materialist creed ("I believe what I see, and no more"); Margaret's attempt to comfort Bessy through her Christian faith sounds vain before their bitter deprivation (sc. 87; *NS* 90-91).

(b) Scenes 108-10/120-22 In answer to Margaret's inquiry about Milton's social friction—"I see two classes dependent on each other in every possible way, yet each evidently regarding the interest of the other as opposed to their own" (sc. 108; *NS* 118)—, Thornton, ridiculing her informant, i.e. Higgins (sc. 108; *NS* 119), explains his policy of governing his hands: he permits them no "independent action during business hours," but respects their independence "for the rest of their time," as he attaches high value to his own independence (sc. 110; *NS* 121). Margaret opposes his despotic control on workers: "The most proudly independent man depends on those around him for their insensible influence on his character—his life" (sc. 110; *NS* 120). Next day, she calls on Higgins at his house to ask why he strikes. To his explanation about the unequal and unfair distribution of wealth, Margaret makes the following reply, which is like a defence of masters: "Surely they will give you a reason for it. It is not merely an arbitrary decision of theirs, come to without reason" (sc. 120; *NS* 134). After making a contemptuous remark on her ignorance of the true situation, Higgins asserts that the strike is carried out "for justice and fair play" (sc. 120; *NS* 135). Margaret, then, hears his description of Thornton: "He's worth fighting wi'. [. . .] as dour as door-nail; an obstinate chap" (sc. 120; *NS* 135). At this visit again, she encourages hopeless Bessy to look at the brighter side of life through her fervent Christian belief: "God is just, and our lots are well portioned out by Him. [. . .] God does not willingly afflict. Don't dwell so much on the prophecies, but read the clearer parts of the Bible" (sc. 121; *NS* 137). Her encouragement bears fruit this time.

(c) Scenes 131/132-34 At one of her nursing visits to Bessy, Margaret asks her if the strike mends the strait condition of workers' poverty; Bessy replies that the

Union says it will, adding the fight between masters and labourers is "like th' great battle o' Armageddon" (sc. 129; *NS* 150-51). On the same day, Thornton pays an evening call to Crompton to offer Margaret something helpful for her invalid mother. His cool and inhumane reply to Hale's inquiry about the origin of working men's "suffering and long-endurance," that it is "entirely logical" for employers as well as employed to "go down into ruin" should trade fail, angers Margaret and makes her feel hardly thankful for his "individual kindness" (sc. 131; *NS* 152-53). Several days later, Margaret hears at Frances Street the miseries of John Boucher, Higgins's neighbour "wi' a sickly wife, and eight childer, none on 'em factory age" (*NS* 134), and perceives the cruelty of the Trade Union (sc. 133; *NS* 154-55).

c. The third vital characteristic of Table 4.3 is that, after the riot scene (ch. 22, vol. 1), the emphasis of the narrative gradually shifts from the conflict between masters and workers to their reconciliation, and from the social problem to the development of the young couple's romance. This alteration of focus halfway through the story, or the novel's two-part structure (Ganz 98, 100-01; Barbara Legh Harman, *Feminine* 69, 71), reveals the author construct's purpose of intermingling the former plot with the latter.[132]

(a) Scenes 182-84/188-90 For example, in contrast to the preceding three pairs in Table 4.3, Scenes 182-84 and 188-90 describing Thornton's visit to Margaret and hers to Higgins respectively is the first pair that brings the romance plot into the foreground of the narrative. Thornton's confession of love to Margaret is depicted in Scene 183 (*NS* 194-96). Soon after the flat rejection of it, she goes to Frances Street to see Bessy, from whom she hears about the ruined strike and Higgins's regret (sc. 188-89; *NS* 198-201).

(b) Scenes 202/206-10 In the afternoon of the following day, Thornton pays a hasty visit to Crompton with his fruit basket for Mrs Hale; Margaret thinks "it would be awkward for both to be brought into conscious collision" (sc. 202; *NS* 214-15). He leaves her house with "Not one word: not one look to Margaret" (sc. 203; *NS* 215), who, having been "shaken by the events of the last two days," i.e. her public protection of Thornton and his love confession, gives "way to the first choking sob" (sc. 203; *NS* 216). Margaret, then, walks "swiftly to the Higgins's house" to see Bessy's dead face (sc. 206; *NS* 218), and invites Higgins to her home to stop him from going to the gin-shop (sc. 209; *NS* 221).

(c) Scenes 285-86/289 From Scene 192 onwards, Gaskell starts the episode of

---

132 The topics of the family conversation the Thorntons have in their house—Margaret's pride and an approaching strike—also imply that the focal point of the novel is the love and industrial plots (scs. 125-27; *NS* 142-46).

Frederick's return—in response to Mrs Hale's wish for seeing her son once again before her death (sc. 192; *NS* 202-04), Margaret writes him a letter (sc. 193; *NS* 204-05). His homecoming results in her lie (sc. 269; *NS* 273), her degradation in Thornton's eyes (sc. 277; *NS* 283), and eventually her recognition of his value (sc. 278; *NS* 284).[133] When Margaret is in "great uneasiness" about her brother, she has Thornton's visit; "the few necessary common-place words" he articulates "in so tender a voice" make her eyes fill with tears (sc. 266; *NS* 271-72). In the next pair of scenes of Thornton's visit at Crampton and Margaret's to Frances Street, the purpose of his visit is just to bring a book for his tutor (sc. 286; *NS* 289). On the following day, Margaret and her father find the tragic effect of the ruined strike at the Higgins's house: starving Boucher's fruitless search for a job (sc. 289; *NS* 293) and his subsequent suicide (sc. 290; *NS* 294).

(d) **Scenes 324-27/332** In the evening talk with Oxford Fellow Bell, Hale, and Margaret, Thornton observes the "last strike, under which I am smarting, has been respectable" (sc. 325; *NS* 335), and makes an impolite remark on Margaret's truthfulness because of jealousy (sc. 326; *NS* 335). Thornton's utterance here indicates again that the narrative is developing with the industrial problem and the couple's romance as its focus. In the ensuing Frances Street scene, Higgins's appreciation of his new master Thornton is related to Margaret and her father (sc. 332; *NS* 339).

(e) **Scenes 338/343** In February 1850, Thornton's occasional visits to Crampton are made for his tutor only, from whom Margaret learns his speaking of her "in the same calm friendly way, never avoiding and never seeking any mention of her name" (sc. 338; *NS* 342). At her April visit to Frances Street in the same year, she finds Higgins's understanding of his master and his "interest in the sacred things" deepened (sc. 343; *NS* 347).

(f) **Scenes 354/367** As for the last pairs of the visiting scenes in Table 4.3, Thornton comes to Crampton as if only to take Mr Bell home, since no clear purpose of his visit is stated (sc. 354; *NS* 356-57). Some days later, Margaret pays a farewell visit to Higgins in vain (sc. 367; *NS* 367).

The above analyses of the third feature of Table 4.3. (a)-(f) demonstrate that the riot scene is the pivot where the focus of the story changes from conflict to recon-

---

133   The significance of Margaret's lie has been one of critics' long-standing disputes: for instance, David (46), C. Gallagher ("the central ethical problem" [175]), Ganz (102), Harman ("It reduces Margaret's excessive sense of moral superiority, eradicates her snobbishness [...], and makes her able truly to connect with others" [*Feminine* 72]), Lansbury (*EG* 46), Elisie B. Michie (136), Stoneman (*EG* 129), Schor (146), and Uglow (It makes "Margaret recognize her need for Thornton" [*EG* 384]). Gaskell herself intimates that her intention in Margaret's lie is to make her humble: "MH has just told the lie, & is gathering herself up after her dead faint; very meek & stunned & humble" (*Letters* 310).

ciliation, not only between the industrial enemies but also between the young couple. As Easson points out, Margaret and Thornton, after her public defence of him, come to enjoy "a gradual process of finding one another" (*EG* 95).

Some critics argue that Gaskell depicts industrial problems from the viewpoint of mill-owners in *North and South* to amend the biased opinions expressed in *Mary Barton*.[134] Judging from the data of Fig 4.6, Fig 4.7, and Table 4.3, however, the labourers' viewpoint is stressed as equally as the masters'. For, what interests her urauthor in this impartial approach to both parties is "a better mutual understanding" between masters and workers, rather than "the triumph of one or other side" (Gérin, *EG* 153). The shift of location in *North and South* reflects the Gaskell construct's meaning to draw the employer's view and the employee's in equilibrium, the process of their reconciliation, and the development of Margaret and Thornton's mutual affection. This author construct's concern is reflected in the stage shifts and Margaret's geographical movement in Milton.

4.5. Plot Interaction

The Gaskell construct advances Thornton's recognition of workers almost in parallel with Margaret's understanding of him. This authorial strategy is illuminated in Fig. 4.9. The five degrees of understanding (from 0 to 4) are determined in relative terms as a convenient method of demonstrating hidden authorial meaning. This section points out the synchronistic rise of the two protagonists' appreciation of their opponents by quoting a few examples from the text.

Margaret encounters Thornton for the first time at a Milton hotel in the middle of November 1848 (ch. 7, vol. 1; sc. 60). The narrator tells us that she looks at him "with proud indifference" (*NS* 63); accordingly, the degree of her liking him is set at zero point here. Thornton's lack of mercy towards workers is still unexpressed at this stage; it appears for the first time when he claims his view at the evening tea in the Hales' home (ch. 10, vol. 1; sc. 80). His sympathy for them, therefore, can be set at the zero level at this time.

Margaret's degree of understanding him slightly goes up when she welcomes him as her father's friend at the above-mentioned tea in "early spring" (*NS* 72) of 1849 (sc. 83). She favours his smile, "the first thing she had admired in this new friend" (*NS* 80), and regards him as "a very remarkable man" (*NS* 88). Here, she is "beginning to lose her early prejudices against tradespeople because of the personal

---

134   Craik, "Lore, Learning and Wisdom" 22; Easson, *EG* 82; Ffrench 59; Ganz 92; Pike 73; Rubenius 153; G. D. Sanders 68; Stoneman, *EG* 126; Whitfield 108; E. Wright, *Mrs Gaskell* 132. E. H. Chadwick disagrees with their claim (142).

appeal of Thornton's honest modest confession of his 'shop-boy' beginnings" (Ganz 91). The comment she makes immediately after—"but personally I don't like him at all" (*NS* 88)—, however, indicates her recognition of his value is still vague and incomplete. Her failure to shake hands with him on his departure (*NS* 86) is a symbolic episode to hint at their spiritual distance.[135] Thornton's level of pity for his workers, on the other hand, remains unchanged since November 1848, for the suffering of the poor being "but the natural punishment of dishonestly-enjoyed pleasure" is his conviction (*NS* 85).

Some months later, one evening in the first half of August 1849, a heated argument about the coming strike breaks out between the Hales and Thornton at Crampton (ch. 15, vol. 1; sc. 109). The young industrialist believes that "despotism is the best kind of government" for workpeople (*NS* 120), while Margaret criticizes his belief by saying "God has made us so that we must be mutually dependent" (*NS* 122). She parts from him with no ill feelings, but does not put out her hand, the symbolic action again in which her antagonism towards him is implied. Both degrees of her appreciation of him and his of workers still keep their previous levels.

Margaret's comprehension of Thornton's value deepens during August 1849 when a significant event takes place on the 21st and the 23rd respectively. At the

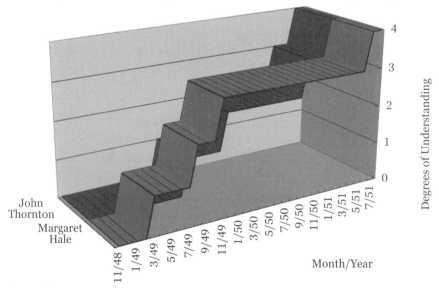

Fig. 4.9. Plot Interaction in *North and South*

[135] The tropological function of their handshaking is pointed out by Uglow (*EG* 374) and Katherine Ann Wildt (97).

Thorntons' dinner party held on the 21st (ch. 20, vol. 1; sc. 143), she shakes hands with him for the first time (*NS* 161), and discovers he has been respected by masters as "a man of great force of character" (*NS* 163). On their way home, in reply to her father's criticism for her prejudice against Thornton, Margaret confesses, "I know he is good of his kind, and by and by I shall like the kind. I rather think I am already beginning to do so" (*NS* 167). Thus, her level of understanding him goes up one point to the second here. It continues to rise inside her heart after the most memorable event in this novel that occurs on 23 August 1849: her public shielding of him from the violence of angry strikers on the doorstep of his house (ch. 22, vol. 1; sc. 162).[136] Thornton's unconscious confession of love to senseless Margaret (*NS* 181), and his subsequent utterance to his mother, "I know she does not care for me. I shall put myself at her feet—I must. If it were but one chance in a thousand—or a million—I should do it" (*NS* 189), are indications of the intensity of his affection for Margaret. Mrs Thornton's prediction that "As far as love may go she may be worthy of you. It must have taken a good deal to overcome her pride" (*NS* 189) turns out to be true in the end. Despite Margaret's insistence that her conduct was done only from womanly instinct, not from a "particular feeling" for him (*NS* 195), she does begin to have that feeling. Her change is exquisitely portrayed in her continued agitation, such as her "feverish" night on that day (*NS* 191), his strong idea lingering in her mind (*NS* 197), and her being "shaken by the events of the last two days [i.e. her public protection of him and his subsequent declaration of love]" (*NS* 216). Bodenheimer offers a similar analysis of her state of mind: "While Margaret painfully attempts to separate her

Fig. 4.10. "Oh, do not use violence! He is one man, and you are many" (*NS* 178). (Web)

---

136   Critics offer various interpretations of this scene. For instance, Bodenheimer (*Politics* 64), C. Gallagher (172), and Lansbury (*Social Crisis* 111) view Margaret's action as an act of justice; Stoneman (*EG* 128-29) as that of humanitarianism; Harman (*Feminine* 75), Michie (134-36), Nord (*Walking* 173-76), Schor (133) as of "sexual impropriety." Ganz (100) and Gérin (*EG* 152) emphasize its romantic impact.

personal from her morally disinterested self, Gaskell insists on the ambiguity of her actions" (*Politics* 65). In the light that her handshake with him has been used as a barometer of her recognition of him up to this stage, Thornton's rejection of her hand after his confession of love (*NS* 196) is significant, as it indicates the reversal of their situations.[137] Indeed, the initiative in their relationship is to be taken by the mill-owner hereafter.

During Thornton's visit on 27 August, when he brings Mrs Hale a second fruit basket, Margaret feels a deep sense of humility to him, "as if mutely apologising" for her blunt and ungracious refusal of his proposal: "Margaret thought about him more than she had ever done before; not with any tinge of what is called love, but with regret that she had wounded him so deeply—and with a gentle, patient striving to return to their former position of antagonistic friendship" (*NS* 239). Thornton's love for Margaret, although his pride is keenly affronted, has yet to disappear: "It was a stinging pleasure to be in the room with her, and feel her presence" (*NS* 239).

On 28 August, four days after the riot, Frederick appears (*NS* 244); in the small hours of the morning of the 30th, Mrs Hale dies (*NS* 250); on 25 October, or actually the day of her mother's death, 30 August (Gaskell makes a miscalculation here in dating her events), Margaret is annoyed at her brother's holding Thornton in contempt ("I took him for a shopman, and he turns out a manufacturer"), recollecting how she herself did the same at first, when she was unfamiliar with his integrity (*NS* 257). This is a sign of improvement of her regard for Thornton. She reddens in talking about Thornton to her brother (*NS* 257), the sign of her maiden shyness. She then becomes "tongue-tied" in trying to make Frederick understand what kind of person the manufacturer is (*NS* 257)—another sign of the awakening of her love.

Next day, she unexpectedly encounters him at Outwood Station while she is talking with her brother. In answer to Frederick's disparagement of Thornton as "unprepossessing-looking fellow," Margaret defends him by observing, "You would not have thought him unprepossessing if you had seen him with mamma" (*NS* 263). To protect Frederick from arrest, she is forced to lie about her presence at the station later. Discovering her deception is known to Thornton, she feels degraded in his eyes (*NS* 283). She shrinks away from admitting that she places much value on his respect and good opinion (*NS* 284). After this inward struggle comes the narration: "Whenever this idea presented itself to her at the end of a long avenue of thoughts, she turned away from following that path—she would not believe in it" (*NS* 284).

---

137 Michie considers the reversal of Margaret's relationship to Thornton takes place when she sells her honour to him to save her brother (136).

Margaret's emotional battle displays that she has already begun to love him. The same is implied in her subsequent self-interrogation: "How was it that he haunted her imagination so persistently? What could it be? Why did she care for what he thought, in spite of all her pride; in spite of herself? [. . .] What strong feeling had overtaken her at last?" (*NS* 286). By 3 November 1849, Margaret comes to anticipate his visit to understand his opinion of her (*NS* 302): every time the ringing bell is known to be other than Thornton's, she feels "strangely saddened and sick at heart at each disappointment" (*NS* 303).

To Higgins, who inquires about the possibility to find a job in the South, Margaret gives advice to see John Thornton (*NS* 307). Perceiving she is expecting the development of mutual understanding between Higgins and Thornton, Mr Hale says to her, "You are getting to do Mr Thornton justice at last" (*NS* 309). It was two and a half months ago (on 21 August, now on 3 November 1849) or twelve days ago (if Gaskell's error in dating is taken into consideration) when, she was encouraged by her father to do him justice (*NS* 166). His remark leaves her choked up as she regrets that her recognition of Thornton's merits comes too late: "It seems hard to lose him as a friend just when I had begun to feel his value" (*NS* 309). At this point, Thornton feels jealousy, not the disdain as Margaret has anticipated: "he passionately loved her, and thought her, even with all her faults, more lovely and more excellent than any other woman" (*NS* 310).

Wrongly accused of her misdemeanour at Outwood Station by Mrs Thornton, Margaret defends herself by saying, "I have done wrong, but not in the way you think or know about. I think Mr Thornton judges me more mercifully than you" (*NS* 317); hence, she articulates her reliance on him. In reviewing the interview with Mrs Thornton, Margaret meditates, "Why do I care what he thinks, beyond the mere loss of his good opinion as regards my telling the truth or not? I cannot tell" (*NS* 322). Nevertheless, the reader knows that she can tell the answer to her own query: she has begun to love him. Thus, her understanding of the young master reaches the third point in November 1849. Ganz also thinks that Margaret is led to realize her true feeling for Thornton at this stage (102). The brief sketch of the Gaskell construct's plot outline indicates that it is after the episode of Margaret's lie that her heroine notices her love for the industrial master (*Letters* 321).

Frederick has often been regarded as irrelevant to the story.[138] However, his return to England causes Margaret's falsehood and subsequent distress which lead her

---

138   G. D. Sanders (69) and E. Wright (*EG* 144) are most doubtful about his function, while David (15), Harman (*Feminine* 70), C. Gallagher (174–75), Michie (138), and Stoneman (*EG* 124–25) attempt to justify his raison d'être from their own approaches.

"to the realization that she is in love with Thornton" (Harman, *Feminine* 72). Viewed in this light, it is thrown into sharp relief that his episode is intended for the promotion of Margaret's love plot.

On the very day of Margaret's awareness of her true feeling, Thornton's degree of consideration towards his workers rises slightly: he asks Higgins to work at his mill, moved by the operative's humble patience in waiting for five hours to speak to him, and by his selfless fostering of the motherless children of Boucher, his neighbour workman who committed suicide (*NS* 325-26). "Their relationship remains prickly on the surface, but an important trust has been established" is Stoneman's succinct account of the two enemies of the day (*EG* 134). From the ensuing short talk with Thornton outside Mrs Boucher's house, Margaret senses that she may still be loved by him, and becomes jovial: "I might but regain his good opinion—the good opinion of a man who takes such pains to tell me that I am nothing to him. Come poor little heart! Be cheery and brave. We'll be a great deal to one another, if we are thrown off and left desolate" (*NS* 328). Here, the focus of the narrative shifts from how Margaret comes to understand Thornton's value to how he comes to acknowledge her love. The possibility of her love's fulfilment is suggested immediately after that of reconciliation between the industrial master and the Union leader. The Gaskell construct's strategy for combining the two plots reveals itself in this small device.

In November 1849, Adam Bell, his landlord and Margaret's godfather, jokingly deplores Margaret's change, "Her residence in Milton has quite corrupted her. She's a democrat, a red republican, a member of the Peace Society, a socialist—." In reply to him, Margaret observes, "it's all because I'm standing up for the progress of commerce" (*NS* 330). The Oxford fellow responds to her, "you were quite Miltonian and manufacturing in your preferences" (*NS* 333). Margaret's view of Milton has altered from disdain to appreciation, as a result of the advancement of her acknowledgement of Thornton's worth. At this stage, Thornton still loves her "sorely, in spite of himself" (*NS* 331). The narrator, thus, clarifies that their loves have already become mutual. In response to Mr Bell's condemnation of Thornton's impoliteness, Margaret defends him: "He is not vain now [. . .]. Tonight he has not been like himself. Something must have annoyed him before he came here" (*NS* 337). Her remark of sympathy towards him makes Mr Bell suspect that they have "a tendresse for each other" (*NS* 337).

As reciprocal trust grows between Higgins and Thornton, the latter comes to regard the last strike as "respectable" (*NS* 335). One day in winter 1849-50, Higgins tells Margaret Thornton's wisdom: "Sometimes he says a rough thing or two, which is not agreeable to look at at first, but has a queer smack o' truth in it when yo' come to chew it" (*NS* 339). At the same time, he informs her of his master's concern about the education of Boucher's children, i.e. a sign of Thornton's sympathy for workers' destitution. Margaret leaves Higgins's house quickly to avoid encountering him, but later regrets her hasty decision: "for the old friendship's sake she should like to have seen him to-night" (*NS* 339). There is no substantial development in Margaret's love in this period; hence, it is still on Level 3. The tears she sheds after listening to her father's careless misunderstanding of "her real feelings" (*NS* 340) indicate that her affection has grown stronger than she acknowledges herself. "If only Mr Thornton would restore her the lost friendship,—nay, if he would only come from time to time to cheer her father as in former days,—though she should never see him, she felt as if the course of her future life, though not brilliant in prospect, might lie clear and even before her" (*NS* 348)—this quotation reflects Margaret's feeling for Thornton as of April 1850. Around this time, Thornton pays a visit to Helstone, Margaret's village in the South (*NS* 352).

The industrial master's realization of Milton workers' plights increases by one more degree (to Level 2) in April 1850 when he tells Mr Bell his dinner scheme for his workers, referring to his previous enemy Higgins as his "friend" (*NS* 361). He then suggests that a mutual understanding among them has been built up since the special dinner he had with Higgins and his fellows (*NS* 362-63). To Mrs Shaw, who disparages the polluted air and deplores the humble living the Hales have led in Milton, Margaret replies, "I have been very happy here" (*NS* 365). This response is another indication of the personal growth and deeper understanding of Thornton that she has developed. They shake hands on the memorable doorstep one Thursday in the same month when she leaves the Thorntons' house after a farewell visit. Her full recognition of his value is implied in the author construct's device of letting her, not him, be the first to put out a hand: "the offered hand was taken with a resolute calmness, and dropped as carelessly as if it had been a dead and withered flower" (*NS* 370). The metaphor expresses the hidden sorrow of the departing girl.

After that day, more than one year (from April 1850 to summer 1851) passes before they are reunited. Even during the period of separation, the thought of Thornton continues floating somewhere inside Margaret's mind. In her easy and monotonous life on Harley Street, she longs for the busy Milton life: "She was getting surfeited of the eventless ease in which no struggle or endeavour was required. [. . .] There was a strange unsatisfied vacuum in Margaret's heart and mode of life" (*NS* 373). Dixon's report of Thornton's kindness in handling the Crampton house matters (*NS* 374) and Mr Bell's news of the Thorntons (*NS* 376) are the only stimuli to Margaret's interest. In the overnight journey to Helstone, Margaret, deeply regretting the loss of Thornton's respect owing to the falsehood she engaged in even if to save her brother, asks Mr Bell to explain the whole circumstances to the young factory owner if there is a chance (*NS* 398-99). Her wish for her truth being explained is inserted three times henceforth: in the scenes of her waiting for Mr Bell's letter (*NS* 408), of her evening meditation after his death (*NS* 412), and of her decision at Cromer to submit herself to the state of being misunderstood (*NS* 414). Ultimately, the intensity of her desire to regain Thornton's respect mirrors the depth of her love for him.

In this period of dissociation, mutual consideration between the mill-owner and his workers is fostered. The episode of one day in late spring 1851 where Higgins and his fellow worker voluntarily do the neglected piece of work for their master's sake implies that Thornton has won their complete reliance and understanding. Their altered relationship is illustrated in the narrator's summary:

> to the workmen in his mill he spoke not many words, but they knew him by this time; and many a curt, decided answer was received by them rather with sympathy for the care they saw pressing upon him, than with the suppressed antagonism which had formerly been smouldering, and ready for hard words and hard judgments on all occasions. (*NS* 421)

His line of understanding his workers goes up to Level 3.

In summer 1851, Thornton's industrial plot and Margaret's love plot reach the climax. At Edith's dinner party, the bankrupt mill-owner articulates his new conviction that attachment of class to class is impossible without "actual personal contact" (*NS* 432); besides, he tells Margaret about the round-robin he received from Higgins and his fellow workers stating their wish to work for him if he acquires a position to employ men again (*NS* 432). Thornton's remark summarizes the conclusion of the industrial plot. Two days after the party, Margaret realizes that her affection is requited by Thornton (*NS* 435-36).[139]

---

[139] Critics vary in their reading of the final union of the two protagonists (For instance, "Margaret's marriage to Thornton is carefully defined as an economic and social partnership as well as domestic settlement" [Bodenheimer, *Politics* 63]; "the metonymic connection between private and public life" [C. Gallagher 177]; "in which Margaret's idealism is brought to bear on Thornton's materialism in the form of a powerful socioethical project" [Gerard 22]; "The love of Thornton and Margaret symbolizes both the union of North and South and the completion of their respective individual enlightenments" [Pollard, *Mrs Gaskell* 135-36]). Some suggest that the ending hardly exemplifies the final resolution of conflicts between capital and labour (Easson, *EG* 90; Lansbury, *EG* 47; Nord, *Walking* 177; Uglow, *EG* 386; ---,

The examination above demonstrates that Thornton's understanding of his workers heightens as Margaret's for him does, or vice versa.[140] It also shows that "the plots of *North and South* are interwoven from the outset, and [...] remain interwoven at the end" (C. Gallagher 170).

4.6. Conclusion

Our statistical analysis of the novel's structure has cast light on the Gaskell construct's seven formal devices for conveying her meaning. (a) First, Richard Hale's second highest frequency of appearance (55.5%), following his daughter's (95.1%), is caused by the two functions assigned to him: a voluntary intermediary between the industrial enemies Thornton and Higgins, and an involuntary promoter of his daughter's realization of Thornton's value. (b) Second, the symmetrical shift of locations, or Margaret's return to the opening stages in the end of the novel, is intended to provide her with the opportunities for reflection and inner growth as a prerequisite for her final reunion with the industrial master. (c) Third, in the Milton phase, the Gaskell construct sets Thornton's dwelling and Higgins's as the main places of action with almost equal rate (13.3% and 9.9%) to underline her impartial treatment of their plights (in the case of her first so-called industrial fiction *Mary Barton*, 7.5% is given to the capitalist's house, but 28.7% to the trade unionist's). (d) Fourth, also in the Milton phase, 75.0% of Margaret's visits to the Higgins come after Thornton's at her house, which mirrors the authorial meaning to weave the plot through her interlacing with the mill-owner and the mill-hand. (e) Fifth, in the Milton scenes before strikers' attack on the Marlborough mill, Margaret learns about the class conflict and, in conjunction with her father, acts as a mediator between Thornton and Higgins. (f) Sixth, after the riot scene, the focus of the story shifts from conflict to reconciliation not only between the industrial enemies but also between the

---

introduction, *NS* xxx; E. Wright, *Mrs Gaskell* 141). Feminists' study of this finale is divided between positive and negative (Newton sees it as the scene where warring males are domesticated by feminine influence [165-66], while Lenard does as "a disturbing picture of her submission to Thornton and her eventual enclosure within a more narrowly-defined domestic sphere" [132]). Whatever opinions may be advocated, the internal structure of the novel champions the interpretation that the Gaskell construct's aim for this last scene is to integrate the two plots (Pamela Corpron Parker offers a similar reading ["Capitalist Fantasy" 1]). Gaskell's note on the development of the novel's plot implies that Margaret's financial rescue of Thornton prior to their marriage has been planned in advance (*Letters* 310).

140 Parallel movement of the two plots is suggested also by David ("The resolution of the sexual tension between them [Margaret and Thornton] is simultaneous with the resolution of industrial strife" [8]), Easson (*EG* 95), Ffrench ("there are two conflicts which pursue their course along parallel tracks" [62]), Ganz (80), Guy (167), Schor ("the industrial novel and the marriage novel jostle against one another" [144]), and Uglow (*EG* 377).

young couple. (g) Seventh, investigation into the development of the industrial plot and the romance plot illuminates how the reconciliation between Thornton and Higgins and the mutual understanding between Thornton and Margaret progress in parallel.

From the statistical evidence above, we cannot but conclude that the author construct planned from the outset to create this fiction with the two plots as its core. This equality is reflected in the novel's title as well in that North represented by Thornton—"the new industrial England, the England of factories, of urban dirt and urban poverty, of tension between masters and men, of competitiveness and self-help, of frankness and good sense and useful knowledge"—and South by Margaret—"the England of villages and superstition, of classical education and religious orthodoxy, of fixed social relationships, of rural cleanliness and rural poverty, of charm and stagnation" (Lerner 17)—are treated on an equal basis. The novel's even balance of the two plots is noticed and praised by Parthenope Nightingale, Florence's elder sister, in her letter to Gaskell: "I must say what a deal of wisdom there seems to me in 'N. & S.' It has instructed me exceedingly. You hold the balance very evenly and it must be a hard task" (Elizabeth Holdane 105). *North and South* is neither the story of Margaret Hale with the social problems as its nucleus, nor the condition-of-England novel with the heroine's romance and growth as its background. It is the story of two themes with equal emphasis upon each.

North and South has long been classified as an industrial novel owing to their treatment of the social conflict in 1840s. The objective analysis of the structure, notwithstanding, implies such a reading might be at variance with the Gaskell construct's meaning, since, as discussed above, the mutual understanding between the master John Thornton and the trade unionist Nicholas Higgins deepens as Margaret Hale's affection for Thornton increases. If the standard interpretation were defined as the interpretation the author aimed at, as Hirsch insists, then, it would be doubtful whether the conventional reading could be considered as standard. For, it is conducted by means of textual significance which is changeable according to readers or time, whereas our humble quest of authorial meaning is attempted through textual meaning that is permanent once a text is published.

CHAPTER 5 A Topic-Modelling Analysis of Christianity in *The Life of Charlotte Brontë*

5.1. Introduction: Structure and Religion[141]

This paper attempts a literary interpretation of the keywords in Elizabeth Gaskell's *The Life of Charlotte Brontë* revealed through computer-assisted analysis of the text which is in contrast to its conventional interpretations based on critics' subjective intuitions. This so-called "corpus stylistic" analysis pursues two aims—structural and Christian.

The first aim is to unearth any structural designs within texts by means of statistically investigating them, since structure is one of the principal devices for the author construct, or "mental construct" which emerges through careful reading of a text, to convey textual themes. The critical tradition has witnessed literary critiques being conducted principally in terms of critics' subjective concerns. Feminists, for instance, pick out patriarchal elements from a text to argue for "the patriarchal structure of society" and "the rediscovery, and republication, of a whole tradition of books by women 'silenced' by the traditional male canon" (Peck and Coyle 170-71). Psychoanalysts explore "the personal unconsciousness of the writer" in a text which is "a symptomatic reproduction of the author's infantile and forbidden wishes" (Peck and Coyle 186). Deconstructionists "track down within a text the aporia or internal contradiction that undermines its claims to coherent meaning" in order to "reveal how texts can be seen to deconstruct themselves" (Baldick, *Shadow* 52). New Historicists focus on such internal and external factors of a text as "politics, ideology, power, authority and subversion" (Peck and Coyle 184) as they look at "literary works within their historical and political contexts" (Baldick, *Shadow* 150). If interested in a specific topic like "colour," "comic spirit," "evil," the "medical system," or "nature" within a text, critics attempt to analyse it from such perspectives. In such critical methodologies, in short, priority in interpretation is placed on critics' concerns rather than the author's. In contrast, this corpus-stylistics analysis attempts to identify some hidden structures within a text, or the author construct's concealed designs for it, through a statistical analysis of the keywords revealed by concordance as well as topic-modelling tools. These computer-assisted attempts at a literary interpretation of a text with the help of corpus-linguistic techniques provide a unique approach to literary interpretation, as they are performed on the basis of the data obtained through scientific means.

---

[141] This chapter is an updated version of my paper published in *Kumamoto University Studies in Social and Cultural Sciences*, vol. 17.

The second objective of our corpus-stylistic exploration into literary texts is to survey how the Christian doctrine "God's Plan of Salvation" is applied to the depictions of characters' lives. We human beings who lived with God as spirits in the pre-mortal world (Acts 17.29; Rom. 8.16) are born into earth after receiving physical bodies, and only through this may our souls attain the necessary experiences to grow up in preparation for meeting God again; death which separates spirits from bodies is a step on the eternal journey that includes the Resurrection, when spirits will reunite with bodies (1 Cor. 15.13-14, 54; John 5.28-29, 14.19); we can return to our Heavenly Father only through Jesus Christ His son, whom He sent for us to overcome sin and death (John 3.16; Acts 4.10-12).[142]

Literature, sacred or secular, is thus seen as a projection of the Christian doctrine. This view is endorsed by some intellectuals. Nicholas Boyle, for instance, insists that "if we believe the teachings of the Catholic church to be true statements about human life, then we must necessarily expect literature that is true to life to reflect and corroborate them, whether or not it is written by Catholics" (139). The Cambridge professor continues to support the view that all literature reflects the Christian doctrine, asserting that "Even in the works and words that seem to hide God's face, or to spit on it, we can see God revealed at the heart of our world and in our culture" (Boyle 145). "Our literature," T. S. Eliot observes, "is a substitute for religion, and so is our religion" (32). As to the religious function of literature, Evelyn Waugh confesses, his work is "the attempt to represent man more fully which . . . means only one thing, man in his relation to God" ("Evelyn Waugh"). In a summary of the religious aspect of the fiction of two Japanese Christian novelists—Ayako Miura (1922-99), a Protestant, and Shusaku Endo (1923-96), a Catholic—Haruo Katayama, a former professor at Hokkaido University of Education, writes that their literary uniqueness and descriptive methods are rooted in the Bible (39). For Miura herself, fiction writing is an activity to convey God's love to the reader ("We Want to Meet"). Endo, invariably characterised as "the Graham Greene in Japan" (Bull, "A Literary Love Affair"), is described by the British Catholic novelist himself as "one of the century's greatest writers" (Ben Myers, "Shusaku Endo") because of his constant "concern with sin and redemption" and "relentless curiosity about the

---

[142] "Our hope and happiness lie in knowing who we are, where we came from, and where we can go. We are eternal beings, spirit children of an eternal God. Our lives can be compared to a three-act play: premortal life (before we came to earth), mortal life (our time here on earth), and postmortal life (where we go after we die). God has had a plan for our lives since the beginning of the first act—a plan that, if followed, provides comfort and guidance now, as well as salvation and eternal happiness in our postmortal life" ("Our Eternal Life").

sources of human goodness and evil" (Bull, "A Literary Love Affair"). These authors' view of literature as a projection of Christian truth constitutes the background to our research into Christianity in 19th-century British fiction.

Accordingly, this chapter attempts to perform a corpus-stylistic analysis of *The Life of Charlotte Brontë* (hereafter abbreviated *LCB*) chiefly using the free topic-modelling software MALLET to identify certain hidden structural patterns of this biographical fiction, and to investigate the author construct's depiction of Christianity uncovered by topic-modelling exploration.

First of all, the basic concepts of corpus stylistics and topic models will be explained in Section 5.2 to elucidate that the purpose of employing these methods lies in the attempt to make a literary interpretation of a text on the basis of scientific data obtained through computer-assisted means. After explaining the mechanism MALLET uses to find topic models, Section 5.3 focuses on the results of its application to *LCB*. Since MALLET innately produces slightly different results even with the same corpus, operations were carried out ten times and the top-ranking keywords of each operation were selected to make the best objective identification of topic-modelling keywords. The investigation found 19 in total, which reveal one of the running themes of the book—describing the lives of the Brontë family in their Haworth home. The validity of this finding shall be verified in two ways: first, through a quest for semantic information of the topics, and second, through an inspection of the frequencies of the names of the Brontë family members and geographical place names, using AntConc, a free concordance software. The results of a contextual categorisation of all 2,795 examples of the 11 most frequent topic-modelling keywords are illustrated in Section 5.4. The most noteworthy result of this computer-assisted analysis is that these 11 keywords are used in association with the Brontës' "literary career." The uniqueness of this discovery shall be verified by a survey of previous studies of this biographical fiction. Another scrutiny of the data above shall be made in this section to investigate the general tendency of the usage of the keywords bearing the Christian connotation "Religion/Morals," which compose the second-largest category. After the quantitative analysis reported in Section 5.3 and the qualitative interpretation of the results in Section 5.4, Section 5.5 will close this study with a summary of the arguments above, focusing especially on the Gaskell construct's unique depiction of Christianity.

5.2. Topic Models

Corpus stylistics "is concerned with the application of corpus methods to the analysis of literary texts by relating linguistic description with literary appreciation"

(Mahlberg, *Dickens's Fiction* 5; ---, "Digital Forum" 295). The purport of this computer-assisted method is succinctly summarized in the statement of David I. Holmes, a statistician who "applies the techniques of stylometry—the statistical analysis of literary style—to uncover the authorship of anonymous works of literature" ("Using Math"), that the "statistical analysis of a literary text can be justified by the need to apply an objective methodology to works that for a long time have received only impressionistic and subjective treatment" ("Vocabulary Richness" 18).

A topic is defined as a mathematically identified collection of words from which the author is presumed to have selected when composing his/her text:

> Topic modeling programs do not know anything about the meaning of the words in a text. Instead, they assume that any piece of text is composed (by an author) by selecting words from possible baskets of words where each basket corresponds to a topic. If that is true, then it becomes possible to mathematically decompose a text into the probable baskets from whence the words first came. The tool goes through this process over and over again until it settles on the most likely distribution of words into baskets, which we call topics. (Shawn Graham, Scott Weingart, and Ian Milligan, "Getting Started")

According to David M. Blei, topic modelling was initially conceived by computer scientists to find "large archives of documents with thematic information" from the enormous amount of online data: "Topic models are algorithms for discov-

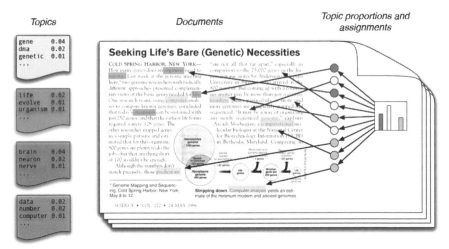

Fig. 5.1. Blei's Image of Topic Model ("Probabilistic" 78)

ering the main themes that pervade a large and otherwise unstructured collection of documents" ("Probabilistic" 77). "Topic modeling algorithms are statistical methods that analyze the words of the original texts to discover the themes that run through them, how those themes are connected to each other, and how they change over time" ("Probabilistic" 77-78).

Topic modelling assumes that any document is made up of topics and words (see Fig. 5.1). For instance, let us imagine we are writing a biography of a novelist. We first determine the topics our biography contains. It probably encompasses such topics as geography, the author's living era, family, education, religion, and main works. We draw heavily from some topics and lightly from others. Weights are then assigned to each topic: 20% of the document will be given to the record of the novelist's family, 30% to his religion, and 10% to his works. Now we extract words from the topics and start to write. The "religion" topic might contain a few irrelevant words like "banana" and "football," which are mixed into the bag mostly by accident. The topic should however include 200 appearances of the word "god," 150 of "christianity," and 100 of "church," for instance. We reach into the "religion" bag for 30% of all the words and put them into the document. In depicting family matters, we pick out such words as "home," "father," and "mother" from the "family" topic bag, and place them on a page. The process is repeated until the document is complete. Thus, the biography ends up as a document containing the prescribed percentage of each topic.[143] "Topic models," in short, "provide a simple way to analyze large volumes of unlabeled text. A 'topic' consists of a cluster of words that frequently occur together. Using contextual clues, topic models can connect words with similar meanings and distinguish between uses of words with multiple meanings" ("Topic Modeling," *Mallet*).

Fig. 5.2. Basic Idea of a Topic-Model Document

[143] This summary of the basic idea of Latent Dirichlet Allocation, the simplest topic model, owes much to Scott B. Weingart's explanation in "Topic Modeling and Network Analysis," Blei's in "Probabilistic" (78-79), and Mark Steyvers & Tom Griffiths' statement that "To make a new document, one chooses a distribution over topics. Then, for each word in that document, one chooses a topic at random according to this distribution, and draws a word from that topic. Standard statistical techniques can be used to invert this process, inferring the set of topics that were responsible for generating a collection of documents" ("Probabilistic Topic Models" 2).

Topic modelling software reverses this procedure and surmises the topics which generated the document. By examining the words used in the biography, the program is able to find the particular collections of word and infer "the distribution over topics that best describes its particular collection of words" (Blei, "Probabilistic" 78). The statistical processing of the frequencies of words is based on the idea that "the more often words are used together within a document, the more related they are to one another" (Weingart, "Topic Modeling").

5.3. Top 19 Keywords
5.3.1. Topic Modelling Analysis

MALLET, a topic-modelling toolkit "takes a single text (or corpus) and looks for patterns in the use of words; it is an attempt to inject semantic meaning into vocabulary," and is designed to find the keywords, or "the words that help define a statistically significant topic," in a text (Graham, et al., "Getting Started").

The application produces the two files "keys" and "composition" in extracting topics from the target corpus (Sample excerpts are shown in Tables 5.1 and 5.2). The "Keys" file contains the Topic Number (0-19), the percentage of topic distribution over the corpus, and the 19 words constituting the topics. The "Composition" file includes the Document ID, document name, and twenty pairs of Topic Numbers and their proportion over the document arranged in accordance with their weights.

While MALLET is useful for the scientific discovery of topics within a corpus, the topic modelling tool "includes an element of randomness," meaning "the keyword lists will look different every time the program is run, even if on the same set of data" (Graham, et al., "Getting Started").[144] In order to make the best objective

Topic NO.	%	WORDS
0	0.11669	bessy tom ll mary mother mrs nathan ve benjamin uncle jem money aunt jenny doctor thou hester home jenkins
1	0.04467	theresa victorine duke amante de bessy castle la madame mark lady tourelle husband room monsieur knew madam french miller
2	0.0835	miss mrs norah hall morton mr dawson openshaw lady dorothy alice squire phillis ethelinda great furnivall house sir lord

Table 5.1. A Sample of "Keys" Generated by MALLET (Extract)

[144] In answer to the question why different locally optimal solutions could be generated in different runs, Neal Audenaert of Texas A&M University states, "The short version is that topic modeling algorithms create estimates of an underlying statistical model of how documents are formed and related (the Bayesian posterior). The models that they estimate involve too many permutations to compute the exact answer." After quoting Blei as saying "That number of possible topic structures, however, is

#doc name topic proportion		1st PROPORTION		2nd PROPORTION		3rd PROPORTION	
ID	DOCUMENT	NO.	%	NO.	%	NO.	%
0	1837_p_Sketches among the Poor No. 1	9	0.358313317	15	0.324639385	3	0.084468311
1	1840_s_Clopton House	4	0.252949344	9	0.178601362	12	0.162466534
2	1847_s_Libbie Marsh's Three Eras	9	0.274744527	3	0.226067698	19	0.172586762
3	1847_s_The Sexton's Hero	9	0.345599681	15	0.200157105	3	0.1817385
4	1848_s_Christmas Storms and Sunshine	0	0.320660108	3	0.240807209	9	0.208228707
5	1849_s_Hand and Heart	3	0.362632011	0	0.28398175	9	0.272300202

Table 5.2. A Sample of "Composition Table" Generated by MALLET (Extract)

identification of the keywords which appear most frequently in the *LCB* topics, therefore, it would be more appropriate to use the averaged data of several runs, rather than the data generated by only one run, or operation. Accordingly, ten topic-modelling operations were run on MALLET and labelled Operations A-J. The top five topics of each operation, or the top 50 out of 200 topics (20 topics multiplied by 10 operations), determined on the basis of their weight points, are given in Table 5.3. Furthermore, to identify the most frequently occurring keywords within the top five topics, as well as the topic containing the highest number of these frequent keywords, the 701 unique words from the 50 topics in Table 5.3 were first sorted by frequency of occurrence. Next, the topics were ranked based on their respective weights. The results are shown in Table 5.4. It is discovered that the top-ranked keywords in the 50 topics are the following 19: "home," "miss," "mr," "brontë," "charlotte," "letter," "day," "great," "made," "good," "haworth," "long," "de," "emily," "character," "time," "life," "thought," and "house." They are integrated into six top-

> exponentially large; this sum is intractable to compute. As for many modern probabilistic models of interest—and for much of modern Bayesian statistics—we cannot compute the posterior because of the denominator, which is known as the *evidence*. A central research goal of modern probabilistic modeling is to develop efficient methods for approximating it. Topic modeling algorithms . . . are often adaptations of general-purpose methods for approximating the posterior distribution" ("Probabilistic" 81), he continues, "These approximations are usually very good, but they typically depend on some degree of randomization. This randomization is different for each computation. Consequently, the final results might converge to different models when run different times. In my (rather limited) experience, the differences across multiple runs are usually minor. If they are not, that might be a good sign that the resulting topic models are of low quality. By low quality, I mean they don't accurately capture what you and I would understand as the relevant topics covered within a collection of documents. So this is not a bug, but a consequence of the mathematical techniques being used."

OPERATION	RANK	TOPIC NO.	WEIGHT	WORDS
A	1	A0	96.43128	miss mr brontë charlotte letter day great made good home haworth long de emily character place mind friend days
A	2	A8	86.72444	time life thought house kind work people la feel till letters left family half knew heard year church things
A	3	A7	6.21093	derived grieve exchange sank start composure stay mun fine lines carlisle rachel appreciation roughly europe bodily brown indignant portrait
A	4	A11	5.20549	soft cherished success combined row person oppressive pensionnat thousands mrs difficulties remote modern palladium refusal sovereign beings ame clinging
A	5	A18	5.016	continues search thin sixteen beatrix periodicals delay afraid entertained double beginning main hungry ceased anticipate exhibition austen windy opium
B	1	B2	144.95209	time brontë mr miss life charlotte great letter day made good long home haworth de thought house emily character
B	2	B14	20.25317	earnestly red repeated falling shows valley establishment fox murmur accordance sincerity managed subdued expensive directed engage explain seat observed
B	3	B16	5.51625	cares finds qualified presses opera guides eloquence advertisements attraction par notions mademoiselle avec analyse sensitive seeking accomplishment disliked oldest
B	4	B17	5.06693	absolutely tabby accounts eyre management attended september recollections beck emanuel cheering reception objections needed occurrence indulgence draught wool iii
B	5	B3	4.98556	stock phrase ranthorpe discriminating multitude particulars visitor summoned rejected beset speed demands eu enjoying shattered moaning remorse wretch humbug
C	1	C7	73.28014	time letter day home de thought emily character friend read years people papa kind father anne part school place
C	2	C18	67.84774	brontë mr miss life great made good house long haworth mind feel make written morning nature dear pleasure things
C	3	C0	61.9926	charlotte sisters write till present il knew visit letters small leave told return power heard half smith end les
C	4	C13	5.53898	donne red submit couple usual sight lodgings vigour selfish burning studying simpler pace range subsequently impending material earned intimating
C	5	C2	4.99396	opera advisable voit suited stern ideal clothing hint despair ye host conjecturing worded forwarded restlessness highest unseen byron hurried

D	1	D5	94.62619	time mr life letter made long haworth de charlotte thought house day character work kind read good years mind
	2	D4	80.92609	brontë miss great home emily place friend people days father part london give visit book papa written family half
	3	D15	6.24683	ms nieces crime brother rising aspect wrung variance cross pronounce arrange anguish contrast deny distress yearned frere christians conflict
	4	D18	5.8986	refusal chambers renewed destitute avail unjust leaf privilege iv top colour bloom germ au rallied compare recreation restored shed
	5	D8	5.01826	stronger measure fortitude striven tenor eyes ball remote ame midsummer decision mist music concerns assembled wealthy coach eighty professional
E	1	E5	100.99754	time mr miss life charlotte letter great day made good long home de thought house emily place kind read
	2	E8	80.52137	brontë character years give feel write till haworth left hope sister subject morning things heard pleasure church dear eyre
	3	E12	5.74882	cut affairs particulars quick exquisitely declare indulged quote accounts merit cambridge illness human pressed reconciled outset devoir appealed noticed
	4	E10	5.16421	ma moments confess remarked daring grateful etait concerned armed burning looked advised foreign states table visitor valley reviving derby
	5	E3	5.02936	treatment emanuel ont qualified absent occasions absolute stimulants mute host tenaciously faut decoration mansion obscurity destiny fluently gaiety thousands
F	1	F5	134.61796	time brontë mr miss life charlotte great letter day made long home haworth good de thought house emily character
	2	F8	40.45522	loved form wished occupied derived likewise subjects invitation wishes holidays afternoon childhood action impressions leur genuine strongly characteristic hold
	3	F17	5.704	serene experienced couple misery perfection sadly unwilling oppressive glass potent evils undoubtedly gardens belgian believing detail replies entire storm
	4	F7	5.24369	failing quickly scarborough stayed stage clerical balzac earning verses alas usual apparent diet noiseless brain ardent gate force motherless
	5	F6	4.96534	closed straight consisting record estrangement amiable impress headache competition lettres excited university indomitable situated deem dropping comprehend libraries transmit
G	1	G4	121.58541	time brontë mr miss life charlotte great letter day made good long home haworth de thought house emily character
	2	G16	53.84984	real des hours returned women stood lines anxiety door grey man girl houses happiness martha gentlemen bring bear offered
	3	G19	5.19055	hair yah personal cared authoress depart peculiarly solitary edge suspect mistake colonel detail render forcibly reside pointing lover touch

CHAPTER 5 A Topic-Modelling Analysis of Christianity in The Life of Charlotte Brontë 153

	4	G15	5.03375	easily relish deeply aux kindest social acting serene strung honourable publishers vigour varied ailment spite dependence pressing merciful prospects
	5	G17	4.97519	profound allusion damp witness displayed disgrace wear comprehend praised temperament proceed conceal earthly principle wrath enclosure proposed strength dead
H	1	H13	130.20532	time brontë mr miss life charlotte day letter great made good long home haworth de thought house emily character
	2	H19	44.89891	low elder month strength wished terrible august white black send forget dreary faithful headache nights progress habits leeds borne
	3	H1	5.21954	highest towns describing france couple companion employed chat spirited arrange undertake calculate holiday harm bought portion roots acted belief
	4	H8	5.0661	crushed ni sont search showing control fewer ensued situations vue revive maid free relish induced discussions robert sate eyre
	5	H6	5.0532	laugh acquired connection beheld resignation spread harassing vigne guild criticism varied experienced combined rate composure waiting cruelty modesty belief
I	1	I19	114.48732	time brontë mr miss life charlotte great letter day made good long haworth de house thought home emily character
	2	I10	61.6454	feel told find bell death glad called love case men home household future reason sort sense stone call close
	3	I11	5.96642	inscription dreams slightly conclusion doubtful brilliant recreation procured se breaking fragment severe proof handsome talk riding square horizon authoress
	4	I0	5.11835	increasing combined brave reliant cet yard romantic sedentary sinking obstinate continued realised informant ll simplicity review sleeplessness beaucoup appreciation
	5	I4	4.929	yielded fixed situated cela perceptions enable heard mounted advisable impunity appreciation arbaletriers yesterday advertising ability inconvenienced forces wasted parle
J	1	J2	124.86325	time brontë mr miss life charlotte great letter day made good home long haworth de thought house emily character
	2	J12	49.57873	year power spirits glad reason began future anxious hard kindness situation grey forget considered road frequently cowan gentlemen view
	3	J9	5.73283	holy inspiration david discussion toute thinks certainty attacks appointed names revived observed ultimate instant grounds blow whereof humbug moved
	4	J0	4.9177	satisfied line features principles affectionately wasted appeal absent displayed occasioned hearty charnock materials william fail mistress figures mind scotland
	5	J14	4.9171	sign wednesday dreams bronchitis assist tyranny entertained altered mills ill volume remind quotation affair walls sold conversation hours penzance

Table 5.3. Top Five Topics in Each of Ten MALLET Operations

ics—B2, F5, H13, J2, G4, and I19—among which the topic with the heaviest weight is B2. This outcome implies that the life of the Brontë family—especially of Charlotte and Emily—in their Haworth home is the most dominant subject of this work. This seemingly trite discovery is further endorsed by the computer-assisted analysis of characters' appearance frequency and geographical place names, as discussed in Section 5.3.2.

In seeking semantic information on the topics, this chapter focuses on only the top two topics (out of 20) of each of the ten MALLET operations, because the probabilities of their distributions occupy more than 70% of each document, or the *LCB* text, on average (see Table 5.5). In Operation B, for example, where the sum of the probabilities of the top two topics is closest to the average of the total 20 topics, Topic B2, containing "time," "brontë," "mr," "miss," "life," "charlotte," "great," "letter," "day," "made," "good," "long," "home," "haworth," "de," "thought," "house," "emily," and "character" as its components (see Table 5.3), seems to denote "the life of Charlotte and Emily Brontë in their Haworth home." This result is almost identical to the conclusion drawn from the above study of the top 19 topic-modelling keywords. Topic B14, on the other hand, having "earnestly," "red," "repeated," "falling," "shows," "valley," "establishment," "fox," "murmur," "accordance," "sincerity," "managed," "subdued," "expensive," "directed," "engage," "explain," "seat," and "observed," as its components, looks like a mixture of words of irrelevant meaning, probably because of the low probability of the topic distribution (2.513%; see Table 5.5). In Operation D, taken as another instance since its top pair of topics shows the least probability difference between them (with the exception of Operation C, whose total probability is significantly lower than the average; see Table 5.5), Topic D5 ("time," "mr," "life," "letter," "made," "long," "haworth," "de," "charlotte," "thought," "house," "day," "character," "work," "kind," "read," "good," "years," and "mind") appears to indicate "Charlotte's life in Haworth." A semantic information of Topic D4 ("brontë," "miss," "great," "home," "emily," "place," "friend," "people," "days," "father," "part," "london," "give," "visit," "book," "papa," "written," "family," and "half") could be "the Brontë family at home and their London visit." Thus, both topics in Operation D highlight the central role of the Brontë family, reinforcing the conclusion we reached earlier after examining the top 19 topic-modelling keywords.

WEIGHT RANK		1	2	3	4	5	6	7	8	9	10	11
INTERNAL RANK		B-1	F-1	H-1	J-1	G-1	I-1	E-1	A-1	D-1	A-2	D-2
TOPIC ID		B2	F5	H13	J2	G4	I19	E5	A0	D5	A8	D4
RANK	WEIGHT	144.9521	134.618	130.2053	124.8633	121.5854	114.4873	100.9975	96.43128	94.62619	86.72444	80.92609
1	home	1	1	1	1	1	1	1	1	0	0	1
2	miss	1	1	1	1	1	1	1	1	0	0	1
2	mr	1	1	1	1	1	1	1	1	1	0	0
2	brontë	1	1	1	1	1	1	0	1	0	0	1
2	charlotte	1	1	1	1	1	1	1	1	1	0	0
2	letter	1	1	1	1	1	1	1	1	1	0	0
2	day	1	1	1	1	1	1	1	1	1	0	0
2	great	1	1	1	1	1	1	1	1	0	0	1
2	made	1	1	1	1	1	1	1	1	1	0	0
2	good	1	1	1	1	1	1	1	1	1	0	0
2	haworth	1	1	1	1	1	1	0	1	1	0	0
2	long	1	1	1	1	1	1	1	1	1	0	0
2	de	1	1	1	1	1	1	1	1	1	0	0
2	emily	1	1	1	1	1	1	1	1	0	0	1
2	character	1	1	1	1	1	1	0	1	1	0	0
2	time	1	1	1	1	1	1	1	0	1	1	0
2	life	1	1	1	1	1	1	1	0	1	1	0
2	thought	1	1	1	1	1	1	1	0	1	1	0
2	house	1	1	1	1	1	1	1	0	1	1	0
20	place	0	0	0	0	0	0	1	1	0	0	1
20	mind	0	0	0	0	0	0	0	1	1	0	0
20	kind	0	0	0	0	0	0	1	0	1	1	0
20	feel	0	0	0	0	0	0	0	0	0	1	0
20	heard	0	0	0	0	0	0	0	0	0	1	0
OCCURRENCE		19	19	19	19	19	19	18	17	16	7	6

Table 5.4. Prominent Topics and Their Most Frequently Used Words in *LCB*

12	13	14	15	16	
E-2	C-1	C-2	C-3	I-2	WORD FREQUENCY
E8	C7	C18	C0	I10	
80.52137	73.28014	67.84774	61.9926	61.6454	
0	1	0	0	1	11
0	0	1	0	0	10
0	0	1	0	0	10
1	0	1	0	0	10
0	0	0	1	0	10
0	1	0	0	0	10
0	1	0	0	0	10
0	0	1	0	0	10
0	0	1	0	0	10
0	0	1	0	0	10
1	0	1	0	0	10
0	0	1	0	0	10
0	1	0	0	0	10
0	1	0	0	0	10
1	1	0	0	0	10
0	1	0	0	0	10
0	0	1	0	0	10
0	1	0	0	0	10
0	0	1	0	0	10
0	1	0	0	0	4
0	0	1	0	0	4
0	1	0	0	0	4
1	0	1	0	1	4
1	0	0	1	0	4
5	10	12	2	2	

RANK	TOPIC NO.	PROBABILITY	OPERATION	PROBABILITY
A1	A0	0.435381	A	0.743578
A2	A8	0.308197		
B1	B2	0.701216	B	0.726346
B2	B14	0.02513		
C1	C7	0.306592	C	0.570859
C2	C18	0.264267		
D1	D5	0.407621	D	0.742953
D2	D4	0.335331		
E1	E5	0.465086	E	0.744984
E2	E8	0.279898		
F1	F5	0.658872	F	0.739604
F2	F8	0.080732		
G1	G4	0.617977	G	0.740872
G2	G16	0.122895		
H1	H13	0.644956	H	0.74577
H2	H19	0.100814		
I1	I19	0.559131	I	0.744281
I2	I10	0.185149		
J1	J2	0.627922	J	0.74395
J2	J12	0.116028		
			AVERAGE	0.72432

Table 5.5. Probability of Distribution of Top 2 Topics of Each of 10 MALLET Operations for *LCB*

5.3.2. AntConc Analysis

To assess the validity of this outcome, an inquiry was conducted on the frequency of appearances of the Brontë family members' names and geographical locations in *LCB* by using the free concordance software AntConc 3.4.1w. Data concerning characters' names and geographical proper nouns was extracted from the Word List tag of AntConc, where a total of 12,608 word types are sorted by their frequency of occurrence. The results for the character names are presented in Table 5.6 and Fig. 5.3, while those for the geographical proper names are shown in Table 5.7 and Fig. 5.4.

Among several structural features unearthed by this AntConc analysis, particularly noteworthy are the following two. (a) First, the character's name which appears most often is Charlotte (539 times), followed by Emily (182 times), Anne (129 times), and Patrick Brontë (102 times). (b) Second, "Brontë," one of the 19 key-

BRONTË FAMILY MEMBERS	WORD TYPES	FREQ	TOTAL FREQ
Patrick Brontë	Reverend Monsieur Brontë	1	102
	Mr Brontë	96	
	Rev Patrick Brontë	1	
	Rev P. Brontë	4	
Mrs Brontë	Mrs Brontë	14	21
	Maria Brontë	1	
	Maria Branwell	2	
	Maria	1	
	Miss Branwell	3	
Elizabeth Branwell	Miss Branwell	16	16
Maria	Maria, eldest daughter	21	27
	Maria Brontë	6	
Elizabeth	Elizabeth, 2nd eldest daughter	11	11
Charlotte	Charlotte	247	539
	Charlotte Brontë	34	
	C. Brontë	19	
	Miss Brontë	170	
	Miss Branwell [sic Miss Brontë]	1	
	C. B. Nicholls	2	
	Mrs Nicholls	1	
	Currer Bell	46	
	Currer	5	
	C. Bell	11	
	C. E. A. Bell	3	
Branwell	Branwell	66	71
	Patrick Branwell	5	
Emily	Emily	160	182
	Emily Brontë	2	
	Emily Jane Brontë	1	
	Ellis Bell	5	
	Ellis	11	
	E. Bell	3	
Anne	Anne	111	129
	Anne Brontë	9	
	Acton Bell	6	
	A. Bell	3	
A. B. Nicholls	Arthur Bell Nicholls	1	23
	Mr Nicholls	22	
Tabby	Tabby [servant]	65	65
TOTAL		1186	1186

Table 5.6. Frequency of Appearance of the Brontë Family Names in *LCB*

ID	AntConc RANK	WORD	FREQ	ID	AntConc RANK	WORD	FREQ
1	106	Haworth	210	18	1910	Lancashire	9
2	189	London	111	19	1961	Scarborough	9
3	339	Brussels	61	20	2015	Cambridge	8
4	411	Yorkshire	50	21	2081	Halifax	8
5	557	Keighley	36	22	2083	Heckmondwike	8
6	664	Leeds	30	23	2299	Filey	7
7	675	England	29	24	2337	Ireland	7
8	748	Bradford	25	25	2485	Ambleside	6
9	778	Cowan	24	26	2716	Oakwell	6
10	1139	Cornhill	16	27	2916	Belgium	5
11	1236	Manchester	15	28	2928	Bruxelles	5
12	1299	Edinburgh	14	29	2935	Casterton	5
13	1384	Europe	13	30	3098	Huddersfield	5
14	1586	Dewsbury	11	31	3144	Liverpool	5
15	1632	Penzance	11	32	3367	Westmoreland	5
16	1808	Scotland	10	33		others	105
17	1902	Hartshead	9		TOTAL		878

Table 5.7. Frequency of Occurrence of Geographical Place Names in *LCB*

words of heaviest weight in the topic modelling analysis, is used especially for Charlotte (Miss Brontë 170 times, Charlotte Brontë 34, C. Brontë 19), Patrick (Mr Brontë 96 times, Rev P. Brontë 4, Rev Patrick Brontë 1, Reverend Monsieur Brontë 1), Maria (Mrs Brontë 14 times, Maria Brontë 1), Anne (Anne Brontë 9 times), and Emily (Emily Brontë 2 times, Emily Jane Brontë 1). Charlotte Brontë's prominence in the Gaskell construct's narrative may seem inevitable, given that the book is her biography; similarly, the emphasis on her family members is unsurprising for the same reason. It is an intriguing discovery, however, that "emily" has the second highest occurrence rate, followed by "anne" in third, their father in fourth, "branwell" in fifth, and "tabby" in sixth.

A comparison of the results of the MALLET and AntConc analyses demonstrates the validity of the topic-modelling data in three ways. (a) First, Charlotte's centrality revealed by the MALLET analysis is confirmed by the AntConc keyword analysis, by which her highest frequency in appearance was uncovered. (b) Second, the significance of "emily," one of the top 19 most heavily weighted keywords in the topic-modelling investigation, is corroborated by the AntConc text mining, in

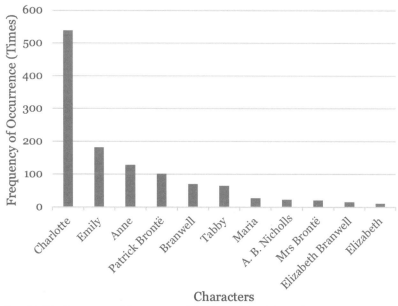

Fig. 5.3. The Frequency of Occurrence of the Brontë Family Members in *LCB*

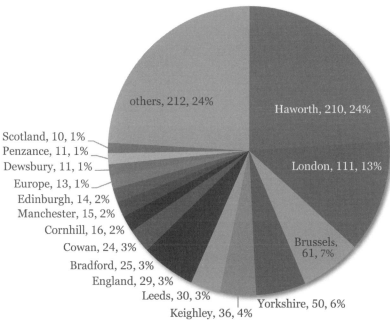

Fig. 5.4. The Frequency of Occurrence of Geographical Place Names in *LCB*

CHAPTER 5 *A Topic-Modelling Analysis of Christianity in* The Life of Charlotte Brontë   161

which it shows the second most frequent occurrence among the Brontë family's names. (c) Third, the frequencies of occurrence of the words "anne" and "branwell" are lower than that of "emily" in both the AntConc and the MALLET's examinations.

A survey of *LCB*'s Word List provided by AntConc reveals that, out of the total 878 proper nouns of geographical places, "Haworth" appears most often, or 210 times (23.9%), followed by "London" 111 times (12.6%), "Brussels" 61 times (6.9%), and "Yorkshire" 50 times (5.7%) (See Table 5.7 and Fig. 5.4). Thus, the topic-modelling outcome concerning the leading role of Haworth is likewise confirmed by the AntConc analysis.

5.3.3. Unique Discoveries

The MALLET and AntConc analyses of the *LCB* text shed light on the dominant structure depicting Charlotte Brontë with Haworth as the background of her life. This discovery, however humble it might seem, is significant for the following three reasons. (a) First, scientific (or objective) confirmation of the central figure and stage is established. (b) Second, the outcome of the statistical investigation accords with traditional (or subjective) criticism of the text (for instance, E. H. Chadwick 252; Easson, *EG* 132; ---, introduction, *LCB* ix; Pollard, *Mrs Gaskell* 152-53; Yamawaki 227; see Section 5.4.2 for details). (c) Last but not least, the results of the computer-assisted methods exactly match Gaskell's confession of her intention in writing this biographical fiction (*Letters* 348, 349, 361, 369, and 396; *LCB* 15, 440; see the same section for details). This third reason may offer evidence to refute the stringent critiques of anti-intentionalist scholars regarding the claim made by intentionalist hermeneutists that the author construct's meaning can be discerned through meticulous analysis of a text's formal design. The importance of this finding may not rest solely in the discovery itself, which is relatively conventional, but rather in the alignment between the formal structure and the authorial meaning. This alignment denotes that computational methods can accurately trace the author construct's conceptual framework for writing.

5.4. Results of Contextual Categorisation
5.4.1. Overview

This section will discuss the results of a contextual categorisation of the 2,795 examples associated with the top 11 topic-modelling keywords. Our objective is to identify the Gaskell construct's implicit or explicit references to Christian elements, based on the mathematically derived and relatively objective data.

The procedure for selecting the top 11 topic-modelling keywords is outlined as follows. Our current corpus consists of the five most heavily weighted topics selected from the 20 topics generated by each of the ten MALLET operations (i.e., 5 topics × 10 operations = 50 topics in total). This corpus includes 950 word tokens, as each topic contains 19 words (i.e., 19 words × 50 topics), and 564 word types. Since our research purpose is to detect the Gaskell construct's references to Christianity from the mathematically obtained data, all 564 word types were first inspected one by one according to their occurrence in the King James version of the Holy Bible, in order to isolate those words in the list with biblical connotations. This inspection reveals that 349 of the 564 words appear in the Scriptures. These words are then arranged in descending order of frequency in the table of the 50 most heavily weighted topics. As a result, the identified keywords are not only the top-ranked topic-modelling keywords but also those that appear in the Bible. Table 5.9 presents the results of this inspection, along with each keyword's frequency of occurrence in both *LCB* and the Bible. The eight words—"miss," "mr," "brontë," "charlotte," "haworth," "de," "emily," and "character"—are excluded from the final list of the target keywords, as they do not appear in the Scriptures. This exclusion aligns with the primary objective of this research, which is to explore the Gaskell construct's description of Christian truth.

ID	KEYWORD	NO. OF EXAMPLES
1	home	214
2	time	495
3	life	311
4	great	249
5	letter	247
6	day	246
7	made	224
8	good	217
9	long	214
10	thought	192
11	house	186
TOTAL (Times)		2,795

Table 5.8. Top 11 Topic-Modelling Keywords and Their Numbers of Examples in *LCB*

All examples of the top 11 keywords generated by MALLET are grouped into categories based on the connotations they bear in their respective contexts and/or according to the contexts themselves. For instance, the following citation which includes the keyword "home" is classified under the "unhappiness" category, as it centres on Charlotte's disorder, distress, and anxiety.

> There were causes for distress and anxiety in the news from **home**, particularly as regarded Branwell.[145]

---

145 Elizabeth Gaskell, *The Life of Charlotte Brontë*, edited by Angus Easson, Oxford UP, 2001, p. 207. Subsequent page references are to this edition and will be inserted parenthetically in the text with the abbreviation *LCB*. Keywords in the quotations from *LCB* are emphasized by bold letters hereafter.

CHAPTER 5 *A Topic-Modelling Analysis of Christianity in* The Life of Charlotte Brontë 163

ID	Frequency of Appearance in Top 50 Topics	Total Rank	Topic No.	Internal Rank	Keywords	Frequency of Occurrence in *LCB*	Frequency of Occurrence in the Bible
1	11	10	A0	10	home	214	51
2	10	5	A0	5	letter	247	37
3	10	6	A0	6	day	246	1743
4	10	7	A0	7	great	249	962
5	10	8	A0	8	made	224	1405
6	10	9	A0	9	good	217	720
7	10	12	A0	12	long	214	212
8	10	20	A8	1	time	495	623
9	10	21	A8	2	life	311	450
10	10	22	A8	3	thought	192	81
11	10	23	A8	4	house	186	2024
12	4	16	A0	16	place	159	716
13	4	17	A0	17	mind	141	95
14	4	24	A8	5	kind	149	45
15	4	28	A8	9	feel	112	7
16	4	35	A8	16	heard	91	641
17	3	18	A0	18	friend	143	53
18	3	26	A8	7	people	145	2143
19	3	29	A8	10	till	108	169
20	3	33	A8	14	half	91	136
21	3	38	A8	19	things	86	1162
22	3	200	C7	10	read	144	70
23	3	201	C7	11	years	137	539
24	3	251	C13	4	couple	6	10

Table 5.9. Top-Ranked Topic-Model Keywords Appearing in the Bible in *LCB*

For the next example, taken from a quotation featuring "time" as its node, the most appropriate connotation/context group would be "literary career," as it depicts the initial phase of Charlotte's emergence as a novelist.

> Messrs. Smith and Elder again forwarded a copy of "Jane Eyre" to the Editor, with a request for a notice. This **time** the work was accepted. (*LCB* 259)

The third instance, an excerpt from the 311 examples featuring the keyword "life" as their node, includes narratorial commentary on Charlotte's trust in God and is

ID	CONNOTATION/CONTEXT	FREQ	ID	CONNOTATION/CONTEXT	FREQ
1	literary career	386	23	school plan	33
2	religion/morals	271	24	building	31
3	unhappiness	217	25	career	30
4	health	207	26	narratorial comment	28
5	personality	174	27	affection	25
6	friendship	150	28	evils	23
7	Yorkshire	133	29	human beings	23
8	education	122	30	politics	19
9	book reading	93	31	social problems	19
10	visiting	87	32	biography	11
11	death	80	33	clothing	11
12	marriage	71	34	food	9
13	happiness	69	35	greeting	8
14	duty	65	36	money	8
15	literature	65	37	family	5
16	Brussels life	55	38	feminism	5
17	governess	49	39	Penzance	3
18	talent	44	40	imagination	2
19	domestic life	43	41	Mama's letters	2
20	letter writing	39	42	mesmerism	2
21	nature	39	43	freedom	1
22	London	38		TOTAL (Times)	2,795

Table 5.10. Summary of the Categorisation of the 2,795 Examples of the 11 Topic-Modelling Keywords in *LCB*

therefore classified under the "religion/moral" category:

> If her trust in God had been less strong, she would have given way to unbounded anxiety, at many a period of her life. As it was, we shall see, she made a great and successful effort to leave "her times in His hands." (*LCB* 94)

This process was repeated for the 2,795 examples of all 11 topic-modelling keywords. The results are summarized in Table 5.10 and visualised in the pie chart in Fig. 5.5. We must admit here that the classification process might not necessarily have been carried out with full objectivity, as determining the most appropriate category of connotation/context requires subjective judgement, and this selection is

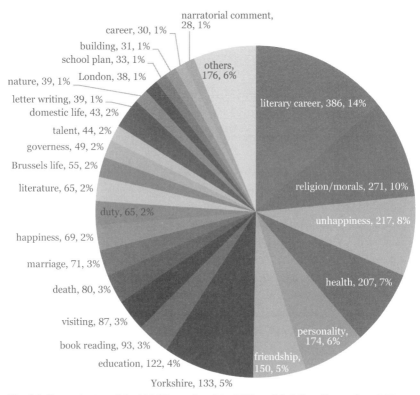

Fig. 5.5. Categorisation of the 2,795 Examples of the 11 Topic-Modelling Keywords in *LCB*

sometimes exacting and tough. For example, in the following quotation with "life" as its node, which has been classified into the category of "unhappiness" connotation/context, the first three sentences depict Charlotte's depressive frustration, but the last sentence her positive attitude towards her life.

> Meantime, life wears away. I shall soon be thirty; and I have done nothing yet. Sometimes I get melancholy at the prospect before and behind me. Yet it is wrong and foolish to repine. (*LCB* 220)

A similar context is created in the next citation, which begins with Charlotte's negative feelings towards life, but ends with her self-confirmation of her positive decision.

> Leave home!—I shall neither be able to find place nor employment, perhaps,

too, I shall be quite past the prime of **life**, my faculties will be rusted, and my few acquirements in a great measure forgotten. These ideas sting me keenly sometimes; but, whenever I consult my conscience, it affirms that I am doing right in staying at home. (*LCB* 248)

The decision was made according to the implication of the sentences nearer to the node, but we cannot but admit that this is tinted with subjectivity.

Another example of a similarly complicated situation is found in the quotation depicting Charlotte's kind concern about her father's health with the word "letter" as its node:

It may easily be conceived that two people living together as Mr. Brontë and his daughter did, almost entirely dependent on each other for society, and loving each other deeply (although not demonstratively)—that these two last members of a family would have their moments of keen anxiety respecting each other's health. There is not one **letter** of hers which I have read, that does not contain some mention of her father's state in this respect. Either she thanks God with simple earnestness that he is well, or some infirmities of age beset him, and she mentions the fact, and then winces away from it, as from a sore that will not bear to be touched. (*LCB* 350-51; emphasis added)

Which group of connotation/context should this example be placed into? Would "health" be most suitable, as Charlotte and her father have "keen anxiety respecting each other's health"? Or would "(filial) duty" be most appropriate, as the letter contains her "mention of her father's state"? Or how about "affection," since her letter is the manifestation of their "loving each other deeply"? The "religion/morals" group is a fourth option, as is implied by the passage that "she thanks God with simple earnestness that he is well." The "letter" in the citation above appears to encompass any of these connotations. Our decision was made in favour of the "affection" group, because Charlotte's concern about her father's health is the central topic of the sentence which contains the node, and also because the phrase "each other" appears as many as three times in this citation.

Such being the case, the collected data simply reveals the probability or general tendency in the author construct's choice of words. However, even this limited insight can lead to some intriguing findings that would be difficult to uncover through a conventional reading of the text.

The most noteworthy result of this computer-assisted analysis would be that the topic-modelling keywords that most frequently appear are used in association with the Brontës' literary career (14%). The second top category is "religion/morals" (10%), followed by the third "unhappiness" (8%), the fourth "health" (7%), and the fifth "personality" (6%).

The earliest reference to the Brontë sisters' "literary career" is their father's discovery of their talent "to invent and act little plays of their own" (*LCB* 47). In their infancy, Rev. Brontë's gift of "wooden soldiers" to Branwell (*LCB* 70) stimulated their imagination to create the Gondal/Anglia chronicles, and their devotion to the imaginary world continued even as late as their late 20s (Lyn Pykett 73). The narrator inserts young Charlotte's letter to the fictional editor of her magazine to emphasize "her powers of creation" (*LCB* 71). The sisters' nightly walks in the parsonage room is "the time for discussing together the plots of their novels" (*LCB* 117). The following is a narratorial summary of the young Brontës' pursuit of a literary career: "They had tried their hands at story-writing, in their miniature magazine, long ago; they all of them 'made out' perpetually. They had likewise attempted to write poetry" (*LCB* 117). Charlotte's letter to Poet Laureate Robert Southey asking his opinion of her poems and Branwell's to William Wordsworth for a similar request (*LCB* 118) are also examples showing their literary ambition. When Charlotte was 30 years old, a collection of the sisters' poems was published.[146] Notwithstanding "the ill-success of their poems—the three sisters were trying that other literary venture [i.e. publication of prose works]" (*LCB* 244). In 1847, Charlotte made her debut as a novelist at the age of 31, Emily at 29, and Anne 27 (*LCB* xxxv-xxxvi). Since around the publication of *Jane Eyre* began Charlotte's association with celebrities such as G. H. Lewes the literary critic (*LCB* 266-67), W. M. Thackeray the novelist (*LCB* 326), Harriet Martineau the social theologist (*LCB* 327), George Smith the publisher (*LCB* 259), W. S. Williams her reader (*LCB* 258), and Elizabeth Gaskell (*LCB* 352).[147] Charlotte Brontë's growing literary career is evident in the meticulous care she took while crafting her third novel *Shirley*. As noted, "the fame she had acquired imposed upon her a double responsibility" (*LCB* 315), indicating that the success of her earlier works placed greater pressure on her to meet rising expectations. The

---

146 "During the whole **time** that the volume of poems was in the course of preparation and publication, no word was written telling anyone, out of the household circle, what was in progress" (*LCB* 162). This is another instance of "time" being used in the context of "literary career."

147 Recollecting her first visit to Haworth, Gaskell writes, "We were so happy together; we were so full of interest in each other's subjects. The day seemed only too short for what we had to say and to hear. I understood her life the better for seeing the place where it had been spent—where she had loved and suffered" (*LCB* 440). This instance including "life" as its focal keyword is categorised into the "literary career" group as it describes Charlotte's friendship with the novelist Gaskell.

publication of her fourth novel *Villette* (*LCB* 423) further solidified her reputation as an established and respected novelist. This brief overview brings to light the fact that narratorial references to the Brontës' "literary career" are woven throughout the text, appearing from its opening chapters to its conclusion, illustrating the continuous and evolving nature of their professional journeys.

5.4.2. Previous Studies

Few previous studies have pointed out this aspect of the biographical fiction—"literary career" as its key subject—since critics proceed with their analyses principally in line with Gaskell's fundamental plan of writing—i.e. to achieve her two ultimate goals by means of two policies, or to emphasize Charlotte's domesticity and piety through the depiction of her circumstances and quotations of her own words.

The urauthor Gaskell's first and foremost purpose for writing this book was to focus on Charlotte Brontë as a domestic woman rather than a professional novelist. She confessed in her often-quoted letter to George Smith, a publisher, dated 31 May 1856, that her object was to make the world honour Charlotte Brontë the woman as much as they admire Currer Bell the writer (*Letters* 345).[148] Her distinction between Charlotte's public life as a novelist and her private life as a domestic woman is made explicit when she narrates, "Henceforward Charlotte Brontë's existence becomes divided into two parallel currents—her life as Currer Bell, the author; her life as Charlotte Brontë, the woman" (*LCB* 271). Acknowledging this principal object of the biography, Alan Shelston observes that it "is Charlotte Brontë the suffering woman rather than Currer Bell the successful author who had attracted Mrs. Gaskell's attention from the start" (introduction, *LCB* 24). Jenny Uglow remarks that the central theme of Gaskell's memoir is "the conflicting yet *converging* lives of woman and artist" (*EG* 407). Easson also makes the following statement in line with Gaskell's distinction between woman and novelist: "Charlotte had suffered doubly as a woman. In her personal life, she knew deprivation and loss, while in her artistic life, despite her fame, she had been taunted as coarse and had none of the advantages that a man might take for granted" (introduction, *LCB* xxi). Even the feminist readings by d'Albertis (*Dissembling* 43) and P. C. Parker ("Constructing" 73, 80) are affected by this distinction; in summary of the latter's argument, Susan VanZanten Gallagher observes "By publishing the details of Brontë's private life, Gaskell also publicised the dilemma of the female author, torn between the conflict-

---

148 This letter is quoted, for instance, in Duthie, *Themes* 105; Ganz 187; Uglow, *EG* 309; and E. Wright, *Mrs Gaskell* 149.

ing demands of domestic life and professional ambition" (9).

The Gaskell construct's second goal was to spotlight her friend's Christian integrity, forbearance, and sense of duty; or, to quote her own words, to "show what a noble, true, and tender woman Charlotte Brontë really was" (*LCB* 419). Her impression of Charlotte's virtuous personality was confirmed after she read a bunch of her letters sent by Ellen Nussey, Charlotte's old friend: "she was one to study the path of duty well, and, having ascertained what it was right to do, to follow out her idea strictly" (*Letters* 370). The Gaskell construct's concern in the depiction of her friend's selflessness is shown in her quotation from Charlotte's friend Mary Taylor's summary of her life:

> She thought much of her duty, and had loftier and clearer notions of it than most people, and held fast to them with more success. [...] All her life was but labour and pain; and she never threw down the burden for the sake of present pleasure. (*LCB* 457)

"Reading Mary's letter," Easson remarks, "Gaskell found no new insight, rather a confirmation, but she seized on it as one more witness to the justice she tried for" (*EG* 142). Valerie Sanders affirms that one of the things Harriet Martineau most admired about Charlotte Brontë was "her integrity of character" (73).

This second objective has sparked significant interest among critics. For instance, they pay attention to Charlotte's femininity (Rebecca Fraser, *Brontës* 268-69, 353; Hopkins, *EG* 198), and her not being "coarse" (Suzann Bick 135; Easson, *EG* 150; Easson, "Getting It Right" 2; Hopkins, *EG* 198; McVeagh, *EG* 25; Stoneman, *EG* 39; Uglow, introduction, *LCB* xii). Peterson notes that "Gaskell emphasises duty not only because it was an esteemed Victorian virtue, but also because it helped to disprove charges that the author of *Jane Eyre* was 'unwomanly' and 'unchristian'" (63). Moreover, critics have highlighted Brontë's outstanding personality (Bick 129-30; Bonaparte 243; Brodetsky 79; E. H. Chadwick 242; Brenda Colloms 2; Enid L. Duthie, *Themes* 137; Easson, *Critical Heritage* 390; Fraser, *Brontës* x, 491; Ganz 187; Gérin, *CB* 574; Lansbury, *Social Crisis* 155; McVeagh, *EG* 25, 29; Pollard, *Mrs Gaskell* 146; Shelston, introduction, *LCB* 36), her Christian virtue (Bick 118, 119; E. H. Chadwick 242; Easson, *EG* 148, 155; Easson, *Critical Heritage* 380; Hopkins, *EG* 198, Pollard, *Mrs Gaskell* 159), and her loyal fulfilment of familial duties (Duthie, *Themes* 129; Peterson 63; Rubenius 59-60; Spencer, *EG* 17-18, 71). Some critics point out that the Gaskell construct's emphasis on Charlotte's Christian integrity stems from her desire to vindicate her friend from the charge of coarseness and unwomanliness levelled at her by contemporary reviewers (Gérin, *EG* 164, 194; Gérin, introduction vii; Hopkins 198; Spencer, *EG* 69).

These two goals were to be attained by two means—first, by stressing the leading role of her environment in forming her character, and second, by making the best use of Charlotte's own words to narrate her life.

The first policy is expressed in her letter to George Smith dated 4 June 1855: "I could describe the wild bleakness of Haworth & speaking of the love & honour in which she was held there" (*Letters* 348). It is suggested also in her letter to the same correspondent dated 18 June 1855: "her home, and the circumstances [. . .] must have had so much to do in forming her character" (*Letters* 349), in her letter to Ellen Nussey dated 24 July 1855: "the circumstances [. . .] made her what she was" (*Letters* 361), in her letter to an unknown correspondent dated 23 Aug 1855: "I want to know all I can respecting the character of the population she lived amongst,—the character of the individuals amongst whom she was known" (*Letters* 369), and in her letter to Ellen Nussey dated 9 July 1856: "truth and the desire of doing justice to her compelled me to state the domestic peculiarities of her childhood, which (as in all cases) contribute so much to make her what she was" (*Letters* 396). In her letter dated autumn 1856, one of Gaskell's reasons for focusing on Haworth and Yorkshire is elucidated: "in her [Charlotte's] case more visibly than in most her circumstances made her faults, while her virtues were her own" (*Letters* 416).

This first approach to writing is hinted at within the book itself. For example, at the beginning of Chapter 2 of *LCB*, the narrator explains:

> For a right understanding of the life of my dear friend, Charlotte Brontë, it appears to me more necessary in her case than in most others, that the reader should be made acquainted with the peculiar forms of population and society amidst which her earliest years were passed, and from which both her own and her sisters' first impressions of human life must have been received. I shall endeavour, therefore, before proceeding further with my work, to present some idea of the character of the people of Haworth, and the surrounding districts. (15)

This intent is further implied in her recollection of her first visit to Haworth: "I understood her [Charlotte's] life the better for seeing the place where it had been spent—where she had loved and suffered" (*LCB* 440). Gaskell's perception of the circumstantial influence of Haworth on Charlotte's life in her first visit to the village is summarized by Haldane: "The silence and calm of the simple, ordered life at the

Haworth parsonage made a deep impression on the woman used to bustle and action" (149).

Indeed, descriptions of Yorkshire, including Haworth, are sprinkled throughout the biography. The narrative opens with the change of scenery from Keighley to Haworth and ends with Haworth mourners' visits to Charlotte's grave. This setting of Yorkshire as the background of Charlotte's life has been acknowledged by some critics (for instance, E. H. Chadwick 252; Easson, *EG* 132; Pollard, *Mrs Gaskell* 152; Yamawaki 227). Easson explains that the reason for Gaskell's insertion of the topic-modelling keywords associated with Yorkshire, or "the world of Haworth and the West Riding," into the text is "partly to show that it was not Charlotte's nature but her environment that was rude and wild" (introduction, *LCB* ix). So does Pollard in insisting that Gaskell indicates "the possible influence of environment upon character" (153), and that "Mrs Gaskell considered that Haworth and Charlotte's home exercised an influence both strong and baneful" (*Mrs Gaskell* 159). At one time Haworth becomes a place of comfort ("The strong yearning to go home came upon her" [*LCB* 205]), and at others that of pain ("Nothing happens at Haworth; nothing, at least, of a pleasant kind" [*LCB* 249])—this feature is also pointed out by certain critics (Brodetsky 28; Hopkins, *EG* 174; Lansbury, *Social Crisis* 140, 146).

The significance of the Haworth descriptions in the *LCB* text is proven one way or another by our statistical analysis, in which the group of keywords associated with Yorkshire is ranked seventh (see Table 5.10 and Fig. 5.5). This result provides an objective piece of evidence to verify the correctness of the above critics' subjective readings, and the appropriateness of our computer-assisted approach as well, because it also provides a correspondence between the qualitative and quantitative interpretations of the text.

The second approach to writing—to narrate Charlotte's life in her own words—is articulated in her reply to Ellen Nussey dated 6 Sept 1855: "I am sure the more fully she—Charlotte Brontë—the *friend*, the *daughter*, the *sister*, the *wife*, is known, and known where need be in her own words, the more highly will she be appreciated" (*Letters* 370).[149]

In short, the Gaskell construct's principle of drawing Charlotte Brontë's life is to appeal her Christian integrity—her perseverance, her goodness as a dutiful daughter—to the public by means of attributing the coarseness of her works to the

---

149 Gaskell's second policy of writing is pointed out by the following critics: E. H. Chadwick 221, 223; the urauthor Gaskell assumes the role of "spectator narrator" (Duthie, *Themes* 108, 189); Gail Mcgrew Eifrig 71; Haldane 166; "Everywhere respect is shown for primary documents" (Hopkins, *EG* 199); Lansbury, *Social Crisis* 136; McVeagh 25, 27; G. D. Sanders 92; Uglow, introduction xv; E. Wright 151.

environment which fostered her life. This principle is elucidated in Gaskell's letter to John M. F. Ludlow, a Christian socialist (*Further Letters* 305), dated 7 June 1853, which is brimful with her compassion for her friend:

> I should like to tell you a good deal about Miss Brontë,—& her wild sad life,—and her utter want of any companionship[.] I mean literally *companionship*,—for she lives alone, (although in the house with an old blind father); the last of six children,—in ill-health; & after all she is so much better, & more faithful than her books. [. . .] She puts all her naughtiness into her books; when the suffering that falls so keenly on one of her passionate nature, pierces her too deeply 'sits by her bed & stabs her when she awakes' (to use her own words,) & when others could go to some friend, & claim sympathy & receive strength her only way of relieving herself is by writing out what she feels, & so getting quit of it. [. . .] she *does* cling to God, as to a father, in her life & in herself—but somehow she only writes at her morbid times. (*Further Letters* 90-91)

Previous critics of this memoir have offered their interpretations more or less in line with this general principle. As further instances, "As its author said, her aim was to 'show what a noble, true and tender woman Charlotte Brontë was.' This aim is intermingled with the continual indication of Mrs Gaskell's sorrow for Charlotte's lot and regret for what in better surrounding she might have become" (Pollard, *Mrs Gaskell* 159). Peterson views the theme of the text as "Gaskell's presentation of Brontë as a gifted writer, plagued by poverty and ill health, but faithful to both her womanly duty and her literary gift" (68). Therefore, while what our corpus-stylistic analysis has disclosed—the Brontë sisters' pursuit of literary career as a hidden but pervasive theme—might be a modest discovery in the sense that it is a commonplace subject for biographical works, its uniqueness lies in the fact that it has been brought to light through this topic-modelling analysis of the *LCB* text.

5.4.3. Religion/Morals

It is an intriguing result that categorisation of the top-ranked topic-modelling keywords identified by fairly scientific means illustrates the group of "Religion/Morals" connotation/context as the second-largest category in *LCB*. This section focuses on this group to investigate the Gaskell construct's mode of description of Christianity.

For this purpose, classification of the 271 examples of the "Religion/Morals" group according to the connotations they bear or the contexts they create is carried out. The results shown in Table 5.12 and Fig. 5.6 demonstrate that the topic-mod-

ID	1			2			3		
KEYWORD	"home"			"time"			"life"		
DIVISION	CONTEXT	FREQ	%	CONTEXT	FREQ	%	CONTEXT	FREQ	%
CONTEXT/CONNOTATION/ASSOCIATION	unhappiness	31	14.486	literary career	81	16.364	literary career	46	14.791
	health	28	13.084	health	40	8.081	unhappiness	44	14.148
	duty	23	10.748	religion/morals	39	7.879	religion/morals	41	13.183
	happiness	19	8.879	education	36	7.273	personality	26	8.36
	friendship	12	5.607	unhappiness	36	7.273	book reading	21	6.752
	personality	9	4.206	personality	30	6.061	death	12	3.859
	literary career	8	3.738	domestic life	27	5.455	health	12	3.859
	Yorkshire	8	3.738	Yorkshire	27	5.455	marriage	12	3.859
	death	7	3.271	talent	24	4.848	Yorkshire	12	3.859
	education	6	2.804	visiting	23	4.646	biography	11	3.537
	marriage	6	2.804	friendship	21	4.242	duty	9	2.894
	visiting	6	2.804	letter writing	17	3.434	education	9	2.894
	nature	5	2.336	death	16	3.232	narratorial comment	9	2.894
	school plan	5	2.336	happiness	15	3.03	career	7	2.251
	affection	4	1.869	governess	14	2.828	friendship	6	1.929
	Brussels life	4	1.869	career	12	2.424	Brussels life	5	1.608
	career	4	1.869	marriage	10	2.02	governess	5	1.608
	domestic life	4	1.869	Brussels life	8	1.616	letter writing	5	1.608
	London	4	1.869	duty	7	1.414	happiness	4	1.286
	evils	3	1.402	nature	3	0.606	literature	3	0.965
	family	3	1.402	imagination	2	0.404	domestic life	2	0.643
	governess	3	1.402	Mama's letters	2	0.404	social problems	2	0.643
	politics	3	1.402	politics	2	0.404	talent	2	0.643
	religion/morals	3	1.402	book reading	1	0.202	affection	1	0.322
	literature	2	0.935	feminism	1	0.202	feminism	1	0.322
	book reading	1	0.467	mesmerism	1	0.202	human beings	1	0.322
	building	1	0.467	TOTAL	495	100	London	1	0.322
	letter writing	1	0.467				money	1	0.322
	Penzance	1	0.467				nature	1	0.322
	TOTAL	214	100				TOTAL	311	100

4 "great"			5 "letter"			6 "day"		
CONTEXT	FREQ	%	CONTEXT	FREQ	%	CONTEXT	FREQ	%
literary career	34	13.655	literary career	76	30.769	unhappiness	32	13.008
religion/morals	23	9.237	friendship	26	10.526	literary career	29	11.789
book reading	21	8.434	literature	14	5.668	health	25	10.163
personality	19	7.631	religion/morals	13	5.263	Yorkshire	17	6.911
Yorkshire	18	7.229	marriage	13	5.263	religion/morals	17	6.911
London	15	6.024	personality	11	4.453	friendship	15	6.098
unhappiness	14	5.622	unhappiness	11	4.453	visiting	14	5.691
education	10	4.016	Brussels life	10	4.049	death	12	4.878
health	10	4.016	health	9	3.644	marriage	9	3.659
nature	10	4.016	governess	7	2.834	Brussels life	7	2.846
friendship	9	3.614	visiting	7	2.834	education	7	2.846
human beings	9	3.614	death	6	2.429	nature	7	2.846
talent	8	3.213	letter writing	5	2.024	personality	6	2.439
building	7	2.811	duty	4	1.619	governess	6	2.439
happiness	6	2.41	education	4	1.619	human beings	6	2.439
social problems	6	2.41	happiness	4	1.619	duty	5	2.033
death	5	2.008	politics	4	1.619	happiness	5	2.033
literature	5	2.008	affection	3	1.215	literature	4	1.626
duty	4	1.606	book reading	3	1.215	letter writing	3	1.22
school plan	3	1.205	London	3	1.215	affection	3	1.22
Brussels life	2	0.803	school plan	3	1.215	domestic life	3	1.22
evils	2	0.803	domestic life	2	0.81	evils	3	1.22
feminism	2	0.803	money	2	0.81	book reading	2	0.813
marriage	2	0.803	Yorkshire	2	0.81	school plan	2	0.813
politics	2	0.803	building	1	0.405	talent	2	0.813
career	1	0.402	evils	1	0.405	clothing	2	0.813
family	1	0.402	freedom	1	0.405	London	1	0.407
narratorial comment	1	0.402	social problems	1	0.405	social problems	1	0.407
TOTAL	249	100	talent	1	0.405	career	1	0.407
			TOTAL	247	100	TOTAL	246	100

ID	7			8			9		
KEYWORD	"made"			"good"			"long"		
DIVISION	CONTEXT	FREQ	%	CONTEXT	FREQ	%	CONTEXT	FREQ	%
CONTEXT/CONNOTATION/ASSOCIATION	literary career	24	10.714	religion/morals	81	37.327	health	22	10.28
	personality	20	8.929	health	31	14.286	unhappiness	21	9.813
	education	19	8.482	personality	13	5.991	literary career	16	7.477
	literature	16	7.143	friendship	11	5.069	religion/morals	16	7.477
	religion/morals	14	6.25	greeting	8	3.687	friendship	15	7.009
	friendship	13	5.804	literary career	8	3.687	Yorkshire	14	6.542
	health	13	5.804	literature	7	3.226	education	10	4.673
	visiting	13	5.804	book reading	5	2.304	personality	9	4.206
	book reading	10	4.464	happiness	5	2.304	nature	8	3.738
	unhappiness	9	4.018	Yorkshire	5	2.304	book reading	7	3.271
	marriage	7	3.125	building	4	1.843	building	7	3.271
	affection	6	2.679	education	4	1.843	death	7	3.271
	Brussels life	6	2.679	food	4	1.843	letter writing	7	3.271
	evils	6	2.679	marriage	3	1.382	literature	7	3.271
	Yorkshire	6	2.679	money	3	1.382	affection	6	2.804
	duty	5	2.232	narratorial comment	3	1.382	visiting	6	2.804
	food	5	2.232	career	2	0.922	Brussels life	5	2.336
	school plan	5	2.232	clothing	2	0.922	human beings	5	2.336
	building	4	1.786	London	2	0.922	happiness	4	1.869
	clothing	4	1.786	politics	2	0.922	duty	3	1.402
	governess	3	1.339	unhappiness	2	0.922	governess	3	1.402
	death	2	0.893	visiting	2	0.922	narratorial comment	3	1.402
	London	2	0.893	Brussels life	1	0.461	clothing	2	0.935
	narratorial comment	2	0.893	domestic life	1	0.461	London	2	0.935
	politics	2	0.893	duty	1	0.461	marriage	2	0.935
	social problems	2	0.893	feminism	1	0.461	school plan	2	0.935
	career	1	0.446	governess	1	0.461	career	1	0.467
	happiness	1	0.446	human beings	1	0.461	domestic life	1	0.467
	mesmerism	1	0.446	letter writing	1	0.461	evils	1	0.467
	money	1	0.446	nature	1	0.461	politics	1	0.467
	nature	1	0.446	school plan	1	0.461	social problems	1	0.467
	talent	1	0.446	talent	1	0.461	TOTAL	214	100
	TOTAL	224	100	TOTAL	217	100			

Table 5.11. Contextual Categorisation of the Total 2,795 Examples of the Top 11 Topic-

10 "thought"			11 "house"		
CONTEXT	FREQ	%	CONTEXT	FREQ	%
literary career	37	19.27	literary career	27	14.52
personality	24	12.5	Yorkshire	22	11.83
book reading	19	9.896	visiting	13	6.989
religion/morals	19	9.896	friendship	11	5.914
friendship	11	5.729	education	10	5.376
death	8	4.167	unhappiness	10	5.376
health	8	4.167	health	9	4.839
education	7	3.646	building	7	3.763
literature	7	3.646	narratorial comment	7	3.763
unhappiness	7	3.646	personality	7	3.763
school plan	5	2.604	school plan	7	3.763
Brussels life	4	2.083	death	5	2.688
happiness	4	2.083	governess	5	2.688
evils	3	1.563	London	5	2.688
London	3	1.563	religion/morals	5	2.688
marriage	3	1.563	evils	4	2.151
narratorial comment	3	1.563	marriage	4	2.151
talent	3	1.563	social problems	4	2.151
visiting	3	1.563	book reading	3	1.613
governess	2	1.042	Brussels life	3	1.613
nature	2	1.042	domestic life	3	1.613
social problems	2	1.042	duty	3	1.613
Yorkshire	2	1.042	happiness	2	1.075
affection	1	0.521	Penzance	2	1.075
career	1	0.521	politics	2	1.075
duty	1	0.521	talent	2	1.075
human beings	1	0.521	affection	1	0.538
money	1	0.521	clothing	1	0.538
politics	1	0.521	family	1	0.538
TOTAL	192	100	nature	1	0.538
			TOTAL	186	100

Modelling Keywords in *LCB*

ID	RELIGION or MORALS	NUMBER OF OCCURRENCE	PERCENTAGE
1	goodness	113	41.697
2	faith	74	27.306
3	church	64	23.616
4	prayer	7	2.583
5	Christmas	5	1.845
6	Bible	3	1.107
7	charity	2	0.738
8	evilness	2	0.738
9	human lots	1	0.369
	TOTAL	271	100.00

Table 5.12. Categorisation of the 271 Examples of the "Religion/Morals" group in the Topic-Modelling Analysis of *LCB*

elling keywords in this group appear most frequently in the connotation or context of "goodness" (41.7%), followed by "faith" (27.3%), and "church" (23.6%), and, let us note, scarcely appear in that of "evilness" (0.7%).

For instance, the following extract narrates "goodness" of Rev. Brontë, who is nearly blind:

> (a) Under his **great** sorrow he was always patient. As in times of far greater affliction, he enforced a quiet endurance of his woe upon himself. (*LCB* 241)

Another extract from the "goodness" sub-category explains Charlotte's integrity in her efforts to conceal her aversion to a gentleman:

> (b) I hated to talk with him—hated to look at him; though as I was not certain that there was substantial reason for such a dislike, and **thought** it absurd to trust to mere instinct, I both concealed and repressed the feeling as much as I could; and, on all occasions, treated him with as much civility as I was mistress of. (*LCB* 156-57)

The servants' praise of Charlotte's "goodness" is the essence of the following quotation:

> (c) They tell of one **long** series of kind and thoughtful actions from this early period to the last weeks of Charlotte Brontë's life. (*LCB* 47)

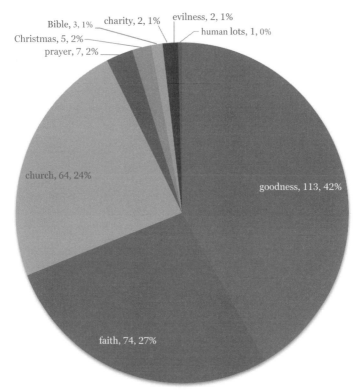

Fig. 5.6. Categorisation of the 271 Examples of the "Religion/Morals" group in the Topic-Modelling Analysis of *LCB*

The purport of the citation below is Anne's "goodness":

> (d) [It] was her custom to bear whatever was unpleasant with mild steady patience. She was a very sincere and practical Christian, but the tinge of religious melancholy communicated a sad shade to her brief blameless **life**. (*LCB* 281)

Acknowledging Charlotte's "absence of hope" (*LCB* 94) in her school-day letters, the narrator emphasizes her fervent "faith":

> (e) If her trust in God had been less strong, she would have given way to unbounded anxiety, at many a period of her **life**. As it was, we shall see, she **made** a **great** and successful effort to leave "her times in His hands." (*LCB*

94-95)

Charlotte's unwavering "faith" in God is demonstrated also in the extract below depicting one of the dreary winters she passed.

> (f) Sleepless, I lay awake night after night, weak and unable to occupy myself. I sat in my chair day after day, the saddest memories my only company. It was a **time** I shall never forget; but God sent it, and it must have been for the best. (*LCB* 404)

It is also reflected in the urauthor Gaskell's citation of Charlotte, which records Charlotte's strict view on people's lots in life:

> (g) She smiled, and shook her head, and said she was trying to school herself against ever anticipating any pleasure; that it was better to be brave and submit faithfully; there was some **good** reason, which we should know in **time**, why sorrow and disappointment were to be the lot of some on earth. It was better to acknowledge this, and face out the truth in a religious faith. (*LCB* 442)

Anne's letter to Ellen Nussey written prior to their departure to Scarborough records her abiding "faith" in God:

> (h) Under these circumstances, I think there is no **time** to be lost. I have no horror of death: if I **thought** it inevitable, I think I could quietly resign myself to the prospect, in the hope that you, dear Miss ----, would give as much of your company as you possibly could to Charlotte, and be a sister to her in my stead. (*LCB* 302)

The next example, which delineates Rev. Grimshaw's religious life, is classified in the "church" sub-group.

> (i) [He] went to engage in religious exercises in the **house** of a parishioner, then **home** again to pray; thence, still fasting, to the church, where, as he was reading the second lesson, he fell down, and, on his partial recovery, had to be led from the church. (*LCB* 24)

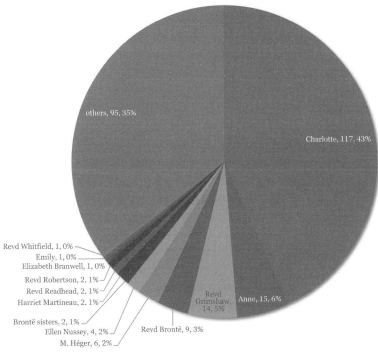

Fig. 5.7. Characters Associated with Sub-Categories of the "Religion/Morals" Group in the Topic-Modelling Analysis of *LCB*

The following is grouped in the "church" sub-category, as it describes Rev. Grimshaw's establishment of a chapel.

> (j) He had built a chapel for the Wesleyan Methodists, and not very **long** after the Baptists established themselves in a place of worship. Indeed [. . .] the people of this district [Yorkshire] are "strong religionists." (*LCB* 25)

A further investigation into the characters who are associated with the "Religion/Morals" category indicates that 117 extracts out of the total 271 (43.2%) are associated with Charlotte, 15 (5.5%) with Anne, 14 (5.2%) with Rev. Grimshaw, a "curate of Haworth" (*LCB* 23), and 9 (3.3%) with Rev. Patrick Brontë (see Table 5.13 and Fig. 5.7). The method of investigation is straightforward. All 271 examples within the "Religion/Morals" group were reorganized based on the central character drawn in each case. For instance, among the ten quotations above, (a) is linked to Rev. Brontë, (b), (c), (e), (f), and (g) to Charlotte, (d) and (h) to Anne, and (i) and

ID	CHARACTERS	NUMBER OF OCCURRENCE	PERCENTAGE
1	Charlotte	117	43.173
2	Anne	15	5.535
3	Rev. Grimshaw	14	5.166
4	Rev. Brontë	9	3.321
5	M. Héger	5	1.845
6	Ellen Nussey	4	1.476
7	Brontë sisters	2	0.738
8	Harriet Martineau	2	0.738
9	Rev. Readhead	2	0.738
10	Rev. Robertson	2	0.738
11	Elizabeth Branwell	1	0.369
12	Emily	1	0.369
13	Rev. Whitfield	1	0.369
14	others	96	35.424
	TOTAL	271	99.999

Table 5.13. Characters Associated with Sub-Categories of the "Religion/Morals" Group in the Topic-Modelling Analysis of *LCB*

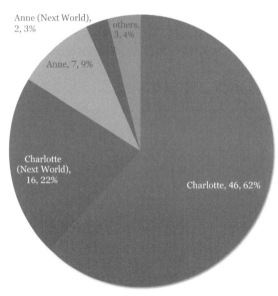

Fig. 5.8. Characters' Belief in the Next World Depicted in the "Faith" Sub-Category in the Contextual Analysis of the Top Topic-Modelling Keywords of *LCB*

(j) to Rev. Grimshaw. The results confirm that the Gaskell construct primarily focuses on highlighting the goodness, integrity, faith, and piety of Charlotte Brontë.

Another intriguing feature of the Gaskell construct's description of her protagonist's Christianity is her stress on Charlotte's belief in the eternal life. Out of 74 extracts from the sub-group of "faith" connotation, 62 examples (83.3%) are associated with Charlotte, from which the description of her belief in the next world amounts to 16 examples (21.6%) (see Fig. 5.8). A few instances should suffice to signify Charlotte's trust in God.

> I read Anne's **letter** to you; it was touching enough, as you say. If there were no hope beyond this world,—no eternity, no **life** to come,—Emily's fate, and that which threatens Anne, would be heart-breaking. (*LCB* 304)

The next is Charlotte's remark after Branwell's death:

> He is in God's hands now; and the All-Powerful is likewise the All-Merciful. A deep conviction that he rests at last—rests well, after his brief, erring, suffering, feverish **life**—fills and quiets my mind now. (*LCB* 289)

Charlotte's belief in the next world appears in her report of Emily's death to Ellen Nussey:

> We feel she is at peace. No need now to tremble for the hard frost and the keen wind. Emily does not feel them. She died in a **time** of promise. We saw her taken from **life** in its prime. But it is God's will, and the place where she is gone is better than that she has left. (*LCB* 293)

Anne's belief in the eternal life is implied in the citation below which explains Charlotte's reason for burying Anne's body in Scarborough:

> [The] afflicted sister decided to lay the flower in the place where it had fallen. She believed that to do so would accord with the wishes of the departed. She had no preference for place. She **thought** not of the grave, for that is but the body's goal, but of all that is beyond it. (*LCB* 310)

In the extract below, Rev. Brontë is quoted as recollecting his childhood education for his daughters:

> Lastly, I asked the oldest [Maria] what was the best mode of spending **time**; she answered, "By laying it out in preparation for a happy eternity." (*LCB* 48)

These five extracts show the Brontës' firm belief in the immortality of the soul, one of the principal teachings of the Christian doctrine. In recognition of this aspect of the Brontë sisters, Marianne Thormählen states, "The works, in poetry and fiction, of all three Brontë sisters reflect the conviction that the passion of love is never simply bounded by the span of human life on earth" (*Religion* 90).

Finally, a brief examination of two examples of human beings' wickedness from the "Evilness" sub-category will conclude this contextual analysis of the top 11 topic-modelling keywords. The first example opens with Charlotte's introduction to a husband and wife in a miserable state:

> You remember Mr. and Mrs. ---? Mrs. --- came here the other **day**, with a most melancholy tale of her wretched husband's drunken, extravagant, profligate habits. She asked Papa's advice; there was nothing she said but ruin before them. (*LCB* 156)

In the subsequent section of this letter, Charlotte expresses "instinctive aversion" (*LCB* 156) towards such a morally corrupt husband.

The second example of evilness involves Charlotte's account of her bitter experience as a governess, spotlighting the vices present in supposedly honourable human nature.

> She said that none but those who had been in the position of a governess could ever realise the dark side of "respectable" human nature; under no **great** temptation to crime, but daily giving way to selfishness and ill-temper, till its conduct towards those dependent on it sometimes amounts to a tyranny of which one would rather be the victim than the inflicter. (*LCB* 135-36)

The Gaskell construct's uses of topic-modelling keywords with the "evilness" connotation constitute less than one percent of her total use of keywords from the "Religion/Morals" connotation/context group. In other words, over 99% of the total examples in the "Religion/Morals" category do not relate to any notions of human "evilness" or wrongdoing. This implies her trust in the fundamental goodness of the human spirit. If so, her writing aligns with God's Plan of Salvation, which holds the scriptural concept that only good spirits are permitted to come to earth (Heb. 12.9; Rom. 8.16; Rev. 12.7–11).

5.5. Conclusion: Gaskell as a Christian Missionary

What has been clarified in our topic-modelling analysis of the *LCB* text can be summarized by the following nine points.

(a) Ten operations of MALLET on the *LCB* text disclose the top rank keywords are the following 19: "home," "miss," "mr," "Brontë," "charlotte," "letter," "day," "great," "made," "good," "haworth," "long," "de," "emily," "character," "time," "life," "thought," and "house"; this word set implies that the most dominant subject of this work is the life of the Brontë family—especially of Charlotte and Emily—in their Haworth home.

(b) A conventional search for semantic information on the topics yielded by the MALLET operations uncovers the centrality of the Brontë family in Haworth. Their visit to London could be another key topic.

(c) An AntConc scrutiny of the frequency of the names of Brontë family members and geographical places clarifies that Charlotte appears most often (539 times), followed by Emily (182 times), Anne (129 times), and Patrick Brontë (102 times), and that "Haworth" occurs most frequently, 210 times (23.9% of the total 878 geographical proper nouns), followed by "London" 111 times (12.6%), "Brussels" 61 times (6.9%), and "Yorkshire" 50 times (5.7%).

(d) The MALLET and AntConc analyses of the *LCB* text throw light upon its overarching structure of presenting Charlotte Brontë's life against the backdrop of Haworth. Although this may seem a trite discovery, it is crucial for three reasons. First, it provides a mathematical confirmation of the central figure and setting. Second, the findings from the computer-assisted analysis accord with conventional reading of the text. Third, the results of the statistical exploration closely accord with Gaskell's authorial intent in writing this memoir. This third reason may serve as evidence against anti-intentionalist critics' persistent dismissal of the intentionalist hermeneutists' view that an author construct's meaning for a text could be discerned through careful examination of its structural design.

(e) The consequences of a contextual categorisation of the total 2,795 examples of the top 11 topic-modelling keywords (the eight words—"miss," "mr," "brontë," "charlotte," "haworth," "de," "emily," and "character"—that do not appear in the Bible are excluded from the list, since an inquiry into the Gaskell construct's use of Christian vocabulary is one of our chief concerns) reveal that they are most frequently employed in association with the Brontës' literary career (14%), followed by "religion/morals" (10%), "unhappiness" (8%), "health" (7%), and "personality" (6%).

(f) A survey of the narratorial references to the Brontës' "literary career" confirms that they are scattered throughout the *LCB* text. The uniqueness of this discovery is verified through a review of previous studies conducted mostly in line with the Gaskell construct's paramount scheme of writing, i.e. to highlight Charlotte's domesticity and piety through the description of her circumstances and quotations of her own words.

(g) Classification of the 271 examples in the "Religion/Morals" group demonstrates that the topic-modelling keywords occur most persistently in the connotation/context of "goodness" (41.7%), followed by "faith" (27.3%), and "church" (23.6%), but scarcely occur in that of "evilness" (0.7%). That is, more than 99% of the total examples are not related to "evilness" of human nature or activities. The Gaskell construct's trust in the fundamental goodness of the human spirit may imply that her plan of writing corresponds to God's Plan of Salvation, according to which only good spirits are allowed to come to earth to receive physical bodies.

(h) An investigation into the topic-modelling keywords of the "Religion/Morals" category reveals that 117 extracts out of the total 271 (43.2%) are associated with Charlotte, 15 (5.5%) with Anne, 14 (5.2%) with Rev. Grimshaw, and 9 (3.3%) with Rev. Patrick Brontë. The result confirms that the Gaskell construct's principal concern is to delineate the goodness, integrity, faith, and piety of Charlotte Brontë.

(i) In addition, out of 74 extracts from the sub-category of the "faith" connotation/context under the "Religion/Morals" group, 62 examples (83.3%) are associated with Charlotte, of which descriptions of her belief in the next world amount to 16 examples (21.6%). This survey hints not only at the Brontë family's firm belief in the immortality of the soul but also the Gaskell construct's emphasis on Charlotte's belief in eternal life.

In conclusion, this study's topic-modelling analysis of Christianity in *LCB* confirms the Gaskell construct's emphasis on Charlotte's staunch Christian faith. d'Albertis asserts that Gaskell's work was written to hasten the realisation of "a collective or social ideal of the coming 'Kingdom of God'" (*LCB* 30), and that she viewed "all work, domestic and literary, as [. . .] a charge from God to write for the use and service of others" (qtd. in Parker, *Constructing* 79). This study substantively claims that the biographical fiction was written to accomplish this Christian mission.

CHAPTER 6 *Lois the Witch*: The Story of Christian Fortitude

6.1. Introduction[150]

In discussing the theme of this short novel, critics have paid much attention to the terror of the external circumstances surrounding Lois Barclay, the 18-year-old English girl falsely prosecuted and hanged as a witch in the 17th-Century Salem, Massachusetts, rather than to the integrity of her inner self. For instance, "[Gaskell] earnestly sought to point up the devastating consequences of prejudice and mass hysteria on the lives of innocent people" (Ganz 217); "'Lois the Witch' is not a study of the occult in Salem, but the delineation of a religious fanaticism leading irresistibly to mass lunacy and bloody persecution" (Lansbury, *EG* 53); "Gaskell's first examination of Calvinism as a morbid social phenomenon" (Lansbury, *Social Crisis* 158); "Gaskell is concerned above all with how scandal is produced and spread throughout society" (Marilena Saracino 202); "she emphasises the gullibility of people who are used to deferring to authority" (Stoneman, *EG* 59); "Lois is the victim of public ignorance and fear of the unknown, but also of men's desire and women's vindictiveness" (Uglow, *EG* 475);[151] and the story concerns "the innocent victim of slanderous tongues and more inhuman misbeliefs" (Ward, introduction, vol. 7 xxv).

To examine if these readings truly represent the authorial meaning, we are comparing the story with *Lectures on Witchcraft*, one of its significant sources, by Charles W. Upham, junior pastor of Salem First Church, in the next two sections. Section 6.2 first explains the creation procedure of the chronology of *Lois the Witch*, then attempts a statistical analysis of Gaskell's manipulation of Upham's first lecture on witchcraft.[152] Upham's book consists of two lectures. The second lecture is excluded from statistical analysis since the collection of "additional facts and considerations, that should be taken into view, previous to pronouncing a judgment, or forming an opinion respecting the conduct and characters of the persons connected with" the tragedy (*LW* 9) offers only indirect connection with the plot development of the novella. The first lecture, "a historical narration of the proceedings in Salem" (*LW* 9), presents direct connection. Section 6.3 details Gaskell's manoeuvres through comparative analysis of quotations from both texts. The result of comparison conducted

---

150 This chapter is the original version of my paper published in *Kumamoto Studies in English Language and Literature*, vol. 50.
151 Uglow offers another reading in which focus is shifted from Lois's circumstances to the heroine herself: "her story is an appeal against the hypocrisy of those who distort the word of God for their own, ill-understood ends—a prayer on behalf of women, a feminine rereading of the Litany from the Book of Common Prayer" (*EG* 479).
152 Page references to this book are cited parenthetically in the text using the abbreviation *LW*.

in the above two sections discloses three features: (a) Upham's attempt to elucidate the fallaciousness of Salem witch consternation by rationalist interpretation of the phenomena,[153] (b) his evident influence on Gaskell's composition of this short fiction, and (c) her initial design to stress the Christian virtues of the innocent victim. In Section 6.4, our scrutiny of its plot reveals that the principal focus is placed on Lois's spiritual triumph over her surrounding threats, i.e. her Christian perseverance. Based on the results of statistical investigation into the story, the concluding Section 6.5 casts doubt on critics' views of the theme of fiction, and assumes that the authorial meaning lies rather in Lois's Christian integrity than in the encircling people's cruelty of forcing her to innocent death.

6.2. Chronology and Statistical Comparison
6.2.1. Chronology for *Lois the Witch*

The chronology of *Lois the Witch* is generally in parallel with the history of the Salem tragedy delineated in Upham's first lecture, but not exactly (See The Comprehensive Chronology for *Lois the Witch* in Appendix 1).

His review of the tragedy starts from "the year 1691, about six months previous to the commencement of the witchcraft delusion" (*LW* 11), centring on "the witchcraft delusion of 1692" (*LW* 6), and ends with the 1712 erasure of the church record of excommunication of a witch (*LW* 123-25), followed by the jurors' declaration of regret for their mistaken judgement in witch trials (*LW* 126-29; *Salem Witchcraft* 641-42), and Judge Sewall's annual prayer (*LW* 129-30; *Salem Witchcraft* 614-15).

Lois arrives at Boston in "May" of "1691," (*CP* 105),[154] and comes to help her aunt's spinning before "a month" elapses after her coming to the Hickson house, that is, June 1691 (*CP* 128). When the "first of November" is near at hand (*CP* 131), probably on the night of 31 October 1691, Lois's talk of English Halloween frightens her cousin Prudence, and "before the late November morning light" (*CP* 132-33), or early next morning, her uncle dies. Then, the narrator describes the "strange, and haunted, and terrific" (*CP* 139) "winter life in Salem in the memorable time of 1691-2" (*CP* 138-39). Abigail and Hester Tappau are possessed by the evil spirit

---

153 Upham himself expresses his purposes in the lectures in four ways: (a) to learn from the errors of Salem ancestors (*LW* 3-6, 118), (b) to know the real character of the witchcraft delusion, "without which the design of providence in permitting it to take place cannot be accomplished" (*LW* 7), (c) to show that the excitement is so powerful as to "pervert [...] the hearts even of good men to violence, and fill them with all manner of bitterness" (*LW* 70-71, 90), and (d) to stress the virtue of humble penitence (*LW* 118-19). Upham is principally sympathetic towards erroneous ancestors (*LW* 8, 19-20).

154 Elizabeth Gaskell, "Lois the Witch," Cousin Phillis *and Other Tales*, 105. Page references are hereafter included parenthetically in the text with the abbreviation *CP*.

"one day towards the end of the month of February" (*CP* 148-49) of 1692, as the three girls in Upham's first lecture.[155] Hota, Pastor Tappau's Indian servant and the first innocent victim in the story, is executed probably on a Sunday in March 1692 (*CP* 168),[156] while, in Upham's lecture, the "first victim, an old woman" is put to death on "the tenth of June" (*LW* 30). Lois is "sentenced to be hanged" on the following Monday (*CP* 181); Nattee, the Indian servant of the Hicksons, is imprisoned on "the Wednesday afternoon" (*CP* 188) of the same week; and on the next morning, Thursday of "April" (*CP* 189) of "1692" (*CP* 191), Nattee and Lois are hanged (*CP* 190).[157] The story closes with Captain Holdernesse's interview with Hugh Ralph Lucy, Lois's fiancé, of "1713" (*CP* 190), in which the Captain talks about the 1712 erasure of the church record of excommunication against the Salem witches (*CP* 190).

The survey of the urauthor Gaskell's timeline suggests that, while she uses the actual historical events as the backbone of her fiction and Upham's information as its context, she relies on her imagination to create the inner world of her novella.

6.2.2. Statistical Comparison between Upham's Text and Gaskell's

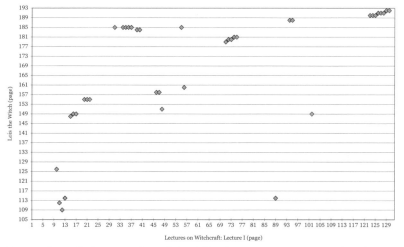

Fig. 6.1. Gaskell's Quotation from Upham's First Lecture in *Lois the Witch* (Page)

155 "Near the close of the month of February, 1692, two female children, belonging to the family of the Rev. Mr Parris, one, his daughter Elizabeth, represented to have been but nine, and the other his niece, Abigail Williams, twelve years old, together with a young female of the neighborhood, named Ann Putnam, began to act in a strange and unaccountable manner" (*LW* 16-17).
156 The date is surmised by counting backward from Lois's execution day, a Thursday of April, 1692.
157 The date of execution of Mary Easty, Lois's supposed model, on the other hand, is not specified (*LW* 92-95).

The scatter diagram titled "Fig. 6.1. Gaskell's Quotation from Upham's First Lecture in *Lois the Witch* (Page)" is designed to track her pattern of citing Upham's text.[158] Lozenge marks indicate the pages of *Lois the Witch* that contain clear excerpts from Upham's records. For instance, his references to the ministerial conflict and the first possession of Revd Samuel Parris's daughters (*LW* 16-17) are incorporated into the pages 148-49 of Gaskell's story. Similarly, Upham's statements at the end of the first lecture, which includes the blotting out of the church record of a witch's excommunication, the jurors' declaration of regret, and Judge Sewall's prayer (*LW* 123-30), are faithfully quoted on the final few pages of the novella (*CP* 190-92).

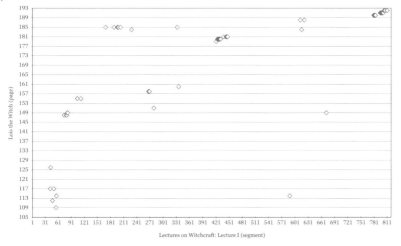

Fig. 6.2. Gaskell's Quotation from Upham's First Lecture in *Lois the Witch* (Segment)

"Fig. 6.2. Gaskell's Quotation from Upham's First Lecture in *Lois the Witch* (Segment)" was created to obtain more accurate data on her manoeuvre. The lozenge markers in this figure illustrate the correlation between segments in the novella and those in Upham's lecture. Segment 425 of his lecture (*LW* 72), for instance, corresponds with Segment 1455 of *Lois the Witch* (*CP* 130), as both contain the passage: "The prisoners were placed about seven or eight feet from the justices, and the ac-

---

158 The data are sourced from "Appendix 3: Gaskell's Manipulation of Upham's *First Lecture on Witchcraft*." In the table, Upham's lecture is divided into 822 segments, principally by the unit of independent clauses, marked by either a full stop or a semicolon in longer sentences. Gaskell's *Lois the Witch* turns out to comprise 1692 segments when divided by the same method, but this table is not included in this study because of its voluminous length. Accordingly, the pages on the Y-axis of Fig. 6.2. represent those that include the *Lois the Witch* segments.

cusers between the justices and them." Likewise, Segment 798 in the lecture (*LW* 126) aligns with Segment 1680 of the novella (*CP* 191), as both share the passage: "We confess that we ourselves were not capable to understand, nor able to withstand, the mysterious delusions of the powers of darkness, and prince of the air."

The two conspicuous features revealed by both scatter diagrams are (a) Gaskell's development of plot in line with Upham's arrangement of records, and (b) her modest dependence upon his text, or her originality in crafting her story. As regards the first feature, Upham begins with a brief statement about the purpose of his lectures, then describes the topography and history of New England, followed by a detailed analysis of the witchcraft delusion from its inception to its end, and concludes with accounts of the repentant. The Gaskell construct mirrors this sequence in constructing her plot. With regard to the second feature, her citations are drawn from 39 out of the total 132 pages of Upham's first lecture—approximately 29.5%—or from 62 out of the total 822 segments, representing 7.5% (See Appendix 3).

The next Section 6.3 conducts further investigation into these two features to unearth the authorial manipulation of Upham's text.

6.3. Comparison with the Source

In 1831, Charles W. Upham (1802-75), the Harvard-graduate pastor of the First Church of Salem, published two lectures on the witch perturbation which took place in 1692 in his village (Brian F. Le Beau ix). His object was, according to his own Preface to *LW*, (a) "to diffuse the blessings of knowledge," (b) to prevent fanaticism, superstition, and an "unrestrained exercise of imagination and passion," and (c) "to establish the effectual dominion of true religion and sound philosophy" (vi-vii). The book (especially his first lecture) is doubtlessly "the only true source for the historical material" (Easson, *EG* 215) in *Lois the Witch*, as demonstrated unequivocally through the subsequent comparison between the novella and its source. Upham's book is identified as a significant source for this fiction also by E. H. Chadwick (89-91), Anne Henry Ehrenpreis (99), Margaret Homans (317), Stoneman (*EG* 59), J. G. Sharps (*Observation* 316), and Uglow (*EG* 475). By examining the similarities and dissimilarities between Gaskell's story and Upham's lecture, therefore, we can uncover the strategies the Gaskell construct employed in crafting her narrative. The outcome of this comparison should offer valuable insights into her intended theme for this short novel.

The most notable feature disclosed through comparison is that the Gaskell construct draws heavily from Upham not only in her description of the social, political, and religious backdrop of 1690s Salem, but also in her creation of several key characters including the heroine Lois, her accuser Prudence Hickson, and Pastor Nolan. The Unitarian minister's influence on Gaskell and her art of fiction will be explored under five headings: 6.3.1. The Atmosphere of New England, 6.3.2. Witch Trials, 6.3.3. Victims with Christian Fortitude, 6.3.4. The Penitent, and 6.3.5. The Rationalist Interpretation of the Witch Panic. Section 6.3.6. will provide a summary of the analysis.

6.3.1. The Atmosphere of New England

The Gaskell construct modifies Upham's descriptions of New England to emphasize its petrifying atmosphere. The following are some examples of her modification.

(a) His description of the mysterious forests surrounding the colonies—"Wide, deep, solemn forests covered the hills, hung over the unfrequented roads, and frowned upon the scattered settlements. These forests were still the abode of wild beasts and of the Indians, in the terror of whose strange customs and warlike propensities [. . .]" (*LW* 10)—is cited particularly in the early stage of Gaskell's story where Lois's settlement in New England is depicted (*CP* 105, 117, 126, 127, 189, and 190). The similarities between both writers' accounts of the hazardous forests are pointed out also by J. G. Sharps (*Observation* 318). After consolidating Upham's two sentences into a single line—"this old forest, girdling round the settlement, was full of dreaded and mysterious beasts, and still more to be dreaded Indians, stealing in and out among the shadows"—, the Gaskell construct then adds the phrase, "intent on bloody schemes against the Christian people" (*CP* 126), to intensify the terror of the Indians.

(b) Upham's account of a day-long hazardous journey from Boston to Salem appears in *Lois the Witch* when Lois is on her way to her uncle's house;[159] to that description, the urauthor Gaskell enhances the sense of danger by adding the phrase, "and the road was reputed so dangerous" (*CP* 117), further emphasizing its insecurity.

(c) The threats of French retaliation are alluded to in Captain Holdernesse's chat with Lois during their travel to Widow Smith's inn,[160] followed by the narrator's remark: "the people here are raging like heathens" (*CP* 109). This addition

---

159 "To travel from Boston to Salem, for instance, which the ordinary means of conveyance enable us to do at present in less than two hours, was then the fatiguing, adventurous and doubtful work of an entire day" (*LW* 12); "it was a good day's journey to Salem, and the road was reputed so dangerous that it was ill tarrying a minute longer than necessary for refreshment" (*CP* 117).

160 "A recent expedition against Canada had exposed the colonies to the vengeance of France" (*LW* 12); "The French colonists, too, are vowing vengeance for the expedition against Canada, and the people here are raging like heathens—at least, as like as godly folk can be—for the loss of their charter" (*CP* 109).

further amplifies the sense of horror.

(d) Upham's statement on the Essex people's self-guarding against Indians—"the county of Essex was ordered to keep four scouts or companies of minutemen, consisting each of six persons, constantly in the field, to guard the frontiers against the savage enemy" (*LW* 11)—is incorporated into Widow Smith's evening talk at her inn almost word for word: "In county of Essex the folk are ordered to keep four scouts, or companies of minute-men; six persons in each company; to be on the look-out for the wild Indians" (*CP* 112). The bizarre stories leave Lois "breathless" (*CP* 113) with fear. The Gaskell construct inserts this table-talk scene not merely to stress New England's horrifying ambience and the colonists' potential animosity towards the Native Americans, but also to let these things foreshadow the ensuing tragic fate awaiting our heroine, as hinted at in Captain Holdernesse's warning to her: "thou hast come to a country where there are many perils" (*CP* 114).

(e) Upham's accounts of the situation preceding the witch turmoil, including the leading patriarchs' deaths (*LW* 15) and the subsequent feud between the Salem minister Samuel Parris and his congregation (*LW* 16) are cited almost as they stand by the Gaskell construct. For example, Upham's expression "Within a short time the town had lost almost all its venerable fathers and leading citizens, the men whose councils had governed and whose wisdom had guided them from the first years of the settlement of the place" (*LW* 15) is converted into the urauthor Gaskell's "The town of Salem had lost by death, within a very short time preceding the commencement of my story, nearly all its venerable men and leading citizens—men of ripe wisdom and sound counsel" (*CP* 148).

(f) It is worth noting, however, that she transforms the controversy between Parris and his congregation into a conflict between the old Pastor Tappau and his young rival Pastor Nolan. This dispute is also connected to the domestic tensions within the Hickson family, especially between Grace, a supporter of Tappau, and her 19-year-old daughter Faith, an adherent of Nolan (*CP* 148). Because Upham offers only a vague explanation for the causes of this congregational discord and Parris's conflict with Revd George Burroughs,[161] the Gaskell construct's adaptation high-

---

161 "Mr Parris invited the neighboring ministers to assemble at his house and unite with him in devoting a day to solemn religious services, and to devout supplications to the throne of Mercy, for rescue from the power of the great enemy of souls" (*LW* 20-21); "At length a day was appointed when, after solemn fasting and prayer, Mr Tappau invited the neighbouring ministers and all godly people to assemble at his house, and unite with him in devoting a day to solemn religious services, and to supplication for the deliverance of his children, and those similarly afflicted, from the power of the Evil One" (*CP* 155). Despite drawing the persecuted minister as "a victim to the prejudice and hatred engendered in a parochial controversy some years before" (*LW* 101-02), Upham gives only abstract reasons for this controversy:

lights her meaning to introduce the young pastor Nolan. This character serves as a catalyst for the unfolding dynamics: Faith's jealousy towards Lois, Lois's genuine assistance with Faith's affection for Nolan, and Lois's uprightness in the face of her spiteful cousin's groundless suspicions about her own relationship with the pastor. To create her own story, indeed, the Gaskell construct makes Nolan "a tall, pale young man" (*CP* 141),[162] although Burroughs is "of small and dark complexion" (Upham, *Salem Witchcraft* 417) and old.[163] That Nolan is modelled after Burroughs is hinted at in the narratorial comment: "He was a good and truly religious man, whose name here is the only thing disguised" (*CP* 143).

(g) "A black man" who appears in Upham's record of the execution of Revd Burroughs[164] is adapted in Grace Hickson's speech about Abigail Tappau in Satan's possession: "Abigail screeched out that he stood at my very back in the guise of <u>a black man</u>" (*CP* 149; emphasis added).

(h) The numbers of the accused,[165] the episode of a courageous young man who helps her mother to escape,[166] the reference to the man pressed to death,[167] and the

---

"violent and heated dissensions, too common in our religious societies at all times," adding that the divided parties are "Parris on the one side, and a large portion of his congregation on the other" (*LW* 16). That Burroughs is Parris's opponent can be surmised only when these quotations are read in contrast. He is "the only minister tried and convicted" of witchcraft (David Levin 213); his name appears in the list of twenty innocent victims (*LW* 34). His integrity in the scenes of his forgiveness and execution, detailed on pp. 101-04 in *LW* and pp. 518-19 of *Salem Witchcraft*, is mentioned only briefly as Nolan's uprightness in Gaskell's novella (*CP* 143, 185).

162 Nolan is about thirty, for the difference in age between the 18-year-old Lois (*CP* 181) and him is "not above a dozen years" (*CP* 164).
163 "He had passed the prime of life" (*LW* 101).
164 "To meet and turn back this state of feeling, the accusers cried out, that they saw the evil being standing behind him in the shape of <u>a black man</u>, and dictating every word he uttered" (*LW* 102; emphasis added).
165 "During the prevalence of this fanaticism, twenty persons lost their lives by the hand of the executioner. [...] Besides these, fifty-five persons escaped death by confessing themselves guilty, one hundred and fifty were in prison, and more than two hundred others accused." (*LW* 34-35); "The dire statistics of this time tell us, that fifty-five escaped death by confessing themselves guilty, one hundred and fifty were in prison; more than two hundred accused, and upwards of twenty suffered death, among whom was the minister I have called Nolan, who was traditionally esteemed to have suffered through hatred of his co-pastor" (*CP* 185).
166 "One adventurous and noble spirited young man found means to effect his mother's escape from confinement, fled with her on horseback from the vicinity of the jail, and secreted her in the Blueberry Swamp, not far from Tapley's brook in the Great Pasture; he protected her concealment there until after the delusion had passed away, provided food and clothing for her, erected a wigwam for her shelter, and surrounded her with every comfort her situation would admit of. The poor creature must, however, have endured a great amount of suffering, for one of her larger limbs was fractured in the all but desperate enterprise of rescuing her from the prison" (*LW* 35-36); "One young man found means to effect his mother's escape from confinement, fled with her on horseback, and secreted her in the Blueberry Swamp, not far from Taplay's Brook, in the Great Pasture; he concealed her here in a wigwam which he built for

fact of even dogs being indicted[168]—are put into the story as they are to depict the increasing horror of witches and the uncontrollable furore against them. Among Upham's list of twenty innocent victims are included "Rev George Burroughs of Wells" and "Mary Easty of Topsfield" (*LW* 34), the models of Pastor Nolan and Lois Barclay.

6.3.2. Witch Trials

After recounting the clerical dissension, Upham moves on to the witch panic which broke out in February 1692. Gaskell adopts the same procedure,[169] but differs from him in the treatment of the first bewitched people. In the Salem history, they are Pastor Parris's nine-year-old daughter Elizabeth, his twelve-year-old niece Abigail Williams, and Ann Putman, a young neighbour (*LW* 16-17), but in Gaskell's story, they are Pastor Tappau's daughters Hester and Abigail. This alteration highlights Tappau's paternal anguish and his desperate efforts to save his daughters, as indicated in the following quotation: his prayer became "violent and passionate, as was to be looked for in the father of children, whom he believed to suffer so fearfully from the crime he would denounce before the Lord" (*CP* 169).

On a Saturday, in March 1692, a meeting is called by Tappau to pray for God's mercy and for the deliverance of his afflicted daughters from Satan (*CP* 155). Hester's reference to her father's old Indian servant as her tormentor[170] and his subsequent whipping Hota into confession of her sin[171] are borrowed from the historical facts. The confessions of the accused, including their signing Satan's red book and their baptism by the Devil at Newbury Falls, are taken up into Hota's confession.[172]

---

her shelter, provided her with food and clothing, and comforted and sustained her until after the delusion had passed away. The poor creature must, however, have suffered dreadfully, for one of her arms was fractured in the all but desperate effort of getting her out of prison" (*CP* 185).

167 "One man refusing to put himself on trial was pressed to death agreeably to the provisions of the English law" (*LW* 31); "One old man, scorning the accusation, and refusing to plead at his trial, was, according to the law, pressed to death for his contumacy" (*CP* 185).

168 "Several dogs were accused of witchcraft, [...] suffered the penalties of the law, and are recorded among the subjects of capital punishment" (*LW* 36-37); "Even dogs were accused of witchcraft, suffered the legal penalties, and are recorded among the subjects of capital punishment" (*CP* 185).

169 "It was while this conflict was going on, and in the midst of all this local trouble and general distress, that the great and awful tragedy began. / Near the close of the month of February, 1692 [...]" (*LW* 16); "Such was the state of things in the township when, one day towards the end of the month of February [...]" (*CP* 148-49).

170 The pretended sufferers "first accused [...] an Indian woman attached to Mr Parris' family" (*LW* 22); "Hester [...] moaned out the name of Hota, her father's Indian servant" (*CP* 155).

171 The "old Indian woman [...] was whipped by Mr Parris until she consented to make a confession" (*LW* 56); "Hota was well whipped by Pastor Tappau ere she was brought to confession" (*CP* 160).

172 The alleged witches "declared that they signed his little red book [...], were present at his impious sacraments, and had ridden on sticks through the air. [...] [Satan] was accustomed to baptize his converts

On the Sunday afternoon, after the execution of Hota, another prayer meeting is organized at Tappau's house, where Lois is accused as a witch by Prudence, Faith's younger sister. Her examiners—Cotton Mather (the leading minister of witch prosecution), John Hathorn and Jonathan Curwin (magistrates)—are characters modelled on real examiners.[173] Upham's critical tone against Mather is neutralized in *Lois the Witch*, for the Gaskell construct's purpose of letting him appear is only "to achieve historical authenticity" (Ganz 217), not to reproach him for his avid involvement into witch hunting, which Upham himself somehow attempts to.[174] Likewise, his references to a few righteous citizens who denounced the proceedings of witch accusation (*LW* 25) and to a virtuous lady who contributed to the cessation of the appalling fanaticism (*LW* 32-33) [175] are omitted in *Lois the Witch*; if cited,

at Newbury Falls" (*LW* 46-47); "Hota had confessed all—had owned to signing a certain little red book which Satan had presented to her—had been present at impious sacraments—had ridden through the air to Newbury Falls" (*CP* 158). Satan's red book signed by a witch is mentioned also in the testimony of Sarah Carrier, a 7-year-old witch suspect (*LW* 79).

173   Soon "after our arrival Mr Hathorn and Mr Curwin, &c, went to the meetinghouse, which was the place appointed for that work" (*LW* 71); "The next day, she was led before Mr Hathorn and Mr Curwin, justices of Salem, to be accused legally and publicly of witchcraft" (*CP* 179-80). In Elder Hawkins's talk, the urauthor Gaskell introduces another real minister (*CP* 114): Mr Noyes, the junior pastor of the First Church in Salem and one of the most active witch persecutors (*LW* 89-92).

174   Upham's criticism of Cotton Mather is explicit when Mather expresses his scepticism about the innocence of Revd Burroughs standing on the gallows: "'While Mr Burroughs was on the ladder,' a contemporary writer observes, 'he made a speech for the clearing of his innocency, with such solemn and serious expressions as were to the admiration of all present, his prayer was so well worded and uttered with such composedness and such fervency of spirit, as was very affecting, and drew tears from many, so that it seemed to some that the spectators would hinder the execution.' To meet and turn back this state of feeling, the accusers cried out, that they saw the evil being standing behind him in the shape of a black man, and dictating every word he uttered. And the famous Cotton Mather, minister of the North Church in Boston, who was declared by Dr Colman to have been the most learned man he ever knew, and who combined an almost incredible amount of vanity and credulity, with a high degree of cunning and policy; an inordinate love of temporal power and distinction, with every outward manifestation of piety and Christian humility, and a proneness to fanaticism and superstition with amazing acquisitions of knowledge, and a great and remarkable genius, rode round in the crowd on horseback, haranguing the people, and saying that it was not to be wondered at, that Mr Burroughs appeared so well, for that the devil often transformed himself into an angel of light!" (*LW* 102-03). Upham makes repeated insertions of his criticism on Cotton Mather: "There is some ground for suspicion that he was instrumental in causing the delusion in Salem; at any rate, he took a leading part in conducting it" (*LW* 107); "And in order the more effectually to give the impression that he was rather opposed to the proceedings, he quotes those portions of the paper that recommended caution and circumspection, leaving out those other passages, in which it was vehemently urged to carry the proceedings on—'speedily and vigorously'!" (*LW* 109-10).

175   The delusion in Salem ended when Mrs Hale, a clergyman's wife, reputed for her "genuine and distinguished virtues," had been prosecuted. The "whole community was convinced that the accusers had perjured themselves"; thus, "a close was put to one of the most tremendous tragedies in the history" (*LW* 32-33).

	Lectures on Witchcraft 72–73		*CP* 180–81
(a)	The prisoners were called in one by one, and as they come in, were cried out at, &c.	(a)′	And when the prisoners were brought in, they were cried out at by the abhorrent crowd.
		(b)	*The two Tappaus, Prudence, and one or two other girls of the same age were there, in the character of victims of the spells of the accused.*
(c)	The prisoners were placed about seven or eight feet from the justices, and the accusers between the justices and them; the prisoners were ordered to stand right before the justices,	(c)′	The prisoners were placed about seven or eight feet from the justices, and the accusers between the justices and them; the former were then ordered to stand right before the justices.
		(d)	*All this Lois did at their bidding, with something of the wondering docility of a child, but not with any hope of softening the hard, stony look of detestation that was on all the countenances around her, save those that were distorted by more passionate anger.*
(e)	with an officer appointed to hold each hand, lest they should therewith afflict them; and the prisoners' eyes must be constantly on the justices; for if they looked on the afflicted, they would either fall into fits, or cry out of being hurt by them.	(e)′	Then an officer was bidden to hold each of her hands, and *Justice Hathorn* bade her keep her eyes continually fixed on him, for this reason—which, however, was not told to her—lest, if she looked on *Prudence*, the girl might either fall into a fit, or cry out that she was suddenly and violently hurt.
		(f)	*If any heart could have been touched of that cruel multitude, they would have felt some compassion for the sweet young face of the English girl, trying so meekly to do all that she was ordered, her face quite white, yet so full of sad gentleness, her grey eyes, a little dilated by the very solemnity of her position, fixed with the intent look of innocent maidenhood on the stern face of Justice Hathorn. And thus they stood in silence, one breathless minute.*
(g)	After an examination of the prisoners, who it was afflicted these girls, &c, they were put upon saying the Lord's prayer, as a trial of their guilt.	(g)′	Then they were bidden to say the Lord's Prayer.
		(h)	*Lois went through it as if alone in her cell; but, as she had done alone in her cell the night before, she made a little pause, before the prayer to be forgiven as she forgave. And at this instant of hesitation—as if they had been on the watch for it—they all cried out upon her for a witch, and when the clamour ended the justices bade Prudence Hickson come forwards. Then Lois turned a little to one side, wishing to see at least one familiar face;*

(i)	After the afflicted seemed to be out of their fits, they would look steadfastly on some one person, and frequently not speak; and then the justices said they were struck dumb, and after a little time would speak again;	(i)'	but when he eyes fell upon *Prudence*, the girl stood stock-still, and answered no questions, not spoke a word, and the justices declared that she was struck dumb by witchcraft.
(j)	then the justices said to the accusers, Which of you will go and touch the prisoner at the bar? Then the most courageous would adventure, but before they had made three steps, would ordinarily fall down as in a fit; the justices ordered that they should be taken up and carried to the prisoner, that she might touch them, and as soon as they were touched by the accused, the justices would say, they are well, before I could discern any alteration; by which I observed that the justices understood the manner of it.	(j)'	Then some behind took *Prudence* under the arms, and would have forced her forwards to touch Lois, possibly esteeming that as a cure for her being bewitched. But *Prudence* had hardly been made to take three steps before she struggled out of their arms, and fell down writhing as in a fit,
		(k)	*calling out with shrieks, and entreating Lois to help her, and save her from her torment.*

Table 6.1. Comparison between the Two Texts in *Lois the Witch* A

these references would diminish the impact of Lois's integrity, as her steadfast Christian faith under cruel adversity becomes less remarkable.

Upham's account of witches' transformation into mice[176] is incorporated into Nolan's evening talk about an elder's experience of kicking a mouse into crying "like a human creature in pain" (*CP* 151).

In Lois's examination scene (*CP* 179-81), the Gaskell construct draws heavily from the 24 May 1692 account of Jonathan Cary, a respectable citizen whose wife was persecuted as a witch; this statement is, according to Upham, "a lively view of the methods of examination and of the sufferings of the accused" (*LW* 71). The ur-author Gaskell's careful manipulation of Cary's account becomes evident when the two texts are juxtaposed. For clarity, corresponding segments are labelled with matching letters, such as (a) and (a)', while phrases uniquely crafted by the urauthor Gaskell are italicised.

In the above paired extracts demonstrating distinct similarity between the two texts, there are still some differences, which provide certain keys to understanding authorial meaning. For instance, Segment (d) emphasizes Lois's docility under

---

[176] "It was, believed that when the witches found it inconvenient from any cause to execute their infernal designs upon those whom they wished to afflict, by going to them in person, they transformed themselves into the likeness of some animal, such as a cat, rat, mouse or toad" (*LW* 48). A mouse as a figure of Satan's transformation is mentioned also in Upham's second lecture (*LW* 187).

helpless circumstances, while Segment (f) highlights her meekness, gentleness, and innocence. These additions serve to underscore the chief protagonist's inherent goodness and to evoke readers' compassion. In Segment (h), the narrator describes Lois's momentary hesitation when repeating the verse from the Lord's Prayer: "And forgive us our debts, as we forgive our debtors" (Matt. 6.12). The onlookers immediately cry out "Witch!" on her, since it was believed that witches were incapable of reciting the prayer (*CP* 170).[177] The true reason for her pause, however, is her desire to confirm that she can genuinely forgive her fellow creatures, just as she did the previous night in the gaol when she cried over their cruelty (*CP* 179). This contrast between the superficiality of the public mind and the depth of Lois's soul brings to light the Gaskell construct's meaning to stress her heroine's sincerity. Segment (k) is inserted to dramatize the helplessness of Lois's situation.

Upham's quotation from Cary's account continues. The following extracts appear immediately after the above.

	Lectures on Witchcraft 74–75		*CP* 181
(l)	And now, instead of one accuser they [the afflicted] all came in, and began to tumble down like swine [...].	(l)'	Then all the girls began 'to tumble down like swine' (to use the word of an eye-witness [John Cary]) and to cry out upon Lois and her fellow prisoners.
(m)	She [Cary's wife] was forced to stand with her arms stretched out.	(m)'	These last were now ordered to stand with their hands stretched out,
		(n)	*it being imagined that if the bodies of the witches were arranged in the forms of a cross they would lose their evil power.*
(o)	I requested that I might hold one of her hands, but it was denied me; then she desired me to wipe the tears from her eyes, and the sweat from her face which I did; then she desired she might lean herself on me, saying she should faint.	(o)'	By-and-by Lois felt her strength going, from the unwonted fatigue of such a position, which she had borne patiently until the pain and weariness had forced both tears and sweat down her face, and she asked in a low, plaintive voice, if she might not rest her head for a few moments against the wooden partition.
(p)	Justice Hathorn replied she had strength enough to torment these persons, and she should have strength enough to stand.	(p)'	But Justice Hathorn told her she had strength enough to torment others, and should have strength enough to stand.
		(q)	*She sighed a little, and bore on, the clamour against her and the other accused increasing every moment; the only way she could keep herself from utterly losing consciousness was by distracting herself from present pain and danger, and saying to herself verses of the Psalms as she could remember them, expressive of trust in God.*

Table 6.2. Comparison between the Two Texts in *Lois the Witch* B

177 Witches' inability to read the Lord's Prayer is noted also in Upham's second lecture (*LW* 186).

The urauthor Gaskell's near-verbatim reliance on Upham's book is unmistakable in this comparison as well. Her short additions to Segment (o)' underline Lois's admirable patience, while her insertion of Segment (q) highlights Lois's virtuous piety.

The received notion Upham refers to that witches cannot weep is mentioned twice in Gaskell's story, both to stress the brutality of witch trials and to evoke the reader's sympathy towards Lois.[178]

6.3.3. Victims with Christian Fortitude

Among twenty innocent victims recorded by Upham, the person that attracted Gaskell's utmost attention is Mary Easty, a dignified and upright victim who chose innocent death rather than dishonourable life (*LW* 92-95). She is the model for Lois Barclay.

Upham eulogises Easty's excellence of character: "Her mind appears to have been uncommonly strong and well cultivated, and her heart the abode of the purest and most Christian sentiments" (*LW* 92-93). Her letter, "a striking and affecting specimen of good sense, of Christian fortitude, of pious humility, of noble benevolence, and of the real eloquence of the heart" (*LW* 93), is also a selfless appeal to the judges and ministers to save any more guiltless blood from being shed (*LW* 93, 94).

> "The Lord above knows my innocence then, and likewise doth now, as at the great day will be known by men and angels. [. . .] by my own innocency I know you are in the wrong way" (*LW* 94); "the Lord alone, who is the searcher of all hearts, knows, as I shall answer it at the tribunal seat, that I know not the least thing of witchcraft, therefore I cannot, I durst not belie my own soul." (*LW* 95)

Her integrity is akin to Lois's refusal to comply with the judges' demand for a false confession: "Sirs, I must choose death with a quiet conscience, rather than life to be gained by a lie. I am not a witch. I know not hardly what you mean when you say I am" (*CP* 184). Easty's unwavering conviction that her innocence will be vindicated on Judgement Day is echoed in Lois's reply to Grace: "Aunt! I will meet you

---

[178] "It was the received opinion that a person in confederacy with the evil one could not weep" (*LW* 39); "If she had had strength to cry, it might—it was just possible that it might—have been considered a plea in her favour, for witches could not shed tears, but she was too exhausted and dead" (*CP* 181); "The tears streaming down from below the coarse handkerchief tightly bound over her eyes. [. . .] 'Look!' said one of these [visitors to her dungeon]. 'She is weeping. They say no witch can weep tears'" (*CP* 184).

there [the judgment-seat]. And there you will know my innocence of this deadly thing" (*CP* 188).

To note, however, is that the family background and age of the historical figure are altered in the fictional account. Mary Easty had "her husband, children and friends" (*LW* 95) and was executed at the age of fifty seven or eight (*Salem Witchcraft* 356). In contrast, Lois, a lonely orphan, dies at eighteen (*CP* 181). This change reflects the urauthor Gaskell's meaning to intensify the sense of pity surrounding Lois's plight and to underscore the tragedy of her heroic death.

Notably, no quotations are drawn from the Salem minister's detailed account of Margaret Jacobs, a young penitent accuser who was coerced into giving false testimony against the accused and later retracted her testimonies out of guilty conscience (*LW* 59-64). Nor are there references to the six courageous women who, having been forced to confess their guilt, later renounced their confessions even at the risk of being executed (*LW* 66-69), or to Mrs Hale, whose "genuine and distinguished virtues" helped cease the awful witchcraft delusion (*LW* 32-33). Also omitted are (a) Margaret Jacobs's visit to Revd Burroughs the day before his execution to confess her false testimony against him and beg his pardon (*LW* 101), (b) the pastor's gracious offer of pardon and his prayer with the repentant (*LW* 101), and (c) the profound remorse of the witch prosecutor Revd Noyes, who "publicly confessed his error; never concealed a circumstance, never excused himself; visited, loved, blessed the survivors whom he had injured, asked forgiveness always, and consecrated the residue of his life to bless mankind" (*LW* 122-23). The Gaskell construct's narrative focuses solely on highlighting Lois's Christian fortitude, which would be diminished if other characters' virtues were described alongside hers.

6.3.4. The Penitent

The author's meaning is subtly revealed through her manipulation of the First Church's record, dated 2 March 1712, concerning the church's efforts to erase the stigma of witchcraft, the conscientious jurors' declaration of repentance, and Judge Sewall's annual observation of the prayer day. All these elements are quoted nearly verbatim in the closing pages of *Lois the Witch*. In 1713, twenty-one years after Lois's death, Captain Holdernesse visits Hugh Ralph Lucy to deliver the news that the

---

179 "Humbly requesting that the merciful God would pardon whatsoever sin, error or mistake was in the application of that censure, and of that whole affair, through our merciful High Priest, who knoweth how to have compassion on the ignorant, and those that are our of the way" (*LW* 124-25); "humbly requested the merciful God would pardon whatsoever sin, error, or mistake was in the application of justice, through our merciful High Priest, who knoweth how to have compassion on the ignorant, and those that are out of the way" (*CP* 190).

excommunication against the Salem witches was lifted at the sacramental meeting,[179] and that Prudence demonstrated her deep remorse for her malicious testimony against Lois.[180] Unsuccessful in assuaging Lucy's grief for his fiancée's loss, Holdernesse shares a third piece of news:[181] the name of Grace Hickson was among those who signed the declaration of repentance. Finding this attempt also fails to console Lucy, the Captain, as a final attempt, speaks of Justice Sewall's profound remorse and annual prayer of atonement.[182] Lucy, however, can only express his regret, stating that no amount of repentance can bring Lois back. Nonetheless, he pledges soon after that he will join the penitent judge in prayer for the rest of his life, believing that "She would have willed it so" (*CP* 193).

A comparison between Upham's description and Gaskell's sheds light on the following three key authorial manoeuvres—(a) her insertion of Prudence's repentance, modelled after the accuser Ann Putnam's from page 125 of his book (Thus we know that the model of Prudence Hickson is Ann Putnam), (b) her inclusion of Grace's name among the signatures of the penitent jurors; and (c) her expansions of Upham's descriptions—transforming "he" into "an old, old man with white hair,"

180 "The records of that church contain a most touching and pungent declaration of sorrow and repentance, made thirteen years afterwards, by Ann Putnam, already mentioned as one of the principal accusers" (*LW* 125); "He also said, that Prudence Hickson—now woman grown—had made a most touching and pungent declaration of sorrow and repentance before the whole church, for the false and mistaken testimony she had given in several instances, among which she particularly mentioned that of her cousin Lois Barclay" (*CP* 191).

181 "We whose names are underwritten, being in the year 1692 called to serve as jurors in court at Salem, on trial of many who were by some suspected guilty of doing acts of witchcraft upon the bodies of sundry persons:—We confess that we ourselves were not capable to understand, nor able to withstand, the mysterious delusions of the powers of darkness, and prince of the air; but were for want of knowledge in ourselves, and better information from others prevailed with to take up with such evidence against the accused, as, on further consideration and better information, we justly fear was insufficient for the touching the lives of any, (Deut. xvii. 6,) whereby we fear, we have been instrumental, with others, though ignorantly and unwittingly, to bring upon ourselves and this people of the Lord, the guilt of innocent blood; which sin, the Lord saith in scripture, he would not pardon, (2 Kings, xxiv 4,) that is, we suppose, in regard of his temporal judgments. We do, therefore, hereby signify to all in general, (and to the surviving sufferers in special) our deep sense of, and sorrow for, our errors, in acting on such evidence to the condemning of any person; and do hereby declare, that we justly fear that we were sadly deluded and mistaken; for which we are much disquieted and distressed in our minds; and do therefore humbly beg forgiveness, first of God, for Christ's sake, for this our error; and pray that God would not impute the guilt of it, to ourselves, nor others; and we also pray that we may be considered candidly, and aright by the living sufferers, as being then under the power of a strong and general delusion, utterly unacquainted with, and not experienced in matters of that nature. We do heartily ask forgiveness of you all, whom we have justly offended; and do declare, according to our present minds, we would none of us do such things again, on such grounds, for the whole world; praying you to accept of this, in way of satisfaction for our offence, and that you would bless the inheritance of the Lord, that he may be entreated for the land—*Foreman*, Thomas Fisk, William Fisk, John Bachelor, Thos. Fisk, Jun. John Dane, Joseph Evelith,

and extending his phrase "a written confession, acknowledging the error" to "a written confession, which he had once or twice essayed to read for himself, acknowledging his great and grievous error" (*CP* 192). All these alterations are designed to emphasize the profound remorse of both the accusers and the judge. This thematic intent is further evident in her faithful adoption of four entire records from Upham, particularly in her meticulous transcription of the third and fourth records.

The Gaskell construct's repeated references to the repentant is brought in to emphasize the profundity of Lucy's indignation against them. However, he ultimately accepts Holdernesse's suggestion to forgive them, influenced by of Lois's spirit of tolerance. The Gaskell construct, thus, underscores Lois's Christian integrity, as Lucy's decision to forgive reveals that his resentment is smaller in scale than her broad-mindedness. Lucy's final resolution to pardon his fiancée's accusers despite his smouldering indignation against them is closely linked with the verse of the Lord's Prayer: "And forgive us our debts, as we forgive our debtors" (Matt. 6. 12). Lois shows momentary hesitation while reciting it, reflecting on whether "she might be sure that in her heart of hearts she did forgive" her accusers (*CP* 179), and repeats the brief pause twice (*CP* 179, 180), highlighting her modesty and sincerity. The Gaskell construct's aim for this final scene, accordingly, is to bring the integrity of Lois's soul into sharp relief. As Ward notes, this ending reflects the urauthor

---

Thomas Pearly, Sen. John Peabody, Thomas Peikins, Samuel Sayer, Andrew Eliot, H. Hernck, Sen" (*LW* 127-29); "We, whose names are undersigned, being, in the year 1692, called to serve as jurors in court of Salem, on trial of many who were by some suspected guilty of doing acts of witchcraft upon the bodies of sundry persons; we confess that we ourselves were not capable to understand, nor able to withstand, the mysterious delusions of the powers of darkness, and prince of the air, but were, for want of knowledge in ourselves, and better information from others, prevailed with to take up with such evidence against the accused, as, on further consideration, and better information, we justly fear was insufficient for the touching the lives of any (Deut. xvii. 6), whereby we feel we have been instrumental, with others, though ignorantly and unwittingly, to bring upon ourselves and this people of the Lord the guilt of innocent blood; which sin, the Lord saith in Scripture, he would not pardon (2 Kings xxiv. 4), that is, we suppose, in regard of his temporal judgments. We do, therefore, signify to all in general (and to the surviving sufferers in special) our deep sense of, and sorrow for, our errors, in acting on such evidence to the condemning of any person; and do hereby declare, that we justly fear that we were sadly deluded and mistaken, for which we are much disquieted and distressed in our minds, and do therefore humbly beg forgiveness, first of God for Christ's sake, for this our error; and pray that God would not impute the guilt of it to ourselves nor others; and we also pray that we may be considered candidly and aright by the living sufferers, as being then under the power of a strong and general delusion, utterly unacquainted with, and not experienced in, matters of that nature. We do heartily ask forgiveness of you all, whom we have justly offended; and do declare, according to our present minds, we would none of us do such things again on such grounds for the whole world; praying you to accept of this in way of satisfaction for our offence, and that you would bless the inheritance of the Lord, that he may be entreated for the land. Foreman, THOMAS FISK, &c." (*CP* 191-92).

Gaskell's abhorrence of injustice and her deep belief in the power of forgiveness: "no principle which influenced her was stronger than her abhorrence of injustice, and no conviction held by her was so much part of herself as the belief, that what is most divine in man is the forgiveness of those who sin against him" (introduction, vol. 7 xxiv).

Upham observes, "Human virtue never shines with more lustre than when it rises amidst the imperfections, or from the ruins of our nature, arrays itself in the robes of penitence, and goes forth with earnest and humble sincerity to the work of reformation and restitution" (*LW* 119), offering this as his rationale for incorporating the accounts of the repentant. Thus, he further notes that Justice Sewall was rewarded for his remorse (*LW* 130-31). The Gaskell construct, notwithstanding, excludes this episode, likely because her use of Upham's accounts aims to stress Lois's Christian virtues rather than focus on the rewards of repentance.

182 "He observed annually in private a day of humiliation and prayer, during the remainder of his life, to keep fresh in his mind a sense of repentance and sorrow for the part he bore in the trials. On the day of general fast, he rose in the place where he was accustomed to worship, the Old South in Boston, and in the presence of the great assembly, handed up to the pulpit a written confession, acknowledging the error into which he had been led, praying for the forgiveness of God and his people, and concluding with a request to all the congregation to unite with him in devout supplication, that it might not bring down the displeasure of the Most High, upon his country, his family, or himself. He remained standing during the public reading of the paper. [. . .] The good and gracious God be pleased to save New England and me, and my family" (*LW* 129-30); "on the day of the general fast, appointed to be held all through New England, when the meeting-houses were crowded, an old, old man with white hair had stood up in the place in which he was accustomed to worship, and had handed up into the pulpit a written confession, which he had once or twice essayed to read for himself, acknowledging his great and grievous error in the matter of the witches of Salem, and praying for the forgiveness of God and of his people, ending with an entreaty that all then present would join with him in prayer that his past conduct might not bring down the displeasure of the Most High upon his country, his family, or himself. That old man, who was no other than Justice Sewall, remained standing all the time that his confession was read; and at the end he said, 'The good and gracious God be pleased to save New England and me and my family.' And then it came out that, for years past, Judge Sewall had set apart a day for humiliation and prayer, to keep fresh in his mind a sense of repentance and sorrow for the part he borne in these trials, and that this solemn anniversary he was pledged to keep as long as he lived, to show his feeling of deep humiliation" (*CP* 192).
183 "As it is one of the leading designs of these lectures to shew to what an extent of error and passion, even good men may be carried, when they have abandoned their reason, and relinquished the exercise of their judgment, and given themselves over to the impulses of imagination and feeling, I am bound, painful as it is to do it, to present to your notice some instances of glaring misconduct and inhumanity, that marked the proceedings of the magistrates, judges, ministers and other principal citizens" (*LW* 70-71); "one of the leading designs of these lectures, which, as has before been observed, is to show that there is power in a popular delusion and a general excitement of the passions of a community to pervert the best of characters, turn the hearts even of good men to violence, and fill them with all manner of bitterness" (*LW* 90).

6.3.5. The Rationalist Interpretation of the Witch Panic

Upham consistently argues that human errors, not devilish powers, are the cause of the Salem witch panic.[183] For instance, the accusations by Pastor Parris's young girls are attributed to their "wicked perjury and wilful malice [...], the mysterious energies of the imagination, the power of enthusiasm, the influence of sympathy, and the general prevalence of credulity, ignorance, superstition and fanaticism" (*LW* 51). The psychology of accusers is presented as something inevitable: "It is obvious, that during the prevalence of the fanaticism, it was in the power of every man to bring down terrible vengeance upon his enemies, by pretending to be bewitched by them" (*LW* 53). The urauthor Gaskell follows Upham's rationalist stance in her portrayal of the prosecution of Hota and Lois, two alleged witches, as well as in her frequent descriptions of supernatural phenomena. The Gaskell construct's application of Upham's "rationalist analysis of witchcraft trials" is highlighted also by Uglow (*EG* 475).

Faith Hickson, who suffers from "the bitter pain of jealousy" (*CP* 147) over Pastor Nolan's affection for her, receives an enigmatic comfort from Nattee, her family's Indian servant:

"Hush thee, hush thee, prairie bird! How can he build a nest, when the old bird has got all the moss and the feathers? Wait till the Indian has found means to send the old bird flying far away." (*CP* 147)

Nattee here means:

"Pastor Nolan [he] cannot settle in Salem [build a nest] if Pastor Tappau [the old bird] enjoys the support of the rich [the moss][184] and leading congregants [the feathers],[185] so that Faith [prairie bird] should wait until she [the Indian] manages to expel Tappau from the church [to send the old bird flying far away]."

"To this end," explains Marie D. Bacigalupo, "Nattee conspires with Tappau's Indian servant, Hota, to place some strategically hidden strings among the minister's household effects" (336). A couple of months later, i.e. in February 1692, Grace comes back from a prayer meeting held at Tappau's house with the terrifying report that the minister's household "is defiled by a malicious spirit that produces strange sounds, shatters his crockery and bewitches his daughters" (Bacigalupo 336-37). The

---

184 The "moss" means "money," as in the proverb: a rolling stone gathers no moss ("moss," OED, 3rd ed.).
185 To wear feathers means to assume the powers of the bird (J. C. Cooper 65).

suggestion that the perpetrator is Hota emerges twice in the conversation Faith and Lois have one day in March 1692. (a) First, in Lois's awareness of the servant's plot: "[O]nce I met her [Nattee] in the dusk, just close by Pastor Tappau's house, in company with Hota, his servant—it was just before we heard of the sore disturbance in his house—and I have wondered if she had aught to do with it" (*CP* 153; emphasis added). (b) Second, in Faith's secret—tempted to disclose the truth about the fuss in Tappau's household to her English cousin, Faith urges her, "promise me never to tell living creature, and I will tell you a secret" (*CP* 154); having her request rejected by the frightened Lois, she adds in displeasure, "[your terrors] if you had listened to me, might have been lessened, if not entirely done away with" (*CP* 154).

The rationalist explanation of Hota's execution continues. At the prayer meeting held at Tappau's house on a Saturday, March 1692, the Indian servant is named as a witch by Hester. On their way home, only Faith looks "uneasy and disturbed beyond her wont" (*CP* 156) among the Hicksons: she is guilt-ridden for having inadvertently caused the misfortune to Hota, the collaborator in her intrigue with Nattee against Tappau. On that evening, after learning of Hota's acknowledgement of her being a witch, Nattee implores her mistress's family for help: "Mercy, mercy, mistress, everybody! Take care of poor Indian Nattee, who never do wrong, but for mistress and the family!" (*CP* 157). She is afraid that she might be indicted if her involvement in Faith's deception were disclosed by Hota. After hearing the details from Nattee, Faith turns colourless, and retreats with her to the kitchen, probably for the consultation about their countermeasures. Lois overhears the word "torture" from their conversation, which later turns out to refer to Tappau's whipping of his servant to confession (*CP* 160). Hota admits the trickery she employed to break her master's crockery; but, the gossips of Salem pay little attention to "such intelligible malpractices" with "the nature of earthly tricks" rather than "of spiritual power" (*CP* 158). Grace's detailed news of Hota's confession prompts "flushed and restless" Faith to question her about its "more extraordinary parts" (*CP* 159) as if to soothe her qualms. On the night prior to Hota's hanging, Faith asks Lois to deliver a letter "concerning life and death" (*CP* 162, 163) to Nolan early in the following morning, hoping to save Hota and relieve her guilty conscience "for her part in Hota's victimization" (Bacigalupo 339). However, on the Sunday morning, overcome by jealousy over Lois's seemingly pleasant talk with Nolan, Faith retrieves her unread letter about "an old woman's life" (*CP* 165) from the pastor. This act ultimately seals Hota's

---

186 "Faith and Nattee," remarks the narrator, "seemed more bound together by love and common interest, than any other two among the self-contained individuals comprising this household" (*CP* 141).

fate, making her a victim to Faith's conspiracy.

Accordingly, the mysterious friendship between Faith and Nattee[186] functions as a narrative device for elucidating the background of Hota's execution from the rationalist perspective. At the same time, the Gaskell construct's device for retaining the bizarre and horrible atmosphere of Salem can be detected in the above outline. The contents of Faith's letter are virtually hidden from the reader as if to leave open Hota's possibility of being a witch.

Gaskell's rationalist perspective is implied in the fact that Lois's death is triggered by man-made causes, mainly by Prudence's malice. Her love of attracting people's attention is highlighted twice in the text. First, while surrounded by Grace, Faith, and Lois, Prudence, after giving "a loud scream of terror" at her English cousin's talk about Halloween tricks, pretends to be more frightened than she actually is, "from the pleasure she received at perceiving herself the centre of attention" (*CP* 132). Second, on the way home from the prayer meeting at Pastor Tappau's house where Hester named Hota as a witch, Prudence, envious of the minister's daughter who attracted the attention of distinguished ministers and so many people in spite of being at the same age as Prudence herself, wonders how long she might "wriggle before great and godly folk would take so much notice of" her (*CP* 156-57). These quotations offer a hint for understanding why she is suddenly possessed by an evil spirit in the middle of the large crowd, including the distinguished minister Dr Cotton Mather. Duthie gives a similar explanation to the real cause of Prudence's condition: "It has been self-induced out of an exhibitionist desire to attract as much notice as the Tappau children" (*Themes* 143-44).

The urauthor Gaskell's rationalist perspective on Lois's tribulation is further illustrated in her description of Prudence's injury to her arm. On the Sunday morning in March 1692, in stealing away for Hota's hanging site in disregard of Lois's advice to stay at home, the wicked child falls at the door and bruises her arm. In response to her jealous sister Faith's malevolent remark to her ("Take care, another time, how you meddle with a <u>witch</u>'s things" [*CP* 168; emphasis added]), Prudence spitefully accuses her English cousin, calling her "Witch Lois!" (*CP* 168; emphasis added). Interrupting Lois's kind offer to treat her injury, furthermore, Prudence confesses to Faith, "I am afeard of her in very truth" (*CP* 168). In the fatal prayer meeting that afternoon, Prudence makes a false testimony: "<u>Witch</u> Lois, witch Lois, who threw me down only this morning, and turned my arm black and blue," and bares her arm to show her mark (*CP* 173). Lois protests, "I was not near you," yet her defence is reckoned only as "fresh evidence of her diabolical power" (*CP* 173). As with the case of Hota, the Gaskell construct is equivocal about Lois's witchery, because of her plan to retain the supernatural tenor in her depiction of Salem:

> That evil child [...] bade them [the ministers] keep the witch away from her; and, indeed, Prudence was strangely convulsed when once or twice Lois's perplexed and wistful eyes were turned in her directions. Here and there girls, women uttering strange cries, and apparently suffering from the same kind of convulsive fits that which had attacked Prudence, were centres of a group of agitated friends, who muttered much and savagely of witchcraft, and the list which had been taken down only the night before from Hota's own lips. (*CP* 173-74)

The examination above indicates that Prudence's "pathological desire for attention" (Ganz 219) and the bruise on her arm are deliberately inserted to provide a ratiocinative explanation for her sudden possession by demons and her unjust condemnation of Lois. In his psychological analysis of such accusers like Prudence, Upham posits, "[i]t was perhaps their original design to gratify a love of notoriety or of mischief, by creating a sensation and excitement in their neighborhood, or at the worst to wreak their vengeance upon one or two individuals who had offended them" (*LW* 51-52). His rationalist portrayal of the Salem witch terror is reflected in the Gaskell construct's own.

However, Upham's conjecture that the accusers' personal vindictiveness is one of the causes for creating innocent victims is cautiously adopted by the novella's narrator: "How much of malice, distinct, unmistakable personal malice, was mixed up with these accusations, no one can now tell" (*CP* 185). This narrative strategy implies the Gaskell construct's design to keep the bizarreness of the Salem witch turmoil and its ratiocinative explanation in delicate balance. Lois's rectitude and nobility are spotlighted as she steadfastly retains her Christian faith even amidst the satanic chaos surrounding her.

6.3.6. Summary

The Gaskell construct's adoption of Upham's strategy is recognizable not only in the narrative's setting and characters—such as political and social unrest in New England, conflicts within the Salem Church, the description of the witch panic and trials, Lois's virtuous choice of innocent death over dishonourable life, and the records of penitents who admitted their errors for the first time in twenty-one years—, but also in the rationalist interpretation of witchcraft. At the same time, a comparison between the two texts discloses the Gaskell construct's original contributions: Lois's background, Captain Holdernesse, Widow Smith, old Hannah's prophecy, the Hickson family (with the exception of Prudence), their psychological abnormalities, their Indian servant Nattee, the secret bond between Faith and Nattee, and Hugh Lucy's grief and eventual forgiveness.

"[T]he whole of this witchcraft transaction was a delusion, having no foundation whatever but in the imaginations and passions, and [. . .] all the accused both the condemned and the pardoned were entirely innocent" (*LW* 57)—this is Upham's principal position. He attempts to demonstrate it primarily through explicating the witch panic from the rationalist angle. Our survey of the Gaskell construct's manipulation of historical facts confirms that she has taken the same strategies to depict Lois's tragedy. This approach is particularly evident in her depiction of Faith's conspiracy and unrequited love as the backdrop of Hota's execution, and in her portrayal of Prudence's malice and Faith's jealousy as the driving forces behind Lois's unjust condemnation.

On the other hand, the Gaskell construct's constant allusion to the goodness of the supposed witch, who adheres to the teachings of Christ even in sombre and devastating circumstances, is a distinctive aspect of her narrative.[187] Lois's orphanage, the frightening tales of Indians, pirates, and witches introduced at Widow Smith's inn, the realization of old Hannah's prediction, and psychological abnormalities of the Hicksons,[188] all serve to highlight her distressing predicament. The more dire her situation is, the nobler her action appears to the reader's eyes.

Worthy of mention is the Gaskell construct's deliberate preservation of Salem bizarreness, such as the mysterious feasibility of Hota's witchery and the convulsive fits experienced by the accusing girls when gazed at by Lois. Her tactic is effective to lessen the predominance of the rationalist perspective in favour of the mystical, and, ultimately, to stress Lois's Christian virtues which stand out when contrasted with the diabolic forces around her.

The most significant difference between Upham and Gaskell lies in their purposes. Upham reviews the Salem history to emphasize that human errors are the

---

[187] Indeed, Upham honours the integrity of innocent victims, stating, "It is the most melancholy reflection suggested by this awful history, that those only suffered whose principles were so strong, that even the fear of death, combined with the love of life, could not persuade them to utter a falsehood" (*LW* 59). He also notes that "most of them exhibited a remarkably Christian deportment throughout the dreadful scenes they were called to encounter from their arrest to their execution" (*LW* 92). But his references to these victims are fleeting.

[188] Their peculiarity, especially the three children's, is discussed by Bacigalupo (327-29), Bonaparte (116), Brodetsky (85), Duthie (*Themes* 142-43), Easson (*EG* 215), Ganz (219), E. Wright (*Mrs Gaskell* 167-68), and T. Wright (64). Duthie (*Themes* 143), Easson (*EG* 215), and Hopkins (*EG* 257) view the family as an epitome of the extraordinary society.

cause of the witchcraft delusion and to extract moral lessons from the past.[189] In contrast, the urauthor Gaskell centres on delineating the Christian fortitude of her heroine. For her, Upham's historical account serves merely as the background of her story.

6.4. The Structure of the Story

The purpose of this section is to elucidate the Gaskell construct's meaning for her characters through a statistical analysis of their appearance rate and of their involvement in the storyline.

According to the development of the plot, the story can be divided into six—Part 1: Boston Pier (*CP* 105-09; scs. 1-3), Part 2: Widow Smith's Inn (*CP* 109-17; scs. 4-7), Part 3: Hickson Family (*CP* 117-48; scs. 8-44), Part 4: Hota's Hanging (*CP* 148-68; scs. 45-60), Part 5: Lois's Hanging (*CP* 168-90; scs. 61-75), and Part 6: Aftermath (*CP* 190-93; scs. 76-77). Part 1 depicts Lois's arrival at Boston, her meditation on her past, and Captain Holdernesse's practical advice about how to survive in New England. Part 2 centres on the horrifying ambience of New England about which the heroine learns at Widow Smith's inn. Part 3 covers her intermingling with the Hickson family. In the next two Parts, the topic moves on to witch trials, first Hota's prosecution and execution, then Lois's. Part 6 describes Hugh Ralph Lucy's visit to Salem, his inconsolable grief, and his resolution to forgive the repentant twenty-one years after the tragic event.

Part	1. Boston Pier	2. Widow Smith's Inn	3. Hickson Family	4. Hota's Hanging	5. Lois's Hanging	6. Aftermath
Pages	4.5	8.5	32.5	22	23	3
Percent	4.9	9.1	34.5	23.5	24.6	3.2

Table 6.3. Page Allocation in *Lois the Witch*[190]

The investigation into page allocation to each Part is one of the most effective methods for understanding the author's formal scheme. "Table 6.3. Page Allocation in *Lois the Witch*," composed on the data in the scene percentage column of "The

---

189 "It shall also be my purpose to lead your minds into such a train of reflections, as will enable you to draw the lesson it was intended by providence to convey from this sad history; to educe from it important illustrations and suggestions respecting our moral and intellectual nature, to cause light to shine forth from its dark folds and beam upon our path, and to confirm us in a grateful sense of the blessings we enjoy, in the possession of enlightened reason, in the clearer revelation of truth, and in the discoveries of science" (*LW* 118).

190 The total number of parts is 93.5 pages, even though the text consists of 89 pages. The discrepancy arises from our method of counting pages in half-a-page units.

Part		Lois Barclay	Grace	Manasseh	Faith	Prudence
1	active	3	0	0	0	0
	referred	0	1	1	1	1
	subtotal	3	1	1	1	1
	%	42.9	14.3	14.3	14.3	14.3
2	active	4	0	0	0	0
	referred	0	0	0	0	0
	subtotal	4	0	0	0	0
	%	100	0	0	0	0
3	active	32	14	13	17	10
	referred	2	12	12	12	12
	subtotal	34	26	25	29	22
	%	25	19.1	18.4	21.3	16.2
4	active	25	13	10	14	12
	referred	0	6	4	4	4
	subtotal	25	19	14	18	16
	%	27.2	20.7	15.2	19.6	17.4
5	active	0	0	0	0	0
	referred	2	1	0	0	1
	subtotal	2	1	0	0	1
	%	50	25	0	0	25
Total	active	64	27	23	31	22
	referred	4	20	17	17	18
	total	68	47	40	48	40
	%	28	19.3	16.5	19.8	16.5

Table 6.4. Protagonists Focused in *Lois the Witch*

Comprehensive Chronology for *Lois the Witch*,"[191] illustrates 82.6% of the total pages are given to Parts 3-5, and 48.1% to Parts 4-5 dealing with the witch tumult. This outcome reveals that the fiction's focal point is placed on Lois's interaction with the Hickson family and on the delineation of the two alleged witches' misfortunes.[192] Further analyses of the story's design throw the Gaskell construct's meaning into sharper relief.

"Table 6.4. Protagonists Focused in *Lois the Witch*," a device based on the data from the "Main Characters" column of the Comprehensive Chronology, displays

191 See Appendix 1. The table consists of the story's chronology and the result of the inspection of stage shifts and major characters' activity. If a character appears in a particular scene, the corresponding cell is coloured dark grey; if he/she is only referred to by other characters, the cell is tinged light grey. This is a device for taking a bird's-eye view of the structure of the story.
192 Structurally, therefore, "the interim at the Boston lodging house serves as a prologue" (Bacigalupo 322).

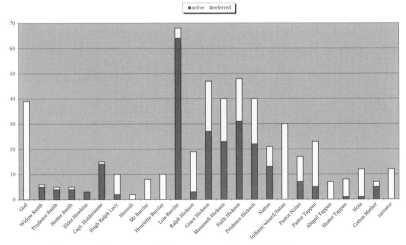

Fig. 6.3. Characters' Frequency of Appearance in *Lois the Witch*

the appearance rate of the protagonist in comparison with the other four main characters. "Fig. 6.3. Characters' Frequency of Appearance in *Lois the Witch*" is the illustration of the data taken from the total boxes of the Chronology. Table 6.4 and Figure 6.3 reveal three distinctive features of the structure of this tale. (a) First, Lois appears most often not merely throughout the whole narrative but also in each individual Part. (b) Second, the Hickson family—Grace, Manasseh, Faith, and Prudence—follows the heroine in terms of the appearance rate. (c) Third, references to God and Satan (including Indians, wizards, witches, and devils) [193] come after the Hicksons in frequency. These three formal aspects, in conjunction with the development of the plot, denote that Lois's intermingling with the four Hicksons under satanic circumstances forms the pivot of the structure, and that the heroine's triumph over the five threats—Grace, Manasseh, Faith, Prudence, and Satan/Indian— is the theme the Gaskell construct aims to convey. The following examination of Lois's goodness should help assess the validity of this assumption.

"Fig. 6.4. Lois's Christian Fortitude in *Lois the Witch*" illustrates the fluctuations in her Christian integrity along with the rising and falling threats posed by her five menaces. One day in May 1691, Lois arrives at Boston Pier (*CP* 105-09; scs. 1-3). She decides to leave her home village in England not merely to fulfill her mother's

---

[193] These four characters are grouped together, as it was the received notion of the 17th century Salem that Satan appears under the disguise of an Indian (*LW* 47). Some New Englanders affirm that Indians are "in league with Satan" (*CP* 115) or "evil powers" (*CP* 126). Indians themselves confess their alliance with Satan (*CP* 126).

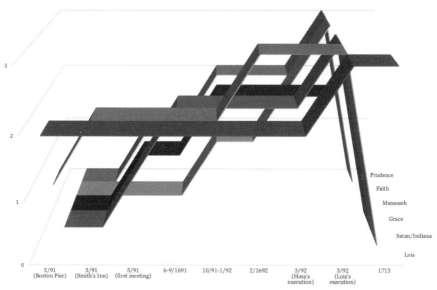

Fig. 6.4. Lois's Christian Fortitude in *Lois the Witch*

wish but also to avoid becoming a source of quarrel between her fiancé, Hugh Ralph Lucy, and his father, a rich miller who disapproves of the match due to her destitute background as a clergyman's daughter. Although she fears that his fiancé's love might wane during their separation, she resolves to leave "all in God's hands" (*CP* 108). This level of discernment places her goodness at the second degree for convenience's sake. At this point, there is no direct reference to Satan except allusions to the mysterious "forests" where Indians are believed to lurk (*CP* 107, 117) and to the "French colonists" in league with Indians (*CP* 109, 114). Hence, the perils of Satan are set at Level 1. No references are made to the other four menaces; accordingly, their levels remain at zero.

At Widow Smith's Inn (*CP* 109-17; scs. 4-7), Lois's goodness is hinted at through the kind and friendly welcome she receives from the proprietor, who has a sure "instinct" for choosing trustworthy guests (*CP* 109). As there is no substantial change in Lois's behaviour, her goodness level remains unchanged. Red Indians' danger and New England's peculiarities discussed at the supper table aggravate the sinister atmosphere surrounding Lois; thus, the Satan/Indians threat goes up by one point. The Hickson family has yet to appear; hence, their threat levels remain at the lowest point.

A couple of days later, the scene shifts from Boston to Salem (*CP* 117-24; scs. 8-14). Soon after their first meeting, momentary animosity arises between Lois and

CHAPTER 6 Lois the Witch: *The Story of Christian Fortitude*   213

her aunt. Lois's defence against Grace's "implied insult to her father" (*CP* 119-20) is approved by Captain Holdernesse, one of the most rational and sensible characters in the story, described as "a healthy norm against which Puritan aberrations can be judged" (J. G. Sharps, *Observation* 322). Another conflict takes place between them during Lois's first interview with her uncle. At her aunt's open criticism of his weakened force of spirit, Lois responds with a flash of indignation, and incurs a stern reprimand from Grace. Although it is righteous anger, Lois quickly seeks to be humble, recognising the troubles her aunt must have suffered until then, and hopes that "this little misunderstanding would soon pass away" (*CP* 122). As a result, the level of Grace's threat is raised to the first degree, while Lois's virtue remains at the second. Although Manasseh protects his English cousin from his mother's intimidation (*CP* 120), his "deep-set eyes furtively watching her" makes Lois "uncomfortable" (*CP* 121),[194] so that the level of his threat rises to the first degree. Prudence's potential danger is hinted at by her "impish antics" (*CP* 120), for imps are generally believed to be under the control of witches (*LW* 48); her threat is thus set at Level 1. Manasseh's prayer for "strength to combat Satan" (*CP* 123) implies the prevalence of the external danger of Satan/Indians; their threat thus stays at its previous level. No mention is made of Faith's peril; hence, her threat level is still at zero.

During the first few months after her arrival (*CP* 124-30; scs. 15-23), that is, approximately from June to September of 1691, Grace and Manasseh, both Puritans, are critical of Lois's Anglicanism: Grace is sarcastic and contemptuous, while Manasseh is simply angry about his cousin's ideas but still more friendly towards her than his mother is (*CP* 125-26). Given these dynamics, it should be reasonable to assume that their threat levels remain unchanged. The narrator's reference to the old forest "full of dreaded and mysterious beasts, and [...] dreaded Indians" and Nattee's tales of the Indian wizards that make "Lois's blood run cold" (*CP* 126) indicate that the external threat of Satan/Indians still looms around the heroine, so that its threat level remains at the previous point. Nattee's arms, "all pinched black and blue by the impish child," make Lois fear Prudence "as of one possessed" (*CP* 127); besides, she is "deceitful, mocking, and so indifferent to the pain or sorrows of others" as to be called "almost inhuman" (*CP* 129). These passages imply her potential hazardousness and foreshadow her eventual downfall to devilish possession. Prudence's peril, accordingly, is set on the former level. Faith, on the other hand, with whom Lois is "the most intimately associated in her uncle's house" (*CP* 128), still poses no threat,

---

194   The danger of his becoming a greater menace is foreshadowed in the phrase: "[h]is eyes thoughtfully fixed on vacancy, as if he saw a vision, or dreamed dreams" (*CP* 123).

keeping her threat level at zero point. Lois tries "in her sweet, simple fashion to cheer her cousin up" when Faith is depressed in gloomy silence (*CP* 128). Her kindness is further stressed in the scene where Faith declares her hatred against Tappau, the first minister of the Salem church: "Lois was sorry for this strong bad feeling; instinctively sorry, for she was loving herself, delighted in being loved, and felt a jar run through her at every sign of want of love in others" (*CP* 129). Her virtue hence remains at Level 2.

The danger surrounding her continues to escalate throughout the autumn and winter of 1691-92 (*CP* 131-48; scs. 24-44). On the night of 31 October, Lois, "in her instinctive, well-intentioned efforts to bring some life and cheerfulness into the monotonous household," shares English girls' innocent Halloween tricks with Faith (*CP* 131), which put Prudence in extreme horror. Startled by her scream, Grace comes into the girls' bedroom, where Prudence implores her mother to take Lois away. Faith pinches her sister harshly to calm her, but Lois "more tenderly" tries "to soothe" her, and reassuringly says "I will stay by thee till thou hast gone off into slumber" (*CP* 132). Despite her tenderness, Prudence calls her "wicked English witch!" (*CP* 132). This scene starkly contrasts Lois's mercifulness with Prudence's maliciousness. Lois's goodness remains consistent, so her virtue stays at Level 2,[195] while the Prudence's threat is elevated to the same level. After the death of Ralph Hickson, Lois's uncle, on the early morning of 1 November,[196] Manasseh's menace towards Lois starts to exhibit substantial increase: despite her categorical rejection, he repeatedly tries to persuade her to accept his proposal, insisting that it is "Lord's will" (*CP* 134-37, 139-40, 144-48). His threat level, hence, rises to Level 2. Meanwhile, perilousness and supernaturalism in Salem are still common: "there was much to tell upon the imagination in those days, in that place, and time. [. . .] [A]t the beginning of the long winter season, such whispered tales, such old temptations and hauntings, and devilish terrors, were supposed to be peculiarly rife" (*CP* 138). The Satan/Indians threat, therefore, is kept at the second level.

One day after "Christmas 1691" (*CP* 140), Grace's threat, together with her son's, is hinted at in the sketch of delightful Lois, who succeeds in leaving Faith and Nolan alone in the keeping-room: "her growing dread of Manasseh's wild ominous

---

195 Another example of Lois's goodness is her recollection of Nolan's prayer to suppress her own momentary anger against Faith (*CP* 144).
196 The early disappearance of Ralph Hickson, the only person in his household that poses no threat to Lois, probably stems from the Gaskell construct's deliberate scheme to exclude him from the prosecution of his beloved niece, and to heighten the reader's attention to her growing vulnerability and helplessness under the increasing danger.

persistence in his suit, <u>her aunt's coldness</u>, her own loneliness, were all forgotten, and she could almost have danced with joy" (*CP* 142; emphasis added). Furthermore, Grace's hostility is suggested in her "supreme contempt" (*CP* 146) for her niece-in-law as well as in her insult: "I value thee not, save as a medicine for Manasseh" (*CP* 147). At the same time, however, her scolding of Manasseh for his proposal to Lois relieves his English cousin from much of the distress caused by his advances (*CP* 147). Hence, the level of Grace's peril remains at the previous point. Faith, who has been described as having "a warm heart, hidden away somewhere under her moody exterior" (*CP* 133), begins to feel jealous of Lois for receiving more attention from Nolan than she attracts (*CP* 144, 147). Her "vehemence of unrequited love" (*CP* 147) is somewhat a symptom of her emotional instability. The degree of her threat rises to Level 1 here.

The peril of Satan/Indians jumps up to the top level in one day towards the end of February 1692 (*CP* 148-51; scs. 45-46) when Grace brings to her family the news that Tappau's two daughters have been possessed (*CP* 149). Nolan's evening talk about an elder's experience of kicking a mouse into crying out "like a human creature in pain" (*CP* 151) is introduced to amplify the sense of terror. Indeed, "all the family" huddles "together in silent fear" on that night (*CP* 151). Faith's harbouring jealousy is intimated in the line: "Faith and Lois sat with arms entwined, as in days before the former had become jealous of the latter" (*CP* 151). Prudence's acute interest in "the creatures that were abroad, and the ways in which they afflicted others" (*CP* 151) portends her eventual possession which will occur in the ensuing month. There are no specific references to Lois's goodness or to the threats of Grace and Manasseh in this section. Therefore, no changes are made to the levels of the other five factors, except for the increase in the Satan/Indians threat.

From early March 1692 to the morning of Hota's execution on a Sunday later that month (*CP* 151-68; scs. 47-60), the levels of all four menaces remain unchanged, except for Faith's, which goes up. One of the most succinct descriptions of the prevalence of Satan's peril appears in Lois's following remark to Faith: "this country is worse than ever England was, even in the days of Master Matthew Hopkinson, the witch-finder. I grow frightened of every one" (*CP* 153). Thus, the menace of Satan/Indians remains at the highest level. During this period, more detailed delineation than ever is given to Lois's Christian faith. For example, she rebukes Faith's defence of Nattee's retaliatory use of supernatural powers by alluding to Matt. 5.44: "we are told to pray for them that despitefully use us, and to do good to them that persecute us" (*CP* 154). It echoes the biblical call for "charity for enemies," one of the story's key themes, embodied in the Lord's prayer: "forgive us our debts, as we forgive our debtors" (Matt. 6.12). Her Christian humility is also underlined: "I often do very wrong, but, perhaps, I might have done worse, if the holy form had not been observed" (*CP* 154). Her compassion extends even to Hota, a supposed accomplice of Satan: "she remembered the tender spirit of the Saviour, and allowed herself to fall into pity" (*CP* 159). In reply to Nolan's request to pray for the Indian servant, Lois confesses that she has been doing so since the previous night, adding her Christian belief: "I would not have her entirely God-forsaken" (*CP* 164). Her "pure, grave face" soothes the pastor's disquieted soul (*CP* 164-65). She expresses her compassion even towards hazardous Manasseh by grieving "for his depressed state of mind, anxious to soothe and comfort him" (*CP* 161). These instances of Lois's Christian virtues keep her goodness at Level 2. The increase of Prudence's threat is hinted at when Lois shrinks from "the cruel, eager face of the young girl" who is eager to see Hota hanged (*CP* 160), and also when she shudders at the shout of the impish American cousin: "Witch Lois! Witch Lois! [. . .] I'm afeard of her in very truth" (*CP* 168). The menace of paroxysmal Manasseh is brought to light in the scenes where Lois runs away from him "like a panting, hunted creature" (*CP* 162) and where his mental illness is disclosed to be the cause for his prophetic revelations (*CP* 161, 162, 166). The danger of Prudence and Manasseh is serious enough to keep them at the second level. Out of burning jealousy, Faith calls Lois a "witch" for the first time (*CP* 168), when her threat reaches Level 2. Grace's level of hazardousness remains at Level 2, since she gradually shows signs of reconciling herself to the idea of marrying her son to Lois (*CP* 161).

During five days after Hota's execution, the narrative shifts focus to Lois's own prosecution and execution (*CP* 168-90; scs. 61-75). Prudence is possessed by the devilish spirit in the midst of Cotton Mather's sermon, and names her English cousin as her torturer (*CP* 171-73). Lois, astounded and tongue-tied, attempts to defend herself by asking her aunt for help. The "stern, harsh, unloving" Grace, however, returns a cold reply: "It is for God to judge whether thou are a witch, or not. Not for me" (*CP* 173). Lois then looks at Faith for assistance, but learns immediately that "no good word" is "to be expected from her gloomy face and averted eyes" (*CP* 173). As Ehrenpreis astutely observes, "a complex blend of fear, jealousy, and spite drives the members of her foster family to accuse" and "abandon" Lois (99). At this point, the threats of Grace and her daughters reach the highest level. Manasseh's perilousness is retained at Level 2, because he tries to protect Lois by arguing against Cotton Mather (*CP* 175). In an effort to save him and her family from disgrace, Grace conceals his perennial insanity and suicide attempt from the congregation, and comes to endorse the belief that both Manasseh and Prudence have fallen prey to Lois's supposed witchcraft (*CP* 176-77). His mental disorder, accordingly, is used to intensify Grace's role as a threat to our heroine. The collective menace of the Hickson family is articulated by Lois in her passing recollection in the dungeon: "every angry thought against her neighbour, against the impertinences of Prudence, against the overbearing authority of her aunt, against the persevering crazy suit of Manasseh, the indignation [...] at Faith's injustice" (*CP* 178). This reflection highlights how deeply the hostility of her foster family has contributed to her tragic situation.

Despite "the open accusation of Prudence and the withheld justification of her aunt and Faith," however, Lois demonstrates remarkable compassion in her feeling that she can still love them (*CP* 179). In the examination scene, she obeys her justices' directions with "the wondering docility of a child" (*CP* 180), and bears physical tortures while reciting "verses of the Psalms" which are "expressive of trust in God" (*CP* 181). Her "indomitable spirit" (Saracino 213) is powerfully conveyed when, urged by the elders to admit her guilt so that they can spare her life, she responds, "I must choose death with a quiet conscience, rather than life to be gained by a lie" (*CP* 184). Her kindness is notably contrasted with Grace's cold-heartedness in the scene of her aunt's unexpected call at her cell: "Grace did not know how often her want of loving-kindness had pierced the tender heart of the stranger under her roof; nor did Lois remember it against her now. Instead, Lois's memory was filled with grateful thoughts of how much that might have been left undone, by a less conscientious person, her aunt had done for her" (*CP* 186-87). Her Christian fortitude reaches its peak when she comforts Nattee, her inmate, by recounting her "the marvellous and sorrowful story of one who died on the cross for us and for our sakes" (*CP* 189). The continuous emphasis on Lois's Christian virtue elevates her goodness to the highest level, Level 3.

In the final phase depicting the aftermath of the Salem witch panic (*CP* 190-93; scs. 76-77), it becomes clear that the witchcraft panic was a delusion: Both Prudence and Grace express their deep regret for the roles in the persecution of the innocent girl. Hence, their threat level drops to zero. Only Lois's goodness preserves its highest point, because it is her pious Christian faith that inspires Hugh Ralph Lucy to forgive the repentant. This ending underscores Lois's enduring influence even after death.

Some may argue that my tracing Lois's Christian fortitude against her five threats throughout the plot contains a tinge of subjectivity, implying that the fluctuations in each bar of Fig. 6.4 could show minor variations depending on the perspective of the investigator. I acknowledge the potential for such variations. Nonetheless, I maintain that the overall shapes of the six elements—a steady ascent towards the climax—should remain consistent, because what is illuminated in this analysis is the core structure of this short fiction. That is, Lois is delineated as a virtuous, morally steadfast character, or "an ideal" shared by "all of Gaskell's good young women" (Maureen Teresa Reddy, *Elizabeth Gaskell's Short Fiction* 45), from the outset of the story, and her Christian fortitude gradually intensifies as the levels of her menaces go up. The gradual elevation of both Lois's virtue and the danger posed by her environment creates a central tension that drives the narrative. The authorial meaning of making the Hickson family a persistent menace to Lois is reinforced by the narratorial statement, which underscores Lois's struggle to find acceptance in the household: "It was hard up-hill work for Lois to win herself a place in this family" (*CP* 124). Despite her efforts, her value seems only recognized by her uncle: "To him she could give pleasure, but apparently to no one else in that household" (*CP* 125). This dynamic amplifies the sense of isolation and adversity Lois faces, which the Gaskell construct uses to further showcase her protagonist's unwavering Christian integrity amidst increasing hardships.

6.5. Conclusion

Upham's fundamental position on the witch prosecution is that it is "the effect of deliberate design" (*LW* 104). The investigation into the Gaskell construct's handling of his recount of the witchcraft delusion reveals both her affinity with and her divergence from this Salem minister's perspective. While Upham attributes the witchcraft delusion to a calculated intent, the urauthor Gaskell construes the catastrophe through the ratiocinative lens, with the stress on the innocent girl's integrity navigating frightening circumstances. Our examination of Lois's evolving relationships with the five central characters along the plot development sheds light on her unflinching faith in God: her goodness is depicted from the beginning to the end, and, as the threat around her intensifies, so does the prominence of her Christian fortitude.[197]

Ultimately, our comparative study of the story with its source and our enquiry into its structure produce the same result: Lois's Christian virtue is at the heart of the narrative. We cannot but conclude, therefore, that the true meaning of Gaskell's

---

[197] This contrastive form has been noticed by at least two critics: "The mass hysteria and inhumanity of the inhabitants of Salem form a poignant contrast with the well-balanced, warm-hearted young English girl, as her death draws inexorably nearer" (Brodetsky 85); "[s]he is the contrast to those around her, the decent person who is perplexed, frightened, but whose faith and upbringing are strong enough to resist the taint" (E. Wright, *Mrs Gaskell* 170).

work lies not in the depiction of the atrocious hazardousness of the mass hysteria but in the heroine's steadfast fortitude amidst overwhelming adversity. Ward's interpretation of *Lois the Witch* is close to ours, as both emphasize Lois's Christian virtue. The critic observes that "Mrs Gaskell cannot forget where all contradictions are reconciled, and all sorrows healed; for Lois's true lover is most true to her, and to the spirit in which she suffered, when he prays for forgiveness for those that brought her to her cruel death" (introduction, vol. 7 xix). This note highlights the Gaskell construct's focus on forgiveness and redemption even amid the profound injustice Lois endures.

CONCLUSION

Our statistical analysis of the structures of Gaskell's five works reveals her author construct's formal devices which have been overlooked by previous critics.

In *Mary Barton*, the appearance rate of John Barton is lower than that of his daughter Mary and her lover Jem Wilson. This outcome implies that less focus is placed on John's struggle against industrial masters and more on Mary's romance. The real Gaskell as person may have intended to depict the industrial conflict, but what the Gaskell construct is actually concerned with is primarily Mary's love.

In *Ruth*, the Gaskell construct has three distinct objectives: (a) to condemn seducers of their irresponsibility, (b) to offer the seduced a chance for redemption, and (c) to awaken Victorian society to Samaritan duties. The Bellinghams, the Bensons, and the Bradshaws, who personify "shallowness," "conscience," and "Pharisaism," serve as tools to achieve her purposes, which are fully realized in the novel's final three chapters. If Ruth's story ended without her death, the urauthor's purposes would be accomplished only partially. Therefore, Ruth's martyrdom is not her misstep but the logical conclusion of the narrative.

In *North and South*, the character who comes after Margaret Hale in the appearance rate is not John Thornton, the mill-owner, but her father Richard Hale. This result reveals Mr Hale's dual role of mediation between Thornton and his daughter Mary, and between Thornton and the trade unionist Nicholas Higgins. This authorial contrivance, along with the analysis of topographical shifts and the plot development, throws into sharp relief the Gaskell construct's goal of advancing both political and romantic narratives in parallel.

A digital humanities approach was employed to uncover the authorial meaning for *The Life of Charlotte Brontë*. A topic-modelling analysis of Christian themes in the biography reveals the Gaskell construct's emphasis on Charlotte Brontë's staunch Christian faith nurtured in her home village Haworth. The MALLET and AntConc analyses of the keywords further illuminate the biography's overarching structure, which presents Charlotte's life against the backdrop of Haworth. The survey also highlights the Gaskell construct's portrayal of the Brontë family's belief in the immortality of the soul and Charlotte's conviction in eternal life.

In *Lois the Witch*, the comparison of the fiction with its source material reveals the Gaskell construct's meaning to construe the Salem witchcraft from a rationalist perspective with a stress on Lois's integrity under terrifying circumstances. In addition, the analysis of the progress of Lois's relationship with the five key characters throughout the plot discloses her unwavering faith in God. Thus, the meaning of the

Gaskell construct is presumably to describe Lois's fortitude rather than the external horror surrounding the innocent victim.

As long as critics ignore the key structural components and fail to take a bird's-eye view of the whole in forming their interpretations, the current situation of the literary arena, or the "critical anarchy" where subjectivism predominates, will remain unresolved. One subjective reading will be superseded by another sooner or later, but interpretation founded on objective evidence will not. The outcomes obtained through the arguments above, concerning the Gaskell construct's structural schemes and authorial meanings, should survive for the benefit of "subsequent critics" (Kroeber, *Styles* 180). If there is one thing I can boast in this study, it would be my commitment to the "interpreter's degree of concern with being faithful to authorial intent" (Irwin, *Intentionalist Interpretation* 32).

To conclude this study, I would like to highlight three principles of Gaskell's fiction that have emerged so far.

(a) **Character prominence and appearance rate**: The characters' appearance rate rises in parallel with the increase of the significance of their assigned roles; to put it in another way, a character who appears to be the main protagonist exhibits the highest rate of appearance.[198]

(b) **Persistent Christian themes**: God is a constant presence in all of Gaskell's novels. Her frequent incorporation of Christian messages, moral teachings, biblical references, and characters' prayers to God, underscores her identity as a fundamentally Christian writer.[199]

(c) **Narrative technique evolution**: The insertion of narrator's comments becomes less frequent in her later novels than in her earlier ones; this change probably implies a maturation of the Gaskell construct's narrative technique and a greater reliance on the narrative itself to convey meaning.[200]

This scientific approach to fiction started from my reservations about the prevalence of subjectivism in the current critical domain and from my quest for the absolute interpretation of a novel. The best objective interpretation of a text should be attained if analysis is focused on its structure that remains physically unchanged once a text is produced. The most effective formal elements should be time, charac-

---

[198] This criterion applies to all novels of Jane Austen without exception (Kroeber, *Styles* 234).

[199] The appearance rate of God is as follows: 33.5% in *Mary Barton* (86 out of 257 scenes), 33.6% in *Ruth* (81 out of 241), 12.6% in *North and South* (57 out of 451), 20.3% in *Sylvia's Lovers* (88 out of 434), and 6.9% in *Wives and Daughters* (32 out of 463).

[200] The appearance rate of the narrator is as follows: 24.9% in *Mary Barton* (64 out of 257 scenes), 12.9% in *Ruth* (31 out of 241), 0.7% in *North and South* (3 out of 451), 3.0% in *Sylvia's Lovers* (13 out of 434), and 3.2% in *Wives and Daughters* (15 out of 463).

ters, and place, all essential to every realist fiction. Since my ultimate goal is to detect the authorial meaning in Gaskell's entire body of fiction, including *Cranford*, *Sylvia's Lovers*, *Cousin Phillis*, and *Wives and Daughters*, through statistical analysis of their structures, this dissertation serves only as an interim report.

APPENDIX 1 Comprehensive Chronologies

The Comprehensive Chronology for *Mary Barton* (1848)

Legend:
- active
- referred
- non-appearance
- dead
- Mary's adventurous days (scs 120–210) are highlighted in grey.

Locations:
- A: Alice's house
- B: Barton's house
- C: Carsons' house on Dunham Street
- D: Davenport's cellar on Berry Street
- GHF: Green Heys Fields
- L: Legh's house
- Lv: Liverpool
- S: on the street
- W: Wilson's house at Ancoats
- J: narrator's comment on John
- M: narrator's comment on Mary
- N: narrator's neutral comment

Part	Chapter	Year (page)	Month (page)	Day (page)	Time Inferred — Number	Range	Length	Percent	Stage	Mary Barton	Mrs Barton	Esther	George Wilson	Jane Wilson	Jem	Alice	Will	Margaret	Job Legh	Mrs Davenport	Sally Leadbitter	Harry	John Carson	John Barton	narrator	Brief Summary of Each Scene (Boxes of important events are coloured.)
I	1	1834	5	one day (2)	1	1–3	2.5	0.53	GHF																J	Workmen and their family on Green Heys Fields
I	1	1834	5	one day (2)	2	4–5	1.5	0.32																	N	Barton and Wilson meet at the stile.
I	1	1834	5	one day (2)	3	5–9	4.5	0.96																		Barton and Wilson talk about missing Esther.
I	1	1834	5	one day (2)	4	9–11	1.5	0.32																		Jem (17) snatches a kiss from Mary (13).
I	2	1834	5	one day (2)	5	11–12	1.5	0.32	B																	On the way to Barton's home
I	2	1834	5	one day (2)	6	12–15	2.5	0.53																	N	Preparation for the tea at the Bartons
I	2	1834	5	one day (2)	7	15–16	2.0	0.43																		Mary invites Alice to the tea.
I	3	1834	5	one day (2)	8	16–18	1.5	0.32	B																	A tea-party at the Bartons
I	3	1834	5	one day (2)	9	18	0.5	0.11																		Mrs Barton's kind words to Alice
I	3	1834	5	one day (2)	10	18–19	0.5	0.11																		Barton asks his neighbour help for his wife in labour.
I	3	1834	5	one day (2)	11	19	0.5	0.11																		Barton calls for the doctor.
I	3	1834	5	one day (2)	12	19–22	3.0	0.64	B																	The death of Mrs Barton
I	3	1837 (26)			13	22–26	3.5	0.75																	J	Barton becomes an active trades' unionist.
I	4	1838 (28)	winter	one day (30)	14	26–28	2.5	0.53																	M	Mary (16) is apprenticed to Miss Simmonds.
I	4	1838	winter	one day (30)	15	28–30	1.0	0.21																		Mary, Esther, Barton, George and Jem Wilsons
I	4	1838	winter	one day (30)	16	30	0.5	0.11																		Mary's acceptance of Alice's invitation for tea
I	4	1838	winter	one day (30)	17	30–31	1.0	0.21	A																N	Alice's preparation at home
I	4	1838	winter	one day (30)	18	32	1.0	0.21																	N	Mary's first meeting with Margaret
I	4	1838	winter	one day (30)	19	32–37	4.5	0.96																		Alice's talk about her old days including Will
I	4	1838	winter	one day (30)	20	37–40	2.5	0.53	L																J	Margaret sings "The Oldham Weaver."
I	4	1838	winter	one day (30)	21	40	0.5	0.11	L																	Job Legh's return home
I	5	1838	winter	one day (30)	22	40–42	1.5	0.32																	N	Weavers full of scientific knowledge
I	5	1838	winter	one day (30)	23	42–45	3.0	0.64																		Mary's first meeting with Job Legh
I	5	1838	winter	one day (30)	24	45	0.5	0.11	B																	Mary tells her father about her evening visit.

226

Brief Summary	narrator	Barton	Carson	Harry	Sally	Mrs D	Job	MJ	Will	Alice	Jem	JW	GW	Esther	Mrs B	Mary	God	Stage	Percent	Length	Range	Number	Day	Month	Year	Chapter	Part
Mary's relationship with Job, Margaret, Harry, & Jem	M																		0.32	1.5	45–47	25		winter			
Jem's love for Mary supported by Barton																		B	0.21	1.0	47–48	26	one evening			5	
Black frost and bleak east wind																			0.11	0.5	48	27		2 (48)			
Margaret asks Mary for helping skirts making.																			0.21	1.0	48–49	28	one evening				
Mary and Margaret's talk over stitching																			0.53	2.5	49–51	29					
Mary knows Margaret may become blind.																		B	0.53	2.5	51–54	30					
The two girls leave for the burning Carsons' mill.																			0.21	1.0	54	31	one evening				
Jem saves his father from the fire at Carsons' mill.	M																	C	1.6	7.5	54–62	32			1839 (97)		I
Margaret tells Barton Jem's heroic rescue.	N																	B	0.11	0.5	62	33					
Fire's influence on masters and workers	J																		0.32	1.5	63–65	34				6	
George Wilson's visit to Barton for money																			0.21	1.0	65–66	35	one evening				
Wilson and Barton help the starving Davenports.	J																	D	1.81	8.5	66–70	36		3 (64)			
Barton goes to a druggist's shop.	J																		0.21	1.0	70–71	37					
Wilson and Barton help the Davenports.																		D	0.64	3.0	71–74	38					
Wilson's visit to the Carsons' house																			0.43	2.0	74–76	39					
Comfortable life of the Carsons																		C	0.32	1.5	76–78	40					
Wilson asks John Carson for an infirmary order.																			0.21	1.0	78–79	41	next day				
The death of Ben Davenport																		D	0.21	1.0	79–80	42					
Mary comforts Mrs Davenport.																			0.11	0.5	81–82	43					
Mary begins to make a mourning gown for Mrs D.																			0.11	0.5	82	44	a few days later				
Ben Davenport's funeral	J																	D	0.11	0.5	82–83	45					
Mrs Davenport's recovery																			0.11	0.5	83–84	46					
The Wilson twins become ill.	N																	B	0.21	1.0	84	47	one day	3 or 4		7	
Margaret tells Mary the state of the Wilsons.																			0.11	0.5	84–85	48					
Mary's visit to Jane Wilson; the twins' deaths																			0.43	2.0	85–87	49					
Alice tells Mary God is against planning.																		W	0.21	1.0	87–88	50					
Jem's expression of gratitude vexes Mary.																			0.43	2.0	88–90	51	next morning				
Mary's reasons for preferring Harry Carson to Jem																		B	0.53	2.5	90–92	52					
Mary's comfort catches hold of Jem's memory.																			0.11	0.5	92	53					
Jem on his way to Barton's house																			0.11	0.5	93	54	one Sunday (93)	4		8	
Mary leaves Jem for her room upstairs.	M																	B	0.21	1.0	93–94	55					
Jem is left alone to listen to Barton's talk of politics.																			0.32	1.5	94–96	56					
Alienation between the classes deepens.																			0.32	1.5	96–97	57		spring			
Barton, a delegate to the Chartist petition																			0.21	1.0	97–98	58		5			
Neighbours' demands on Parliament	J																	B	0.64	3.0	98–101	59	one night				

APPENDIX 1 Comprehensive Chronologies 227

Brief Summary	narrator	Barton	Carson	Harry	Sally	Mrs D	Job	MJ	Will	Alice	Jem	JW	GW	Esther	Mrs B	Mary	God	Stage	Percent	Length	Range	Number	Day	Month	Year	Chapter	Part
Barton and Mary talk about Jane Wilson.		■														■			0.21	1.0	101–02	60	same as above	5	1839 (97)	8	I
Mary's resolution not to meet Harry	N															■			0.43	2.0	102–04	61	next morning				
George Wilson's death; Mary avoids meeting Harry.													■						0.64	3.0	104–07	62	one evening			9	
Margaret enters; Sally leaves.					■														0.11	0.5	107	63		7			
Margaret's debut as a singer								■											0.85	4.0	107–11	64					
Barton's return home from London		■																	0.43	2.0	111–13	65	next evening				
Mary asks Job to come and cheer her father.							■									■			0.11	0.5	113–14	66					
Barton's unsuccessful petition in London		■																	0.64	3.0	114–17	67					
Job's experiences in London							■												2.35	11.0	117–27	68					
Job reads Bamford's poem.							■												0.53	2.5	127–29	69					
Mary copies the poem on a valentine sheet from Jem.																■			0.11	0.5	129	70	next day (129)				
Deepening distress		■																B	0.75	3.5	130–33	71					
Distress surrounding Mary																■			0.43	2.0	133–35	72		1	1840	10	
Barton opium-addicted; desperate trade unionists		■																B	0.21	1.0	135–36	73					
Barton tells Mary to visit Jane next day.																■		W	0.11	0.5	136	74	one evening				
Mary's visit to Jane Wilson																■			1.28	6.0	136–42	75	next day				
Mary's thought about Jem and Harry																■			0.11	0.5	142	76					
Mary attends a trades' union meeting.																■		S	0.11	0.5	142–43	77					
Esther's warning against Mary is unheard by Barton.		■												■					0.32	1.5	143–45	78					
Esther's prayer for saving Mary														■					0.11	0.5	145	79					
Esther is imprisoned.														■					0.11	0.5	145	80					
Barton searches for Esther in vain.		■																B	0.21	1.0	146–47	81					
Barton upbraids Mary for the loss of Jem.		■														■			0.32	1.5	147–48	82				11	
Jem determines to offer Mary a proposal of marriage.	M										■								0.11	0.5	148–49	83	one day				
Mary rejects Jem's proposal of marriage.											■					■		B	0.53	2.5	149–51	84		2			
Mary discovers Jem is the man she truly loves.	M															■			0.53	2.5	151–54	85					
Mary serves irritable Barton breakfast.		■														■			0.11	0.5	154	86	next day				
Mary's determination to avoid Harry																■			0.21	1.0	154–55	87	two days				
Sally's visit to Mary's house					■											■			0.32	1.5	155–56	88					
Sally takes Mary to the meeting spot.					■											■		B	0.11	0.5	156–57	89	one evening				
Harry's vicious intentions are revealed.				■															0.75	3.5	157–61	90					
Harry tells Sally he won't give up Mary.				■	■														0.21	1.0	161–62	91					
Harry and Jem's contrastive approaches to Mary				■							■					■		S	0.32	1.5	162–64	92				12	
Barton uses Mary's money for opium.		■																	0.11	0.5	164	93					

228

	Brief Summary
94	Mary confides her love for Jem to Margaret.
95	Margaret gives Mary a sovereign.
96	Barton and Mary enjoy an extravagant meal.
97	Mary's visit to Mrs Wilson proud of Jem
98	Alice's return from the post-office
99	Will Wilson's appearance
100	Will drops in on Mary to take her to Job Legh's.
101	Will entertains his new friends with his tales.
102	Mary's talk with Alice
103	Mary's worries about Barton, Harry, and Jem
104	Esther's release from prison
105	Esther's confession of her past to Jem
106	Esther's pleading with Jem to save Mary
107	Jem walks home downcast.
108	Jem enters his house downcast.
109	Jem's resolution to do the duty of a brother
110	Barton becomes a Chartist as well as a Communist.
111	Mutual distrust between masters and workers
112	Harry will not give up Mary, who cannot see Jem yet.
113	Mary notices Will's love for Margaret.
114	Jem's search for Harry Carson
115	The scuffle between Harry and Jem
116	Masters waiting for the interview with workmen
117	Negotiations between employers and employees
118	Harry draws a caricature of worker delegates.
119	Workers' assembly; Barton's speech; assassin chosen
120	Will's farewell visit to Mary
121	Barton comes home; Will leaves for Liverpool.
122	Barton is restless and fierce.
123	Job Legh's interest in Barton's Glasgow mission
124	Job Legh's criticism of the Trade Union
125	Barton leaves for Glasgow.
126	Barton helps an Irish child.
127	Job talks to Mary about Margaret's walking alone.
128	Margaret comes; Alice's paralytic stroke

	narrator	Barton	Carson	Harry	Sally	Mrs D	Job	MJ	Will	Alice	Jem	JW	GW	Esther	Mrs B	Mary	God
94																✓	
98	N																
99																	
100	N																
101																	
103	M																
104	N																
109	J																
110	J																
115	M																
116	J																

Stage	Percent	Length	Range	Number	Day	Month	Year	Chapter	Part
B	0.64	3.0	164–67	94	4			12	I
B	0.21	1.0	167–68	95					
	0.11	0.5	168–69	96					
W	0.43	2.0	169–70	97	5			13	
	0.21	1.0	170–71	98					
	0.21	1.0	171–72	99					
B	0.32	1.5	173–74	100					
L	1.60	7.5	174–82	101	9 (173)				
	0.21	1.0	182	102					
B	0.43	2.0	182–83	103		3	1840	14	
	0.75	3.5	184–86	104					
S	0.75	3.5	186–89	105	10				
	0.11	0.5	190–93	106					
	0.11	0.5	193	107					
W	0.53	2.5	194	108	11				
J	0.53	2.5	194–97	109					
J	0.75	3.5	197–200	110			15		
	0.21	1.0	200–04	111					
	0.21	1.0	204	112					
S	0.21	1.0	204–06	113	14 (204)				
	0.96	4.5	206–07	114					
hotel	0.43	2.0	207–11	115	15				
	0.53	2.5	211–13	116					
	0.21	1.0	214–16	117			16		
	1.49	7.0	216–17	118	16 Tues				
	1.07	5.0	217–24	119					II
B	0.11	0.5	224–29	120					
	0.21	1.0	229	121					
	0.21	1.0	229–30	122					
	0.21	1.0	230–31	123	18 Thurs (224, 251, 273, 300)			17	
	0.11	0.5	231–32	124					
S	0.64	3.0	232–33	125					
B	0.32	1.5	233	126					
			233–34	127					
			234–36	128					

APPENDIX 1 Comprehensive Chronologies 229

Brief Summary	narrator	Barton	Carson	Harry	Sally	Mrs D	Job	MJ	Will	Alice	Jem	JW	GW	Esther	Mrs B	Mary	God	Stage	Percent	Length	Range	Number	Day	Month	Year	Chapter	Part
Everything seems going wrong for Mary.																▓		B	0.11	0.5	236	129				17	
Three Miss Carsons' talk about Harry																			0.64	3.0	237-40	130	18 Thurs			18	
N Harry's body is brought home.				✕														C	0.53	2.5	240-42	131					
John Carson knows the death of his son.			▓																0.43	2.0	242-44	132					
John Carson sees his son's dead face.			▓																0.43	2.0	244-46	133					
Carson's inquiry into the cause of Harry's death			▓																0.21	1.0	246-47	134					
Carson comforts his wife in deep sorrow.			▓																0.43	2.0	247-49	135					
Carson's talk with the superintendent			▓																0.11	0.5	249-50	136					
J Carson swears vengeance on the murderer.																			0.21	1.0	250-51	137		3	1840		II
N Mary falls into a sleep at dawn.																▓		B	0.11	0.5	251	138	19 Fri (250)			19	
Mary knows Margaret has gone to Wilson's at Job's.																		L	0.11	0.5	251	139					
Mary hastens to follow Margaret's steps.																			0.21	1.0	251-52	140					
M Mary enters Wilson's house.																		W	0.53	2.5	252-53	141					
Mary sees Alice dreaming of her childhood scenes.										▓									0.64	3.0	253-55	142					
Mary hears Harry's death from Sally.					▓														0.32	1.5	255-58	143					
N Jem Wilson is detected as a suspected murderer.											▓							W	0.21	1.0	258-59	144					
A disguised policeman's visit to Jane												▓						S	0.53	2.5	259-61	145					
Jem's arrest											▓							W	0.11	0.5	261-62	146					
Jane Wilson knows her son's arrest.												▓						S	0.75	3.5	262-64	147			20 Sat (300)	20	
Mary in sorrow, desolation, and anger																▓			0.85	4.0	264-65	148					
Mary hastens to the Wilsons' house.																▓			0.32	1.5	265-66	149					
Mary knows Jem is in gaol, blamed for flirtation.												▓							0.11	0.5	266-69	150					
Mary gives some food to a hungry Italian boy.																▓		B	0.21	1.0	269-70	151				21	
Mary's self-reproach, and anxious sympathy for Jem																▓			1.17	5.5	270-72	152					
Mary's dream of her mother																▓			1.28	6.0	272	153					
N Mary falls into the arms of Esther.														▓		▓			0.85	4.0	272-73	154					
Esther's motive in seeking her niece														▓				L	0.32	1.5	273-79	155				22	
N Esther's midnight interview with Mary														▓		▓			0.21	1.0	279-85	156					
N The scrap of paper reveals the true murderer.																▓			0.75	3.5	285-89	157					
Mary goes out with a jug to take water.																▓		W	0.53	2.5	289-90	158					
N Mary determines to ask for Job's help.																			0.11	0.5	290-91	159					
N Mary asks Job for advice about saving Jem's life.						▓										▓			0.11	0.5	291-95	160					
Mary's interview with Jane Wilson												▓				▓				3.5	295-97	161					
Mary goes upstairs to see the dying Alice.										▓						▓				2.5	297-98	162					
To prove Jem's innocence is Mary's first priority.																▓		S		0.5	298	163					

230

Brief Summary	narrator	Barton	Carson	Harry	Sally	Mrs D	Job	MJ	Will	Alice	Jem	JW	GW	Esther	Mrs B	Mary	God	Stage	Percent	Length	Range	Number	Day	Month	Year	Chapter	Part
To save Jem without involving Barton's suspicion	M																	B	0.53	2.5	298–301	164	20 Sat			23	II
Mary receives a subpoena.	N																		0.32	1.5	301–02	165					
Mary asks Job about the subpoena she received.																		L	0.43	2.0	302–04	166					
Margaret begins to love Mary again and helps her.																			0.64	3.0	304–07	167					
Mary and Margaret during Job's visit to a lawyer																			0.75	3.5	307–10	168					
Job's arrangement about a lawyer for Jem																			0.32	1.5	310–12	169					
Mary determines to inquire after Jem.																			0.11	0.5	312–13	170					
Jane also receives a subpoena; Alice is unconscious.	N																	B	0.53	2.5	313–15	171				24	
Mary alone looks after the sleeping Alice and Jane.	N																		0.32	1.5	315–17	172					
Mary looks at Alice and Jane.	J																		0.21	1.0	317–18	173					
Mary tells Alice her plans for seeking out Will.	M																	W	0.32	1.5	318–19	174					
Mary fetches the doctor for Alice and Jane.																			0.11	0.5	319–20	175					
Mary wins the doctor's consent about J's unfit travel.																			0.43	2.0	320–22	176		3	1840		
Mary tells Job her fear about Jane's strength.																			0.11	0.5	322	177	21 Sun (317)				
Mary returns to her home.																		L	0.11	0.5	323	178					
Sally's unsympathetic visit																			0.43	2.0	323–25	179				25	
Mary's belief in Jem's innocence																		B	0.21	1.0	325–26	180					
Sally and Job with mutual looks of dislike																			0.11	0.5	326–27	181					
Job tells Mary Mr Bridgenorth's opinion.																			0.11	0.5	327	182					
Jane's determination to go to the trial																		W	0.75	3.5	327–31	183					
Margaret: "Let Mary go find Will."	N																	L	0.21	1.0	331–32	184					
On the train, talks of two lawyers' clerks about the case																			0.43	2.0	332–34	185				26	
In Liverpool, Mary knows Will sailed this morning.																			0.43	2.0	334–36	186				27	
Mary knows she may be able to catch Will.																			0.64	3.0	336–39	187	22 Mon (332)				
Mary sits in a boat to catch the *John Cropper*.	N																	Liverpool	1.17	5.5	339–45	188					
Mary's message is heard by Will.																			1.28	6.0	345–51	189				28	
Ben Sturgis takes Mary home.																			0.53	2.5	351–53	190					
Jem's attorney inclines to think him innocent.																			0.85	4.0	354–58	191				29	
Job finds Mary's action of the day at Will's lodging.																			0.43	2.0	358–60	192					
Job explains the current situation to Jane.																			0.32	1.5	360–62	193					
Job's consultation with Mr Bridgenorth, the lawyer																			0.11	0.5	362	194				30	
Job visits Mrs Jones, Will's landlady.																			0.21	1.0	362–63	195					
Job deceives Jane to assure her of her son's safety.																			0.43	2.0	363–65	196					

APPENDIX 1 Comprehensive Chronologies 231

Brief Summary	narrator	Barton	Carson	Harry	Sally	Mrs D	Job	MJ	Will	Alice	Jem	JW	GW	Esther	Mrs B	Mary	God	Stage	Percent	Length	Range	Number	Day	Month	Year	Chapter	Part
Job returns to his lodging.																			0.11	0.5	365	197	22 Mon		1840	31	II
Job is anxious about Mary.																			0.11	0.5	366	198					
Mary spends the night at the Sturgises's house.																			1.07	5.0	366–71	199		3		32	
Mary's sleepless night; the trial day																			0.11	0.5	371	200	23 Tues				
Mr Carson before the trial																		J	0.21	1.0	372–73	201					
Jem's letter to Job																			0.53	2.5	373–75	202					
The trial begins.																			0.43	2.0	375–77	203					
Jane Wilson's testimony																		N	0.43	2.0	377–79	204					
Evidence against Jem																			0.11	0.5	379–80	205					
Mary's testimony																		N	1.28	6.0	380–86	206					
Job looks about for Mary.																			0.21	1.0	386–87	207					
Will's testimony; Jem wins "Not Guilty."																		J	1.17	5.5	387–93	208					
After the trial																			0.21	1.0	393–94	209	24			33	
Delirious Mary, Jem has divined the true murderer.																			0.32	1.5	394–95	210					
Job's advice to Jem to return home to see Alice																		M	0.53	2.5	395–98	211					
Jem goes to see her mother.																			0.11	0.5	398–99	212					
Jem, Jane, and Will return to Manchester.																		N	0.21	1.0	399	213	25 (399)				
The death of Alice Wilson																			0.11	0.5	399–400	214					
Alice's funeral; Jem's request to Margaret																		W	0.43	2.0	400–02	215	28 Sun (400, 407)				III
Jem persuades Jane to accept Mary as his wife.																			0.64	3.0	402–05	216					
Jem visits Margaret to receive her bundle for Mary.																		W	0.43	2.0	405–07	217					
Jem happens to see John Barton entering his house.																		L	0.32	1.5	407–08	218	29				
Jem nurses Mary at the Sturgises's house.																		S	0.75	3.5	409–12	219	one day				
Mary gradually recovers.																		Lv	0.21	1.0	412–13	220					
Jem and Mary return home.																			0.11	0.5	413–15	221					
Mary asks Jem to let her and her father alone.																			0.32	1.5	415–16	222	5[?]				
Mary's reunion with her father																		B	0.21	1.0	416–17	223					
Mary purchases necessities for her father's comfort.																			0.11	0.5	417–18	224				34	
Mary drops in on Job and Margaret.																		L	0.32	1.5	418–19	225					
Mary stays at home with her father.																			0.11	0.5	419	226					
Barton's agony; Mary nurses him.																		B	0.21	1.0	419–20	227	7 (420)				
Jem requests Mary to meet his mother.																		L	0.11	0.5	420–21	228		4 (433)			
Sally's unsympathetic visit																			0.43	2.0	421–22	229					
Mary hears from Sally about Jem's dismissal.																		B	0.21	1.0	423	230	8 (421)				
Barton's request for Jem's visit to him at eight																		S	0.43	2.0	423–24	231					
Jem discloses to Mary his plan of emigration.																			0.11	1.0	424–26	232					
Jane Wilson gives Mary a hearty welcome.																		W	0.21	1.0	426–27	233				35	

Brief Summary	Barton's confession of his guilt	A little girl's words of forgiveness for a boy	Carson reads the Bible.	B's degradation after stopping following the Bible	Job goes home; Jem to buy some alleviation	Barton dies in Carson's arms.	Carson leaves Barton's house.	Mary becomes an orphan.	Jem hides the truth from his mother for Mary's sake.	Jem's talk with his former master	Jem's visit to Mary	A note from Carson	Jane's condolatory visit to Mary	Jane's innate generosity towards Mary	Carson's reasons for summoning Job and Jem	Carson's enquiry about the details of the murder	Carson learns the Spirit of Christ.	The emigration plan is arranged.	Mary and Jem talk about Esther.	Jem's search for Esther in vain	Esther comes to Mary's house to die.	Job and Margaret come; Esther's death	Esther's burial	Mary and Jem live a happy life in Canada.
narrator	J	N												N	N									N
Barton						X																		
Carson																								
Harry																								
Sally																								
Mrs D																								
Job																								
MJ																								
Will																								
Alice																								
Jem																								
JW																								
GW																								
Esther																						X		
Mrs B																								
Mary																								
God																								
Stage	B	S	C		B				W	B	L		B		C		W	B		B				Canada
Percent	1.17	0.43	0.32	0.32	0.11	0.11	0.11	0.21	0.43	0.32	0.11	0.11	0.11	0.43	0.32	1.71	0.21	0.21	0.32	0.21	0.21	0.11	0.11	0.32
Length	5.5	2.0	1.5	1.5	0.5	0.5	0.5	1.0	2.0	1.5	0.5	0.5	0.5	2.0	1.5	8.0	1.0	1.0	1.5	1.0	1.0	0.5	0.5	1.5
Range	427-33	433-35	435-36	436-38	438	438	439	439-40	440-42	442-43	443-44	444	444-45	445-47	447-49	449-57	457-58	458-59	459-60	460-61	461-62	462-63	463	463-64
Number	234	235	236	237	238	239	240	241	242	243	244	245	246	247	248	249	250	251	252	253	254	255	256	257
Day	8			9				10 (442, 455)					10						one evening	next day				
Month	4																							late autumn
Year	1840																							1842 or 43 [?]
Chapter	35			36								37						38						
Part	III																							

APPENDIX 1 *Comprehensive Chronologies* 233

64	0	64	32.9	0	32.9	narrator
54	72	126	19.7	32	51.7	Barton
22	23	45	10.7	12.1	22.8	Carson
10	69	79	3.9	36.2	40.1	Harry
12	8	20	4.1	2.6	6.7	Sally
10	11	21	5.3	3.8	9.1	Mrs D
46	34	80	22.5	11.6	34.1	Job
35	29	64	18	8.8	26.8	MJ
11	32	43	6.6	15.5	22.1	Will
27	38	65	10.7	15.2	25.9	Alice
58	90	148	24	39	63	Jem
43	50	93	17.6	24.2	41.8	JW
16	26	42	8.5	13.6	22.1	GW
8	21	29	3.7	10.7	14.4	Esther
8	25	33	2.7	11.5	14.2	Mrs B
160	50	210	64.9	20.6	85.5	Mary
0	86	86	0	50.7	50.7	God
						Stage
					100.03	Percent
		468.5				Length
						Range
						No.
	Times			%		
Active	Referred	Total Appearance	Active	Referred	Total Appearance	

234

The Comprehensive Chronology for *Ruth* (1853)

Legend:
- active
- referred
- non-appearance
- dead
- A: Abermouth
- E: Eccleston
- P: Pen tre Voelas

		Scene				Time Inferred			
Main Characters	Brief Summary of Each Scene (Boxes of important events are coloured.)	Stage	Percent	Length	Range	Number	Day (page)	Month (page)	Year (page)	Chapter	Volume

Character / Scene #	1	2	3	4	5	6	7	8	9	10	11	12	13	14	15	16	17	18	19	20	21	22	23	24
narrator																								
Mr Davis																								
Mr Farquhar																								
Elizabeth Bradshaw																								
Mary Bradshaw																								
Jemima Bradshaw																								
Richard Bradshaw																								
Mrs Bradshaw																								
Mr Bradshaw																								
Sally																								
Faith Benson																								
Thurstan Benson																								
Leonard																								
Ruth Hilton																								
Mrs Hilton																								
Mr Hilton																								
Henry Bellingham																								
Mrs Bellingham																								
Jenny Wood																								
Mrs Mason																								
God																								

Scene Summaries:
1. The history of an eastern assize-town
2. Seamstresses' hard work
3. Jenny's comfort of Ruth
4. Ruth becomes a selected apprentice.
5. Mrs Mason's complaint of Ruth's frock
6. Ruth's first meeting with Bellingham
7. At dawn, the milliners come home.
8. Ruth's baseless morning dream
9. In the morning, Mrs Mason is cross.
10. Jenny gives Ruth a chance to go out.
11. Bellingham saves Tom.
12. Bellingham gives Ruth his purse.
13. The adventure fills Ruth's mind.
14. Jenny's illness is the predominant subject.
15. Mrs Wood comes to look after Jenny.
16. Ruth's third meeting with Bellingham
17. Farewell to Jenny, warning and wisdom
18. Bellingham attends service.
19. Bellingham's moral defects
20. Ruth's five months at Mrs Mason's
21. How Ruth has become apprenticed
22. Bellingham does not come to St Nicholas.
23. Ruth enjoys talking with Bellingham.
24. Ruth's one-hour ramble with Bellingham

Stage: Fordham (108)

Percent: 0.54 | 1.08 | 0.22 | 0.43 | 0.22 | 0.87 | 0.22 | 0.11 | 0.33 | 0.11 | 0.54 | 0.87 | 0.11 | 0.22 | 0.11 | 0.43 | 0.11 | 0.11 | 0.43 | 0.76 | 0.11 | 0.11 | 0.22

Length: 2.5 | 5.0 | 1.0 | 2.0 | 1.0 | 4.0 | 1.0 | 0.5 | 1.5 | 0.5 | 2.5 | 4.0 | 0.5 | 1.0 | 0.5 | 2.0 | 0.5 | 0.5 | 2.0 | 3.5 | 0.5 | 0.5 | 1.0 | 0.22

Range: 1–3 | 3–8 | 8–9 | 9–11 | 11–12 | 12–17 | 17–18 | 18 | 18–20 | 20 | 20–23 | 23–27 | 27–28 | 28–29 | 29 | 29–31 | 31 | 31 | 31–33 | 33–36 | 36–39 | 39 | 39–40 | 40–41

Day (page): one day | next day | Sunday | next Sunday | next two Sundays | next Sunday | next Sunday

Month (page): 1 (3) | 2 (40)

Year (page): 1828

Chapter: 1 | 2 | 3

Volume: 1

APPENDIX 1 Comprehensive Chronologies 235

Brief Summary	Bellingham arranges a walk to Milham.	Ruth's secret joy of seeing her home	Walking to Milham Grange	Ruth goes on her way home.	Unexpected encounter with Mrs Mason	Acquiescence to Bellingham's directions	Bellingham and Ruth in North Wales	Even rain is a pleasure to Ruth.	Bellingham and Ruth play cards.	Ruth encounters a deformed gentleman.	Bellingham despises the little hunchback.	"She's a bad naughty girl."	Ruth sees the deformed gentleman.	Bellingham and Ruth's sauntering	Bellingham falls into a brain fever.	Mrs Bellingham is sent for.	Ruth's selfless nursing of Bellingham	Mrs Bellingham comes; Ruth excluded.	Ruth's first meeting with Mrs Bellingham	Ruth's selfless patience	Bellingham agrees to leave Ruth.	Mrs Bellingham's note and fifty pounds	Ruth goes out to catch the carriage.	Ruth's third meeting with Benson	Benson persuades Ruth to stay at his inn.	Benson and Mrs Hughes look after Ruth.	Benson writes a note to Mrs Bellingham.	Mr Jones sees Ruth at Mrs Hughes's inn.	Mrs Bellingham's reply to Benson	Benson summons Faith.	Benson takes care of Ruth.	Faith's reply arrives.	Faith's arrival at Mrs Hughes's inn	Faith's talk about home affairs
narrator																																		
Dav																																		
Far																																		
EB																																		
MB																																		
JB																																		
RB																																		
Ms B																																		
Mr B																																		
Sal																																		
FB																																		
TB																																		
Leo																																		
RH																																		
Mrs H																																		
Mr H																																		
HB																																		
Mrs B																																		
JW																																		
Mas																																		
God																																		
Stage	Fordham										Llan-dhu (62, 110)										P			Llan-dhu										
Percent	0.65	0.11	1.41	0.43	0.22	1.41	0.76	0.11	0.22	0.65	0.11	0.33	0.22	0.43	0.22	0.65	0.11	1.08	0.43	0.11	0.87	0.33	0.33	0.98	0.54	0.33	0.54	0.11	0.54	0.11	0.11	0.11	0.65	0.11
Length	3.0	0.5	6.5	2.0	1.0	6.5	3.5	0.5	1.0	3.0	0.5	1.5	1.0	2.0	1.0	3.0	0.5	5.0	2.0	0.5	4.0	1.5	1.5	4.5	2.5	1.5	2.5	0.5	2.5	0.5	0.5	0.5	3.0	0.5
Range	41–44	44	45–51	51–53	53–55	55–61	61–65	65	65–66	66–70	70	70–72	72–73	73–75	75–76	76–79	79–80	80–85	85–87	87	87–91	91–93	93–94	94–99	99–101	101–03	103–05	105–06	106–08	108–09	109	109–10	110–13	113–14
Number	25	26	27	28	29	30	31	32	33	34	35	36	37	38	39	40	41	42	43	44	45	46	47	48	49	50	51	52	53	54	55	56	57	58
Day	one day (41)	Sunday (45)					one day	next day (65)		next day			next day					one day (80)	next day	many days	Tuesday				Wednesday						two days		Saturday (109)	
Month	5 (123)																				7 (61)													
Year	1828																																	
Chapter	3	4					5			6			7					8			9			10					11					
Volume	1																																	

236

Brief Summary	narrator	Dav	Far	EB	MB	JB	RB	Ms B	Mr B	Sal	FB	TB	Leo	RH	Mrs H	Mr H	HB	Mrs B	JW	Mas	God	Stage	Percent	Length	Range	Number	Day	Month	Year	Chapter	Volume
Faith looks after Ruth.											▓	▓		▓									0.43	2.0	114–15	59	Saturday	7	1828	11	1
Brief talk between Ruth and Faith											▓	▓		▓									0.11	0.5	115–16	60	Sunday				
The Bensons' talk about Ruth's treatment											▓	▓		▓								Llan-dhu (131)	1.3	6.0	116–22	61					
Indecisive Faith looks after Ruth.											▓	▓		▓									0.11	0.5	122	62	Wednesday (123)				
The Bensons' talk about Ruth's future											▓	▓		▓									0.76	3.5	123–26	63				12	
Ruth rejects to accept the fifty pound.											▓	▓		▓									0.33	1.5	126–27	64	one day				
Ruth's watch is helpful to pay the cost.											▓	▓		▓									0.33	1.5	127–29	65	next day	8			
The sale of Ruth's watch											▓	▓		▓									0.11	0.5	129	66	Wednesday				
Ruth is to be called Mrs Denbigh.											▓	▓		▓									0.33	1.5	129–31	67	Thursday				
Ruth finishes stitching the black gown.											▓	▓		▓									0.11	0.5	131	68	Friday			13	
Journey to Eccleston										▓	▓	▓		▓									0.54	2.5	131–34	69					
Arrival at the Benson's house										▓	▓	▓		▓									1.3	6.0	134–40	70	Saturday	9 (190)			
Clean house; wedding ring										▓	▓	▓		▓									0.87	4.0	140–44	71				14	
Sally cuts Ruth's hair for widow's cap.										▓	▓	▓		▓									0.43	2.0	144–46	72					
Sally hears Ruth's true story.										▓	▓	▓		▓									0.54	2.5	146–48	73	Sunday (150)				
Mrs and Miss Bradshaw's visit					▓	▓		▓		▓	▓	▓		▓									0.43	2.0	149–50	74					
Sunday school at the Bensons'										▓	▓	▓		▓									0.22	1.0	150–51	75					
Bradshaw praises Ruth.						▓					▓	▓		▓									0.87	4.0	151–55	76	Tuesday (155)			15	
Bradshaw's gift for Ruth arrives.						▓				▓	▓	▓		▓								Eccleston	0.65	3.0	155–58	77					
Ruth becomes Bradshaw's favour.						▓				▓	▓	▓		▓									0.33	1.5	158–60	78					2
Ruth sighs with remembrance.											▓	▓		▓									0.22	1.0	160	79					
The birth of the child										▓	▓	▓	▓	▓									0.43	2.0	160–62	80	Leonard's birthday	11			
Ruth's judgement of his father										▓	▓	▓	▓	▓									0.33	1.5	162–64	81		2 (437)	1829	16	
Sally and Faith take care of Ruth.										▓	▓	▓	▓	▓									0.11	0.5	164	82	one night				
Sally's story of her sweethearts										▓	▓	▓	▓	▓									1.3	6.0	164–70	83	one day	3			
Ruth's proposal of earning her livelihood											▓	▓	▓	▓									0.54	2.5	170–72	84	one day				
Ruth in mournful regretful recollections												▓	▓	▓									0.11	0.5	173	85					
Sally's talk improves Ruth.										▓	▓	▓	▓	▓									0.87	4.0	173–77	86	one day	summer			
Ruth starts to learn under Thurstan.											▓	▓	▓	▓									0.22	1.0	177	87					
The plan for the baby's baptism											▓	▓	▓	▓									0.22	1.0	178–79	88				17	
Leonard's christening					▓	▓					▓	▓	▓	▓									0.43	2.0	179–81	89	one day	8 (178)			
Jemima goes home for permission.						▓																	0.11	0.5	181	90					
Jemima's admiration of Ruth					▓	▓					▓	▓	▓	▓									0.54	2.5	181–84	91					
Leonard is Ruth's grandfather's name.					▓	▓					▓	▓	▓	▓									0.54	2.5	184–86	92					
Ruth's brightness; Jemima's admiration					▓	▓					▓	▓	▓	▓									0.33	1.5	186–88	93					

APPENDIX 1 *Comprehensive Chronologies* 237

Brief Summary	Ruth's first evening at the Bradshaws	Sally's talk to Ruth about her will	Possibility of Ruth's independence	The job of governess is offered to Ruth.	Leonard's whipping and its consequence	Faith's grey hair	Changes in Benson, Sally, and the house	Increase of dignity in Ruth's face	Detailed introductions of the Bradshaws	Talk between Richard and Jemima	Mary and Elizabeth Bradshaw	Ruth's ordinary day at happy home	Jemima and Farquhar's relationship	Mary and Elizabeth's interest in their love	Bradshaw lectures Jemima.	Jemima and Farquhar's relationship	Bradshaw's request for Ruth's help	Jemima and Farquhar's states of mind	Bradshaw's invitation comes.	Ruth's evening at the Bradshaws'	Jemima knows her father's manoeuvring.	Jemima's repulse and alienation	Wild strawberries gathering	Elizabeth's fainting fit	Ruth takes her share of nursing.	Jemima's jealous dislike grows up.	Abermouth is chosen for Elizabeth.	Bradshaw supports the Liberal Donne.	From Eccleston to Abermouth	Preparation for welcoming Donne	Discussion about bribery	Benson's sermon and stinging conscience	Ruth's dream and Leonard's dream	Ruth receives two letters at Eagle's Crag.	Reasons for the visit to Abermouth	Donne resembles a race-horse.
narrator																																				
Dav																																				
Far					▓				▓		▓	▓	▓	▓		▓		▓		▓			▓													
EB									▓		▓			▓									▓	▓												
MB									▓		▓			▓									▓													
JB					▓				▓	▓		▓	▓	▓	▓	▓	▓	▓	▓	▓	▓	▓	▓	▓		▓	▓	▓								
RB					▓				▓	▓		▓			▓		▓		▓	▓			▓	▓			▓	▓		▓	▓	▓				
Ms B									▓			▓								▓			▓	▓												
Mr B																																				
Sal		▓					▓																													
FB						▓	▓																													
TB					▓	▓	▓																													
Leo					▓		▓					▓													▓											
RH	▓	▓	▓	▓	▓	▓	▓	▓				▓					▓			▓			▓	▓	▓				▓				▓	▓		
Mrs H																																				
Mr H																																				
HB																													▓							
Mrs B																																				
JW																																				
Mas																																				
God																																				
Stage									Eccleston													A					E			A		E				
Percent	0.43	1.19	0.11	0.87	0.54	0.22	0.43	0.43	0.33	0.11	0.11	0.65	0.33	0.33	1.08	0.22	0.65	0.33	1.19	0.65	0.54	0.87	0.22	0.22	0.11	0.22	0.11	0.54	0.22	0.22	0.76	0.11	0.11	0.33	0.54	0.33
Length	2.0	5.5	0.5	4.0	2.5	1.0	2.0	2.0	1.5	0.5	0.5	3.0	1.5	1.5	5.0	1.0	3.0	1.5	5.5	3.0	2.5	4.0	1.0	1.0	0.5	1.0	0.5	2.5	1.0	1.0	3.5	0.5	0.5	1.5	2.5	1.5
Range	188–89	190–96	196	196–200	201–04	204–07	207–08	208–10	210–12	212–14	214	214	214–17	217–19	219–24	224–25	225–28	228–29	229–31	231–36	236–39	239–41	241–45	245–46	246–47	248	248–49	249–51	252–53	253–54	254–57	257–58	258	258–60	260–63	263–64
Number	94	95	96	97	98	99	100	101	102	103	104	105	106	107	108	109	110	111	112	113	114	115	116	117	118	119	120	121	122	123	124	125	126	127	128	129
Day	one evening	one afternoon		Monday			autumn (208)			(212)					Friday (239)					a few days after (229)		next day (236)	one day	next day (245)	many days after					one day		next day			one day	
Month	8	9		2 (196)					12						4 (218)								8 (245)						9 (247, 267)							
Year	'29	'30			1835 (201, 207)																		1836													
Chapter	17	18			19										20								21										22			
Volume																	2																			

238

Brief Summary	One more reason for the visit	Eagle's Crag is ready for the welcome.	Ruth invites her pupils to a walk.	Ruth recognizes Donne as Bellingham.	Ruth is astounded.	Ruth's agonized meditation	Ruth soothes Elizabeth into sleep.	Ruth decides to leave her fate in God.	Donne's recognition of Ruth	Donne talks to Ruth on the way to church.	Ruth's meditation in the church	On their walk home	Donne's wish to talk with Ruth	Ruth asks Donne to read a passage.	Donne knows Leonard is his child.	Ruth's fear of losing Leonard	A letter from Faith	A letter from Donne	Ruth is absent from afternoon church.	Ruth's meeting with Donne	Ruth's struggle	Donne is elected as an MP.	The letters from Jemima and Faith	The seaside party's arrival at Eccleston	Bradshaw's regret about bribery	Farquhar is weary of Jemima.	Life in the Chapel-house; Leonard is safe.	Ruth's feeling of insecurity	Farquhar thinks of Ruth for a wife.	Ruth senses Jemima's dislike of her.	The afternoon at the Bensons	Mrs Bradshaw's love for Jemima	Mrs Pearson's talk about Ruth Hilton	Jemima's afternoon discovery	Ruth is in Jemima's power.	Jemima's observation of Ruth begins.
narrator																																				
Dav																																				
Far																																				
EB																																				
MB																																				
JB																																				
RB																																				
Ms B																																				
Mr B																																				
Sal																																				
FB																																				
TB																																				
Leo																																				
RH																																				
Mrs H																																				
Mr H																																				
HB																																				
Mrs B																																				
JW																																				
Mas																																				
God																																				
Stage	E			Abermouth																					Eccleston											
Percent	0.22	0.11	0.22	0.54	0.65	0.54	0.22	0.11	0.76	0.43	0.43	0.54	0.43	0.33	0.11	0.22	0.43	0.11	2.06	0.33	0.11	0.11	0.33	0.22	0.87	0.11	0.11	0.43	0.33	0.22	0.98	0.76	0.33	0.22		
Length	1.0	0.5	1.0	2.5	3.0	2.5	1.0	0.5	3.5	2.0	2.0	2.5	2.0	1.5	0.5	1.0	2.0	0.5	9.5	1.5	0.5	0.5	1.5	1.0	4.0	0.5	0.5	2.0	1.5	1.0	4.5	3.5	1.5	1.0		
Range	264–65	265–66	266–67	267–69	269–72	272–75	275	276	276–79	279–81	281–83	283–86	286–88	288–90	290	290–91	291–93	293–94	294	294–303	304–05	305	306	306	307–08	308–09	309–13	313–14	314	314–16	316–17	317–18	318–22	323–26	326–27	328–29
Number	130	131	132	133	134	135	136	137	138	139	140	141	142	143	144	145	146	147	148	149	150	151	152	153	154	155	156	157	158	159	160	161	162	163	164	165
Day			Saturday (266) 24						Sunday 25 (283)						Monday 26		Thu 29 (293)	Fri 30 (293)		Sun 2 (294, 304)			few days later	the next day				autumn/winter (313, 314)		(314, 315)		Saturday (316, 317, 324)				
Month				9																10								5				6 (324)				
Year						1836																									1837					
Chapter	22			23											24										25											26
Volume					2																				3											

APPENDIX 1 Comprehensive Chronologies 239

Brief Summary	Richard's annual home visit	Jemima's heart has not forgotten jealousy.	Jemima's agony	The plan of Wednesday expedition	Morning lessons at the Bradshaws	Ruth's secret is disclosed.	Ruth's secret has spread abroad.	Ruth's confession of her sin to Leonard	Bradshaw's note arrives.	Bradshaw's interview with Benson	The severance of the tie	Benson stops Ruth leaving the house.	Benson asks Sally to make a cup of tea.	Benson's interview with Ruth	Benson cheers Leonard.	Benson's interview with Faith	Faith comforts Ruth.	Change in acquaintances' behaviours	Benson's talk with Jemima in the street	Trials to Ruth and Leonard	Farquhar's visit to Benson	Leonard goes for newspapers.	Jemima's engagement to Farquhar; the return of Richard	Mary and Elizabeth are sent to school.	Few depressing events in the Bensons	Sally's offer of her savings	Hearing Jemima's engagement	Leonard is Ruth's only hope.	Jemima's visit on the eve of her wedding	Ruth looks after Ann Fleming.	Ruth tells Jemima of her being a nurse.	Ruth's reputation as a nurse spreads.	Ruth feels the lapse of life and time.
narrator																																	
Dav																																	
Far		■																			■				■								
EB	■																																
MB	■																																
JB	■		■	■		■																											
RB	■																																
Ms B																																	
Mr B						■																											
Sal														■																			
FB																■	■																
TB																																	
Leo							■	■							■					■		■						■					
RH						■		■				■		■			■			■										■		■	■
Mrs H																																	
Mr H																																	
HB																																	
Mrs B																																	
JW																																	
Mas																																	
God																																	
Stage																Eccleston																	
Percent	0.65	0.33	0.22	0.22	1.08	0.11	1.08	0.11	0.11	0.98	0.11	0.22	0.22	1.08	0.22	0.65	0.11	0.11	0.33	0.76	0.87	0.11	0.65	0.11	0.33	0.76	0.33	0.33	0.65	0.11	0.54	0.54	0.33
Length	3.0	1.5	1.0	1.0	5.0	0.5	5.0	0.5	0.5	4.5	0.5	1.0	1.0	5.0	1.0	3.0	0.5	0.5	1.5	3.5	4.0	0.5	3.0	0.5	1.5	3.5	1.5	1.5	3.0	0.5	2.5	2.5	1.5
Range	329–32	332–33	334	334–35	335–36	336–41	341	342–47	347	347–52	352	352–53	353–54	354–59	359–60	360–63	363	363–64	364–65	365–69	369–73	373	373–76	376	376–78	378–81	381–83	383–84	384–87	387	387–90	390–92	392
Number	166	167	168	169	170	171	172	173	174	175	176	177	178	179	180	181	182	183	184	185	186	187	188	189	190	191	192	193	194	195	196	197	198
Day				Wednesday (335)															one day (365)			a month after						13 (384)			one evening (387)	summer (392)	
Month				8 (334)																			8 (376)	12 (376)				8	9/10	11			
Year				1837																			1838 (372, 376)					1839				1840	
Chapter		26				27													28					29								30	
Volume												3																					

240

Brief Summary	Farquhar's visit to the Bensons	Farquhar writes to the Insurance Co.	Bradshaw's angry letter to the Co.	The visit of Smith, the insurance clerk	Richard's forgery is disclosed.	Mrs Bradshaw's visit to Benson	Farquhar's prompt action	Benson's meditation	Jemima's visit to Benson	Benson's interview with Bradshaw	Bradshaw in a swoon; coach overturned	Bradshaw resumes his work.	Farquhar's visit to Benson	Farquhar's handling of Richard's income	The life of Ruth and Leonard	Richard is improving in Glasgow.	Bradshaw attends Benson's service.	Social background of the year	The threat of typhus fever	Decision to work in the fever-ward	Ruth tells Leonard of her purpose.	Ruth leaves for the fever-ward.	Benson's report of Ruth	"I am her son!"	Ruth's return home	The strong tie between Ruth and Leonard	Jemima's invitation to the Abermouth trip	The rector brings the note of thanks.	Sally's commotion about the rector's visit	Davis's talk about Leonard and Donne	Ruth's decision and Davis's secret	Ruth begins to nurse Donne.	Donne's recovery and Ruth's decline	Ruth is carried into the Bensons' house.	The decline of Ruth
narrator																																			
Dav																															▓			▓	
Far	▓	▓		▓			▓			▓			▓	▓																					
EB																																			
MB																																			
JB																																			
RB																																			
Ms B																																			
Mr B																																			
Sal																																			
FB	▓			▓		▓																													
TB	▓			▓																															
Leo																																			
RH	▓																																	▓	
Mrs H																																			
Mr H																																			
HB																																			
Mrs B																																			
JW																																			
Mas																																			
God																																			
Stage																	Eccleston																		
Percent	0.33	0.11	0.87	0.76	0.98	0.43	0.65	0.11	0.22	0.22	0.33	0.33	0.54	0.11	0.22	0.22	0.11	0.22	0.22	0.65	0.11	0.22	0.11	0.33	0.11	0.11	0.43	0.65	0.22	0.76	0.65	0.22	0.54	0.11	0.43
Length	1.5	0.5	4.0	3.5	4.5	2.0	3.0	0.5	1.0	1.0	1.5	1.5	2.5	0.5	1.0	1.0	0.5	1.0	1.0	3.0	0.5	1.0	0.5	1.5	0.5	0.5	2.0	3.0	1.0	3.5	3.0	1.0	2.5	0.5	2.0
Range	392-94	394	394-98	399-402	402-06	406-08	408-11	411-12	412-13	413-14	414-15	416-17	417-20	420	420-21	421-22	422	422-23	423-24	424-27	427	427-28	428	429-30	430-31	431	431-32	432-35	435-36	436-40	440-42	443	444-46	446	446-48
Number	199	200	201	202	203	204	205	206	207	208	209	210	211	212	213	214	215	216	217	218	219	220	221	222	223	224	225	226	227	228	229	230	231	232	233
Day	one day	next morning	29 (400)	1		2			6 (412)						one day	Sunday		one day (425)			one evening	some weeks after			next day, or 14 (438)			17 (444)			
Month	9					10 (403, 406)									10 (421)		summer / early autumn	9								10 (432)			
Year	1840		1841	1842 (431) / ?1840 (437)	
Chapter	30	31	32	33	34	35
Volume	3

APPENDIX 1 *Comprehensive Chronologies* 241

						Active	Referred	Total	Active %	Referred %	Total %	Brief Summary
The death of Ruth						32	0	32	13.3	0	13.3	narrator
	Leonard under the Farquhars' care					11	0	11	4.6	0	4.6	Dav
		Donne looks at Ruth's dead face.				32	24	56	13.3	10.0	23.2	Far
			Benson's interview with Donne			40	22	62	16.6	9.1	25.7	EB
						35	23	58	14.5	9.5	24.0	MB
						59	20	79	24.5	8.3	32.8	JB
						5	28	33	2.1	11.6	13.7	RB
						25	26	51	10.4	10.8	21.2	Ms B
						45	48	93	18.7	19.9	38.6	Mr B
						49	11	60	20.3	4.6	24.9	Sal
						69	26	95	28.6	10.8	39.4	FB
						101	30	131	41.9	12.4	54.3	TB
						53	54	107	22	22.4	44.4	Leo
						160	46	206	66.4	19.1	85.5	RH
						0	25	25	0	10.4	10.4	Mrs H
						0	5	5	0	2.1	2.1	Mr H
				Benson's preparation for the sermon		42	57	99	17.4	23.7	41.1	HB
						4	13	17	1.7	5.4	7.1	Mrs B
						9	6	15	3.7	2.5	6.2	JW
				Benson's funeral sermon		10	10	20	4.1	4.1	8.2	Mas
					Bradshaw's first touch on Leonard	0	81	81	0	33.6	33.6	God
					Eccleston							Stage
0.11	0.11	0.54	0.54	0.22	0.11	0.43	0.22					Percent
0.5	0.5	2.5	2.5	1.0	0.5	2.0	1.0					Length
448–49	449–50	450–52	452–54	455	455–56	456–58	458					Range
234	235	236	237	238	239	240	241					Number
one day		three days after (450)		Saturday (456)	Sunday (456)	Monday (458)		Times		%		Day
								Total Appearance		Total Appearance		
1842		11 (432, 449)						Active		Active		Month
35								Referred		Referred		Year
		36										Chapter
3												Volume

242

The Comprehensive Chronology for *North and South* (1854–55)

■ active ☐ referred ▨ non-appearance ⊠ dead

Scenes 1–56: before Margaret moves to Milton
Scenes 57–371: where Margaret lives in Milton
Scenes 372–451: after Margaret leaves Milton

Cra: Crampton, Milton (the Hales)
Har: Harley Street, London (the Lennoxes)
Mar: Marlborough St, Milton (the Thorntons)
Str: on the street

Cro: Cromer, Norfolk
Hel: Helstone, Hampshire
Mil: Milton
Tra: on a train

Fra: Frances Street, Milton (the Higginses)
Hes: Heston
Out: at Outwood Station, Milton

Lon: London
Oxf: Oxford

Volume	Chapter	Year	Month	Day	Time Inferred	Number	Range	Length	Percent	Stage	Main Characters	Brief Summary of Each Scene (Boxes of important events are coloured.)
1	1	1848	7 (27)		one evening	1	5–6	1.0	0.22	Har	Anna Shaw, Edith	Edith goes into an after-dinner nap.
						2	6–8	2.0	0.45			Margaret hears Mrs Shaw's talk.
						3	8–9	1.0	0.22			Margaret's recollection in the nursery
						4	9	0.5	0.11			Margaret as a shawl-bearer
						5	9–10	1.0	0.22			Entrance of Henry Lennox and Edith
						6	10–13	3.0	0.67			Talk between Henry and Margaret
						7	13–14	1.5	0.34			The arrival of Captain Lennox
	2		9			8	15–17	2.0	0.45	Tra		Margaret travels home with her father.
						9	17–18	1.0	0.22			The forest is Margaret's pride.
						10	18	0.5	0.11			Mrs Hale's complaint about Helstone
						11	18–19	1.0	0.22			Margaret's contempt for trades
						12	19–20	1.0	0.22			Margaret's evenings in Helstone
						13	20–21	1.0	0.22			Frederick's whereabouts
						14	21	0.5	0.11			Mr Hale's absence of mind
	3		10	15		15	21–22	0.5	0.11	Hel		Margaret's determination to sketch
						16	22	0.5	0.11			Henry Lennox's visit is announced.
						17	22–23	1.0	0.22			Margaret's inquiry about the Lennoxes
						18	23	0.5	0.11			Henry's scrutiny of the drawing room
						19	23–24	0.5	0.11			Margaret tells Mrs Hale Henry's visit.
						20	24	0.5	0.11			Mrs Hale's greeting to Henry
						21	24–25	1.0	0.22			Margaret takes Henry out for sketching.

Main Characters: Narrator, God, Anna Shaw, Edith, Captain Lennox, Henry Lennox, George Leonards, Adam Bell, Dixon, Frederick Hale, Maria Hale, Richard Hale, Margaret Hale, Mrs Boucher, John Boucher, Mary Higgins, Bessy Higgins, Nicholas Higgins, Fanny Thornton, Mrs Thornton, John Thornton

APPENDIX 1 Comprehensive Chronologies 243

Brief Summary	Mr Hale's comments on Henry's sketch	Pears for dessert	Mrgrt, Henry, Mr Hale gathering pears	Henry's confession of love	Margaret and Henry come upon Mr Hale.	Henry leaves Helstone soon afterwards.	Margaret's reflection	Brief tea time at the Hales	Mr Hale's reason for leaving Helstone	Margaret will tell her mother the news.	"We must go to Milton."	Mr Hale will be a private tutor.	Margaret responds to her mother's calling.	Margaret is a good listener.	Margaret looks back what happened today.	Margaret and Mr Hale: the Lord's Prayer	She spends a miserable and restless night.	Mr Hale will not be at home till evening.	Margaret tells her mother his decision.	Margaret's efforts to soothe her mother	Margaret cries on bed.	Margaret's upbraiding of Dixon	Preparation for moving under way	Margaret urges Mr Hale to show his plan.	Margaret startled into decisions	Margaret's plan of removal sanctioned	Margaret is the director of the removal.	Margaret remembers Henry in the garden.	Margaret enters the house.	Margaret encourages Hale: No hesitation.	Departure from Helstone	The Hales happen to see Henry Lennox.	The Hales stay at a London hotel.	The Hales arrive at Heston, a seaside town.	They spend there a fortnight (66).
Narrator																																			
God																																			
Anna Shaw																																			
Edith																																			
Capt Lennox																																			
Henry Lennox																																			
George Leonards																																			
Adam Bell																																			
Dixon																																			
Frederick Hale																																			
Mrs Hale																																			
Mr Hale																																			
Margaret																																			
Mrs Boucher																																			
John Boucher																																			
Mary Higgins																																			
Bessy Higgins																																			
Nicholas Higgins																																			
Fanny Thornton																																			
Mrs Thornton																																			
John Thornton																																			
Stage												Hel																			Lon			Hes
Percent	0.22	0.22	0.11	0.56	0.22	0.11	0.11	0.11	0.89	0.34	0.11	0.45	0.11	0.22	0.22	0.11	0.11	0.11	0.56	0.11	0.11	0.34	0.22	0.22	0.11	0.22	0.22	0.22	0.11	0.22	0.11	0.11	0.11	0.11	0.11
Length	1.0	1.0	0.5	2.5	1.0	0.5	0.5	0.5	4.0	1.5	0.5	2.0	0.5	1.0	1.0	0.5	0.5	0.5	2.5	0.5	0.5	1.5	1.0	1.0	0.5	1.0	1.0	1.0	0.5	1.0	0.5	0.5	0.5	0.5	0.5
Range	25-26	26-27	27-28	28-30	30-31	31	31-32	32	32-36	36-37	37-38	38-40	40	41-42	42	42-43	43	43-44	44-46	46-47	47	47-48	49	49-50	50-51	51-52	52-53	53-54	54-55	55-56	56	56-57	57	58	58-59
Number	22	23	24	25	26	27	28	29	30	31	32	33	34	35	36	37	38	39	40	41	42	43	44	45	46	47	48	49	50	51	52	53	54	55	56
Day				15													16						22? (49)					the last Helstone day		next day		next day			
Month							10																							early 11					
Year	1848
Chapter	3			4					5														6									7			
Volume	1

Brief Summary	Margaret and Mr Hale go to Milton.	Their house-hunting in Milton	At the hotel entrance	Margaret's first meeting with Thornton	Mr Hale comes back to meet Thornton.	Crampton, the most healthy suburb	Father and daughter return to Heston.	The obnoxious wallpapers were gone.	The Hales are settled in Milton.	Margaret reads Edith's letter.	An assistant servant hardly found	Thornton is Hale's favourite pupil.	Difference of opinion on Milton workers	A servant has to be searched by Margaret.	Margaret walks around Milton for a girl.	Miltoners are outspoken but innocent.	Margaret meets Nicholas and Bessy.	Mrgrt knows they live in Frances Street.	Milton becomes a brighter place for Mrgrt.	Mr Hale invites Thornton to tea.	Margaret's contempt on John	Mrs Thornton's anxiety and hatred	Thornton reaches Crampton.	Thornton's first visit to the Hales' house	Thornton's talk about his past experience	Margaret fails to shake hands with John.	The Hales' views of Thornton exchanged	Mrs Hale's health is declining.	Margaret is busy searching for a servant.	Margaret meets Bessy.	Christian Margaret vs materialist Nicholas	Mrs Thornton will visit the Hales.	Thornton wishes his mother to be civil.	Mrs Thornton's manner to her children	Mrs Thornton's tenderness to weak Fanny
Narrator																																			
God																																			
Anna Shaw																																			
Edith																																			
Capt Lennox																																			
Henry Lennox																																			
George Leonards																																			
Adam Bell																																			
Dixon																																			
Frederick Hale																																			
Mrs Hale																																			
Mr Hale																																			
Margaret																																			
Mrs Boucher																																			
John Boucher																																			
Mary Higgins																																			
Bessy Higgins																																			
Nicholas Higgins																																			
Fanny Thornton																																			
Mrs Thornton																																			
John Thornton																																			
Stage		Mil		Hes					Cra						Mil				Cra				Mar			Cra			Mil		Fra			Mar	
Percent	0.11	0.34	0.11	0.45	0.11	0.22	0.11	0.11	0.22	0.11	0.45	0.11	0.22	0.11	0.11	0.11	0.11	0.34	0.11	0.22	0.22	0.45	0.11	1.34	0.22	0.11	0.45	0.22	0.11	0.22	0.45	0.22	0.11	0.11	0.11
Length	0.5	1.5	0.5	2.0	0.5	1.0	0.5	0.5	1.0	0.5	2.0	0.5	1.0	0.5	0.5	0.5	0.5	1.5	0.5	1.0	1.0	2.0	0.5	6.0	1.0	0.5	2.0	1.0	0.5	1.0	2.0	1.0	0.5	0.5	0.5
Range	59	59-61	61	61-63	63-64	64-65	65	65-66	66-68	68	68-69	69	69-70	70-71	71-72	72	72-74	74	74-75	75-76	76-78	78	78-84	84-85	85-86	86-88	88-89	89	89-90	90-92	92-93	93-94	94-95	95	
Number	57	58	59	60	61	62	63	64	65	66	67	68	69	70	71	72	73	74	75	76	77	78	79	80	81	82	83	84	85	86	87	88	89	90	91
Day		one day			one day (65)												one day (72)		next day (74)									several days		one day (89)				next day	
Month		mid 11					winter										early spring (72)												late spring/ early summer						
Year	1848													1849																					
Chapter	7				8					9			10				11							12											
Volume	1																																		

APPENDIX 1 Comprehensive Chronologies 245

Brief Summary	John's kindness to Mrs Hale	"Who are the Hales?"	Talks in the Hales' drawing-room	Talk between Margaret and Fanny	Mrs Thornton is proud of Milton.	"At any rate John must be satisfied now."	Margaret on the way to Bessy's house	Bessy suffers from fluff and noise.	Milton life is affecting Mrs Hale's health.	Mrgrt and her father worry about Mrs H.	Mrs Hale becomes tenderer to Margaret.	A detailed story of Frederick's mutiny	Margaret oppressed with gloom	Mr Hale's anxiety about his wife's health	A return call of Mr Hale and Margaret	Mrs Thornton takes pride in her son.	Thornton's view of masters and men	Despotism is Thornton's policy.	We must be mutually independent.	Dr Donaldson sees Mrs Hale.	Margaret knows her mother is dying.	Dr Donaldson: Margaret is like a queen.	The dread should be kept from Mr Hale.	Mrs H's wish to meet her son once again	Margaret asks Dixon for help.	Talk between Margaret and Dixon	Dixon loves Mrs Hale, Fred, and Margaret.	Margaret on her way to Bessy	Higgins and Margaret discuss the strike.	Margaret comforts Bessy.	For Bessy, Margaret is an angel.	Mrs Hale's fatal condition is kept secret.	Mrs Thornton's invitation accepted	The Thorntons' talk about Margaret's pride	Thornton may employ Irish hands.	The time limit of fortnight for strikers
Narrator																																				
God																																				
Anna Shaw																																				
Edith																																				
Capt Lennox																																				
Henry Lennox																																				
George Leonards																																				
Adam Bell																																				
Dixon																																				
Frederick Hale																																				
Mrs Hale																																				
Mr Hale																																				
Margaret																																				
Mrs Boucher																																				
John Boucher																																				
Mary Higgins																																				
Bessy Higgins																																				
Nicholas Higgins																																				
Fanny Thornton																																				
Mrs Thornton																																				
John Thornton																																				
Stage	Mar		Cra		Mil	Str	Fra			Cra							Str	Sra				Cra					Str			Fra			Cra		Mar
Percent	0.11	0.11	0.11	0.22	0.22	0.11	0.89	0.11	0.22	0.11	0.89	0.11	0.22	0.34	0.89	0.11	0.67	0.22	0.89	0.11	0.11	0.45	0.11	0.11	0.45	0.11	0.34	0.11	0.11	0.89	0.11	0.34	0.22	0.56	0.45	0.11
Length	0.5	0.5	0.5	1.0	1.0	0.5	4.0	0.5	1.0	0.5	4.0	0.5	1.0	1.5	4.0	0.5	3.0	1.0	4.0	0.5	0.5	2.0	0.5	0.5	2.0	0.5	1.5	0.5	0.5	4.0	0.5	1.5	1.0	2.5	2.0	0.5
Range	95	95-96	96	97	97-98	98-99	99-103	103-04	104-05	105	105-09	109	110-11	111-12	112-16	116-19	119-20	120-24	124-25	125-27	127	127	127-29	129	129-31	131	131-32	132-36	136-38	138	139-40	140-41	141-44	144-45	145-46
Number	92	93	94	95	96	97	98	99	100	101	102	103	104	105	106	107	108	109	110	111	112	113	114	115	116	117	118	119	120	121	122	123	124	125	126	127
Day		the same day as above			some days			one evening			next day (110)												next day (124)							
Month	late spring/ early summer								8 (171)							
Year	1849
Chapter	12		13		14		15				16							17				18
Volume	1

246

Brief Summary	Mrs Hale's concern about Margaret's dress	To Bessy, Margaret looks like an angel.	Nicholas comes back; he is now on strike.	Thornton's kindness and mercilessness	Margaret's visit to the Higginses	Argument between Higgins and Boucher	Margaret gives Bessy money for Boucher.	Mrgrt tells her mother Boucher's agony.	A basket for the Bouchers is planned.	Mr Hale's visit to the Bouchers	Mr Hale will see Boucher himself.	Bessy is still weak.	Margaret is dressed for the party.	Sumptuousness of the dinner-table	Mrs Thornton is proud of her son.	Thornton's first handshake with Margaret	Thrntn respected; masters' view of strike	Thrntn's "gentleman" differs from Mrgrt's.	Masters' talk about the strike	Margaret should do justice to Thornton.	Mrs Hale has been dying.	Mr Hale sees his wife lying in the bed.	Mr Hale knows his wife's true condition.	Mrs Hale attended to by the three	Margaret's overnight nursing her mother	Mrs Hale is recovered temporarily.	Mrs Hale becomes feverish before night.	"Borrow a water-bed for Mrs Hale."	Margaret is struck with crowded people.	Margaret enters Thornton's yard.	Fanny's explanation of the situation	In nearness of terror	John Thornton returns from the mill.	Mrgrt tells Thornton to speak to strikers.	Mrgrt protects him from the savage mob.	Expression of love to the swooned Mrgrt
Narrator																																				
God					■																									■						
Anna Shaw																																				
Edith	■																																			
Capt Lennox																																				
Henry Lennox																																				
George Leonards																																				
Adam Bell																																				
Dixon																								■	■	■	■	■								
Frederick Hale																																				
Mrs Hale	■							■	■												■	■	■	■	■	■	■	■								
Mr Hale								■	■	■	■										■	■	■	■	■	■	■	■								
Margaret	■	■	■	■	■	■	■	■	■	■		■	■	■		■		■		■	■	■	■	■	■	■	■	■	■	■	■	■	■	■	■	■
Mrs Boucher						■		■																												
John Boucher						■																														
Mary Higgins			■	■	■																															
Bessy Higgins		■	■	■	■		■					■																								
Nicholas Higgins			■	■	■	■																														
Fanny Thornton															■																■					
Mrs Thornton															■				■																	
John Thornton				■											■	■	■	■	■														■	■	■	■
Stage	Cra	Fra	Cra		Fra		Cra			Fra	Cra	Fra	Cra							Mar					Str				Cra					Str		Mar
Percent	0.22	0.67	0.22	0.34	0.11	0.34	0.34	0.22	0.11	0.11	0.11	0.11	0.22	0.22	0.34	0.22	0.22	0.22	0.22	0.45	0.11	0.11	0.22	0.11	0.11	0.11	0.11	0.11	0.22	0.11	0.11	0.11	0.22	0.34	0.67	0.11
Length	1.0	3.0	1.0	1.5	0.5	1.5	1.5	1.0	0.5	0.5	0.5	0.5	1.0	1.0	1.5	1.0	1.0	1.0	1.0	2.0	0.5	0.5	1.0	0.5	0.5	0.5	0.5	0.5	1.0	0.5	0.5	0.5	1.0	1.5	3.0	0.5
Range	146-48	148-51	151	151-53	153-54	154-55	155-56	157-58	158	158	158-59	159	159-60	160	160-61	161-62	162-63	163-64	164-65	166-67	167-68	168	168-69	169-70	170	170-71	171	171	171-72	172-73	173	173-75	175-76	176-77	177-80	180-81
Number	128	129	130	131	132	133	134	135	136	137	138	139	140	141	142	143	144	145	146	147	148	149	150	151	152	153	154	155	156	157	158	159	160	161	162	163
Day	14 Thurs (151)			20 (153) Tues (154) or Wed													21 Wed (154) or Thurs (151)				22		23						24 (171)							
Month																			8 (171)																	
Year																			1849																	
Chapter	19			20													21											22								
Volume																			1																	

APPENDIX 1 Comprehensive Chronologies 247

Brief Summary	Mrs Thornton comes downstairs.	Thrntn's talk with Irish workers in the mill	Mrs Thornton nurses Margaret.	Mrs Thornton goes out for a doctor.	Fanny knows Mrgrt's holding her brother.	Mrs Thornton fetches the doctor.	Mr Lowe takes Margaret to her home.	Thornton is visiting police and Crampton.	Thornton thinking of Margaret	Mrs Thornton's request for him to return	Mrs Thornton feels the pang of jealousy.	Margaret returns home.	Margaret looks back on what happened.	The arrival of the water-bed	Mr Hale: "Good night, Margaret."	Margaret is sleepless: sense of shame	Margaret, unrefreshed, yet rested	Thornton's effort to forget the Thorntons	Dixon announces Thornton's visit.	Thornton's confession of love to Margaret	Margaret's self-defence	Margaret's comparison of two offers	The threat of Thornton's enduring love	Margaret goes to Bessy's house.	Margaret reads a Bible chapter for Bessy.	Bessy's talk about the aftermath of the riot	Margaret leaves the dying girl.	Mrs Hale's visit to Oxenham	Mrs Hale's wish for meeting Frederick	Margaret writes a letter to Frederick.	Her father approves of her deed.	Thornton's omnibus ride	Mrs Thornton's works to be done	Mrs Thornton's jealousy	Thornton in tears still loves Margaret.	T's handling of the aftermath of the strike
Narrator																																				
God																																				
Anna Shaw																																				
Edith																																				
Capt Lennox																																				
Henry Lennox																																				
George Leonards																																				
Adam Bell																																				
Dixon																			■																	
Frederick Hale																																				
Mrs Hale															■														■							
Mr Hale															■																					
Margaret	■		■		■		■					■	■		■	■	■			■	■			■	■	■	■		■	■	■					
Mrs Boucher																																				
John Boucher																																				
Mary Higgins																																				
Bessy Higgins																									■	■										
Nicholas Higgins																																				
Fanny Thornton			■		■			■																												
Mrs Thornton	■	■	■	■		■																											■	■	■	
John Thornton		■						■	■	■	■							■	■	■	■	■	■									■			■	■
Stage			Mar															Cra										Fra				Cra	Str	Mil	Mar	Mil
Percent	0.11	0.11	0.11	0.11	0.34	0.11	0.22	0.11	0.45	0.11	0.11	0.11	0.22	0.11	0.11	0.11	0.11	0.11	0.11	0.89	0.11	0.22	0.11	0.11	0.11	0.45	0.11	0.22	0.45	0.11	0.22	0.34	0.11	0.34	0.34	0.22
Length	0.5	0.5	0.5	0.5	1.5	0.5	1.0	0.5	2.0	0.5	0.5	0.5	1.0	0.5	0.5	0.5	0.5	0.5	0.5	4.0	0.5	1.0	0.5	0.5	0.5	2.0	0.5	1.0	2.0	0.5	1.0	1.5	0.5	1.5	1.5	1.0
Range	181	181	181-82	182	182-84	184-85	185	185-87	187-88	188	188-89	189-90	190-91	191	191	191-92	192	192	192-93	193-96	196	197-98	198	198	198-199	199-201	201	201-02	202-04	204-05	205-06	207-08	208-09	209-10	210-12	212-13
Number	164	165	166	167	168	169	170	171	172	173	174	175	176	177	178	179	180	181	182	183	184	185	186	187	188	189	190	191	192	193	194	195	196	197	198	199
Day				24																25 (192)												26 Mon				
Month																	8																			
Year																	1849																			
Chapter			22				23					24					25												1					2		
Volume									1																							2				

248

Brief Summary	Dr Donaldson: Mrs Hale is dying.	Thornton purchases a fruit basket.	Thornton's brief visit to the Hales	The Hales: Margaret is prejudiced.	Bessy died this morning.	Mary: Bessy's last words	Margaret finds Bessy's death was peaceful.	Nicholas is stopped to go drinking.	Nicholas searched missing workers.	Margaret invites Nicholas home.	Margaret tells Mary her arrangement.	Margaret takes Nicholas home.	Margaret asks Dixon about Mrs Hale.	Margaret asks Mr Hale to meet Nicholas.	Mrs Hale's regret about calling Frederick	Nicholas and Mr Hale talking in his study	Nicholas is not an infidel.	Discussion on the strike	Mr Hale, mediator; the Union's tyranny	Higgins joins the Hales in family prayer.	Margaret reads Edith's letter.	Margaret reads it to her mother.	Another offering of fruit for Mrs Hale	In preparation for Frederick's return home	M thinks about T more than before.	Mrs Thornton pays a visit to Mrs Hale	Mrs Thornton's promise to Mrs Hale	Margaret and Dixon's planning	The house is still and quiet.	The muffled doorbell rings.	In the afternoon, Frederick comes back.	Margaret leads Mr Hale to his study.	Margaret prepares refreshment.	Margaret brings refreshment to the study.	Mrs Hale has yet to meet Frederick.	Margaret's observation of Frederick
Narrator																									■											
God				■			■						■					■								■				■						■
Anna Shaw																					■															
Edith																					■															
Capt Lennox																																				
Henry Lennox																																				
George Leonards																																				
Adam Bell																																				
Dixon		■	■										■															■	■	■	■	■	■	■		
Frederick Hale																															■	■	■	■		■
Mrs Hale		■	■										■		■					■		■	■	■		■	■	■								
Mr Hale		■	■	■										■		■	■	■	■	■	■	■	■	■							■	■		■		
Margaret		■	■	■			■			■	■	■	■	■		■	■	■	■	■	■	■	■	■	■			■	■	■	■	■	■	■		■
Mrs Boucher																																				
John Boucher																																				
Mary Higgins					■	■					■																								■	
Bessy Higgins					✕																															
Nicholas Higgins								■	■	■		■				■	■	■	■	■																
Fanny Thornton																																				
Mrs Thornton																										■	■									
John Thornton		■	■																																	
Stage	Str	Mil		Cra							Fra					Str													Cra							
Percent	0.22	0.11	0.22	0.11	0.22	0.11	0.22	0.11	0.45	0.22	0.11	0.11	0.11	0.22	0.34	0.11	0.67	0.56	0.67	0.11	0.45	0.11	0.11	0.34	0.11	0.34	0.34	0.11	0.11	0.11	0.22	0.22	0.11	0.11	0.11	0.22
Length	1.0	0.5	1.0	0.5	1.0	0.5	2.0	1.0	0.5	0.5	0.5	0.5	0.5	1.5	0.5	3.0	2.5	3.0	0.5	2.0	0.5	0.5	1.5	1.5	1.5	1.5	0.5	0.5	0.5	1.0	1.0	0.5	0.5	1.0
Range	213–14	214	214–15	215–16	216–17	217	218	218–20	220–21	221–22	222	222	222	223	223–25	225	225–28	228–30	230–33	233	234–36	236	236	236–38	238–39	240–41	241–42	242–43	243	243–44	244	244–45	245–46	246	246–47	247–48
Number	200	201	202	203	204	205	206	207	208	209	210	211	212	213	214	215	216	217	218	219	220	221	222	223	224	225	226	227	228	229	230	231	232	233	234	235
Day							26											27 (234)						28 (240)												
Month																	8																			
Year																	1849																			
Chapter		2						3								4							5													
Volume																	2																			

APPENDIX 1 Comprehensive Chronologies 249

Brief Summary	Mrs Hale takes Frederick's hands.	M's talk to F about their dying mother	Fred does something perpetually.	Mrs Hale dies before the morning comes.	Frederick's violent cry	Margaret reads the chapter of consolation.	Margaret helps Dixon prepare breakfast.	Breakfast is ready.	Mr Hale's advice about the funeral	Dixon's account of meeting with Leonards	Margaret tells Frederick of Dixon's fear.	Mr Hale joins the talk: Fred must go.	Frederick glances at Thornton.	For Miss Barbour's sake, clear your name.	Margaret recommends Henry Lennox.	Margaret writes to Henry Lennox.	Frederick takes his last look at his mother.	Margaret and Frederick reach the station.	Margaret bows to Thornton.	Margaret and Fred walk on the platform.	Leonards falls from the platform.	Margaret hears railway officials' talk.	Margaret takes the train to go home.	Margaret: I shall go to the funeral.	Mrs Thornton's offer of a carriage	Frederick remains in London.	Dixon's talk with Thornton at the funeral	Nicholas and Mary at the funeral	No information of the interview given to M	Margaret is motherless.	Thornton's visit to the Hales	Dixon comes to fetch Margaret downstairs.	Mrgrt is wanted by a police-inspector.	Mrgrt denies her presence at the station.	Hale and Thornton knitted together
Narrator																																			
God																																			
Anna Shaw																																			
Edith																																			
Capt Lennox																																			
Henry Lennox																																			
George Leonards																																			
Adam Bell																																			
Dixon																																			
Frederick Hale																																			
Mrs Hale				✕																															
Mr Hale																																			
Margaret																																			
Mrs Boucher																																			
John Boucher																																			
Mary Higgins																																			
Bessy Higgins																																			
Nicholas Higgins																																			
Fanny Thornton																																			
Mrs Thornton																																			
John Thornton																																			
Stage				Cra															Out				Cra			Mil				Cra					
Percent	0.11	0.34	0.11	0.11	0.22	0.11	0.22	0.11	0.11	0.11	0.22	0.11	0.22	0.45	0.11	0.22	0.11	0.22	0.11	0.22	0.11	0.11	0.22	0.34	0.11	0.22	0.11	0.11	0.11	0.11	0.11	0.11	0.67	0.22
Length	0.5	1.5	0.5	0.5	0.5	1.0	0.5	0.5	0.5	0.5	1.0	0.5	1.0	2.0	0.5	1.0	0.5	1.0	0.5	1.0	0.5	0.5	1.0	1.5	0.5	1.0	0.5	0.5	0.5	0.5	0.5	0.5	3.0	1.0
Range	248–49	249–50	250	250	250–51	251	251–52	252	252–53	253–55	255–56	256	256–57	257–59	259–60	260–61	261–62	262–63	263	263–64	264	264–65	265	266–67	267	267–69	269	269–70	270	271	271–72	272	272–75	275–76
Number	236	237	238	239	240	241	242	243	244	245	246	247	248	249	250	251	252	253	254	255	256	257	258	259	260	261	262	263	264	265	266	267	268	269	270
Day	28	29				30				25							26 Thurs (261, 272, 278, 283, 316)							27 Fri (260)		28 Sat			29 Sun–31 Tues		31 Tues				
Month	8															10 (251)																			
Year	1849
Chapter	5				6							7											8				9						10		
Volume	2

250

Brief Summary	Two causes of Margaret's anxiety	Thornton knows Margaret is in difficulty.	Thornton decides to help out Margaret.	George Watson's meditation	The Hales before receiving Watson's call	Margaret's interview with Watson	She is degraded in Thornton's eyes.	M values T's respect and good opinion.	Dixon brings Margaret her brother's letter.	Summary of Frederick's letter	Why does she care for what T thinks?	Margaret shows Mr Hale Frederick's note.	Mr Hale looks after his daughter.	Let us visit the Higginses tomorrow.	Mr Hale: Thornton may bring a book.	The expected book arrives.	Mr Hale relapses into melancholy.	Mr Hale and Margaret visit the Higginses.	Higgins's defence of the Union	Boucher's body is brought in.	M tells Mrs Boucher her husband's death.	Margaret is the active commander.	Mgrt places Johnnie in his mother's arms.	Nicholas refuses to meet the Hales.	Mr Hale and Margaret visit Mrs Boucher.	Margaret's longing for Thornton's respect	Instead of expected Thrntn, Hggns comes.	Margaret and Mr Hale welcome Higgins.	Dixon's complaint	Higgins's wish to help Mrs Boucher	Higgins gives up working in South.	The Hales advises him to meet Thornton.	Higgins is proud; Margaret does T justice.	Thrntn feels jealousy, not disdain, for M.	Mrs Thornton's determination	Thornton's love for Margaret
Narrator																																				
God																																				
Anna Shaw																																				
Edith																																				
Capt Lennox																																				
Henry Lennox																																				
George Leonards																																				
Adam Bell																																				
Dixon																																				
Frederick Hale																																				
Mrs Hale																																				
Mr Hale																																				
Margaret																																				
Mrs Boucher																																				
John Boucher																																				
Mary Higgins																																				
Bessy Higgins																																				
Nicholas Higgins																																				
Fanny Thornton																																				
Mrs Thornton																																				
John Thornton																																				
Stage	Cra	Str	Mar						Cra									Str				Fra				Str				Cra					Mar	
Percent	0.22	0.34	0.34	0.11	0.22	0.22	0.22	0.11	0.11	0.22	0.22	0.11	0.22	0.11	0.11	0.11	0.11	0.89	0.34	0.45	0.34	0.11	0.11	0.34	0.34	0.22	0.11	0.11	0.22	0.34	0.22	0.11	0.22	0.78	0.11
Length	1.0	1.5	1.5	0.5	1.0	1.0	1.0	0.5	0.5	1.0	1.0	0.5	1.0	0.5	0.5	0.5	0.5	4.0	1.5	2.0	1.5	0.5	0.5	1.5	1.5	1.0	0.5	0.5	1.0	1.5	1.0	0.5	1.0	3.5	0.5
Range	276-77	277-79	279-80	280-81	281	282-83	283	283-84	284	284-85	285-86	286	286-87	287-88	288	288-89	289	289	289	289-94	294-95	295-97	297-99	299	299	300-01	301-03	303-04	304	304-05	305-07	307-08	308-09	309-10	310-14	314
Number	271	272	273	274	275	276	277	278	279	280	281	282	283	284	285	286	287	288	289	290	291	292	293	294	295	296	297	298	299	300	301	302	303	304	305	306
Day	31					1										2									3 (300)								one day			
Month	10															11																				
Year	1849																																			
Chapter	10									11										12										13						
Volume	2																																			

APPENDIX 1 Comprehensive Chronologies 251

Brief Summary	Mrs Thornton feels M's indiscretion.	Mrs Thornton remonstrates Margaret.	Margaret, being hurt, quits Mrs Thornton.	Thornton's daily annoyance	Thornton rejects Higgins's wish for a job.	Margaret is aware of her love for Thrntn.	Coming back from the country, M meets H.	Margaret visits dying Mrs Boucher.	Mrgrt's talk with N about his application	Thornton's unexpected visit to Higgins	Thornton gives Higgins work at his mill.	The talk between Thornton and Margaret	Margaret: I might regain his good opinion.	Margaret is merry this afternoon.	Letters come from Mr Bell and Edith.	Mr Bell's visit to Crampton	Thrntn loves Mrgrt, in spite of himself.	B and T: Talk about business transaction	Which is better, Milton or Oxford?	M's change of subject; repentant Thornton	Thornton's resolution to avoid Margaret	B's condemnation of T; M's defence of T	Mr Bell's suspect: Are they lovers?	Mr H has no intention of leaving Milton.	Boucher children brought up by Higgins	Higgins's evaluation of Thornton	Margaret wishes for seeing Thornton.	Mr Hale regrets cessation of intercourse.	Mr Hale: Did Thornton care for you?	Talk about the Lennoxes and Frederick	M: Father should have the change of air.	Thrntn's occasional visits to Mr Hale	Married Frederick becomes a trader.	Mr Hale's difficulty in breathing	Margaret's regrets and determination
Narrator																																			
God																																			
Anna Shaw																																			
Edith																																			
Capt Lennox																																			
Henry Lennox																																			
George Leonards																																			
Adam Bell																																			
Dixon																																			
Frederick Hale																																			
Mrs Hale																																			
Mr Hale																																			
Margaret																																			
Mrs Boucher																								✕											
John Boucher																																			
Mary Higgins																																			
Bessy Higgins																																			
Nicholas Higgins																																			
Fanny Thornton																																			
Mrs Thornton																																			
John Thornton																																			
Stage	Mar	Cra	Mar	Cra				Fra				Str			Cra		Mar			Cra						Fra					Cra				
Percent	0.11	0.67	0.11	0.67	0.34	0.11	0.11	0.22	0.11	0.11	0.56	0.22	0.11	0.11	0.22	0.22	0.11	0.11	0.67	0.22	0.11	0.11	0.11	0.11	0.11	0.11	0.22	0.11	0.22	0.11	0.22	1.0	0.22	0.11	0.22
Length	0.5	3.0	0.5	3.0	1.5	0.5	0.5	1.0	0.5	0.5	2.5	1.0	0.5	0.5	1.0	1.0	0.5	0.5	3.0	1.0	0.5	0.5	0.5	0.5	0.5	0.5	1.0	0.5	1.0	0.5	1.0	1.0	1.0	0.5	1.0
Range	314	314–17	317	318	318–21	321–23	323	323–24	324	324–27	324–27	327–28	328	328	328–29	330–31	331–32	332	332–35	335–36	336	336–37	337	337–38	338	338–39	339	339	340	340–41	341–42	342–43	343–44	344	344–45
Number	307	308	309	310	311	312	313	314	315	316	317	318	319	320	321	322	323	324	325	326	327	328	329	330	331	332	333	334	335	336	337	338	339	340	341
Day	the same day as above	next day						some days later				one day					next day		one day		one evening						one day								
Month		11																							winter (338)					2	3			4	
Year	1849																													1850					
Chapter	13	14						15																						16					
Volume	2																																		

252

Brief Summary	Fanny will marry Mr Watson.	Higgins sings a Methodist hymn.	Margaret thinks about her future.	Talk between Mr Hale and Mr Bell	Mr Bell is shocked by his sudden death.	Mr Bell happens to meet Thornton.	Margaret senses why Mr Bell has come.	Margaret has no appetite.	Bell decides to ask for Mrs Shaw's help.	Mrs Shaw decides to go to Milton.	Mrs Shaw arrives at "that horrid place."	Margaret weeps on her aunt's shoulder.	Dixon's attempt to dismiss Thornton	Thornton invites Bell to his house.	Thornton's regret about Margaret's Milton	Fanny trying wedding clothes	Mr Bell's arrival at the Thorntons	Mrs Thornton welcomes Mr Bell.	Bell's impertinent question to Thornton	Thornton's dinner scheme for his workers	Mrs Shaw's intention to take Mrgrt home	Mr Bell's plan of financial aid for Mrgrt	M: I have been very happy in Milton.	Margaret disposing Mr Hale's books	Margaret's wish for two farewell visits	Margaret's call at Higgins's house	Margaret shakes hands with Thornton.	Captain Lennox's arrival	Margaret gives Higgins her father's Bible.	Margaret's easy but monotonous life	Edith's sympathy for Margaret	Edith's proposal of dinners unattractive	Margaret's inactive course of the day	Dixon's report of Milton	Margaret sitting alone while meditating
Narrator																																			
God																																			
Anna Shaw									▓	▓	▓	▓									▓														
Edith																													▓						
Capt Lennox																												▓							
Henry Lennox																																			
George Leonards																																			
Adam Bell			▓	▓	▓	▓	▓		▓					▓	▓		▓	▓	▓	▓		▓													
Dixon													▓																					▓	
Frederick Hale																																			
Mrs Hale																																			
Mr Hale				✕																															
Margaret	▓	▓	▓	▓			▓	▓				▓	▓								▓	▓	▓	▓	▓	▓	▓		▓	▓	▓	▓	▓		▓
Mrs Boucher																																			
John Boucher																																			
Mary Higgins		▓																							▓										
Bessy Higgins																																			
Nicholas Higgins		▓																											▓					▓	
Fanny Thornton																▓																			
Mrs Thornton																		▓																	
John Thornton						▓								▓	▓		▓	▓	▓	▓							▓								
Stage	Cra	Fra	Cra	Oxf	Tra		Cra		Har	Mil		Cra			Str			Mar			Cra					Fra		Mar		Cra				Har	
Percent	0.22	0.22	0.22	0.45	0.11	0.56	0.11	0.11	0.11	0.22	0.11	0.11	0.11	0.11	0.22	0.11	0.11	0.11	0.34	0.56	0.11	0.11	0.22	0.11	0.11	0.11	0.34	0.22	0.11	0.22	0.11	0.11	0.11	0.11	0.11
Length	1.0	1.0	1.0	2.0	0.5	2.5	0.5	0.5	0.5	1.0	0.5	0.5	0.5	0.5	1.0	0.5	0.5	0.5	1.5	2.5	0.5	0.5	1.0	0.5	0.5	0.5	1.5	1.0	0.5	1.0	0.5	0.5	0.5	0.5	0.5
Range	345–46	346–47	347–48	348–50	350	350–53	353	353–54	354	354–55	355	355–56	356	356–57	357–58	358	358	359	359–61	361–63	363–64	364	365	365–66	366–67	367	368–69	369–70	370	370–71	372–73	373	373–74	374	374
Number	342	343	344	345	346	347	348	349	350	351	352	353	354	355	356	357	358	359	360	361	362	363	364	365	366	367	368	369	370	371	372	373	374	375	376	377
Day	the same day as above	next day		next day											next day (356)							Tues (365)	Wed (364)		Thurs									Tues evening	
Month											4																			6 (372,373, 376)					
Year	1850
Chapter	16				17										18														19						
Volume	2

APPENDIX 1 Comprehensive Chronologies 253

Brief Summary	Mr Bell's goodwill visit	Henry Lennox's appearance	Bell introduced to the Lennoxes & Shaw	Henry's criticism of Hale; Bell's defence	Mr Bell's dream of his Helstone holiday	Frederick's exoneration is difficult.	Mr Bell's invitation of M to Helstone	Mrs Shaw's consent to the project	Margaret and Mr Bell leave for Helstone.	A gentleman's visit last winter/ this spring	Mrs Purkis, the landlady, about new Vicar	Margaret and Mr Bell set out for walk.	Margaret and Mr Bell to Susan's house	Betty Barnes' roasting of the cat	Margaret must go and see Susan.	M's old pupils grown into great girls	The parsonage so altered, inside and out	Margaret and Mr Bell returning to the inn	M ponders: There was change everywhere.	Margaret: I told a lie.	Margaret's confession of her lie	Margaret's request to Mr Bell	Margaret: Nothing had been the same.	A brighter view of things comes.	Margaret: O Helstone!	Margaret's impression of the Helstone visit	Dixon brings some pieces of Milton news.	Mrgrt wonders if Mr Bell went to Milton.	Mr Bell's secret plan of visiting Cadiz	Bell's plan might be a fancy of moment.	Margaret's love for Edith's boy Sholt	Opinions and tastes different from Henry's	Margaret is disinterested in dinner parties.	Henry's confidential talk with Margaret	No intelligence of Mr Bell going to Milton	Mr Bell's letter: he must be ill.
Narrator																																				
God																																				
Anna Shaw			■		■																															
Edith			■																													■	■			
Capt Lennox																																				
Henry Lennox		■	■	■																												■	■	■		
George Leonards																																				
Adam Bell	■	■	■	■	■	■	■	■	■			■	■					■				■						■	■	■					■	■
Dixon																											■	■								
Frederick Hale						■																														
Mrs Hale																																				
Mr Hale																																				
Margaret	■	■	■			■	■	■	■	■		■	■		■	■	■	■	■	■	■	■	■	■	■	■	■	■	■	■	■	■	■	■	■	■
Mrs Boucher																																				
John Boucher																																				
Mary Higgins																																				
Bessy Higgins																																				
Nicholas Higgins																																				
Fanny Thornton																																				
Mrs Thornton																																				
John Thornton																																				
Stage		Har		Str	Lon		Har			Tra									Hel												Har					
Percent	0.45	0.45	0.22	0.34	0.11	0.22	0.11	0.11	0.22	0.34	0.11	0.22	0.34	0.11	0.11	0.34	0.22	0.11	0.34	0.22	0.11	0.22	0.11	0.11	0.11	0.22	0.11	0.22	0.11	0.22	0.11	0.45	0.45	0.11	0.11	0.22
Length	2.0	2.0	1.0	1.5	0.5	1.0	0.5	0.5	1.0	1.5	0.5	1.0	1.5	0.5	0.5	1.5	1.0	0.5	1.5	1.0	0.5	1.0	0.5	0.5	0.5	1.0	0.5	1.0	0.5	1.0	0.5	2.0	2.0	0.5	0.5	1.0
Range	374–76	376–78	378–79	379–81	381–82	382–83	383	383–84	384–85	385–87	387	387–88	388–89	389–90	390–91	391–92	392–93	393	393–94	394–95	395–97	397–99	399–400	400–01	401	402–03	403	404–05	405	405–06	407–08	408	408–09			
Number	378	379	380	381	382	383	384	385	386	387	388	389	390	391	392	393	394	395	396	397	398	399	400	401	402	403	404	405	406	407	408	409	410	411	412	413
Day	the same day as above		Wed									Thurs												Fri (383)	a few days	one day						One day (407)			one morning	
Month						6																				summer						8 (408)				
Year	1850
Chapter	19		20						21																	22						23				
Volume	2

254

Brief Summary	A letter from Wallis, Mr Bell's servant	Margaret: I'm going to Oxford.	Captain Lennox accompanies Margaret.	Mr Bell died in the previous night.	Margaret and Captain Lennox come home.	Margaret's wish for Thornton's respect	Margaret may be Mr Bell's heiress.	Margaret is Mr Bell's residuary legatee.	Edith's teasing of Henry	M agrees to spend a holiday at Cromer.	Margaret's hope about Thornton vanished.	The holidays soothe and revive Margaret.	Edith: Henry Lennox should be invited.	Henry is impressed by Margaret's change.	Henry's love for Margaret rekindled	Margaret fulfils her seaside resolve.	Margaret's decision to be independent	Edith's plan for the marriage of M and H	Failure in America affects Milton mills.	Thornton: mutual understanding promoted	A secret help of Higgins and his fellow	Margaret's wish is fulfilled by Higgins.	Could Thornton stand the loss of fortunes?	Thornton is tempted by a speculation.	Thornton asks for biblical comfort.	Thornton's decision to refuse speculation	Thornton in bankruptcy	Edith is looking for Margaret.	Henry's request for bringing T to dinner	H tells M T's reason for coming to town.	Margaret's reunion with Thornton	At dinner: Margaret watches T's face.	Thornton's talk of his failure in business	T tells Margaret Higgins's round-robin.
Narrator																																		
God																																		
Anna Shaw																																		
Edith																																		
Capt Lennox																																		
Henry Lennox																																		
George Leonards																																		
Adam Bell	X																																	
Dixon																																		
Frederick Hale																																		
Mrs Hale																																		
Mr Hale																																		
Margaret																																		
Mrs Boucher																																		
John Boucher																																		
Mary Higgins																																		
Bessy Higgins																																		
Nicholas Higgins																																		
Fanny Thornton																																		
Mrs Thornton																																		
John Thornton																																		
Stage	Har	Har	Oxf	Har	Har	Har	Har	Har	Har	Har	Har	Cro	Cro	Cro	Har	Har	Har	Har	Mil	Mil	Mil	Mil	Mar	Mar	Mar	Mar	Mar	Har	Har	Har	Har	Har	Har	Har
Percent	0.11	0.11	0.11	0.11	0.11	0.11	0.11	0.11	0.11	0.11	0.11	0.11	0.11	0.11	0.22	0.11	0.11	0.11	0.22	0.56	0.11	0.34	0.11	0.34	0.22	0.11	0.11	0.11	0.22	0.11	0.11	0.22	0.34	0.11
Length	0.5	0.5	0.5	0.5	0.5	0.5	0.5	0.5	0.5	0.5	0.5	0.5	0.5	0.5	1.0	0.5	0.5	0.5	1.0	2.5	0.5	1.5	0.5	1.5	1.0	0.5	0.5	0.5	1.0	0.5	0.5	1.0	1.5	0.5
Range	409-10	410	410-11	411	411-12	412-13	413	413	413-14	414	414-15	415	415	415-16	416-17	417	417-18	418-19	419-21	421	421-23	423	423-24	425	425-26	426	427	427-28	428-29	429	430	431-32	432-33
Number	414	415	416	417	418	419	420	421	422	423	424	425	426	427	428	429	430	431	432	433	434	435	436	437	438	439	440	441	442	443	444	445	446	447
Day		one day	one day	one day	a wk afterwards	one day	one day	one day	one day	more than one week	more than one week	more than one week	more than one week	more than one week									one day	One day (423)	Next day (425)	Next day (425)	Next day (425)	one evening	one evening	one evening	one evening	one evening		
Month		8	8	8		9	9	9	9					10 (415)						late spring (420)											summer (427)			
Year	1850																			1851														
Chapter	23				24															25							26							
Volume	2																																	

APPENDIX 1 *Comprehensive Chronologies* 255

	M to H: Can I speak to you tomorrow?	Henry: Miss Hale would not have me.	Recognition of mutual love	Happy ending with humour						Brief Summary
					3	0	3	0.7	0	0.7	Narrator
					0	57	57	0	20.2	20.2	God
					22	53	75	3.9	12	15.9	Anna Shaw
					25	52	77	4.1	11.6	15.7	Edith
					14	33	47	2.2	8.9	11.1	Capt Lennox
					31	35	66	6.9	8.2	15.1	Henry Lennox
					1	20	21	0.1	5.7	5.8	George Leonards
					43	38	81	10.1	9	19.1	Adam Bell
					66	40	106	11.6	9.2	20.8	Dixon
					22	60	82	3.9	17.1	21	Frederick Hale
					64	104	168	14.6	25.2	39.8	Mrs Hale
					138	100	238	32.1	23.4	55.5	Mr Hale
					359	68	427	80.3	14.8	95.1	Margaret
					6	15	21	1.5	5.0	6.5	Mrs Boucher
					4	27	31	1.3	8.9	10.2	John Boucher
					11	16	27	3.0	4.1	7.1	Mary Higgins
					16	23	39	5.7	5.4	11.2	Bessy Higgins
					34	39	73	10.7	10.2	20.9	Nicholas Higgins
					21	24	45	4.7	7.5	12.2	Fanny Thornton
					37	45	82	10.2	11.3	21.5	Mrs Thornton
					77	113	190	22.5	27.1	49.6	John Thornton
		Har									Stage
	0.11	0.22	0.45	0.11						99.42	Percent
	0.5	1.0	2.0	0.5			447.5				Length
	433	433–34	434–36	436							Range
	448	449	450	451							Number
the same day as above	next day		next day		Times			%			Day
	summer				Active	Referred	Total Appearance	Active	Referred	Total Appearance	Month
1851											Year
26	27										Chapter
2											Volume

256

The Comprehensive Chronology for *Lois the Witch* (1859)

Legend: active | referred | non-appearance | dead | B: Barford

		Chapter	1										2						
		Year	1661	1674	1678	1689	1690–91			1691									
	Time Inferred	Month								5 (105)						6 (128)			
		Day	(106)	(181)	(115)	(130, 140, 148)	(105–08)			one day			a couple of days later (117)		next morning			one day (129)	
	Scene	Number	1	2	3	4	5	6	7	8	9	10	11	12	13	14	15	16	17	18	19
		Range	105	105–08	108–09	109–10	110–11	111–15	115–17	117–18	118–19	119–20	120–21	121–23	123	123–24	124–26	126	126–28	128	128–29
		Length	1.0	2.5	1.0	1.5	1.0	4.0	2.0	1.0	1.0	1.5	1.0	1.5	1.0	0.5	1.5	0.5	1.5	0.5	0.5
		Percent	1.1	2.7	1.1	1.6	1.1	4.3	2.1	1.1	1.1	1.6	1.1	1.6	1.1	0.5	1.6	0.5	1.6	0.5	0.5
		Stage						Boston								Salem					
Main Characters		God																			
		Widow Smith																			
		Prudence Smith																			
		Hester Smith																			
		Elder Hawkins																			
		Capt. Holdernesse																			
		Hugh Ralph Lucy																			
		Hannah																			
		Mr Barclay																			
		Henrietta Barclay																			
		Lois Barclay																			
		Ralph Hickson																			
		Grace Hickson																			
		Manasseh Hickson																			
		Faith Hickson																			
		Prudence Hickson																			
		Nattee																			
		Satan/Indians																			
		Pastor Nolan																			
		Pastor Tappau																			
		Abigail Tappau																			
		Hester Tappau																			
		Hota																			
		Cotton Mather																			
		narrator																			
	Brief Summary of Each Scene (Boxes of important events are coloured.)		Barclay, Barford minister	The birth of Lois	Old Hannah's curse	Tappau vs. Nolan	Lois's background	The arrival at Boston	Lois's recollections	On the way to Widow Smith's	Widow Smith's welcome	Preparation for a meal	Tales of horror	Lois's tale of old Hannah	To Salem	Lois's arrival at the Hicksons	Ungracious reception	Waiting for Grace's return	Lois's meeting with her uncle	Supper	Farewell to Capt. Holdernesse	Grace's sarcasm	Manasseh is friendly.	Nattee's weird tales	Lois's friendship with Faith	Pastoral visits

APPENDIX 1 Comprehensive Chronologies 257

Brief Summary	nar	CM	Hot	HT	AT	PT	PN	S/I	Nat	PH	FH	MH	GH	RH	LB	HB	MrB	Han	HRL	CH	EH	HS	PS	WS	God	Stage	Percent	Length	Range	Number	Day	Month	Year	Chapter
Faith hates Tappau.																											0.5	0.5	129	20		10	1691	2
Faith's secret																											0.5	0.5	129-30	21	the same day as above			
Faith's attachment to Nolan																											0.5	0.5	130	22				
Lois's interest in Faith's love																											0.5	0.5	130	23				
Lois's talk of Halloween																											1.1	1.0	131	24				
Prudence's scream of terror																											1.1	1.0	131-32	25	31 (131, 132-33)			
Ralph Hickson's death															✕												0.5	0.5	132-33	26				
Bereaved family's responses																											0.5	0.5	133	27	1 (132-33)	11		
Manasseh's intention																											0.5	0.5	133-34	28	3 (133)			
Lois avoids Manasseh.																											1.1	1.0	134-35	29	next few days			
Manasseh's search for Lois																											0.5	0.5	135	30	one day (135)			
Manasseh's proposal																											2.1	2.0	135-37	31		12		
Winter of devilish terrors																											1.1	1.0	137-39	32				
Manasseh's approach																											1.1	1.0	139-40	33	one day (139)			
Necessity of assistant pastor																											0.5	0.5	140	34				
Nolan's return is discussed.																											0.5	0.5	140	35				
Nattee as Faith's confidant																											0.5	0.5	140-41	36	Christmas (140)			
Nolan's morning visit																											1.1	1.0	141-42	37				
Faith meets Nolan.																										Salem	1.1	1.0	142-43	38				
Pastor Nolan's prayer																											1.1	1.0	143-44	39	one day (141)			
Manasseh's vision																											1.1	1.0	144-45	40				
Manasseh's appeal to Grace																											2.1	2.0	145-47	41				
Faith's love is unrequited.																											0.5	0.5	147	42				
Manasseh's proposals																											0.5	0.5	147-48	43				
Tappau vs. Nolan again																											1.1	1.0	148	44				
Hester and Abigail possessed																											1.6	1.5	148-50	45	one day (148)	2 (149)	1692 (191)	3
Nolan's story and prayer																											1.6	1.5	150-51	46				
The sin of witchcraft																											2.1	2.0	151-53	47				
Lois's fear of Nattee																											1.1	1.0	153-55	48				
The rumour of witchcraft																											0.5	0.5	155	49				
Supplication at Tappau's																											1.1	1.0	155-56	50	Saturday (155)	3		
On their way home																											1.1	1.0	156-57	51				
Hota confessed her sin.																											0.5	0.5	157	52				
Talk about Hota's confession																											4.3	4.0	157-61	53				
Manasseh's evening prayer																											1.1	1.0	161-62	54				
Faith's request to Lois																											1.1	1.0	162-63	55				

258

Brief Summary	Lois's interview with Nolan	Faith's jealousy	The plan for the morning	Manasseh's prophecy	Hota's execution	The prayer meeting	Dr Mather's speech	Prudence's convulsions	Lois is prosecuted as a witch.	Manasseh is mad!	Lois is dragged to the gaol.	Lois in the city gaol	Sentenced to be hanged	Feverish night in the gaol	Lois chooses death.	Historical facts	No one saves Lois.	Manasseh yearns after Lois.	Grace's visit to the gaol	Lois comforts Nattee.	Lois hanged; mad Manasseh	Holdernesse and Lucy come.	21 years later
nar																							
CM					▨	▨	▨	▨															
Hot				✗																			
HT																							
AT												▨											
PT							▨	▨															
PN	▨																						
S/I																							
Nat																					✗		
PH	▨	▨																					
FH	▨	▨																					
MH	▨		▨	▨				▨									▨						
GH	▨		▨	▨				▨									▨						
RH																							
LB	▨	▨	▨	▨	▨	▨	▨	▨	▨	▨	▨	▨	▨	▨	▨			▨	▨	▨	✗		
HB													▨										
MrB													▨										
Han								▨															
HRL																						▨	
CH																						▨	
EH																							
HS																							
PS																							
WS																							
God	▨			▨																			
Stage							Salem																B
Percent	2.1	1.1	0.5	1.1	1.6	0.5	1.6	0.5	2.7	3.2	0.5	2.7	2.1	2.1	1.1	0.5	0.5	3.2	1.1	1.1	1.1	0.5	2.7
Length	2.0	1.0	0.5	1.0	1.5	0.5	1.5	0.5	2.5	3.0	0.5	2.5	2.0	2.0	1.0	0.5	0.5	3.0	1.0	1.0	1.0	0.5	2.5
Range	163-65	165-66	166	166-67	167-68	168-69	169-71	171	171-74	174-77	177	177-79	179-81	181-82	182-85	185	185-86	186	186-88	188-89	189-90	190	190-93
Number	56	57	58	59	60	61	62	63	64	65	66	67	68	69	70	71	72	73	74	75	76	77	78
Day	Sunday (163)									Monday (179)					Tuesday (182)					Wednesday (188)	Thurs. (184, 189)	(190)	(190)
Month				3 spring (182, 183)																	4 (189)	autumn	
Year	1692																						1713
Chapter	3																						

APPENDIX 1 Comprehensive Chronologies 259

0	0	0	5	0	7	0	12	12	0	21.38	21.38	narrator
0	1	0	1	5	0	5	2	7	8.54	2.67	11.21	Cotton Mather
0	0	0	0	1	11	1	11	12	1.07	16.56	17.63	Hota
0	0	0	1	1	6	1	7	8	1.07	12.29	13.36	Hester Tappau
0	0	0	1	0	6	0	7	7	0	12.29	12.29	Abigail Tappau
0	0	0	12	5	6	5	18	23	9.08	19.21	28.29	Pastor Tappau
0	0	5	7	2	3	7	10	17	8.55	10.14	18.69	Pastor Nolan
0	3	0	7	0	20	0	30	30	0	50.22	50.22	Satan/Indians
2	1	8	5	3	2	13	8	21	11.73	8	19.73	Nattee
3	2	9	11	10	5	22	18	40	32.57	22.41	54.98	Prudence Hickson
3	2	16	11	12	4	31	17	48	36.83	22.42	59.25	Faith Hickson
4	2	10	11	9	4	23	17	40	29.91	21.35	51.26	Manasseh Hickson
4	3	12	10	11	7	27	20	47	35.76	26.69	62.45	Grace Hickson
1	7	2	6	0	3	3	16	19	3.73	24.04	27.77	Ralph Hickson
14	0	27	2	23	2	64	4	68	85.98	4.8	90.78	Lois Barclay
0	5	0	2	0	3	0	10	10	0	13.88	13.88	Henrietta Barclay
0	5	0	2	0	1	0	8	8	0	15.49	15.49	Mr Barclay
0	1	0	0	0	1	0	2	2	0	4.81	4.81	Hannah
0	3	0	3	2	2	2	8	10	3.2	14.97	18.17	Hugh Ralph Lucy
12	1	0	0	2	0	14	1	15	20.84	2.67	23.51	Capt. Holdernesse
3	0	0	0	0	0	3	0	3	7.49	0	7.49	Elder Hawkins
4	1	0	0	0	0	4	1	5	9.09	1.07	10.16	Hester Smith
4	1	0	0	0	0	4	1	5	9.09	1.07	10.16	Prudence Smith
5	1	0	0	0	0	5	1	6	10.16	1.07	11.23	Widow Smith
0	9	0	13	0	17	0	39	39	0	67.87	67.87	God
												Stage
										99.9		Percent
						93.5						Length
												Range
												Number
	Times					Times			%			
Active	Referred	Active	Referred	Active	Referred	Total Active	Total Referred	Total Appearance	Total Active	Total Referred	Total Appearance	
1		2		3								

260

APPENDIX 2 Characters' Correlation Diagrams for Gaskell's Fiction

Characters' Correlation Diagram for *Mary Barton*

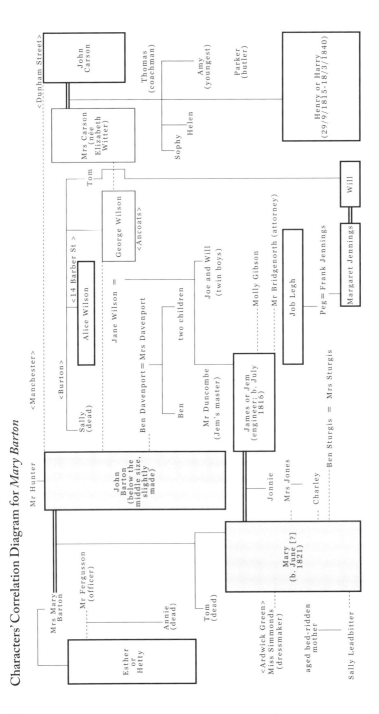

Characters' Correlation Diagram for *Ruth*

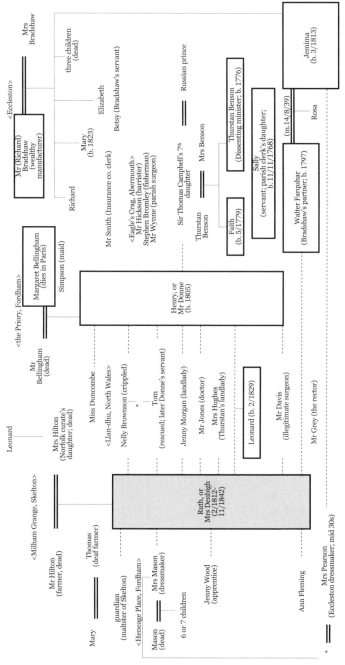

APPENDIX 2 *Characters' Correlation Diagrams for Gaskell's Fiction* 263

Characters' Correlation Diagram for *North and South*

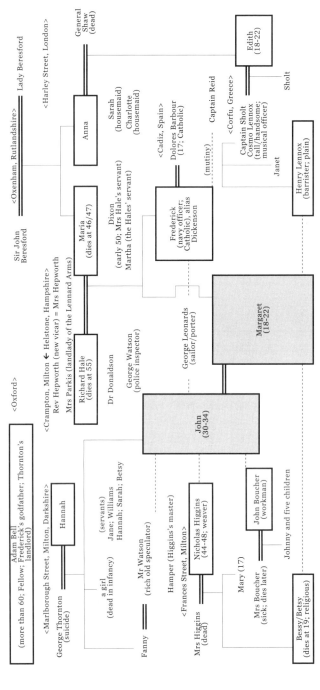

264

Characters' Correlation Diagram for *Lois the Witch*

<Boston>

Widow Smith
— Hester
— Prudence

Elder Hawkins

Hannah Benson
Elijah

old Nance Hickson

Elias Wellcome (errand boy)

Mr Lucy (Miller) = Mrs Lucy

Hugh Ralph

Captain Holdernesse

<Barford, Warwickshire>

a brother (dead)

Mr Barclay (Jacobite minister; dead)

(schoolfellow)

old Clemence (servant)

old Hannah

Henrietta (dead)

Lois (1674–92; hanged at 18) =

<Salem>

Ralph Hickson ═ Grace (past middle age)

Prudence (12 or above)

Manasseh (23/24)

Faith (19?)

Pastor Nolan (30)

Nattee (Indian servant)

Hosea (old out-door servant)

Pastor Tappau
— Hester
— Abigail

Hota (Indian servant; hanged)

Cotton Mather

APPENDIX 2 Characters' Correlation Diagrams for Gaskell's Fiction   265

… APPENDIX 3 Gaskell's Manipulation of Upham's *First Lecture on Witchcraft*

NO.	PAGE	LOIS	SUMMARY	SEGMENT
1	1		purpose	It is one of the distinguishing characteristics of the human being, that he loves to contemplate the scenes of the past, and desires to have his own history borne down to the future—this, like all the other propensities of our nature, is accompanied by faculties to secure its gratification.
2	1		purpose	The gift of speech by which the parent can convey information to the child, and the old transmit intelligence to the young, is an indication that it is the design of the Author of our being, that we should receive from those who are passing away before us, the narrative of their experience, and communicate the results of our own to the generations that are to succeed us.
3	1-2		purpose	All nations have to a greater or less degree been faithful to their trust, in using the gift to fulfil the design of the Creator.
4	2		purpose	It is impossible to name a people who do not possess cherished traditions that have descended from their early ancestors.
5	2		purpose	Although it is generally considered that the invention of a system of arbitrary and external signs to communicate thought, is one of the greatest and most arduous achievements of human ingenuity, yet so universal is, the disposition to make future generations acquainted with our condition and history, a disposition, the efficient cause of which can only be found in a sense of the value of such knowledge, that you can scarcely find a people on the face of the globe, who have not contrived by some means or other, from the rude monument of shapeless rock, to the most perfect alphabetical language, to communicate with posterity, thus declaring as with the voice of nature herself, that it is desirable and proper that all men should know as much as possible, of the character, and actions, and fortunes of their predecessors on the stage of life.
6	3		purpose	It is not difficult to discern the end, for which this disposition to preserve for the future and contemplate the past was imparted to us.
7	3		purpose	If all that we knew were what is taught by our individual experience, our minds would have but little, comparatively, to exercise and expand them, and our characters would be the result of the limited influences embraced within the narrow sphere of our particular relations and circumstances.
8	3		purpose	But now, that our eye is attracted to the observation of those who have lived before us, our materials for reflection and sources of instruction are multiplied.
9	3		purpose	The virtues we admire in our ancestors, not only adorn and dignify their names, but win us to their imitation.
10	3		purpose	Their prosperity and happiness spread abroad a diffusive light that reaches us, and brightens our condition.
11	3		purpose	The wisdom that guided their footsteps becomes at the same time a lamp to our path.
12	3-4		purpose	The observation of the errors of their course, and of the consequent disappointments and sufferings that befel them, enables us to pass in safety, through rocks and ledges, on which they were shipwrecked,—and while we grieve to see them eating the bitter fruits of their own vices and crimes, we can seize the benefits of their experience without paying the price at which they purchased it.
13	4		purpose	In the desire which every man feels to learn the history, and be instructed by the example of his predecessors, and in the accompanying disposition, with the means of carrying it into effect, to transmit a knowledge of himself and his own times to his successors, we discover the wise and admirable arrangement of a providence, which removes the worn out individual to a better country, but leaves the acquisitions of his mind, and the benefit of his experience, as an accumulating and common fund, for the use of his posterity—which has secured the continued renovation of the race, without the loss of the wisdom of each generation.

NO.	PAGE	LOIS	SUMMARY	SEGMENT
14	4		purpose	These considerations suggest a much more adequate and accurate definition of history, than the celebrated one proposed by Bolingbroke—'Philosophy teaching by example.'
15	4-5		definition of history	They inform us that history is rather the instrument by which the results of the great experiment of human life are collected and transmitted from age to age: speaking through the records of history, all past generations become the instructors of the present.
16	5		meaning of history	Since this is the true and proper design of history, it assumes an exalted station among the branches of human knowledge.
17	5		meaning of history	Every community that aspires to become intelligent and virtuous, should cherish it.
18	5		meaning of history	Institutions for the promotion and diffusion of useful information, should have special reference to it.
19	5		purpose	And all people should be induced to look back to the days of their forefathers, to be warned by their errors, instructed by their wisdom, and stimulated in the career of improvement, by the example of their virtues.
20	5		purpose	Under the influence of these views, it has appeared to me, that I could not discharge the duty to which I have here been called, in any way more conducive to the accomplishment of the design of this association, than by presenting to its members a remarkable passage in the history of their ancestors.
21	5-6		purpose	It shall be my design to exhibit the subject in such a light, that the great end of history, just described, may be attained; and that when the whole scene to be disclosed has been spread out before you, you may bear away instruction and improvement from its contemplation.
22	6		purpose	The historian would find a great amount and variety of materials in the annals of this town,—greater perhaps, than in any other of its size in the country.
23	6		purpose	But there is one chapter in our history of preeminent interest and importance.
24	6		witchcraft	The witchcraft delusion of 1692 has attracted universal attention for the last century, and will, in all coming ages, render the name of Salem notable, throughout the world.
25	6		witchcraft	Wherever the name of the place we live in is mentioned, this memorable transaction will be found associated with it, and those who know nothing else of our history, or our character, will be sure to know, and tauntingly to inform us that they know, that we hanged the witches.
26	6-7		purpose	It is surely incumbent upon us to possess ourselves of correct and just views of a transaction, thus indissolubly connected with the reputation of our home, with the memory of our fathers, and of course with the most precious part of the inheritance of our children.
27	7		purpose	I am apprehensive that the community is very superficially acquainted with this transaction.
28	7		purpose	All have heard of the Salem witchcraft—hardly any are aware of the real character of that event.
29	7		purpose	Its mention creates a smile of astonishment, and perhaps a sneer of contempt, or it may be, a thrill of horror for the innocent who suffered, but there is reason to fear that it fails to suggest those reflections and impart that salutary instruction, without which the design of providence in permitting it to take place cannot be accomplished.
30	7		witchcraft	There are, indeed, few passages in the history of any people to be compared with it in all that constitutes the pitiable and tragical, the mysterious and awful.

NO.	PAGE	LOIS	SUMMARY	SEGMENT
31	7		witchcraft	The student of human nature will contemplate in its scenes one of the most remarkable developments which that nature ever assumed; while the moralist, the statesman and the Christian philosopher, will, severally, find that it opens widely before them, a field fruitful in instruction.
32	8		witchcraft	Our ancestors have been visited with unmeasured reproach for their conduct on the occasion.
33	8		purpose of lecture	Sad, indeed, was the delusion that came over them, and shocking was the extent to which their bewildered imaginations and excited passions hurried and drove them on.
34	8		purpose of lecture	Still, however, there are many considerations that deserve to be well weighed before sentence is passed upon them.
35	8		purpose of lecture	And, while I hope to give evidence of a readiness to have everything appear in its own just light, and to expose to view the very darkest features of the transaction, I am confident of being able to bring forward such facts and reflections as will satisfy you, that no reproach ought to be attached to them in consequence of this affair, which does not belong, at least equally, to all other nations, and to the greatest and best men of their times and of previous ages; and in short, that the final predominating sentiment, their conduct should awaken, is not so much that of anger and indignation as of pity and compassion.
36	8-9		1st and 2nd lectures	In order to do justice to the subject, it will be necessary for me to divide it into two lectures;—the first must be devoted to a historical narration of the proceedings in Salem, and the second will present those additional facts and considerations, that should be taken into view, previous to pronouncing a judgment, or forming an opinion respecting the conduct and characters of the persons connected with them.
37	9		historical background	Let us endeavor to carry ourselves back to the state of the colony of Massachusetts one hundred and forty years ago.
38	9		historical background	The persecutions our ancestors had undergone in their own country, and the privations, altogether inconceivable by us, they suffered during the early years of their residence here, acting upon their minds and characters, in cooperation with the influences of the political and ecclesiastical occurrences that marked the commencement of the seventeenth century, had imparted a gloomy, solemn and romantic turn to their dispositions and associations, which was transmitted without diminution to their children, and was strengthened and aggravated by the peculiar circumstances of the period.
39	9-10		age of superstition	It was the triumphant age of superstition.
40	10		age of superstition	The imagination had been expanded by credulity until it had reached a wild and monstrous growth.
41	10		age of superstition	The puritans were always prone to subject themselves to its influence, and New England, at the time to which we have referred, was a most fit and congenial theatre upon which to display its power.
42	10		age of superstition	Cultivation and civilization had made but a partial encroachment upon the wilderness.
43	10	105, 117	forests	Wide, deep, solemn forests covered the hills, hung over the unfrequented roads, and frowned upon the scattered settlements.
44	10	126, 189	forests	These forests were still the abode of wild beasts and of the Indians, in the terror of whose strange customs and warlike propensities, the European settlers were apt to lose sight of all those nobler qualities, which properly regarded and addressed would unquestionably have proved them worthy of the friendship of our ancestors.

NO.	PAGE	LOIS	SUMMARY	SEGMENT
45	10-11		want of confidence	In consequence of a want of confidence and sympathy, and of provocations incident to two races of men of dissimilar habits and feelings, thus thrown into close proximity, conflicts and wars of the most distressing and shocking character soon arose.
46	11		hostility between two races of men	A strongly rooted sentiment of hostility and horror became associated in the minds of the colonists with the name of Indian.
47	11		hostility between two races of men	There was scarcely a village where the marks of savage violence and cruelty could not be pointed out, or an individual whose family history did not contain some illustration of the stealth, the malice, or the vengeance of the savage foe.
48	11	112	Essex, scouts	In the year 1691, about six months previous to the commencement of the witchcraft delusion, the county of Essex was ordered to keep four scouts or companies of minute-men, consisting each of six persons, constantly in the field, to guard the frontiers against the savage enemy, and to give notice of his approach, an event then looked for every hour with the greatest alarm and apprehension.
49	11		Indians' attack on Haverhill	On the fifteenth of March, 1697, five years after the delusion occurred, the Indians struck terror into the hearts of the people of this county, by a sudden attack upon Haverhill, where they burned six houses, and killed or made captive about forty of the inhabitants.
50	12		Little communication	There was but little communication between the several villages and settlements.
51	12	117	from Boston to Salem	To travel from Boston to Salem, for instance, which the ordinary means of conveyance enable us to do at present in less than two hours, was then the fatiguing, adventurous and doubtful work of an entire day.
52	12		the darkest and most desponding period	It was the darkest and most desponding period in the whole history of New England.
53	12		a feverish state of anxiety	The people whose ruling passion then was, as it has ever since been, a love for constitutional rights, had a few years before been thrown into dismay by the loss of their charter, and from that time had been kept in a feverish state of anxiety respecting their future political destinies.
54	12		pirates	In addition to all this, the whole sea coast was infested with hostile privateers—ruthless pirates were continually prowling along the shores.
55	12		historical background	Commerce was nearly extinguished, and great losses had been experienced by men in business.
56	12	109	French vengeance	A recent expedition against Canada had exposed the colonies to the vengeance of France.
57	12-13	114	Indians in alliance with French	The inland frontiers were constantly harassed by the warlike and vengeful incursions of the Indians in alliance with that power.
58	13		Indians in alliance with French	In the year 1708, several hundred Algonquin and St Francis Indians, under the command of French officers, fell upon Haverhill about break of day on the twenty-ninth of August, consigned the town to conflagration and plunder, destroyed property to the amount of one thousand pounds, massacred the minister of the congregation, Mr Rolfe, the commander of the place, Capt. Wainright, together with nearly forty others, and carried off many more into captivity.
59	13		tax	The province was encumbered with oppressive taxes and weighed down by a heavy debt.

NO.	PAGE	LOIS	SUMMARY	SEGMENT
60	13		tax	The sum assessed upon Salem to defray the expenses of the country at large, the year before the witchcraft prosecutions, was one thousand three hundred and fortysix pounds one shilling.
61	13		tax	Besides this there were the town taxes.
62	13-14		tax	The whole amounted no doubt to more than six thousand dollars, exclusive of the support of the ministry, a weight of taxation considering the greater value of money at that time, of which we have no experience and can hardly form an adequate conception.
63	14		tax	The burden pressed directly upon the whole community.
64	14		tax	There were then no great private fortunes, no moneyed institutions, no foreign commerce, few, if any, articles of luxury, and no large capitals to intercept and divert its pressure.
65	14		tax	It was borne to its whole extent by the actual industry of a population of extremely moderate estates, and very limited earnings, and almost crushed it to the earth.
66	14		historical background	The people were dissatisfied with the new charter.
67	14		historical background	They were becoming the victims of political jealousies, discontent and animosities.
68	14		historical background	They had been agitated by great revolutions.
69	14		war	They were surrounded by alarming indications of change, and their ears were constantly assailed by rumors of war.
70	14		prophecies, foreboding	Their minds were startled and confounded by the prevalence of prophecies and forebodings of dark and dismal events.
71	14-15		evil being	At this most unfortunate moment, and as it were to crown the whole, and fill up the measure of their affliction and terror, it was their universal and sober belief, that the evil being himself was in a special manner let loose, and permitted to descend upon them with unexampled fury.
72	15		Salem in 1708	The population of what is now Salem, was at that time and continued, for nearly thirty years afterwards, to be so small, that there was but one religious society in the place.
73	15		Salem in 1708	All the people were accommodated in the meetinghouse of the first church.
74	15		gloom, despondency, trouble, distress	They participated in their full share of the gloom and despondency that pervaded the province, and in addition to that, had their own peculiar troubles and distresses.
75	15	148	loss of fathers and citizens	Within a short time the town had lost almost all its venerable fathers and leading citizens, the men whose councils had governed and whose wisdom had guided them from the first years of the settlement of the place.
76	15-16		loss of fathers and citizens	Only those who are intimately acquainted with the condition of a community of simple manners and primitive feelings, such as were the early New England settlements, can have an adequate conception of the degree to which the people were attached to their patriarchs, the extent of their dependence upon them, and the amount of their loss when they were removed.
77	16		congregation	A separate religious society, had previously been formed in what was then Salem Village, now a part of Danvers.

NO.	PAGE	LOIS	SUMMARY	SEGMENT
78	16		congregation	This congregation, the same at present under the pastoral care of Rev. Mr Braman, lately under that of the estimable Dr Wadsworth, had for a long period been the scene of those violent and heated dissensions, too common in our religious societies at all times.
79	16		strife	The unhappy strife was gradually propagated, until it had spread alienation and bitterness through the whole town, and finally became of such moment, that it was carried up to the General Court and was a topic of discussion and altercation there.
80	16	148	strife, Parris	The parties were the Rev. Samuel Parris on the one side, and a large portion of his congregation on the other.
81	16	148-49	strife, conflict	It was while this conflict was going on, and in the midst of all this local trouble and general distress, that the great and awful tragedy began.
82	16-17	148-49	start of delusion	Near the close of the month of February, 1692, two female children, belonging to the family of the Rev. Mr Parris, one, his daughter Elizabeth, represented to have been but nine, and the other his niece, Abigail Williams, twelve years old, together with a young female of the neighborhood, named Ann Putnam, began to act in a strange and unaccountable manner.
83	17	149	start of delusion	They would creep into holes, and under benches and chairs, put themselves into odd postures, make antic gestures, and utter loud outcries and ridiculous, incoherent and unintelligible expressions.
84	17		start of delusion	The attention of the family was arrested.
85	17		start of delusion	No account or explanation of the conduct of the children could be given, and, in an evil hour physicians were called in and consulted.
86	17		children bewitched	One of the physicians gave it as his opinion that the children were bewitched.
87	17		children bewitched	It is proper, before we proceed any further, to explain what was meant by this opinion.
88	17		definition of witch	There are several words and expressions, that are sometimes used synonymously with witch, although they are not strictly synonymous.
89	17		definition of witch	The following for instance,—diviner, enchanter, charmer, conjurer, necromancer, fortune teller, augur, soothsayer, and sorcerer.
90	17-18		definition of witch	None of these words convey the same idea our ancestors attached to the word witch.
91	18		definition of witch	Witch was sometimes specially used to signify a female, while wizard was exclusively applied to a male.
92	18		definition of witch	A witch was regarded by our fathers, as a person who had made an actual, deliberate and formal compact with Satan, by which compact it was agreed that she should become his faithful subject, and do what she could in promoting his cause, and in consideration of this allegiance and service, he on his part agreed to exercise his supernatural powers in her favor, and communicate to her portion of those powers.
93	18		definition of witch	Thus a witch was considered in the light of a person who had transferred allegiance and worship from God to the Devil.
94	18-19		witch	The existence of this compact was supposed to confer great additional power on the Devil as well as on his new subject, for the doctrine seems to have prevailed, that for him to act with effect upon men, the intervention and instrumentality of human co-operation was necessary, and almost unlimited power was ascribed to the combined exertions of Satan, and those of the human species in league with him.

APPENDIX 3 Gaskell's Manipulation of Upham's **First Lecture on Witchcraft** 273

NO.	PAGE	LOIS	SUMMARY	SEGMENT
95	19		witch	A witch was believed to have the power, through her compact with the Devil, of afflicting, distressing, and rending whomever she would.
96	19		witch	She could cause them to pine away and to suffer almost every description of pain and distress.
97	19		witchcraft	She was also believed to possess the faculty of being present in her shape or apparition at a different place from that which her actual body occupied.
98	19		witchcraft	Indeed, an almost indefinite amount of supernatural ability, and a great freedom and variety of methods for its exercise, were supposed to result from the diabolical compact.
99	19		bewitched	Those upon whom she thus exercised her malignant and mysterious energies, were said to be bewitched.
100	19-20		sympathetic towards ancestors	When I state the fact that these opinions were not merely prevalent among the common people, but were advocated by the learning and philosophy, the science and jurisprudence of the times, none can be surprised at the alarm which it created, when the belief became current, that there were those in the community who had actually entered into this dark confederacy against God and Heaven, Religion and Virtue, and that individuals were beginning to suffer from their infernal power.
101	20		sympathetic towards ancestors	It cannot be considered strange that our fathers should have looked with more than common horror upon persons who had been convicted, as they thought, upon overwhelming evidence of conspiracy with all that was evil, and this treason against all that was good.
102	20		to the narrative	We are now prepared to return to the narrative.
103	20		bewitched children	One or two other young girls in the neighborhood, soon began to exhibit similar indications of being bewitched.
104	20		bewitched children	The families to which the afflicted children belonged, immediately applied themselves to fasting and prayer, invoking the interposition of the Divine Being, to deliver them from the snares and dominion of Satan.
105	20-21	155	Revd Parris	Mr Parris invited the neighboring ministers to assemble at his house and unite with him in devoting a day to solemn religious services, and to devout supplications to the throne of Mercy, for rescue from the power of the great enemy of souls.
106	21		bewitched children	During the exercises of this occasion, one of the children had frequent and violent convulsion fits.
107	21		bewitched children	These events soon became generally known in the village, and through the whole surrounding country.
108	21		bewitched children	The public mind was prepared to sanction the opinion of the physician, and it was universally believed, that the evil one had commenced his operations with a bolder front and on a broader scale than in any previous period.
109	21		bewitched children	Great numbers crowded to the spot to gratify their credulous curiosity, by witnessing the effect of his influence upon the afflicted children—and all were anxious to discover by whose cooperation he thus exercised his malignant power.
110	21		bewitched children	The pretended sufferers were incessantly importuned to declare who afflicted them.
111	21		bewitched children	Who were the witches through whom the evil one acted upon them.
112	21-22		accusation	At length, when they had wrought the people up to a sufficient degree of excitement, they began to select and bring forward their victims.

NO.	PAGE	LOIS	SUMMARY	SEGMENT
113	22	155	Indian servant of Parris	They first accused, or as the phrase was, 'cried out upon,' an Indian woman attached to Mr Parris' family.
114	22		forced confession of Indian	By operating upon the old creature's fears and imagination, and as there is some reason to apprehend, by using severe treatment towards her, she was made to confess that the charge was true, and that she was in league with the devil.
115	22		forced confession of Indian	All can easily imagine the effect of this confession.
116	22		credibility of accusers	It established beyond question or suspicion, the credibility of the accusers, and produced such a thorough conviction of their veracity in the public mind, that if any one still continued to have misgivings or doubts, it seemed to be all in vain, even if he had courage enough to dare to do it, to give them utterance.
117	22		accusation	This state of things emboldened the young girls, and they proceeded to accuse two more decrepid and miserable old women, who were immediately arrested, thrown into prison, and put in irons.
118	22–23		afflicted accusers	In the meantime, new accessions were made to the number of the afflicted accusers, owing either to the inflamed state of the imaginations of the people, which led them to attribute their various diseases and ailments to the agency of witches, to a mere love of notoriety and a passion for general sympathy, to a desire to be secure against the charge of bewitching others, or to a malicious disposition to wreak vengeance upon enemies.
119	23		person accused	The next person accused was carried into the meetinghouse in the village, and confronted with the accusers.
120	23		person accused	As soon as the poor old woman was brought in, they uttered loud screams and fell down upon the floor.
121	23		accusation	If in her terror and despair she happened to clasp her hands, they would shriek out that she was pinching them.
122	23		mark of teeth on flesh	When she pressed in agony her withered lip, they exclaimed that she was biting them, and would show the marks of her teeth upon their flesh.
123	23–24		accusation	If the dreadful excitement of the scene, added to the feebleness of age, exhausted and overcame her, and she happened to lean for support against the side of the pew or the aisle, they would cry out that their bodies were crushed; and if she changed her position, or took a single step, they would declare that their feet were in pain.
124	24		accusation	In this manner they artfully produced a strong conviction in the minds of the deluded magistrates and excited by-standers.
125	24		accusation	On these occasions the proceedings were always introduced by prayer and addresses from the most influential ministers of the vicinity, who were decided in countenancing and active in promoting them.
126	24		sign book with blood	The afflicted, as they were called, did not rest with merely accusing their victims of having bewitched them, but testified on the stand that they had been present with them at their diabolical meetings, had witnessed them partaking in the visible company of Satan, of his blasphemous sacraments, and had seen them sign his book with their own blood.
127	24		examination of the accused	The examination of the accused generally took place, as has always been understood, in the house still standing at the western corner of North and Essex Streets, then the residence of Jonathan Corwin, Esq., at that time an acting magistrate.

NO.	PAGE	LOIS	SUMMARY	SEGMENT
128	24		examination of the accused	His colleague in the magistracy was John Hathorne, Esq.
129	24		great sensation	It may well be supposed that these events would produce a great sensation throughout the colony.
130	24-25		great sensation	They did so.
131	25		rationalist ministers	There was no discordance in the public voice, and although many individuals afterwards endeavored to make it appear that they were untouched by the delusion, I am inclined to think with the late Dr Bentley of Salem, that all honorable men and good citizens would prefer to be considered as participating in the excitement, than as having been free from it, and opposed to it, without ever daring to resist or check or reduce it.
132	25		rationalist ministers	There were, however, a few who were incredulous from the beginning, and have vindicated their claim to that distinction, by openly advocating their opinions at the time.
133	25		rationalist ministers	Among these were the reverend and celebrated Samuel Willard of the Old South church in Boston, who always frowned upon the proceedings, although three of the judges were members of his church; and Major Saltonstall, who publicly expressed his disapprobation by retiring from his seat on the bench.
134	25-26		deluded community	With these and perhaps a few other exceptions, the whole community was convinced of the truth of the accusations, and that there was a dark and diabolical confederacy in the land between Satan and some of the inhabitants, that threatened to overthrow and extirpate religion and morality, and to establish the kingdom of the evil one, in a country which had been dedicated by the prayers, and tears and sufferings of its pious fathers to God and the church.
135	26		delusion spreading	While the delusion was spreading over the colony, its operations were going on with tremendous efficacy in Salem, and the neighboring towns; additions were continually making to the number of the accusers by voluntary accessions, and by those who having been themselves accused, to save their lives, confessed, and became witnesses against others.
136	26		delusion spreading	The prisons in Salem, Cambridge and Boston were crowded with supposed witches.
137	26		delusion spreading	All the securities of society were dissolved.
138	26		delusion spreading	Every man's life was at the mercy of every other man.
139	26-27		domination of Satan	Fear sat on every countenance; terror and distress were in all hearts; silence pervaded the streets; many of the people left the country; all business was at a stand, and the feeling, dismal and horrible indeed, became general, that the providence of God was removed from them, and that they were given over to the dominion of Satan.
140	27		Mrs English's case	To illustrate the condition of society at this dreadful time, I will relate the circumstances connected with the arrest of the wife of Phillip English.
141	27		Mrs English's case	This gentleman was possessed of a very large estate, for that period.
142	27		Mrs English's case	He owned fourteen buildings, a wharf in the lower part of the town, and twentyone sail of vessels;
143	27		Mrs English's case	his dwellinghouse is still standing, and bears the marks of having been constructed upon the best style of that day;

NO.	PAGE	LOIS	SUMMARY	SEGMENT
144	27		Mrs English's case	it is situated at the eastern termination of Essex Street, and is a venerable and curious specimen of our ancient architecture.
145	27		Mrs English's case	Mrs English was a lady of accomplished education and superior endowments.
146	27		Mrs English's case	In consequence of several pecuniary controversies in which her husband had been engaged with the town, and perhaps from a want of sympathy arising from other causes between his family and the poorer people of the place, they were not popular.
147	27-28		Mrs English's case	Many persons entertained jealousies and cherished feelings of aversion towards them.
148	28		Mrs English's case	This was the case with some of the accusers, and they determined to gratify their malignity by getting Mr English and his wife hanged for witchcraft.
149	28		Mrs English's case	They accordingly commenced by accusing Mrs English.
150	28		Mrs English's case	The officer entered her dwelling on the evening of the 21st of April, read his warrant in her bedchamber, and placed guards around the house, intending to carry her to prison the next day.
151	28		Mrs English's case	So utterly hopeless at that time was the condition of any one who might happen to fall under the accusation of witchcraft, that Mrs English considered herself lost.
152	28		Mrs English's case	In the morning she attended the devotions of her family, gave direction for the education of her children, kissed them, clasped them in her arms, commended them to God, bid them farewell, and then committed herself to the sheriff, declaring her readiness to die.
153	28-29		Mrs English's case	Mr English, hoping that by placing himself beyond the reach of the prosecutors, he might more easily promote the release of his wife, either concealed himself or retired from this part of the country.
154	29		Mrs English's case	Several ineffectual attempts were made to arrest him.
155	29		Mrs English's case	Finding, however, that he could not protect or rescue her from the power of the infatuated magistrates, he came forward, voluntarily surrendered himself, and expressed his determination to share her fate.
156	29		Mrs English's case	They found means, however, to effect their escape, and fled to New York.
157	29		Mrs English's case	It ought to be mentioned to the honor of Mr English, and never forgotten by the people of Salem, that, notwithstanding the treatment he and his family had received, he sent from the place of his refuge generous donations to our suffering poor at a season of great distress the next winter.
158	29		Mrs English's case	To the honor of the people too it should be recorded, that when their fanatical delirium had passed away, they welcomed him and his family back with public rejoicings, and did everything in their power to make restitution and compensation for the injury they had inflicted upon them.
159	29-30		special commission	To meet the extraordinary crisis, a special commission was issued to seven of the principal citizens and jurists of the colony, constituting them a court to try the accused persons at Salem.
160	30		special commission	These were the Lieut. Governor, Mr Stoughton, Major Saltonstall, Major Richards, Major Gedney, Mr Wait Winthrop, Capt. Sewall, and Mr Sargeant.

APPENDIX 3 Gaskell's Manipulation of Upham's First Lecture on Witchcraft   277

NO.	PAGE	LOIS	SUMMARY	SEGMENT
161	30		court	They assembled by particular appointment at the court house in Salem, supposed to have stood at the eastern corner of Essex and Washington Streets, on the second of June, 1692.
162	30		execution	The first victim, an old woman, was executed on the tenth of June.
163	30		court	The court then adjourned.
164	30		government's decision	The government during their recess consulted several of the ministers of Boston and its vicinity, respecting the prosecutions, and while they urged the importance of caution and circumspection in the methods of examination, and the admission of testimony, they at the same time decidedly and earnestly recommended that the proceedings should be vigorously carried on.
165	30		prosecutions carried on	And they were vigorously carried on.
166	30		prosecutions carried on	The court sat again on the thirtieth of June, and five more old women were hanged on the nineteenth of July.
167	30-31		the hanged omitted	The Court sat again August fifth, and on the nineteenth of the same month, four men and one woman were hanged.
168	31		the hanged omitted	And on the twentysecond of September, two men and six women were hanged.
169	31		the hanged omitted	Eight more were condemned, but this was the last execution.
170	31	185	the hanged omitted	One man refusing to put himself on trial was pressed to death agreeably to the provisions of the English law.
171	31		accusers become bold	The principal immediate effect of these summary and sanguinary proceedings was to render the accusers more bold, confident and daring;
172	31		accusers become bold	they began to feel that the lives of all the people were in their hands, and seemed at last to have experienced a fiendlike satisfaction in the thought of bringing infamy and death upon the best and most honored citizens of the colony;
173	31		accusers become bold	they repeatedly cried out upon the Rev. Mr Willard, before mentioned, the author of the 'Body of Divinity,' one of the most revered and beloved ministers of the times.
174	31-32		accusers become bold	They accused a member of the immediate family of Dr Increase Mather, who had recently returned from a special embassy to the English court respecting the charter, and was then the President of Harvard College—the man whom Elliott calls 'the father of the New England clergy,'—and whose name and character have been held in veneration by his contemporaries and all succeeding generations.
175	32		accusers become bold	A writer of that period intimates that they accused the wife of the Governor, Sir William Phipps; they even went so far, it is said, as to implicate one of the Judges of the court.
176	32		Mrs Hale's case	But that which finally overthrew their power and broke the spell by which they had held the minds of the whole colony in bondage, was their accusation of Mrs Hale, the wife of the minister of the first church in Beverly.
177	32		Mrs Hale's case	Her genuine and distinguished virtues had won for her a reputation, and secured in the hearts of the people a confidence, which superstition itself could not sully nor shake.
178	32		Mrs Hale's case	Mr Hale had been active in all the previous proceedings;

NO.	PAGE	LOIS	SUMMARY	SEGMENT
179	32		Mrs Hale's case	but he knew the innocence and piety of his wife, and he stood forth between her and the storm he had helped to raise;
180	32		Mrs Hale's case	although he had driven it on while others were its victims, he turned and resisted it, when it burst in upon his own dwelling.
181	32-33		Mrs Hale's case	In crying out upon Mrs Hale, the whole community was convinced that the accusers had perjured themselves, and from that moment their power was destroyed;
182	33		Mrs Hale's case	the awful delusion ceased;
183	33		Mrs Hale's case	the curtain fell, and a close was put to one of the most tremendous tragedies in the history of real life.
184	33		Mrs Hale's case	The wildest storm, perhaps, that ever raged in the moral world, instantly became a calm;
185	33		Mrs Hale's case	the tide that had threatened to overwhelm everything in its fury, sunk back in a moment to its peaceful bed.
186	33		innocent victims	There are few, if any other, instances in history, of a revolution of opinion and feeling, so sudden, so rapid, and so complete.
187	33		bewildered imagination	The images and visions that had possessed the bewildered imaginations of the people, flitted away and left them standing in the clear sunshine of reason, and their senses, and they could have exclaimed, as they witnessed them passing off, in the language of the great master of the drama, and of human nature, but that their rigid puritan principles, would not, it is presumed, have permitted them, even in that moment of rescue and deliverance, to quote Shakespeare—
188	33-34		bewildered imagination	'See they're gone— / The earth has bubbles, as the waters have / And these are some of them: they vanished / Into the air, and what seemed corporal, / Melted as breath into the wind.'
189	34		prevalence of fanaticism	During the prevalence of this fanaticism, twenty persons lost their lives by the hand of the executioner.
190	34		praise of innocent victim's integrity	As they died innocent of the crime imputed to them, and maintained their integrity to the last, preferring to suffer an ignominious and horrible death, rather than increase the delusion of the times, by feigning a confession in order to save their lives, it will be proper to recall their names from oblivion, and while we reverse the sentence that was passed upon them, pay them our tribute of respect for their firmness and veracity, and of pity for their dreadful sufferings and fate.
191	34		innocent victims	I shall mention the places of their usual residence, in order to shew how the delusion pervaded the country.
192	34-35		innocent victims	Rev George Burroughs of Wells, Samuel Wardwell of Andover, Wilmot Reed of Marblehead, Margaret Scott of Rowley, Susanna Marta of Amesbury, Elizabeth How of Ipswich, Sarah Wildes and Mary Easty of Topsfield, Martha Carrier and Mary Parker of Andover, John Proctor, John Willard, Sarah Good, Rebecca Nurse and Martha Cory of Salem Village, George Jacobs, Jr, Alice Parker, Ann Pudeater, Bridget Bishop, alias Oliver, of Salem.
193	35		innocent victims	Giles Cory of Salem was pressed to death.
194	35		innocent victims	Most of these persons were advanced in years, and many of them left large families of children.

NO.	PAGE	LOIS	SUMMARY	SEGMENT
195	35		innocent victims	The following were condemned to death but did not suffer: Abigail Faulkner, Maty Lacy and Ann Foster of Andover, Dorcas Hoar of Beverly, Mary Bndbury of Salisbury, Rebecca Eames of Boxford, Abigail Hobbs of Topsfield, and Elizabeth Proctor of Salem Village.
196	35		55 escaped death	Besides these, fiftyfive persons escaped death by confessing themselves guilty, one hundred and fifty were in prison, and more than two hundred others accused.
197	35	185	son helps mother	One adventurous and noble spirited young man found means to effect his mother's escape from confinement, fled with her on horseback from the vicinity of the jail, and secreted her in the Blueberry Swamp, not far from Tapley's brook in the Great Pasture;
198	35-36	185	son helps mother	he protected her concealment there until after the delusion had passed away, provided food and clothing for her, erected a wigwam for her shelter, and surrounded her with every comfort her situation would admit of.
199	36	185	son helps mother	The poor creature must, however, have endured a great amount of suffering, for one of her larger limbs was fractured in the all but desperate enterprise of rescuing her from the prison.
200	36		termination of excitement	Immediately upon the termination of the excitement, all who were in prison were pardoned.
201	36		termination of excitement	Nothing more was heard of the afflicted or the confessors: they were never called to account for their malicious imposture, and perjury.
202	36		termination of excitement	It was apprehended that a judicial investigation might renew the excitement and delusion, and all were anxious to consign the whole subject as speedily and effectually as possible to oblivion.
203	36		even animals suspected	It should be mentioned before this review of the outlines of the proceedings is concluded, that the diabolical compact was not considered as confined to the human species, but that other animals were suspected of entering into it.
204	36-37	185	dogs	Several dogs were accused of witchcraft, and two, one in Salem Village, the other in Andover, suffered the penalties of the law, and are recorded among the subjects of capital punishment.
205	37		begins to reflect	As soon as the people had recovered from their delusion, they began to reflect and review the whole transaction with a spirit of calmness and discernment.
206	37		rationalist view	Mr Hale of Beverly, wrote a treatise respecting it, in which he offers some reasons that led him to the conclusion that there was error at the foundation of the proceedings.
207	37		rationalist view	The following extract will show that he took a rational view of the subject.
208	37		rationalist view	'It may be queried then, *How doth it appear that there was a going too far in this affair?*
209	37		rationalist view	Answer 1st.
210	37		rationalist view	By the number of the persons accused, it cannot be imagined, that in a place of so much knowledge, so many in so small a compass of land should so abominably leap into the devil's lap at once.
211	37		rationalist view	Answer 2d.
212	37		rationalist view	The quality of several of the accused was such as did bespeak better things, *and things that accompany salvation.*

NO.	PAGE	LOIS	SUMMARY	SEGMENT
213	37-38		rationalist view	Persons whose blameless and holy lives before did testify for them; persons that had taken great pains to bring up *their children in the nurture and admonition of the Lord*, such as we had charity for as for our own souls, and charity,' the good man proceeds, 'is a Christian duty, commended to us in 1 Cor. 13th chap.—Col. 3: 14, and many other places.
214	38		rationalist view	Answer 3d.
215	38		rationalist view	The number of the afflicted by Satan daily increased, till about fifty persons were thus vexed by the devil.
216	38		rationalist view	This gave just ground to suspect some mistake.
217	38		rationalist view	Answer 4th.
218	38		innocent victims	It was considerable, that nineteen were executed, and all denied the crime to the death, and some of them were knowing persons, and had before this been accounted blameless livers.
219	38		innocent victims	And it is not to be imagined, but that if all had been guilty, some would have had so much tenderness as to seek mercy for their souls in the way of confession and sorrow for such a sin.
220	38		rationalist view	Answer 5.
221	38		afflicted grow well	When this prosecution ceased, the Lord so chained up Satan, that the afflicted grew presently well;
222	38-39		accused are quiet	the accused are generally quiet, and for five years since, we have no such molestation by them.'
223	39		rationalist view	Such reasonings as these soon found their way into the minds of the whole community, and it became the melancholy conviction of all candid and considerate persons that much innocent blood had been shed.
224	39		rationalist view	Standing where we do, with the lights that surround us, we look back upon the whole scene as an awful perversion of justice, reason and truth.
225	39		rationalist view	In reviewing the events that have now been related, several topics suggest themselves, which, if we wish to possess a thorough knowledge of the transaction, it will be necessary to consider.
226	39		rationalist view	I shall endeavor to discuss them with as much compression and brevity as possible.
227	39		rationalist view	The evidence by which the convictions were procured is particularly deserving of notice.
228	39		witch can be detected	There were certain signs by which it was thought witches could be detected, and these signs were not only established in the faith of the people, but were to a great extent sanctioned by the courts.
229	39-40	181, 184	witch cannot weep	It was the received opinion that a person in confederacy with the evil one could not weep; those accused were for the most part of an age and condition, which rendered it impossible for them, however innocent they might have been, to escape the fatal effects of this test.

NO.	PAGE	LOIS	SUMMARY	SEGMENT
230	40		witch cannot weep	A poor, haggard, decrepid old woman, was put to the bar, and if she could not weep on the spot, if in consequence of her withered frame, her amazement and indignation at the false and malicious charges by which she was circumvented, her stupified sensibility, her sullen despair, the hopeless horror of her situation, or if from any other cause, the fountain of her tears was closed or dried up, her inability to call them forth at the bid of her malignant prosecutors was regarded as an infallible proof of guilt.
231	40		torture	It was believed that Satan affixed his mark to the bodies of those in alliance with him, and that the point where this mark was made became callous and dead.
232	40		torture	It was the practice to commit the prisoner to the scrutiny of a jury of the same sex.
233	40-41		torture	They would pierce the body with pins, and if, as was to have been expected, particularly in aged persons, any spot could be found insensible to the torture, it was looked upon as visible evidence, ocular demonstration of guilt.
234	41		shave head	In conducting this examination, it was the custom to shave the head of the miserable victim.
235	41		barbarous, inhuman practice	It should be mentioned, that although they were in some instances permitted to be used, these barbarous and inhuman practices were not countenanced by our forefathers to the same extent as in England and all other countries.
236	41		ocular fascination	Then there was the evidence of ocular fascination.
237	41		ocular fascination	The accused and the accusers were brought into the presence of the examining magistrate, and the supposed witch was ordered to look upon the afflicted persons, instantly; upon coming within the glance of her eye, they would scream out, and fall down as in a fit.
238	41		ocular fascination	It was thought that an invisible and impalpable fluid, darted from the eye of the witch, and penetrated the brain of the bewitched.
239	41		ocular fascination	By bringing the witch so near that she could touch the afflicted persons with her hand, the malignant fluid was attracted back into the hand, and the sufferers recovered their senses.
240	41-42		ocular fascination	It is singular to notice the curious resemblance between this opinion, the joint product of superstition and imposture, and the results to which modern science has led us in the discoveries of galvanism and animal electricity.
241	42		ocular fascination	The doctrines of fascination maintained its hold upon the public credulity for a long time, and gave occasion to the phrase, still in familiar use among us, of 'looking upon a person with an evil eye.'
242	42		ocular fascination	Its advocates claimed in its defence the authority of the Cartesian philosophy, but it cannot be considered in an age of science and reason, as having any better support than the rural superstition of Virgil's simple shepherd, who thus complains of the condition of his emaciated flock:—
243	42		ocular fascination	'they look so thin, / Their bones are barely covered with their skin; / What magic has bewitched the woolly dams? / And what ill eyes beheld the tender lambs?'
244	42		rationalist view	If anything strange or remarkable could be discovered in the persons, histories, or deportment of the prisoners, it was permitted to be brought against them in evidence.
245	42-43		Cotton Mather	Cotton Mather was employed to compile and publish a report of some of the trials.
246	43		Burroughs	He adduces the following proof of the guilt of the Rev. Mr Burroughs.

NO.	PAGE	LOIS	SUMMARY	SEGMENT
247	43		Burroughs	'God,' says he, 'had been pleased so to leave this George Burroughs, that he had ensnared himself by several instances which he had formerly given of preternatural strength, and which were now produced against him.'
248	43		Burroughs	He was a very puny man, yet he had often done things beyond the strength of a giant.
249	43		Burroughs	A gun of about seven foot barrel, and so heavy that strong men could not steadily hold it out with both hands;
250	43		Burroughs	there were several testimonies given in by persons of credit and honor, that he made nothing of taking up such a gun behind the lock with but one hand, and holding it out like a pistol at arms' end.
251	43		Burroughs	Yea, there were two testimonies that George Burroughs with only putting the forefinger of his right hand into the muzzle of a heavy gun, a fowling piece of about six or seven foot barrel, did lift up the gun and hold it out at arms' end, a gun which the deponents thought strong men could not with both hands lift up and hold at the butt end as is usual.'
252	44		Upham's comment	I will quote another passage to the same point, from Dr Mather's report.
253	44		Bridget Bishop	It relates to the first trial, that of Bridget Bishop, alias Oliver.
254	44		Bridget Bishop	'There was one very strange thing more with which the court was newly entertained.
255	44		Bridget Bishop	As this woman was under a guard, passing by the great and spacious meetinghouse of Salem,' (the building that preceded the one recently taken down to give place to the present meetinghouse of the first church, and situated on the same spot) 'she gave a look towards the house, and immediately a Demon, invisibly entering the meetinghouse, tore down a part of it, so that though there was no person to be seen there, yet the people, at the noise, running in, found a board which was strongly fastened with several nails, transported unto another quarter of the house.'
256	44		testimony	So far as we have now reviewed the evidence, none has been found that would have been thought to justify a jury, even of that period, in rendering a verdict of guilty.
257	44-45		testimony	But there was much stronger evidence than any we have yet considered, before the jury, that condemned the reputed Salem witches.
258	45		testimony	There were many witnesses who swore that the individuals accused, had afflicted them with pain, destroyed their rest, robbed them of their goods, caused them to pine, and distressed them in a great variety of modes; they produced the identical pins, with which they declared the accused persons had tormented them; these pins were filed away, as usual, with the other evidence, and are at this day to be seen, among the records of the trials, in the office of the clerk of our courts.
259	45		testimony	Some of these witnesses were persons formerly of respectable and irreproachable characters.
260	45		testimony	Their testimony was delivered with great apparent sincerity.
261	45		testimony	In several cases, they swore that they had suffered under the malignant influence for a long period, even of twenty or thirty years.
262	45		testimony	Three or four of the accusers would appear to be thrown into agony by the mere presence of the prisoners, and declared that while giving their evidence in court, they were tormented by them.

NO.	PAGE	LOIS	SUMMARY	SEGMENT
263	45-46		testimony	In one instance, the hands of the witness were tied strongly together by a rope during the delivery of her evidence while on the stand, and she swore that it was done by an invisible agent employed by the prisoner at the bar.
264	46		testimony	But there was one species of evidence that rendered all the rest unnecessary, and overwhelmed the minds of the court, the jury, the public, and, perhaps in many instances, the unhappy prisoners themselves, with conviction.
265	46		confession	The confessions.
266	46		confession	Fiftyfive persons, many of them previously of the most unquestionable character for intelligence, virtue and piety, acknowledged the truth of the charges that were made against them—confessed that they were witches and had made a compact with the devil.
267	46		confession	The records of these confessions have been preserved.
268	46	158	red book	They relate the particulars that attended the interviews the confessing persons had held with the evil one, declared that they signed his little red book, as they described it, were present at his impious sacraments, and had ridden on sticks through the air, several of them in company all the way from Andover to Salem, to a diabolical meeting convened there.
269	47	158	confession	They specify the exact places where the sacraments of the devil were celebrated.
270	47	158	Newbury Falls	It seems that he was accustomed to baptize his converts at Newbury Falls.
271	47		confession	They were organized, as Dr Mather observes, 'much after the manner of a Congregational church.'
272	47		confession	The confessions of the New England witches describe the person and deportment of Satan with considerable minuteness.
273	47		Satan's appearance	He generally appeared to them in the guise of a well dressed black man, and the usual place in which he convened his assemblies, was a wide open field in Salem Village.
274	47		midnight meeting	The hour of meeting was most frequently that of deep midnight.
275	47		Satan's appearance	The received opinion of the age authorized his appearance under a great variety of shapes, sometimes that of a negro, sometimes of an Indian, sometimes of a goat, and sometimes of a huge black dog.
276	47		confessing witch	The confessing witches go on to acknowledge that in the malignant exercise of the power acquired by the compact with Satan, they had actually afflicted the accusers in the manner and form alleged.
277	47-48		Upham's comment	It cannot, indeed, be a matter of surprise to any one that such declarations and confessions had a very powerful effect upon a jury, when the greatest philosophers as well as the common people believed in the reality of witchcraft.
278	48		Upham's comment	This consideration must be borne in mind continually while we contemplate the proceedings.
279	48		Upham's comment	One more circumstance remains to be mentioned in connexion with the evidence.
280	48	150-51	mouse	It was believed that when the witches found it inconvenient from any cause to execute their infernal designs upon those whom they wished to afflict, by going to them in person, they transformed themselves into the likeness of some animal, such as a cat, rat, mouse or toad.
281	48		imp	They also had imps under their control.

NO.	PAGE	LOIS	SUMMARY	SEGMENT
282	48		insect	These imps were generally supposed to bear the resemblance of some small insect, such as a fly or a spider.
283	48		animal	The latter animal was prevailingly considered as most likely to bear this character.
284	48-49		imp	The accused person was closely watched in order that the spider imp might be seen when it approached to obtain its nourishment, as it was thought to do, from the witchmark on her body.
285	49		spider	Within the cells of a prison, spiders were of course often seen.
286	49		spider	Whenever one made its appearance, the guard attacked it with all the zeal and vehemence, with which it was natural and proper to assault an agent of the wicked one.
287	49		spider	If the spider was killed in the encounter, it was considered as an innocent animal, and all suspicion was removed from its character.
288	49		spider	But if it escaped into a crack or crevice of the apartment, as spiders often do when assaulted, all doubt of its guilty connexion with the prisoner was removed, it was set down as beyond question or cavil, her veritable imp, and the evidence of her confederacy with the devil was regarded thenceforward as complete.
289	49		witch can send spectres	It was believed, moreover, that witches could send their own spectres or apparitions or the spectres of those with whom they were confederate to fulfil their commissions.
290	49		impossible defence	It is obvious that where courts of justice, countenanced the popular credulity in maintaining this doctrine, there was no security left to the individual accused.
291	49-50		impossible defence	No matter how clear and certain the evidence adduced by him, that at the time alleged he was absent from the specified place.
292	50		impossible defence	No matter how far distant, whether twenty or twenty thousand miles, it availed him nothing, he was present through his agent or imp.
293	50		impossible defence	When accused of having been present in his own proper bodily shape, it did not break down nor impair in the least the force of the accusation, to prove that at the time he was in another place, at a great distance, for it was immediately contended that he was present in the shape or spectral illusion, by which Satan enabled him to act any and everywhere at once.
294	50		impossible defence	It was impossible to disprove the accusation, however false it might be, and the last defence of innocence was swept away.
295	50		impossible defence	It deserves to be mentioned with respect to this spectral evidence, as it was called, that, although generally admitted in other countries, it never received the unqualified or undisputed sanction of public opinion here.
296	50		Upham's comment	There are two inquiries that must have engaged the meditations of all reflecting persons who have followed me thus far.
297	50-51		accusers	One is this: What are we to think of those persons who commenced and continued the accusations, of the afflicted children and their confederates.
298	51		rationalist view	Shocking as is the view it presents of the extent to which human nature can be carried in depravity, I am constrained to declare, as the result of as thorough a scrutiny as I could institute, my belief that this dreadful transaction was introduced and driven on by wicked perjury and wilful malice.
299	51		rationalist view	The young girls in Mr Parris' family and their associates, on several occasions, indicated by their conduct and expressions that they were acting a part.

NO.	PAGE	LOIS	SUMMARY	SEGMENT
300	51		rationalist view	It may be that, in some instances, the steps they took and the testimony they bore may be explained by referring to the mysterious energies of the imagination, the power of enthusiasm, the influence of sympathy, and the general prevalence of credulity, ignorance, superstition and fanaticism at the time;
301	51		rationalist view	and it is not probable that when they began they had any idea of the tremendous length to which they were finally led on.
302	51-52		rationalist view	It was perhaps their original design to gratify a love of notoriety or of mischief, by creating a sensation and excitement in their neighborhood, or at the worst to wreak their vengeance upon one or two individuals who had offended them.
303	52		accusers	They soon, however, became intoxicated by the terrible success of their imposture, and were swept along by the phrensy they had occasioned.
304	52		accusers are victims	It would be much more congenial with our feelings to believe that these misguided and wretched persons early in the proceedings became themselves victims of the delusion into which they plunged every one else.
305	52		accusers	But we are forbidden to form this charitable judgment by the manifestations of art and contrivance, of deliberate cunning and cool malice they exhibited to the end.
306	52		accusers	Once or twice they were caught in their own snare, and nothing but the blindness of the bewildered community saved them from, disgraceful exposure, and well deserved punishment.
307	52		accusers	They appeared as the prosecutors of almost every poor creature that was tried, and seemed ready to bear testimony against any one, upon whom suspicion might happen to fall.
308	52-53		accusers	It is dreadful to reflect upon the enormity of their wickedness, if they were conscious of imposture throughout.
309	53		accusers	It seems to transcend the capabilities of human crime.
310	53		rationalist view	There is, perhaps a slumbering element in the heart of man, that sleeps forever in the bosom of the innocent and good and requires the perpetration of a great sin, to wake it into action, but which when once aroused, impels the transgressor onward with increasing momentum, as the descending ball is accelerated in its course.
311	53		rationalist view	It may be that crime begets an appetite for crime, which like all other appetites is not quieted but inflamed by gratification.
312	53		rationalist view	It is obvious, that during the prevalence of the fanaticism, it was in the power of every man to bring down terrible vengeance upon his enemies, by pretending to be bewitched by them.
313	53		rationalist view	There is great reason to fear that this was often the case.
314	53-54		accusers	If any one ventured to resist the proceedings, or to intimate a doubt respecting the guilt of the persons accused, the accusers would consider it as an affront to them, and proceed instantly to cry out against him.
315	54		a man in Andover	The wife of an honest and worthy man in Andover, was sick of a fever of which she finally died; during her illness it occurred to him, after all the usual means had failed to cure her, that she might be bewitched.
316	54		a man in Andover	He went directly to Salem Village to ask the afflicted persons there who had bewitched his wife.
317	54		a man in Andover	Two of them returned with him to Andover.

286

NO.	PAGE	LOIS	SUMMARY	SEGMENT
318	54		a man in Andover	Never did a place receive more inauspicious visitors.
319	54		a man in Andover	Soon after their arrival they contrived to get more than fifty of the inhabitants imprisoned, several of whom were afterwards hanged for witchcraft.
320	54		Bradstreet	A Mr Bradstreet, the magistrate of the place, after having committed about forty persons to jail on their accusation, concluded that he had done enough, and declined to arrest any more; the consequence was that they accused him and his wife of being witches, and they had to fly for their lives.
321	54-55		Willard	A person by the name of Willard, who had been employed to guard the prisoners to and from the jail, had the humanity to sympathise with the sufferers, and the courage to express his unwillingness to continue any longer in the odious employment.
322	55		Willard	This was very offensive to the afflicted children.
323	55		Willard	They accordingly charged him with bewitching them.
324	55		Willard	The unhappy man was condemned to death;
325	55		Willard	he contrived to escape from prison;
326	55		Willard	they were thrown into the greatest distress;
327	55		Willard	the news came that he was retaken;
328	55		Willard	their agonies were moderated, and at length he was hanged, and then they were wholly relieved.
329	55		accusers very bad	It should be added, that many of the accusers turned out afterwards very badly, becoming profligate and abandoned characters.
330	55		Burroughs	There is something very dark about the case of Mr Burroughs.
331	55		Burroughs	He had formerly preached as a candidate at Salem Village, and had received an invitation to settle in the ministry of the church in that place.
332	55		Burroughs	While there, he had been brought into collision with some of the inhabitants.
333	55-56	185	Burroughs	There are strong indications of personal malice, arising from this old animosity in the proceedings against him at his trial.
334	56		Parris suspected	After the delusion had passed away, several ecclesiastical councils were convened at Salem Village to compose difficulties that had arisen between Mr Parris, and many of his people.
335	56		Parris suspected	It is evident from the documents connected with the proceedings of these councils, that the disaffected members of his society regarded his conduct in the preceding tragedy with an aversion and horror, that can only be accounted for on the hypothesis, that they suspected him of having acted, not merely under the influence of an indiscreet enthusiasm, but from dishonest and malignant motives.
336	56	160	Indian whipped by Parris	Their suspicion was very much confirmed by the circumstance that the old Indian woman, who, by declaring herself guilty of the charge of witchcraft, first gave credit and power to the accusers, always asserted that she was whipped by Mr Parris until she consented to make a confession.

NO.	PAGE	LOIS	SUMMARY	SEGMENT
337	56-57		Parris forced to resign	But however it may have been with him—and, in the absence of conclusive testimony, we must leave his guilt or innocence to the decisions of a higher tribunal—so strong and deeply rooted were the feelings of disapprobation and aversion towards him which occupied the breasts of his disaffected parishioners, that all attempts on the part of the other churches to produce a reconciliation, and even his own humble and solemn acknowledgment of his error, were unavailing, and he was compelled to resign his situation and remove from the place.
338	57		another inquiry	The other inquiry is this.
339	57		Why did the accused confess themselves guilty?	Since it is, at present, the universal opinion that the whole of this witchcraft transaction was a delusion, having no foundation whatever but in the imaginations and passions, and as it is now certain, that all the accused both the condemned and the pardoned were entirely innocent, how can it be explained that so many were led to confess themselves guilty?
340	57-58		rationalist view	The answer to this question is to be found in those general principles that have led the wisest legislators and jurists to the conclusion that although on their face and at first thought, they appear to be the very best kind of evidence, yet maturely considered, confessions made under the hope of a benefit, and sometimes even without the impulses of such a hope, are to be received with great caution and wariness.
341	58		rationalist view	Here were fiftyfive persons, many of them of worthy characters, many of them professors of religion, who declared themselves guilty of a capital, nay, a diabolical crime, of which we know they were innocent.
342	58		rationalist view	It is probable that the motive of self-preservation influenced most of them.
343	58		rationalist view	An awful death was in immediate prospect.
344	58		rationalist view	They saw no escape from the wiles of their malignant accusers.
345	58		rationalist view	The delusion had obtained full possession of the people, the witnesses, the jury and the court.
346	58		rationalist view	By acknowledging a compact with Satan, they might in a moment secure their lives and liberty.
347	58		rationalist view	Their principles could not withstand the temptation.
348	58		rationalist view	They made a confession and were rewarded by a pardon.
349	58		increase of accusers' authority	Each confession served to heighten the public infatuation, and aggravate the general calamity, by increasing the authority of the accusers.
350	58-59		increase of accusers' authority	The unhappy confessors could not but perceive this, they saw that they had given fresh strength to an arm that was continually stretched out to destroy the innocent.
351	59		moral integrity	The reproaches of conscience in some instances prevailed, and they took back their confessions.
352	59		moral integrity	One man, an inhabitant of Andover, retracted, and was put to death.

NO.	PAGE	LOIS	SUMMARY	SEGMENT
353	59		moral integrity	It is the most melancholy reflection suggested by this awful history, that those only suffered whose principles were so strong, that even the fear of death, combined with the love of life, could not persuade them to utter a falsehood.
354	59		Why did the accused confess themselves guilty?	You cannot, however, receive from any description, I could give you, so satisfactory an explanation of the inducements, that prevailed upon some of the accused to do violence to their moral sense, by confessing a guilt that did not belong to them, as from their own words.
355	59		Margaret Jacobs	The following is the recantation of a young woman who had been prevailed upon to confess and become a witness against the Rev Mr Burroughs and also against her own grandfather, who, mainly upon the strength of her evidence, were condemned and executed.
356	60		Margaret Jacobs	'The humble declaration of Margaret Jacobs, unto the honored court now sitting at Salem, sheweth,—That whereas your poor and humble declarant, being closely confined here in Salem gaol, for the crime of witchcraft, which crime, thanks be to the Lord, I am altogether ignorant of, as will appear at the great day of judgment.
357	60		Margaret Jacobs	May it please the honored court, I was cried out upon by some of the possessed persons, as afflicting them; whereupon, I was brought to my examination, which persons at the sight of me fell down, which did very much startle and affright me.
358	60		Margaret Jacobs	The Lord above knows I knew nothing, in the least measure, how or who afflicted them;
359	60		Margaret Jacobs	they told me, without doubt I did, or else they would not fall down at me;
360	60		Margaret Jacobs	they told me if I would not confess, I should be put down into the dungeon and would be hanged;
361	60		Margaret Jacobs	but if I would confess I should have my life;
362	60-61		Margaret Jacobs	the which did so affright me, with my own vile wicked heart, to save my life, made me make the like confession I did, which confession, may it please the honored courts altogether false and untrue.
363	61		Margaret Jacobs	The very first night after I had made confession, I was in such horror of conscience that I could not sleep, for fear the devil should carry me away for telling such horrid lies.
364	61		Margaret Jacobs	I was, may it please the honored court, sworn to my confession, as I understand since, but then, at that time, was ignorant of it, not knowing what an oath did mean.
365	61		Margaret Jacobs	The Lord, I hope, in whom I trust, out of the abundance of his mercy, will forgive me my false forswearing myself.
366	61		Margaret Jacobs	What I said was altogether false, against my grandfather and Mr Burroughs, which I did to save my life and to have my liberty, but the Lord, charging it to my conscience, made me in so much horror, that I could not contain myself, before I had denied my confession, which I did, though I saw nothing but death before me, choosing rather death with a quiet conscience, than to live in such horror, which I could not suffer.
367	61		Margaret Jacobs	Where, upon my denying my confession, I was committed to close prison, where I have enjoyed more felicity in spirit a thousand times, than I did before in my enlargement.
368	61-62		Margaret Jacobs	And now, may it please your honors, your declarant having in part given your honors a description of my condition, do leave it to your honors' pious and judicious discretions to take pity and compassion on my young and tender years;

NO.	PAGE	LOIS	SUMMARY	SEGMENT
369	62		Margaret Jacobs	to act and do with me as the Lord above and your honors shall see good, having no friend but the Lord to plead my cause for me; not being guilty in the least measure, of the crime of witchcraft, nor any other sin that deserves death from man;
370	62		Margaret Jacobs	and your poor and humble declarant shall forever pray, as she is bound in duty, for your honors' happiness in this life, and eternal felicity in the world to come.
371	62		Margaret Jacobs	So prays your honors' declarant, Margaret Jacobs.'
372	62		Margaret Jacobs	The following letter was written by this same young person to her father.
373	62		Margaret Jacobs	Let it be observed that her grandfather had already been executed upon her false testimony.
374	62		Margaret Jacobs	Her father had saved himself by flying from the country.
375	62		Margaret Jacobs	And her mother was in prison waiting her trial for witchcraft.
376	63		Margaret Jacobs	From the dungeon in Salem prison, August 20th 1692.
377	63		Margaret Jacobs	Honored Father—After my humble duty remembered to you, hoping in the Lord of your good health, as blessed be God I enjoy, though in abundance of affliction, being close confined here in a loathsome dungeon the Lord look down in mercy upon me, not knowing how soon I shall be put to death, by means of the afflicted persons; my grandfather having suffered already, and all his estate seized for the king.
378	63		Margaret Jacobs	The reason of my confinement is this: I having, through the magistrates' threatenings, and my own vile and wretched heart, confessed several things contrary to my conscience and knowledge, though to the wounding of my own soul, (the Lord pardon me for it;) but oh! the terrors of a wounded conscience who can bear?
379	63-64		Margaret Jacobs	But blessed be the Lord, he would not let me go on in my sins, but in mercy, I hope, to my soul, would not suffer me to keep it any longer, but I was forced to confess the truth of all before the magistrates, who would not believe me;
380	64		Margaret Jacobs	but it is their pleasure to put me in here, and God knows how soon I shall be put to death.
381	64		Margaret Jacobs	Dear Father, let me beg your prayers to the Lord on my behalf, and send us a joyful and happy meeting in heaven.
382	64		Margaret Jacobs	My mother, poor woman, is very crazy, and remembers her kind love to you, and to uncle, viz. D. A.
383	64		Margaret Jacobs	So leaving you to the protection of the Lord, I rest your dutiful daughter, MARGARET JACOBS.
384	64		Margaret Jacobs	Her prayer was heard.
385	64		Margaret Jacobs	Her Christian penitence and heroic fortitude were rewarded.
386	64		Margaret Jacobs	A temporary illness prevented her being tried at the appointed time, and before the next sitting of the court, the delusion had passed away.
387	64		Upham's comment	But there can be no doubt that in several cases, the confessing persons sincerely believed themselves guilty.

NO.	PAGE	LOIS	SUMMARY	SEGMENT
388	64		Upham's comment	To explain this, we must look into the secret chambers of the human soul;
389	64		Upham's comment	we must read the history of the imagination, and consider its power over the belief.
390	64–65		Upham's comment	We must transport ourselves to the dungeon, and think of its dark and awful walls, its galling confinement, its clanking chains, its scanty fare, and all its dismal and painful circumstances.
391	65		Upham's comment	We must reflect upon their influence over a terrified and agitated, an injured and broken spirit.
392	65		Upham's comment	We must think of the situation of the poor prisoner, cut off from hope, hearing from all quarters, and at all times, morning, noon and night, that there is no doubt of his guilt, surrounded and overwhelmed by accusations and evidence, gradually, but insensibly mingling and confounding the visions and vagaries of his troubled dreams, with the reveries of his waking hours, until his reason becomes obscured, his recollections are thrown into derangement, his mind loses the power of distinguishing between what is perpetually told him by others and what belongs to the suggestions of his own memory;
393	65		Upham's comment	his imagination at last gains complete ascendency over his other faculties, and he believes and declares himself guilty of crimes, of which he is as innocent as the child unborn.
394	65		Upham's comment	The history of the transaction we have been considering affords a clear illustration of the truth and reasonableness of this explanation.
395	66		six female victims	I will present to you a declaration made by six respectable females, belonging to Andover, who had been induced to confess during the prevalence of the delusion.
396	66		six female victims	It is accompanied by a paper signed by more than fifty of the most respectable inhabitants of that town, testifying to their good character, in which it is said, that 'by their sober, godly and exemplary conversation, they have obtained a good report in the place, where they have been well esteemed and approved in the church of which they are members.'
397	66		declaration by six females, innocent victims	'We whose names are underwritten, inhabitants of Andover; whereas that horrible and tremendous judgment, beginning at Salem Village, in the year 1692, by some called witchcraft, first breaking forth at Mr Parris' house, several young persons being seemingly afflicted, did accuse several persons for afflicting them, and many there believing it so to be, we being informed, that, if a person was sick, the afflicted person could tell what or who was the cause of that sickness.
398	66–67		innocent victims	Joseph Ballard, of Andover, his wife being sick at the same time, he, either from himself, or by the advice of others, fetched two of the persons, called the afflicted persons, from Salem Village to Andover, which was the beginning of that dreadful calamity that befel us in Andover, believing the said accusations to be true, sent for the said persons to come together to the meetinghouse in Andover, the afflicted persons being there.
399	67		innocent victims	After Mr Barnard had been at prayer, we were blind-folded and our hands were laid upon the afflicted persons, they being in their fits, and falling into their fits at our coming into their presence, as they said, and some led us and laid our hands upon them, and then they said they were well, and that we were guilty of afflicting them.
400	67		innocent victims	Whereupon we were all seized as prisoners, by a warrant from the justice of the peace, and forthwith carried to Salem.

APPENDIX 3 Gaskell's Manipulation of Upham's First Lecture on Witchcraft

NO.	PAGE	LOIS	SUMMARY	SEGMENT
401	67-68		innocent victims	And by reason of that sudden surprisal, we knowing ourselves altogether innocent of that crime, we were all exceedingly astonished and amazed, and consternated and affrighted, even out of our reason;
402	68		innocent victims	and our nearest and dearest relations, seeing us in that dreadful condition, and knowing our great danger, apprehended there was no other way to save our lives, as the case was then circumstanced, but by our confessing ourselves to be such and such persons as the afflicted represented us to be, they, out of tenderness and pity, persuaded us to confess, what we did confess.
403	68		innocent victims	And, indeed, that confession, that it is said we made, was no other than what was suggested to us by some gentlemen, they telling us that we were witches, and they knew it, and we knew it, which made us think that it was so;
404	68		innocent victims	and our understandings, our reason, our faculties almost gone, we were not capable of judging of our condition;
405	68		innocent victims	as also the hard measures they used with us, rendered us incapable of making our defence, but said anything, and everything which they desired, and most of what we said, was but in effect a consenting to what they said.
406	68		innocent victims	Some time after, when we were better composed, they telling us what we had confessed, we did profess that we were innocent and ignorant of such things;
407	68-69		innocent victims	and we hearing that Samuel Wardwell had renounced his confession, and was quickly after condemned and executed, some of us were told we were going after Wardwell.
408	69		innocent victims	Mary Osgood, Sarah Wilson, Abigail Barker, Deliverance Dane, Mary Tyler, Hannah Tyler.'
409	69		Upham's comment	The facility with which persons can be persuaded, by perpetually assailing them with accusations of the truth of a charge, even when it is made against themselves, that in reality is not true, has been frequently noticed.
410	69		old female accuser's confession	Addison, in one of the numbers of his Spectator, speaks of it in connexion with our present subject.—
411	69		old female accuser's confession	'When an old woman,' says he 'begins to doat, and grow chargeable to a parish, she is generally turned into a witch, and fills the whole country with extravagant fancies, imaginary distempers, and terrifying dreams.
412	69-70		old female accuser's confession	In the meantime, the poor wretch, that is the innocent occasion of so many evils, begins to be frighted at herself, and sometimes confesses secret commerces, and familiarities that her imagination forms in a delirious old age.
413	70		old female accuser's confession	This frequently cuts off charity from the greatest objects of compassion, and inspires people with a malevolence towards those poor decrepid parts of our species in whom human nature is defaced by infirmity and dotage.'
414	70		Upham's comment	This passage is important, in addition to the bearing it has upon the point under consideration, as describing the state of opinion and feeling in England, twenty years after the fanaticism had passed away in Salem.
415	70-71		Upham's comment	As it is one of the leading designs of these lectures to shew to what an extent of error and passion, even good men may be carried, when they have abandoned their reason, and relinquished the exercise of their judgment, and given themselves over to the impulses of imagination and feeling, I am bound, painful as it is to do it, to present to your notice some instances of glaring misconduct and inhumanity, that marked the proceedings of the magistrates, judges, ministers and other principal citizens.

NO.	PAGE	LOIS	SUMMARY	SEGMENT
416	71		misconduct and inhumanity	A great many irregularities were permitted at the trials, and the most absurd cruelties were practised in all stages of the proceedings.
417	71		methods of examination; sufferings of the accused	The following account given by a respectable citizen of Charlestown, is, no doubt, substantially correct, and presents a lively view of the methods of examination and of the sufferings of the accused.
418	71		Jonathan Cary's observation	'*May 24th.*—I having heard, some days, that my wife was accused of witchcraft; being much disturbed at it, by advice went to Salem Village, to see if the afflicted knew her;
419	71		Jonathan Cary's observation	we arrived there on the twentyfourth of May;
420	71		Jonathan Cary's observation	it happened to be a day appointed for examination;
421	71	179-80	Jonathan Cary's observation	accordingly soon after our arrival Mr Hathorn and Mr Curwin, &c, went to the meetinghouse, which was the place appointed for that work;
422	71		Jonathan Cary's observation	the minister began with prayer, and having taken care to get a convenient place, I observed that the afflicted were two girls of about ten years old, and about two or three others of about eighteen;
423	71		Jonathan Cary's observation	one of the girls talked most, and could discern more than the rest.
424	72	180	Jonathan Cary's observation	The prisoners were called in one by one, and as they come in, were cried out at, &c.
425	72	180	Jonathan Cary's observation	The prisoners were placed about seven or eight feet from the justices, and the accusers between the justices and them;
426	72	180	Jonathan Cary's observation	the prisoners were ordered to stand right before the justices, with an officer appointed to hold each hand, lest they should there with afflict them; and the prisoners' eyes must be constantly on the justices;
427	72	180	Jonathan Cary's observation	for if they looked on the afflicted, they would either fall into fits, or cry out of being hurt by them.
428	72	180	Jonathan Cary's observation	After an examination of the prisoners, who it was afflicted these girls, &c, they were put upon saying the Lord's prayer, as a trial of their guilt.
429	72	180	Jonathan Cary's observation	After the afflicted seemed to be out of their fits, they would look steadfastly on some one person, and frequently not speak; and then the justices said they were struck dumb, and after a little time would speak again, then the justices said to the accusers, Which of you will go and touch the prisoner at the bar?
430	72-73	180	Jonathan Cary's observation	Then the most courageous would adventure, but before they had made three steps, would ordinarily fall down as in a fit;

APPENDIX 3 Gaskell's Manipulation of Upham's First Lecture on Witchcraft 293

NO.	PAGE	LOIS	SUMMARY	SEGMENT
431	73	180	Jonathan Cary's observation	the justices ordered that they should be taken up and carried to the prisoner, that she might touch them, and as soon as they were touched by the accused, the justices would say, they are well, before I could discern any alteration; by which I observed that the justices understood the manner of it.
432	73		Jonathan Cary's observation	Thus far I was only as a spectator; my wife also was there part of the time, but no notice was taken of her by the afflicted, except once or twice they came to her and asked her name.
433	73		Jonathan Cary's observation	But I, having an opportunity to discourse Mr Hale (with whom I had formerly acquaintance), I took his advice what I had best do, and desired of him that I might have an opportunity to speak with her that accused my wife; which he promised should be, I acquainting him that I reposed my trust in him.
434	73-74		Jonathan Cary's observation	Accordingly, he came to me after the examination was over, and told me I had now an opportunity to speak with the said-accuser, Abigail Williams, a girl eleven or twelve years old; but that we could not be in private at Mr Parris' house, as he had promised me;
435	74		Jonathan Cary's observation	we went therefore into the alehouse, where an Indian man attended us, who it seems was one of the afflicted;
436	74		Jonathan Cary's observation	to him we gave some cider;
437	74		Jonathan Cary's observation	he showed several scars, that seemed as if they had been long there, and showed them as done by witchcraft, and acquainted us that his wife, who also was a slave, was imprisoned for witchcraft.
438	74	181	tumble down like swine	And now, instead of one accuser they all came in, and began to tumble down like swine;
439	74		Jonathan Cary's observation	and then three women were called in to attend them.
440	74		Jonathan Cary's observation	We in the room were all at a stand, to see who they would cry out of, but in a short time they cried out, Cary;
441	74		Jonathan Cary's observation	and immediately after a warrant was sent from the justices to bring my wife before them, who were sitting in a chamber near by, waiting for this.
442	74		Jonathan Cary's observation	Being brought before the justices her chief accusers were two girls.
443	74		Jonathan Cary's observation	My wife declared to the justices, that she never had any knowledge of them before that day.
444	74	181	arms stretched out	She was forced to stand with her arms stretched out.
445	74-75	181	Jonathan Cary's observation	I requested that I might hold one of her hands, but it was denied me, then she desired me to wipe the tears from her eyes, and the sweat from her face which I did;

NO.	PAGE	LOIS	SUMMARY	SEGMENT
446	75	181	Jonathan Cary's observation	then she desired she might lean herself on me, saying she should faint.
447	75	181	Jonathan Cary's observation	Justice Hathorn replied she had strength enough to torment these and she should have strength enough to stand.
448	75		Jonathan Cary's observation	I speaking something against their cruel proceedings, they commanded me to be silent, or else I should be turned out of the room.
449	75		Jonathan Cary's observation	The Indian before mentioned was also brought in, to be one of her accusers;
450	75		Jonathan Cary's observation	being come in, he now (when before the justices) fell down and tumbled about like a hog, but said nothing.
451	75		Jonathan Cary's observation	The justices asked the girls, who afflicted the Indian;
452	75		Jonathan Cary's observation	they answered, she, (meaning my wife,) and that she now lay upon him;
453	75		Jonathan Cary's observation	the justices ordered her to touch him, in order to his cure, but her head must be turned another way, lest, instead of curing, she should make him worse, by her looking on him, her hand being guided to take hold of his;
454	75		Jonathan Cary's observation	but the Indian took hold of her hand, and pulled her down on the floor, in a barbarous manner;
455	75		Jonathan Cary's observation	then his hand was taken off, and her hand put on his, and the cure was quickly wrought.
456	76		Jonathan Cary's observation	I being extremely troubled at their inhuman dealings, uttered a hasty speech, "That God would take vengeance on them, and desired that God would deliver us out of the hands of unmerciful men."
457	76		Jonathan Cary's observation	Then her mittimus was writ.
458	76		Jonathan Cary's observation	I did with difficulty and charge obtain the liberty of a room, but no beds in it, if there had been, could have taken but little rest that night.
459	76		Jonathan Cary's observation	She was committed to Boston prison, but I obtained a habeas corpus to remove her to Cambridge prison, which is in our county of Middlesex.
460	76		Jonathan Cary's observation	Having been there one night, next morning the jailer put irons on her legs, (having received such a command) the weight of them was about eight pounds;

NO.	PAGE	LOIS	SUMMARY	SEGMENT
461	76		Jonathan Cary's observation	these irons and her other afflictions soon brought her into convulsion fits, so that I thought she would have died that night.
462	76		Jonathan Cary's observation	I sent to entreat that the irons might be taken off;
463	76		Jonathan Cary's observation	but all entreaties were in vain, if it would have saved her life, so that in this condition she must continue.
464	76–77		Jonathan Cary's observation	The trials at Salem coming on, I went thither to see how things were managed, and finding that the spectre evidence was there received, together with idle, if not malicious stories, against people's lives, I did easily perceive which way the rest would go;
465	77		Jonathan Cary's observation	for the same evidence that served for one would serve for all the rest.
466	77		Jonathan Cary's observation	I acquainted her with her danger; and that if she were carried to Salem to be tried, I feared she would never return.
467	77		Jonathan Cary's observation	I did my utmost that she might have her trial in our own county;
468	77		Jonathan Cary's observation	I with several others petitioning the judge for it, and were put in hopes of it; but I soon saw so much, that I understood thereby it was not intended; which put me upon consulting the means of her escape; which through the goodness of God was effected, and she got to Rhode Island, but soon found herself not safe when there, by reason of the pursuit after her;
469	77		Jonathan Cary's observation	from thence she went to New York along with some others that had escaped their cruel hands; where we found his Excellency Benjamin Fletcher, Esq. Governor, who was very courteous to us.
470	77–78		Jonathan Cary's observation	After this some of my goods were seized in a friend's hands, with whom I had left them, and myself imprisoned by the sheriff, and kept in custody half a day, and then dismissed;
471	78		Jonathan Cary's observation	but to speak of their usage of the prisoners, and the inhumanity shown to them at the time of their execution, no sober christian could bear.
472	78		Jonathan Cary's observation	They had also trials of cruel mockings; which is the more, considering what a people for religion, I mean the profession of it, we have been; those that suffered, being many of them church members, and most of them unspotted in their conversation, till their adversary the devil took up this method for accusing them.
473	78		Jonathan Cary's observation	Jonathan Cary.'
474	78		Martha Carrier's trial	Every idle rumor, everything that the gossip of the credulous or the fertile memories of the malignant could produce, that had an unfavorable bearing upon the prisoner, however foreign it might be from the indictment, was allowed to be brought in evidence before the jury.
475	78		Martha Carrier's trial	A child between five and six years of age was arrested and put into prison.

NO.	PAGE	LOIS	SUMMARY	SEGMENT
476	78		Martha Carrier's trial	Children were encouraged to become witnesses against their parents, and parents against their children.
477	78		Martha Carrier's trial	The following is a part of the testimony borne by a young child against her mother.
478	79		Martha Carrier's trial	Sarah Carrier's confessions, August the 11th, 1692.
479	79		Martha Carrier's trial	'It was asked Sarah Carrier by the magistrates or justices, John Hathorne, Esq, and others; How long hast thou been a witch?
480	79		Martha Carrier's trial	A. Ever since I was six years old.
481	79		Martha Carrier's trial	Q. How old are you now?
482	79		Martha Carrier's trial	A. Near eight years old; brother Richard, says I shall be eight years old in November next.
483	79		Martha Carrier's trial	Q. Who made you a witch?
484	79		Martha Carrier's trial	A. My mother, she made me set my hand to a book.
485	79		Martha Carrier's trial	Q. How did you set your hand to it?
486	79		Martha Carrier's trial	A. I touched it with my fingers, and the book was red, the paper of it was white.
487	79		Martha Carrier's trial	She said she never had seen the black man, the place where she did it was in Andrew Foster's pasture, and Elizabeth Johnson, Jr, was there.
488	79		Martha Carrier's trial	Being asked who was there besides, she answered, her aunt Toothaker, and her cousin.
489	79		Martha Carrier's trial	Being asked when it was, she said, when she was baptized.
490	79		Martha Carrier's trial	Q. What did they promise to give you?
491	79		Martha Carrier's trial	A. A black dog.
492	79		Martha Carrier's trial	Q. Did the dog ever come to you?
493	79		Martha Carrier's trial	A. No.
494	79		Martha Carrier's trial	Q. But you said you saw a cat once: what did that say to you.
495	79-80		Martha Carrier's trial	A. It said it would tear me in pieces, if I would not set my hand to the book.
496	80		Martha Carrier's trial	She said, her mother baptized her, and the devil, or black man was not there, as she saw, and her mother said when she baptized her, Thou art mine forever and ever.
497	80		Martha Carrier's trial	Amen.

NO.	PAGE	LOIS	SUMMARY	SEGMENT
498	80		Martha Carrier's trial	Q. How did you afflict folks?
499	80		Martha Carrier's trial	A. I pinched them, and she said she had no puppets, but she went to them that she afflicted.
500	80		Martha Carrier's trial	Being asked whether she went in her body or her spirit.
501	80		Martha Carrier's trial	She said in her spirit.
502	80		Martha Carrier's trial	She said her mother carried her thither to afflict.
503	80		Martha Carrier's trial	Q. How did your mother carry you when she was in prison?
504	80		Martha Carrier's trial	A. She came like a black cat.
505	80		Martha Carrier's trial	Q. How did you know it was your mother?
506	80		Martha Carrier's trial	A. The cat told me so, that she was my mother.
507	80		Martha Carrier's trial	She said she afflicted Phelps' child last Saturday, and Elizabeth Johnson joined with her to do it.
508	80		Martha Carrier's trial	She had a wooden spear, about as long as her finger, of Elizabeth Johnson and she had it of the devil.
509	80		Martha Carrier's trial	She would not own that she had ever been at the witch meeting at the village.
510	80		Martha Carrier's trial	This is the substance.
511	80		Martha Carrier's trial	Attest. Simon Willard.'
512	81		Martha Carrier's trial	In concluding his report of the trial of the unhappy woman, whose young children were thus induced to become the instruments for procuring her death, Dr Cotton Mather expresses himself in the following language, 'this rampant hag, Martha Carrier, was the person of whom the confessions of the witches, and of her own children among the rest, agreed, that the devil had promised her, she should be Queen of Hell.'
513	81		examination of prisoner	One woman was induced to bear witness against her husband; it was of course false, and it was fatal to him.
514	81		examination of prisoner	Well may we sympathize with Hutchinson, who declares that he shudders while he relates such monstrous violations of the principles of law, as well as nature.
515	81		examination of prisoner	At the examination of the prisoners before the magistrate at the time of their commitment, they were interrogated at great length and minutely;
516	81		examination of prisoner	leading questions were put to them, and they were led to ensnare themselves as much as possible.
517	81		examination of prisoner	The minutes of these examinations were preserved and brought in evidence against them at their trials.
518	81–82		examination of prisoner	Many of them were left upon record, and they exhibit in some cases, an extraordinary degree of sagacity and good sense on the part of the prisoners.

NO.	PAGE	LOIS	SUMMARY	SEGMENT
519	82		Susanna Martin's trial	The following dialogue between Susanna Martin and the magistrate, shews that she did not lack presence and acuteness of mind.
520	82		Susanna Martin's trial	Magistrate. 'Pray what ails these people?'
521	82		Susanna Martin's trial	Martin. 'I don't know.'
522	82		Susanna Martin's trial	Mag. 'But what do you think ails them?'
523	82		Susanna Martin's trial	Martin. 'I do not desire to spend my judgment upon it.'
524	82		Susanna Martin's trial	Mag. 'Don't you think they are bewitched?'
525	82		Susanna Martin's trial	Martin. 'No I do not think they are.'
526	82		Susanna Martin's trial	Mag. 'Tell us your thoughts about them, then.'
527	82		Susanna Martin's trial	Martin. 'No, my thoughts are my own, when they are in, but when they are out, they are another's.
528	82		Susanna Martin's trial	Their master—'
529	82		Susanna Martin's trial	Mag. 'Their master! Who do you think is their master?'
530	82		Susanna Martin's trial	Martin. 'If they be dealing in the black art, you may know as well as I.'
531	82		Susanna Martin's trial	Mag. 'Well, what have you done towards this?'
532	83		Susanna Martin's trial	Martin. 'Nothing at all.'
533	83		Susanna Martin's trial	Mag. 'Why, 'tis you or your appearance.'
534	83		Susanna Martin's trial	Martin. 'I can't help it.'
535	83		Susanna Martin's trial	Mag. 'Is it not your master?
536	83		Susanna Martin's trial	How comes your appearance to hurt these?'
537	83		Susanna Martin's trial	Martin. 'How do I know?'
538	83		Susanna Martin's trial	He that appeared in the shape of Samuel, a glorified saint, may appear in any one's shape.'
539	83		Rebecca Nurse	One circumstance occurred that inflicted a deep and lasting stain upon the pure ermine of justice.
540	83		Rebecca Nurse	The waves of popular fury made one clear breach over the judgment seat.
541	83		Rebecca Nurse	The jury appointed to try Rebecca Nurse brought in a verdict of 'Not Guilty.'

APPENDIX 3 Gaskell's Manipulation of Upham's **First Lecture on Witchcraft** 299

NO.	PAGE	LOIS	SUMMARY	SEGMENT
542	83		Rebecca Nurse	Immediately upon hearing it the malignant and fiendlike accusers uttered a loud outcry in open court!
543	83		Rebecca Nurse	The judges were overcome by the general clamor and intimidated from the faithful discharge of their sacred duty.
544	83		Rebecca Nurse	They expressed their dissatisfaction with the verdict.
545	83-84		Rebecca Nurse	One of the judges declared his disapprobation with great vehemence, another said she should be indicted, anew, and the Chief Justice intimated to the jury that they had overlooked one important piece of evidence.
546	84		Rebecca Nurse	It was this: during the trial, a woman named Hobbs, who had confessed herself a witch, was brought into court, and as she entered, the prisoner turned towards her and said, 'What!
547	84		Rebecca Nurse	do you bring her?
548	84		Rebecca Nurse	she is one of us.'
549	84		Rebecca Nurse	The jury were thus prevailed upon to go out again they soon returned, pronouncing the poor old woman 'Guilty.'
550	84		Rebecca Nurse	After her conviction she addressed the following note to the judges.
551	84		Rebecca Nurse's note	'These presents do humbly shew to the honored court and jury, that I being informed that the jury brought me in guilty, upon my saying that good wife Hobbs and her daughter were of our company; but I intended no otherways, than as they were prisoners with us, and therefore did then, and yet do judge them not legal evidence against their fellow prisoners.
552	84		Rebecca Nurse's note	And I being something hard of hearing, and full of grief, none informing me how the court took up my words, and therefore had no opportunity to declare what I intended, when I said, they were of our company.
553	84		Rebecca Nurse's note	Rebecca Nurse.'
554	84-85		Rebecca Nurse	The governor had intended to grant her a reprieve but upon hearing of his intention the accusers renewed their dismal outcries against her.
555	85		Rebecca Nurse	Several gentlemen of Salem expostulated with the governor, and he was prevailed upon to give orders for her execution, which took place within a few weeks after her conviction.
556	85		an association	The extraordinary conduct of these gentlemen, in preventing the exercise of the executive clemency and discretion on this occasion, is to be explained, it is probable by the following fact recorded by Dr Neal in his History of New England.
557	85		an association	There was an organized association or committee of private individuals in Salem, during the continuance of the delusion, who had undertaken and engaged to find out, and prosecute all suspected persons.
558	85		an association	Dr Neal also informs us that many were arrested and thrown into prison by their interference and influence.
559	85		an association	It is probable that the gentlemen who prevented the reprieve of Mrs Nurse, acted under the authority and by the direction of this association.
560	85-86		Justice Stoughton	The chief justice, Lieutenant Governor Stoughton, seems to have been actuated by a violent prejudice and remarkable zeal against the prisoners.

NO.	PAGE	LOIS	SUMMARY	SEGMENT
561	86		Stoughton's adroitness	The following instance is related by one of his friends and courtiers, Dr Cotton Mather, as illustrative of his adroitness in circumventing and ensnaring an accused individual, in the course of his examination;
562	86		Stoughton's adroitness	it cannot, however, but be regarded by all reflecting and humane persons, as an undignified interference and an unfeeling officiousness on the part of a presiding judge.—
563	86		Stoughton's adroitness	'It cost the court,' says the reporter, 'a wonderful deal of trouble to hear the testimonies of the sufferers;
564	86		Stoughton's adroitness	for when they were going to give in their depositions, they would for a long time be taken with fits, that made them incapable of saying anything.
565	86		prisoner, Rev Burroughs	The chief judge asked the prisoner (Rev. Mr Burroughs,) "who he thought hindered these witnesses from giving their testimonies?"
566	86		prisoner, Rev Burroughs	And he answered, "he supposed it was the devil;"
567	86		Stoughton's adroitness	that honorable person replied, "how comes the devil then to be so loath to have any testimony borne against you?" which cast him into very great confusion.'
568	86–87		Judge Stoughton	The judge and all the people exulted no doubt exceedingly at the success of the stratagem by which the poor prisoner had been thus entrapped and confounded.
569	87		Judge Stoughton	Judge Stoughton does not appear to have recovered from the excitement, into which he was thrown against the supposed witches.
570	87		Judge Stoughton	He never could bear to hear any persons express regret or penitence for the part they had taken in the proceedings.
571	87		Judge Stoughton	When the public delusion had so far subsided, that it became difficult to procure the execution of a witch, he was disturbed and incensed to such a degree, that he abandoned his seat on the bench.
572	87		Judge Stoughton	During a session of the court at Charlestown, in January, 1692-3, 'word was brought in that a reprieve was sent to Salem, and had prevented the execution of seven of those that were there condemned; which so moved the chief judge that he said to this effect.
573	87		Judge Stoughton	"We were in a way to have cleared the land of them, who it is that obstructs the cause of justice, I know not;
574	87		Judge Stoughton	the Lord be merciful to the country;"
575	87		Judge Stoughton	and so went off the bench, and came no more into that court.'
576	87		going off the bench	The executive officers of the law partook of the same spirit.
577	87–88		Giles Cory	It has already been mentioned that Giles Cory seeing that a trial was a mere mockery, and that to put himself to the bar, was to offer himself to be murdered under the forms of law, refused to plead to the indictment.
578	88		Giles Cory	I find by the records of the first church, that some months before, this same Giles Cory, then eighty years of age, made a public profession of religion, acknowledged with penitence the sins of his life, and was admitted to the communion.
579	88		Giles Cory executed	In consequence of his refusing to plead, he was crushed to death.
580	88		Giles Cory	As his aged frame yielded to the dreadful pressure, his tongue was protruded from his mouth.

NO.	PAGE	LOIS	SUMMARY	SEGMENT
581	88		Giles Cory	The demon who presided over the torture, drove it back again with the point of his cane.
582	88		exercise of ferocity	The heart of man once turned to cruelty seems, like the fleshed tiger, to gather new fury in the mere exercise of ferocity.
583	88		exercise of ferocity	We have seen that a physician gave the first impulse to the awful work, by pronouncing the opinion that the pretended sufferers were afflicted by the influence of witches.
584	88		judges and officers	We have also seen that the judges and officers of the law did what they could to drive on the delusion to its height.
585	88–89		instrumental clergy	It ought not in justice to be denied or concealed, that the clergy were also instrumental in promoting the proceedings.
586	89		instrumental clergy	Nay, it must be acknowledged that they took the lead in the whole transaction.
587	89		instrumental clergy	As the supposed agents of all the mischief belonged to the supernatural or spiritual world, which has ever been considered their peculiar province, it was thought that the assistance and cooperation of ministers were particularly appropriate and necessary.
588	89		instrumental clergy	It has been mentioned that the government consulted the ministers of Boston, and the vicinity, after the execution of the first person convicted, and previous to the trial of the others, and that they returned a positive and earnest recommendation to proceed in the good work.
589	89	114	Revd Noyes	Mr Noyes, at that time the junior pastor of the first church in Salem, was one of the most distinguished ministers of the age.
590	89–90		Revd Noyes	There is no reason to doubt that he was justly described in his obituary, in the Boston newspaper, which concludes a glowing account of his eminent gifts and Christian graces in the following terms—'It is no wonder that Salem, and the adjacent parts of the country, as also the churches, university and people of New England, justly esteem him as a principal part of their glory.'
591	90		Upham's remark	It is my painful duty to hold up the conduct of this my predecessor to your pity and amazement;
592	90		Upham's purpose of lectures	if I should fail to do so, I should prove false to one of the leading designs of these lectures, which, as has before been observed, is to show that there is power in a popular delusion and a general excitement of the passions of a community to pervert the best of characters, turn the hearts even of good men to violence, and fill them with all manner of bitterness.
593	90		Rebecca Nurse	Rebecca Nurse, the person whom the jury in the first instance acquitted, but were afterwards induced by the strong disapprobation and rebukes of the judges to condemn, was a member of the first church.
594	90		Rebecca Nurse	On the communion day that intervened between her conviction and execution, Mr Noyes procured a vote of excommunication to be passed against her.
595	90–91		Rebecca Nurse	In the afternoon of the same day, the poor old woman was carried to the 'great and spacious meeting-house' in chains, and there in the presence of a vast assembly, Mr Noyes proclaimed her expulsion from the church, pronounced the sentence of eternal death upon her, formally delivered her over to Satan, and consigned her to the flames of hell.
596	91		Rebecca Nurse	It is related, however, that as soon as the fanaticism had disappeared, the recollection of her excellent character, and virtuous and pious life, effaced the reproach of the spiritual as well as the temporal sentence.

NO.	PAGE	LOIS	SUMMARY	SEGMENT
597	91		Martha Cory	I would mention in this connexion, that Martha Cory, the wife of Giles Cory, was a member of the church in Salem Village.
598	91		Martha Cory	A committee consisting of the pastor, the two deacons, and another member, was sent by the church to the prison, to promulgate to her a doom similar to that to which Rebecca Nurse was consigned, the day after her conviction.
599	91		Parris	Mr Parris declares in the records of the church, that they found her 'very obdurate, justifying herself, and condemning all who had done anything to her just discovery or condemnation.
600	91-92		Martha Cory	Where upon, after a little discourse (for,' says he, 'her imperiousness would not suffer much) and after prayer (which she was willing to decline) the dreadful sentence of excommunication was pronounced against her.'
601	92		Revd Noyes	Mr Noyes was also very active to prevent a revulsion of the public mind or even the least diminution of the popular violence against the supposed witches.
602	92		sympathy	As they all protested their innocence to the moment of death, and as most of them exhibited a remarkably Christian deportment throughout the dreadful scenes they were called to encounter from their arrest to their execution, there was reason to apprehend that the people would gradually be led to feel a sympathy for them, if not to entertain doubts of their guilt.
603	92		Revd Noyes	It became necessary, therefore, to remove any impressions unfavorable to themselves, that might be made by the conduct and declarations of the convicts.
604	92		Revd Noyes	Mr Noyes and others were on the ground continually for this purpose.
605	92		Mary Easty	One of the most interesting persons among the innocent sufferers, was Mary Easty of Topsfield;
606	92		Mary Easty	she was a sister of Rebecca Nurse.
607	92-93		Mary Easty	Her mind appears to have been uncommonly strong and well cultivated, and her heart the abode of the purest and most Christian sentiments.
608	93		Mary Easty	After her conviction, she addressed the following letter to the judges and ministers, by which it appears, that she felt for others more than she did for herself.
609	93		Mary Easty	It is a striking and affecting specimen of good sense, of Christian fortitude, of pious humility, of noble benevolence, and of the real eloquence of the heart.
610	93		Mary Easty	'To the honorable judge and bench now sitting in judicature in Salem, and the reverend ministers, humbly sheweth,—That, whereas your humble and poor petitioner, being condemned to die, doth humbly beg of you to take it into your judicious and pious consideration, that your poor and humble petitioner, knowing my own innocency, (blessed be the Lord for it,) and seeing plainly the wiles and subtilty of my accusers, by myself, cannot but judge charitably of others, that are going the same way with myself, if the Lord step not mightily in.
611	93-94		Mary Easty	I was confined a whole month on the same account that I am now condemned, and then cleared by the afflicted persons, as some of your honors know;
612	94		Mary Easty	and in two days time, I was cried out upon by them again; and have been confined and am now condemned to die.
613	94	188	Mary Easty	The Lord above knows my innocence then, and likewise doth now, as at the great day will be known by men and angels.
614	94		Mary Easty	I petition to your honors, not for my own life, for I know I must die, and my appointed time is set, but the Lord he knows if it be possible that no more innocent blood be shed, which undoubtedly cannot be avoided in the way and course you go in.

NO.	PAGE	LOIS	SUMMARY	SEGMENT
615	94		Mary Easty	I question not but your honors do to the utmost of your powers, in the discovery and detecting of witchcraft and witches, and would not be guilty of innocent blood for the world;
616	94	184	Mary Easty	but by my own innocency I know you are in the wrong way.
617	94		Mary Easty	The Lord in his infinite mercy direct you in this great work, if it be his blessed will, that innocent blood be not shed.
618	94-95		Mary Easty	I would humbly beg of you that your honors would be pleased to examine some of those confessing witches, I being confident there are several of them have belied themselves and others, as will appear, if not in this world, I am sure in the world to come, whither I am going;
619	95		Mary Easty	and I question not but yourselves will see an alteration in these things.
620	95		Mary Easty	They say, myself and others have made a league with the devil;
621	95		Mary Easty	we cannot confess, I know and the Lord knows (as will shortly appear) they belie me, and so I question not but they do others;
622	95	188	Mary Easty	the Lord alone, who is the searcher of all hearts, knows, as I shall answer it at the tribunal seat, that I know not the least thing of witchcraft, therefore I cannot, I durst not belie my own soul.
623	95		Mary Easty	I beg your honors not to deny this my humble petition, from a poor, dying, innocent person, and I question not but the Lord will give a blessing to your endeavours.
624	95		Mary Easty	Mary Easty.'
625	95		Mary Easty	The parting interview of this excellent woman with her husband, children and friends, is said to have been a most solemn, affecting and sublime scene.
626	95		Mary Easty	She was executed with seven others.
627	95		Revd Noyes	Mr Noyes turned towards their bodies and exclaimed with a compassion, that was altogether worthy of an inquisitor, 'What a sad thing it is to see eight firebrands of hell hanging there!!'
628	96		John Proctor	John Proctor of Salem Village, went to court to attend his wife during her examination on the charge of witchcraft; and having rendered himself disagreeable to the prosecuting witnesses by the interest he naturally took in her behalf, was accused by them on the spot, of the same crime, condemned and executed.
629	96		John Proctor	Both he and his wife sustained excellent characters in the village, and in Ipswich where they had formerly resided.
630	96		John Proctor	He wrote the following spirited and interesting letter to the ministers of Boston, requesting to be tried there, and protesting against the proceedings of the court.
631	96		John Proctor	'Salem Prison, July 23, 1692.
632	96		John Proctor	'Mr Mather, Mr Allen, Mr Moody, Mr Willard and Mr Baily,
633	96		John Proctor's letter	'Reverend Gentlemen,—
634	96-97		John Proctor's letter	The innocency of our case, with the enmity of our accusers and our judges and jury, whom nothing but our innocent blood will serve, having condemned us already before our trials, being so much incensed and enraged against us by the Devil, makes us bold to beg and implore your favorable assistance of this our humble petition to his excellency, that if it be possible our innocent blood may be spared, which undoubtedly otherwise will be shed, if the Lord doth not mercifully step in;

NO.	PAGE	LOIS	SUMMARY	SEGMENT
635	97		John Proctor's letter	the magistrates, ministers, juries, and all the people in general, being so much enraged and incensed against us by the delusion of the Devil, which we can term no other, by reason we know in our own consciences, we are all innocent persons.
636	97		John Proctor's letter	Here are five persons who have lately confessed themselves to be witches, and do accuse some of us of being along with them at a sacrament, since we were committed into close prison, which we know to be lies.
637	97		John Proctor's letter	Two of the five are (Carrier's sons) young men, who would not confess anything till they tied them neck and heels, till the blood was ready to come out of their noses, and it is credibly believed and reported this was the occasion of making them confess what they never did, by reason, they said, one had been a witch a month; and another five weeks, and that their mother made them so, who has been confined here this nine weeks.
638	98		John Proctor's letter	My son, Wilham Proctor, when he was examined, because he would not confess that he was guilty, when he was innocent, they tied him neck and heels till the blood gushed out at his nose, and would have kept him so twenty four hours, if one, more merciful than the rest, had not taken pity on him and caused him to be unbound.
639	98		John Proctor's letter	'These actions are very like the Popish cruelties.
640	98		John Proctor's letter	They have already undone us in our estates, and that will not serve their turns without our innocent blood.
641	98		John Proctor's letter	If it cannot be granted that we can have our trials at Boston, we humbly beg that you would endeavor to have these magistrates changed, and others in their room;
642	98		John Proctor's letter	begging also and beseeching you that you would be pleased to be here, if not all, some of you, at our trials, hoping, thereby you may be the means of saving the shedding of our innocent blood.
643	98		John Proctor's letter	Desiring your prayers to the Lord in our behalf, we rest your poor afflicted servants, John Proctor, &c.'
644	98-99		John Proctor	When he was in prison, all his property was attached, everything was taken from his house, his family, consisting of eleven children, were left destitute, even the food that was preparing for their dinner, was carried away by the sheriff.
645	99		John Proctor	After conviction he petitioned for a little more time to prepare to die, but it was denied him.
646	99		John Proctor	He begged Mr Noyes to pray with him, but he refused, unless he would confess that he was guilty!
647	99		John Proctor	His numerous family was not permitted to starve.
648	99		John Proctor	The cruelty that snatched the bread from their mouths was overruled by a merciful providence.
649	99		John Proctor	His descendants, who are found in all parts of the country, occupy at this moment the estate, and cultivate the fields which he owned.
650	99		the prosecutors	The prosecutors were exceedingly anxious to obtain confessions from the convicted, and importuned, harassed and vexed them continually to acknowledge their guilt.
651	99		the public	The public were predisposed to suspect and convict of witchcraft all persons in whose character and conduct, there were any marks of eccentricity or traits of peculiarity.
652	99-100		Sarah Good	Sarah Good had for some time previous to the delusion, been subject to a species of mental derangement, of which sadness and melancholy were the prevailing characteristics.
653	100		Sarah Good	She was accordingly accused of witchcraft and condemned to die.

APPENDIX 3 *Gaskell's Manipulation of Upham's* First Lecture on Witchcraft   305

NO.	PAGE	LOIS	SUMMARY	SEGMENT
654	100		Sarah Good/ Revd Noyes	Mr Noyes urged her very strenuously, at the time of her execution, to confess.
655	100		Sarah Good/ Revd Noyes	Among other things he told her, 'She was a witch, and that she knew she was a witch.'
656	100		Sarah Good/ Revd Noyes	She was conscious of her innocence, and felt that she was injured, oppressed and trampled upon, and her indignation was roused against her persecutors.
657	100		Sarah Good/ Revd Noyes	She could not bear in silence the cruel aspersion, and although she was just about to be launched into eternity, the torrent of her feelings could not be restrained, but burst upon the head of him who uttered the false accusation.
658	100		Sarah Good/ Revd Noyes	'You are a liar,' said she.
659	100		Sarah Good/ Revd Noyes	'I am no more a witch, than you are a wizard;—and if you take away my life, God will give you blood to drink.'
660	100-01		Revd Noyes's death	Hutchinson says that in his day there was a tradition among the people of Salem, and it has descended to the present time, that the manner of Mr Noyes' death strangely verified the prediction thus wrung from the incensed spirit of the dying old woman.
661	101		Margaret Jacobs	I have before related the circumstances connected with the confession and recantation of Margaret Jacobs, the poor girl who was persuaded to be instrumental in procuring the conviction of her grandfather;
662	101		Margaret Jacobs/Revd Burroughs	it was also remarked that she had been a witness against the Rev Mr Burroughs.
663	101		Margaret Jacobs/Revd Burroughs	She obtained permission to visit him the day before his execution, acknowledged that she had belied him, and implored his forgiveness.
664	101		Margaret Jacobs/Revd Burroughs	He freely forgave her, and prayed with her and for her.
665	101		Burroughs	The case of Mr Burroughs is connected with circumstances of uncommon interest.
666	101		Burroughs	He had enjoyed the benefit of a liberal education;
667	101		Burroughs	you will find his name among those who received the honors of Harvard University in the year 1670.
668	101		Burroughs	At the time of his arrest, he was the minister of a congregation in Wells, a town in the state of Maine.
669	101-02		Burroughs	He had passed the prime of life, and, as there is reason to fear, fell a victim to the prejudice and hatred engendered in a parochial controversy some years before.
670	102		Burroughs	He was carried in a cart with other convicts from the jail, which is supposed to have stood on the northern corner of County and St Peter's Streets, the procession probably passing down St Peter's into Essex Street, and thence onward to the rocky elevation, called 'Gallows hill,' about an eighth of a mile towards Danvers, beyond the head of Federal Street, where the executions took place.
671	102		Burroughs	'While Mr Burroughs was on the ladder,' a contemporary writer observes, 'he made a speech for the clearing of his innocency, with such solemn and serious expressions as were to the admiration of all present, his prayer was so well worded and uttered with such composedness and such fervency of spirit, as was very affecting, and drew tears from many, so that it seemed to some that the spectators would hinder the execution.'

NO.	PAGE	LOIS	SUMMARY	SEGMENT
672	102	149	Burroughs	To meet and turn back this state of feeling, the accusers cried out, that they saw the evil being standing behind him in the shape of a black man, and dictating every word he uttered.
673	102–03		Cotton Mather	And the famous Cotton Mather, minister of the North Church in Boston, who was declared by Dr Colman to have been the most learned man he ever knew, and who combined an almost incredible amount of vanity and credulity, with a high degree of cunning and policy; an inordinate love of temporal power and distinction, with every outward manifestation of piety and Christian humility, and a proneness to fanaticism and superstition with amazing acquisitions of knowledge, and a great and remarkable genius, rode round in the crowd on horseback, haranguing the people, and saying that it was not to be wondered at, that Mr Burroughs appeared so well, for that the devil often transformed himself into an angel of light!
674	103		Cotton Mather	This artful declamation, together with the outcries and assertions of the accusers, had the intended effect upon the fanatical multitude.
675	103–04		Burroughs	When the body was cut down it was dragged by the rope to a hollow place, excavated between the rocks, stripped of its garments, and then covered with clothes that had belonged to some poor wretch previously executed, thrown with two others into the hole, trampled down by the mob, and finally left partly uncovered.
676	104		concluded	I have now concluded the narrative of the Salem witchcraft.
677	104		Upham's object	It has been my object to present only those facts that were necessary to give you a correct and adequate view of the transaction, and to enable you to bear away from the contemplation of the dreadful scene, such impressions and reflections as historical and philosophical truth and justice require.
678	104		Upham's determination	It has been my determination to set down nought in malice, and to keep back nothing from partiality.
679	104		Upham's analysis of the cause of the witch delusion	I might proceed to analyze the whole transaction, into the several elementary passions, motives, and intentions, by whose combined, conflicting, or separate influence it was introduced and carried on to its dreadful results.
680	104		Upham's analysis of the cause of the witch delusion	There is much reason to fear that to a great extent it was the effect of deliberate design.
681	104–05		Upham's analysis of the cause of the witch delusion	The peculiar theology of that period presented inducements to ambitious and enthusiastic individuals among the prominent members of the clergy, to bring about a state of things in which their spiritual power would be felt and displayed to a greater extent than before.
682	105		Upham's analysis of the cause of the witch delusion	The frequently repeated wars with the Indians, especially the struggle with the celebrated and heroic Phillip, had produced a relaxed and licentious state of morals and manners among the people.
683	105		Upham's analysis of the cause of the witch delusion	This appears with sufficient clearness from the doings and declarations of the Reforming Synod convened at Boston in 1679.
684	105		Upham's analysis of the cause of the witch delusion	All patriotic, pious and benevolent citizens were distressed at the contemplation of such a state of things, and many attempts were made to arrest the downward movement of society.

NO.	PAGE	LOIS	SUMMARY	SEGMENT
685	105		Upham's analysis of the cause of the witch delusion	It was thought that the only way in which to check it was to restore and increase the influence of the clergy, that through them the community at large might be brought more under the sway of moral and Christian obligation.
686	105		Why did the clergy become so powerful?	The whole machinery of a religious reformation, so far as the methods for producing such an effect had then been discovered, were put into operation simultaneously and on a large scale.
687	105-06		Why did the clergy become so powerful?	In the year 1692, special efforts were made to renew the power of the spirit of the gospel in many of the churches.
688	106		Why did the clergy become so powerful?	The motives of those who acted in these measures were for the most part of the purest and holiest character.
689	106		Why did the clergy become so powerful?	But there were not wanting individuals who were willing to abuse the opportunities offered by the general excitement and awakening thus produced.
690	106		Why did the clergy become so powerful?	It was soon discerned by those ambitious of spiritual influence and domination, that their object could be most easily achieved by carrying the people to the greatest extreme of credulity, fanaticism, and superstition.
691	106		Why did the clergy become so powerful?	Opposition to prevailing vices, and attempts to reform society, were considered at that time in the light of a conflict with Satan himself, and he was thought to be the ablest minister who had the greatest power over the great enemy, who could most easily and effectually avert his blows and counteract his baleful influence.
692	106		Upham's criticism of Mather	Dr Cotton Mather aspired to be considered the great champion of the church, and the most successful combatant against the prince of the power of the air.
693	106-07		Upham's criticism of Mather	He seems to have longed for an opportunity to signalize himself in this particular kind of warfare; seized upon every occurrence that would admit of such a coloring to represent it as the result of diabolical agency; circulated in his numerous publications as many tales of witchcraft as he could collect throughout New and Old England, and repeatedly endeavored to get up a delusion of this kind in Boston.
694	107		Upham's criticism of Mather	He succeeded to some extent.
695	107		Upham's criticism of Mather	An instance of witchcraft was brought about in that place by his management in 1688.
696	107		Upham's criticism of Mather	There is some ground for suspicion that he was instrumental in causing the delusion in Salem;
697	107		Upham's criticism of Mather	at any rate, he took a leading part in conducting it.
698	107		Upham's criticism of Mather	And while there is evidence that he endeavored, after the delusion subsided, to escape the disgrace of having approved of the proceedings, and pretended to have been in some measure opposed to them, it can be too clearly shown that he was secretly and cunningly endeavoring to renew them during the next year in his own parish in Boston.

NO.	PAGE	LOIS	SUMMARY	SEGMENT
699	107-08		Upham's criticism of Mather	I know nothing more artful and jesuitical than his attempts, to avoid the reproach of having been active in carrying on the delusion in Salem, and elsewhere, and, at the same time, to keep up such a degree of credulity and superstition in the minds of the people, as to render it easy to plunge them into it again at the first favorable moment.
700	108		Cotton Mather's self-defence	In the following passages he endeavors to escape the odium that had been connected with the prosecutions.
701	108		Cotton Mather's self-defence	The world knows how many pages I have composed and published, and particular gentlemen in the government know how many letters I have written to prevent the excessive credit of spectral accusations.
702	108		Cotton Mather's self-defence	'In short, I do humbly but freely affirm it, that there is not a man living in this world who has been more desirous than the poor man I, to shelter my neighbors from the inconveniences of spectral outcries: yea, I am very jealous I have done so much that way, as to sin in what I have done;
703	108		Cotton Mather's self-defence	such have been the cowardice and fearfulness, whereunto my regard unto the dissatisfaction of other people has precipitated me.
704	108-09		Cotton Mather's self-defence	I know a man in the world, who has thought he has been able to convict some such witches as ought to die;
705	109		Cotton Mather's self-defence	but his respect unto the public peace has caused him rather to try whether he could not renew them by repentance.'
706	109		Cotton Mather's self-defence	In Dr Mather's life of Sir William Phipps, a man of an exceedingly feeble intellect, and whom he appears to have kept by flattery in complete subserviency to his purposes, he artfully endeavors to take the credit to himself of having doubted the propriety of the proceedings while they were in progress.
707	109		Cotton Mather's self-defence	This work was published without his name, in order that he might commend himself with more freedom.
708	109		Cotton Mather's self-defence	The advice given by the ministers of Boston and the vicinity to the government, has been spoken of already more than once.
709	109		Cotton Mather's self-defence	Cotton Mather frequently took occasion to commend, and magnify the merit of this production.
710	109		Cotton Mather's self-defence	In one of his writings he speaks of 'the gracious words' it contained.
711	109		Cotton Mather's self-defence	In his life of Phipps, he thus modestly takes the credit of its authorship to himself;
712	109		Cotton Mather's self-defence	it was 'drawn up at their (the ministers') desire, by Mr Mather the younger, as I have been informed.'

NO.	PAGE	LOIS	SUMMARY	SEGMENT
713	109-10		Upham's criticism of Mather	And in order the more effectually to give the impression that he was rather opposed to the proceedings, he quotes those portions of the paper that recommended caution and circumspection, leaving out those other passages, in which it was vehemently urged to carry the proceedings on—'speedily and vigorously.'!
714	110		Upham's criticism of Mather	But like other ambitious and grasping politicians, he was anxious to have the support of all parties at the same time.
715	110		Cotton Mather's self-defence	After making court to those who were dissatisfied with the prosecutions, he thus commends himself to all who approved of them.
716	110		Cotton Mather's self-defence	'And why, after all my unwearied cares and pains to rescue the miserable from the lions and bears of hell, which had seized them, and after all my studies to disappoint the devils in their designs to confound my neighborhood, must I be driven to the necessity of an apology?
717	110		Cotton Mather's self-defence	Truly the hard representations wherewith some ill men have reviled my conduct, and the countenance which other men have given to these representations, oblige me to give mankind some account of my behaviour.
718	110-11		Cotton Mather's self-defence	No Christian can (I say none but evil workers can) eliminate my visiting such of my poor flock, as have at any time fallen under the terrible and sensible molestations of evil angels: [sic]
719	111		Cotton Mather's self-defence	let their afflictions have been what they will, I could not have answered it unto my glorious Lord, if I had withheld my just comforts and counsels from them;
720	111		Cotton Mather's self-defence	and if I have also, with some exactness, observed the methods of the invisible world, when they have thus become observable, I have been but a servant of mankind in doing so: [sic]
721	111		Cotton Mather's self-defence	yea, no less a person than the venerable Baxter has more than once or twice in the most public manner invited mankind to thank me for that service.'
722	111		Upham's criticism of Mather	In other passages, he thus continues to stimulate and encourage the advocates of the prosecutions.
723	111		Cotton Mather's self-defence	Wherefore, instead of all apish shouts and jeers at histories which have such undoubted confirmation, as that no man that has breeding enough to regard the common laws of human society will offer to doubt of them;
724	111-12		Cotton Mather's self-defence	it becomes us rather to adore the goodness of God, who does not permit such things every day to befall us all, as he sometimes did permit to befall some few of our miserable neighbors.
725	112		Cotton Mather's self-defence	And is it a very glorious thing that I have now to mention:
726	112		Cotton Mather's self-defence	The devils have with most horrid operations, broke in upon our neighborhood, and God has at such a rate overruled all the fury and malice of those devils, that all the afflicted have not only been delivered, but I hope also savingly brought home unto God, and the reputation of no one good person in the world has been damaged;
727	112		Cotton Mather's self-defence	but instead thereof, the souls of many, especially of the rising generation, have been thereby awakened unto some acquaintance with religion;

NO.	PAGE	LOIS	SUMMARY	SEGMENT
728	112		Cotton Mather's self-defence	our young people, who belonged unto the praying meetings, of both sexes, apart, would ordinarily spend whole nights, by whole weeks together, in prayers and psalms upon these occasions, in which devotions the devils could get nothing, but, like fools, a scourge for their own backs;
729	112–13		Cotton Mather's self-defence	and some scores of other young people, who were strangers to real piety, were now struck with the lively demonstrations of hell evidently set forth before their eyes, when they saw persons cruelly frighted, wounded and starved by devils, and scalded with burning brimstone;
730	113		Cotton Mather's self-defence	and yet so preserved in this tortured state, as that, at the end of one month's wretchedness, they were as able still to undergo another;
731	113		Cotton Mather's self-defence	so that of these also, it might now be said—"Behold they pray."
732	113		Cotton Mather's self-defence	In the whole the devil got just nothing, but God got praises, Christ got subjects, the Holy Spirit got temples, the Church got additions, and the souls of men got everlasting benefits.
733	113		Cotton Mather's self-defence	I am not so vain as to say that any wisdom or virtue of mine did contribute unto this good order of things;
734	113		Cotton Mather's self-defence	but I am so just as to say, I did not hinder this good.'
735	113		Upham's criticism of Mather	From this latter passage it is clear that Dr Mather contemplated the witchcraft delusion as having been the instrument in promoting a revival of religion, and was inclined to boast of the success with which it had been attended as such.
736	113–14		Upham's criticism of Mather	I cannot, indeed, resist the conviction, that, notwithstanding all his attempts to appear dissatisfied, after they had become unpopular, with the occurrences in the Salem trials, he looked upon them with secret pleasure, and would have been glad to have had them repeated again in Boston.
737	114		Upham's criticism of Mather	How blind is man to the future!
738	114		Upham's criticism of Mather	The state of things which Cotton Mather labored to bring about, in order that he might increase his own influence over an infatuated people, by being regarded by them as mighty to cast out and vanquish evil spirits, and as able to hold Satan himself in chains by his prayers and his piety, brought him at length into such disgrace, that his power was broken down, and he became the object of public ridicule and open insult.
739	114		Upham's criticism of Mather	And the excitement that had been produced for the purpose of restoring and strengthening the influence of the clerical and spiritual leaders resulted in effects which reduced that influence to a still lower point.
740	114		Upham's criticism of ministers	The intimate connexion of Dr Mather and other prominent ministers with the witchcraft delusion, brought a reproach upon the clergy from which they have never yet recovered.

NO.	PAGE	LOIS	SUMMARY	SEGMENT
741	115		Upham's ratiocinative analysis of delusion	In addition to the designing exertions of ambitious ecclesiastics, and the benevolent and praiseworthy efforts of those whose only aim was to promote a real and thorough reformation of religion, all the passions of our nature stood ready to throw their concentrated energy into the excitement, (as they ever will do whatever may be its character,) so soon as it became sufficiently strong to encourage their action.
742	115		Upham's ratiocinative analysis of delusion	The whole force of popular superstition, all the fanatical propensities of the ignorant and deluded multitude united with the best feelings of our nature to heighten the fury of the storm.
743	115		Upham's ratiocinative analysis of delusion	Piety was indignant at the supposed rebellion against the sovereignty of God, and was roused to an extreme of agitation and apprehension, in witnessing such a daring and fierce assault by the devil and his adherents upon the churches and the cause of the gospel.
744	115–16		Upham's ratiocinative analysis of delusion	Virtue was shocked at the tremendous guilt of those who were believed to have entered the diabolical confederacy; while public order and security stood aghast, amidst the invisible, the supernatural, the infernal, and, apparently, the irresistible attacks that were making upon the foundations of society.
745	116		Upham's ratiocinative analysis of delusion	In baleful combination with principles, good in themselves, thus urging the passions into wild operation, there were all the wicked and violent affections to which humanity is liable.
746	116		Upham's ratiocinative analysis of delusion	Theological bitterness, personal animosities, local controversies, private feuds, long cherished grudges, and professional jealousies, rushed forward, and raised their discordant voices, to swell the horrible din;
747	116		Upham's ratiocinative analysis of delusion	credulity rose with its monstrous and ever expanding form, on the ruins of truth, reason and the senses;
748	116		Upham's ratiocinative analysis of delusion	malignity and cruelty rode triumphant through the storm, by whose fury every mild and gentle sentiment had been shipwrecked;
749	116		Upham's ratiocinative analysis of delusion	and revenge, smiling in the midst of the tempest, welcomed its desolating wrath as it dashed the mangled objects of its hate along the shore.
750	116–17		Upham's ratiocinative analysis of delusion	It would indeed be worthy the attention of the metaphysician and moralist, to scrutinize this transaction thoroughly in all its periods and branches, to ascertain its causes and to mark its developments.
751	117		Upham's summary	There cannot be a doubt that much valuable instruction would thus be gathered respecting the elements of our nature, and of society.
752	117		Upham's summary	But this is a study which can best be pursued by each individual observer for himself.
753	117		Upham's summary	I relinquish it therefore to the calm consideration and sober reflection of every one who has followed me in the examination and review now brought to a close.

NO.	PAGE	LOIS	SUMMARY	SEGMENT
754	117		Upham's summary	Perhaps you are ready to exclaim that your ancestors were at once, the greatest fanatics, and the greatest barbarians the world ever knew; that they have left a darker stain upon our annals than is to be found elsewhere on all the records of history.
755	117		Upham's summary	And that, instead of being proud of such forefathers, you would rather have been the descendants of any other people.
756	117		unreasonable exclamation	It shall be the purpose of the remaining lecture to show the unreasonableness of such exclamations.
757	117–18		unreasonable exclamation	By giving a history of similar superstitious delusions and proceedings in other countries, by tracing the progress and describing the state of legislation respecting witchcraft, and by presenting a sketch of the condition of science, theology and philosophy at the time, I shall hope to do this.
758	118		Upham's purpose of lectures	It shall also be my purpose to lead your minds into such a train of reflections, as will enable you to draw the lesson it was intended by providence to convey from this sad history; to educe from it important illustrations and suggestions respecting our moral and intellectual nature, to cause light to shine forth from its dark folds and beam upon our path, and to confirm us in a grateful sense of the blessings we enjoy, in the possession of enlightened reason, in the clearer revelation of truth, and in the discoveries of science.
759	118		Upham's purpose of lectures	Partly, however, from an unwillingness to have your minds continue for a day under the impression that must now rest upon them respecting your ancestors, and partly to prepare you for the considerations, in justification, or rather in palliation, of their conduct, to be presented in the remaining lecture, I must exercise your patience for a moment longer.
760	119		lesson from failure	Human virtue never shines with more lustre, than when it rises amidst the imperfections, or from the ruins of our nature, arrays itself in the robes of penitence, and goes forth with earnest and humble sincerity to the work of reformation and restitution.
761	119		lesson from failure	It is the sight of such virtue, we are assured by him who dwells in the bosom of God, that imparts the sublimest joy and raises the loudest strains of thanksgiving in the choirs of heaven.
762	119		lesson from failure	Such virtue did our pious ancestors exhibit when the spell that had bound and perverted them was broken.
763	119		lesson from failure	The government, all its branches acting in concert, issued a proclamation, enjoining a general Fast, and the people were called upon in the following affecting expressions to unite in prayer to God.
764	119		proclamation of fast	By the honorable the Lieutenant Governor, Council and Assembly of his Majesty's province of the Massachusetts Bay, in General Court assembled.
765	119–20		proclamation of fast	Whereas the anger of God is not yet turned away, but his hand is still stretched out against his people in manifold judgments, particularly in drawing out to such a length the troubles of Europe, by a perplexing war;
766	120		proclamation of fast	and more especially respecting ourselves in this province, in that God is pleased still to go on in diminishing our substance, cutting short our harvest, blasting our most promising undertakings more ways than one, unsettling us, and by his more immediate hand snatching away many out of our embraces by sudden and violent deaths, even at this time, when the sword is devouring so many both at home and abroad, and that after many days of public and solemn addressing him;
767	120		proclamation of fast	and although, considering the many sins prevailing in the midst of us, we cannot but wonder at the patience and mercy moderating these rebukes;
768	120		proclamation of fast	yet we cannot but also fear, that there is something still wanting to accompany our supplications: [sic]

NO.	PAGE	LOIS	SUMMARY	SEGMENT
769	120		proclamation of fast	and doubtless there are some particular sins, which God is angry with our Israel for, that have not been duly seen and resented by us, about which God expects to be sought, if ever he again turn our captivity.
770	121–22		proclamation of fast	Wherefore it is commanded and appointed, that Thursday, the fourteenth of January next, be observed as a day of prayer with fasting, throughout this province, strictly forbidding all servile labor thereon; that so all God's people may offer up fervent supplications unto him, for the preservation and prosperity of his Majesty's royal person and government, and success to attend his affairs both at home and abroad; that all iniquity may be put away, which hath stirred God's holy jealousy against this land; that he would show us what we know not, and help us wherein we have done amiss to do so no more; and especially that whatever mistakes on either hand, have been fallen into, either by the body of this people, or any orders of men, referring to the late tragedy, raised among us by Satan and his instruments, through the awful judgment of God, he would humble us therefor, and pardon all the errors of his servants and people, that desire to love his name; that he would remove the rod of the wicked from off the lot of the righteous, that he would bring in the American heathen, and cause them to hear and obey his voice.
771	122		proclamation of fast	'Given at Boston, December 17th, 1696, in the eighth year of his Majesty's reign.
772	122		proclamation of fast	Isaac Addington, Secretary.'
773	122		community's regret	It seems as if the community could not recover from a sense of the injury it had inflicted upon the innocent.
774	122		resolution by Sewall	I find that a resolution was introduced into the General Court, nearly fifty years afterwards, by Major Sewall, a son of the Judge, for the appointment of a committee to make an inquiry into the condition and circumstances of individuals and families, that might have suffered, from the calamity of 1692,' as it was called.
775	122		resolution by Sewall	The resolution was passed unanimously and the house expressed a strong desire to compensate them either by money or a township of land.
776	122–23		resolution by Sewall	The inhabitants of Salem did what they could in the way of restitution and reparation.
777	123		Revd Noyes's regret	Dr Bentley, who has given the most lively and interesting account of the delusion, of any I have seen, says, 'that Mr Noyes came out and publicly confessed his error; never concealed a circumstance, never excused himself; visited, loved, blessed the survivors whom he had injured, asked forgiveness always, and consecrated the residue of his life to bless mankind.'
778	123		the first Church's regret	The first Church, which had anathematized Rebecca Nurse and others, after their conviction and previous to their execution, did all that could be done by way of reparation.
779	123		the first Church's regret	It endeavored to erase the ignominy it had cast upon them, by publicly repealing and reversing its censures, and by recording the following affecting acknowledgment of its error.
780	123	190	the first Church's regret	'*March 2d*, 1712.—

314

NO.	PAGE	LOIS	SUMMARY	SEGMENT
781	123	190	record of Rebecca Nurse's excommunication blotted out	After the Sacrament a church meeting was appointed to be at the Teacher's house, at two o'clock in the afternoon, on the sixth of the month, being Thursday; on which day accordingly, March sixth, they met to consider of the several particulars propounded to them by the Teacher:—viz. 1st, Whether the record of the excommunication of our sister Nurse, (all things considered,) may not be erased and blotted out.
782	123–24	190	record of Rebecca Nurse's excommunication blotted out	The result of which consideration was—That whereas on the third of July, 1692, it was proposed by the elders, and consented to by a unanimous vote of the church, that our sister Nurse should be excommunicated, she being convicted of witchcraft by the court—and she was accordingly excommunicated.
783	124	190	record of Rebecca Nurse's excommunication blotted out	Since which the General Court having taken off the attainder, and the testimony on which she was convicted, being not now so satisfactory to ourselves and others, as it was generally in that hour of darkness and temptation, and we being solicited by her son, Mr Samuel Nurse, to erase and blot out of the church records the sentence of her excommunication—this church having the matter proposed to them by the Teacher, and having seriously considered it, doth consent that the record of our sister Nurse's excommunication be accordingly erased and blotted out, that it may no longer be a reproach to her memory, and an occasion of grief to her children.
784	124–25	190	record of Rebecca Nurse's excommunication blotted out	Humbly requesting that the merciful God would pardon whatsoever sin, error or mistake was in the application of that censure, and of that whole affair, through our merciful High Priest, who knoweth how to have compassion on the ignorant, and those that are out of the way.'
785	125		record of Giles Cory's excommunication blotted out	A similar step was taken in reference to Giles Cory.
786	125		record of Martha Cory's excommunication blotted out	The same course was pursued, as appears from its records, by the church in Salem Village, with reference to the excommunication, of Martha Cory.
787	125		Ann Putnam's repentance	The records of that church contain a most touching and pungent declaration of sorrow and repentance, made thirteen years afterwards, by Ann Putnam, already mentioned as one of the principal accusers.
788	125		general repentance	We have reason to cherish the belief that the unhappy and truly penitent young woman was under the influence, at the time of the prosecutions, of a sincere and complete delusion, without any consciousness or suspicion of error, or the least inclination to injure the innocent.
789	125		general repentance	It is probable that reflecting persons would agree that the jury had acted in conformity with their obligations in convicting the persons accused.
790	125		general repentance	They had sworn to try them according to the law and the evidence.
791	125–26		general repentance	The law was certain;
792	126		general repentance	it was laid down with great positiveness by the court, and not disputed by the prisoners or their friends.

NO.	PAGE	LOIS	SUMMARY	SEGMENT
793	126		general repentance	The jury were bound to take and weigh the evidence that was admitted, and to their minds, it was clear, decisive and overwhelming, offered by persons of good character, and confirmed by a great number of confessions.
794	126		general repentance	If it had been within their province, as it is always declared not to be, to discuss the general principles, and sit in judgment on the particular penalties of law, it would not have altered the case, for at that time not only the common people but the wisest philosophers supported the interpretation of the law that acknowledged the existence of witchcraft, and its sanction that visited it with death.
795	126	191	declaration of regret	Notwithstanding all this, however, so tender and sensitive were the consciences of the jurors that they signed and circulated the following humble and solemn declaration of regret for the part they had borne in the trials.
796	126–27	191	declaration of regret	As the publication of this paper was highly honorable to those who signed it, and cannot but be contemplated with satisfaction by all their descendants, I will repeat their names.
797	127	191	declaration of regret	We whose names are underwritten, being in the year 1692 called to serve as jurors in court at Salem, on trial of many who were by some suspected guilty of doing acts of witchcraft upon the bodies of sundry persons;—
798	127	191	declaration of regret	We confess that we ourselves were not capable to understand, nor able to withstand, the mysterious delusions of the powers of darkness, and prince of the air; but were for want of knowledge in ourselves, and better information from others prevailed with to take up with such evidence against the accused, as, on further consideration and better information, we justly fear was insufficient for the touching the lives of any, (Deut. xvii. 6,) whereby we fear, we have been instrumental, with others, though ignorantly and unwittingly, to bring upon ourselves and this people of the Lord, the guilt of innocent blood; which sin, the Lord saith in scripture, he would not pardon, (2 Kings, xxiv 4,) that is, we suppose, in regard of his temporal judgments.
799	127–28	191	declaration of regret	We do, therefore, hereby signify to all in general, (and to the surviving sufferers in special) our deep sense of, and sorrow for, our errors, in acting on such evidence to the condemning of any person; and do hereby declare, that we justly fear that we were sadly deluded and mistaken; for which we are much disquieted and distressed in our minds; and do therefore humbly beg forgiveness, first of God, for Christ's sake, for this our error; and pray that God would not impute the guilt of it, to ourselves, nor others;
800	128	191	declaration of regret	and we also pray that we may be considered candidly, and aright by the living sufferers, as being then under the power of a strong and general delusion, utterly unacquainted with, and not experienced in matters of that nature.
801	128–29	191	declaration of regret	We do heartily ask forgiveness of you all, whom we have justly offended; and do declare, according to our present minds, we would none of us do such things again, on such grounds, for the whole world; praying you to accept of this, in way of satisfaction for our offence, and that you would bless the inheritance of the Lord, that he may be entreated for the land—
802	129	191	declaration of regret	Foreman Thomas Fisk, William Fisk, John Bachelor, Thos. Fisk, Jun. John Dane, Joseph Evelith, Thomas Pearly, Sen. John Peabody, Thomas Peikins, Samuel Sayer, Andrew Eliot, H. Hernck, Sen.
803	129		Sewall's prayer	The conduct of Judge Sewall claims our particular admiration.
804	129	192	Sewall's prayer	He observed annually in private a day of humiliation and prayer, during the remainder of his life, to keep fresh in his mind a sense of repentance and sorrow for the part he bore in the trials.

NO.	PAGE	LOIS	SUMMARY	SEGMENT
805	129	192	Sewall's prayer	On the day of the general fast, he rose in the place where he was accustomed to worship, the Old South in Boston, and in the presence of the great assembly, handed up to the pulpit a written confession, acknowledging the error into which he had been led, praying for the forgiveness of God and his people, and concluding with a request to all the congregation to unite with him in devout supplication, that it might not bring down the displeasure of the Most High, upon his country, his family, or himself.
806	129-30	192	Sewall's prayer	He remained standing during the public reading of the paper.
807	130		Judge Sewall forgiven	The following passage is found in his diary under the date of April 23d, 1720, nearly thirty years afterwards.
808	130		Judge Sewall forgiven	It was suggested by the perusal of Neal's History of New England.
809	130		Judge Sewall forgiven	'In Dr Neal's History of N. E. its nakedness is laid open in the businesses of the Quakers, Ana-baptists, Witchcraft.
810	130		Judge Sewall forgiven	The Judges names are mentioned p. 502, my confession p. 536, vol. 2.
811	130	192	Judge Sewall forgiven	The good and gracious God be pleased to save New England and me, and my family.'
812	130		Sewall's prayer	There never was a more striking and complete fulfilment of the apostolic assurance, that the prayer of a righteous man availeth much, than in this instance.
813	130		Judge Sewall forgiven	God has been pleased in a remarkable manner to save and bless New England.
814	130		Judge Sewall forgiven	The favor of heaven was bestowed upon Judge Sewall during the remainder of his life.
815	130-31		Judge Sewall forgiven	He presided for many years on the very bench where he committed the error so sincerely deplored by him, and was regarded by all as a benefactor, an ornament and a blessing to his generation;
816	131		Judge Sewall forgiven	while his family have enjoyed to a high degree the protection of Providence from that day to this, they have adorned every profession, and every department of society;
817	131		Judge Sewall forgiven	they have occupied the most elevated stations, have graced in successive generations the same lofty seat their ancestors occupied, have been the objects of the confidence, respect and love of their fellow citizens, and in this vicinity, their name is associated with all that is excellent in the memory of the past, and the observation of the present.
818	131		Upham's summary	Your thoughts, my friends, have been led in the course of this lecture, through scenes of the most distressing and revolting character.
819	131		praise of Judge Sewall	I leave before your imaginations one that is bright with all the beauty of Christian virtue.
820	131-32		praise of Judge Sewall	In the picture that exhibits Judge Sewall standing forth in the house of his God and in the presence of his fellow worshippers, making a public declaration of his sorrow and regret for the mistaken judgment he had co-operated with others in pronouncing, and praying that it might be forgiven—that it might not be followed by evil consequences to himself, his family or his country;
821	132		praise of Judge Sewall	in this picture you have a representation of a truly great and magnanimous spirit, a spirit to which the divine influence of our religion had given an expansion and a lustre, that Roman or Grecian virtue never knew; a spirit that had achieved a greater victory than warrior ever won, a victory over itself, a spirit so noble and so pure that it felt no shame in acknowledging an error, and no humiliation in atoning for an injury.

NO.	PAGE	LOIS	SUMMARY	SEGMENT
822	132		praise of Judge Sewall	If the contemplation of this bright example shall have imparted a glow of emulation to your hearts, your patience in listening, I am sure, will not go unrewarded.
822	62	7.5%	SEGMENT	The frequency of Gaskell's quotations from Upham's first lecture
132	39	29.5%	PAGE	

WORKS CITED

Abrams, M. H. *A Glossary of Literary Terms*. 7th ed., Harcourt Brace College, 1999.
"AntConc." *Laurence Anthony's Website*. Web. 9 March. 2013.
Audenaert, Neal. "Re: [Topic-models] A Bug? MALLET: Different Results under the Same Condition." E-mail to Tatsuhiro OHNO. 9 Jan. 2015.
Bacigalupo, Marie D. *The Short Fiction of Elizabeth Gaskell*. Diss. Fordham U, 1984, UMI, 1985. 8506315.
Baldick, Chris. *In Frankenstein's Shadow: Myth, Monstrosity, and Nineteenth-Century Writing*. Clarendon, 1987.
Barthes, Roland. "The Death of the Author." *Image Music Text*. Edited and translated by Stephen Heath, Fontana, 1977, pp. 142-48.
Basch, Françoise. *Relative Creatures: Victorian Women in Society and the Novel*. Schocken, 1974.
Bible. The King James Version. Scriptures, https://www.churchofjesuschrist.org/study/scriptures/.
Bick, Suzann. *Towards a Female Bildungsroman: The Protagonist in the Works of Elizabeth Gaskell*. 7904373, UMI, 1978.
Bie, Wendy A. "Dramatic Chronology in *Troilus and Criseyde*." *English Language Notes*, vol. 14, 1976, pp. 9-13.
Blei, David M. "Probabilistic Topic Models." *Communications of the Acm*, vol. 55, no. 4, 2012, pp. 77-84. PDF file. 3 Aug. 2013.
Bodenheimer, Rosemarie. *The Politics of Story in Victorian Social Fiction*. Cornell UP, 1988.
    This study of twelve Victorian condition-of-England novels, including *North and South* and *Ruth*, intends to investigate the pattern of narrative in which each novelist attempted to record "a period of unprecedented social change" (5). Bodenheimer reads *North and South* as a story of the female paternalist Margaret Hale's challenge to the paternalist society, and *Ruth* as a pastoral fiction of the eponymous heroine's assimilation into and segregation from nature. As far as Gaskell is concerned, the author's suggestion that a private plot is "a writer's most revealing account of a pubic problem" (7) is correct, because a romance plot and an industrial plot are closely linked in her social-problem novels.
---. "Private Grief and Public Acts in *Mary Barton*." *Dickens Society Annual*, vol. 9, 1981, pp. 195-216.
Reads the novel as "part of Gaskell's grieving process" (214) and as leading, "like Mary's journey," Gaskell "out of the domestic world and into a public one" (214).
Bonaparte, Felicia. *The Gypsy-Bachelor of Manchester: The Life of Mrs. Gaskell's Demon*. UP of Virginia, 1992.
    The ninth biography of Gaskell ever published after her death. The author's purpose is to trace Gaskell's inner self to attempt a metaphorical interpretation of her life and fiction, not to relate her fact-based life as in the conventional method. The author's remark, for example, that what inspired Gaskell to write the biography of Charlotte Brontë was that she saw a reflection of herself in her—and that, therefore, *The Life* is rather an autobiography than a biography—is unique, but convincing. Her analysis of the fiction is subjective. According to her reading of *Ruth*, for example, Leonard, Ruth's illegitimate son, is her lover (228).
Booth, Wayne C. *The Rhetoric of Fiction*. 2nd ed, U of Chicago P, 1983.
Booth, Wayne C., Gregory G. Colomb, and Joseph M. Williams. *The Craft of Research*. U of Chicago P, 1995.
Boyle, Nicholas. *Sacred and Secular Scriptures: A Catholic Approach to Literature*. Darton, Longman,

and Todd, 2004.

Briggs, Asa. *A Social History of England*. 2nd ed., Penguin, 1987.

Brodetsky, Tessa. *Elizabeth Gaskell*. Berg Women's Series, Berg, 1986.

After making a succinct summary of the plot, the author inserts her interpretation of *North and South* into her explanation of the storyline. Especially convincing is her assertion that the use of the same London drawing room highlights the contrast between the inexperienced Margaret and the matured Margaret (56).

Brown, Raymond E. *Responses to 101 Questions on the Bible*. Geoffrey Chapman, 1991.

Burrows, J. F. *Computation into Criticism: A Study of Jane Austen's Novels and an Experiment in Method*. Clarendon, 1987.

Cecil, David. *Early Victorian Novelists: Essays in Revaluation*. Constable, 1934.

Chadwick, Ellis H. *Mrs. Gaskell: Haunts, Homes, and Stories*. Sir Issac Pitman & Sons, 1913.

The first full-scale biography of Gaskell published after her death. The author recounts her life chronologically, dividing chapters according to the place where she lived. The authorial interpretations of Gaskell's works are inserted mainly when places relating to the story are referred to. Her approach is biographical, historical, and impressionistic. Full of photographs.

Chadwick, Esther Alice. Introduction. *North and South*, by Elizabeth Gaskell, Dent, 1914, pp. vii-xiv.

Chapple, J. A. V. "*North and South*: A Reassessment." *Essays in Criticism,* vol. 17, 1967, pp. 461-72.

The author reads the novel as a Bildungsroman rather than an industrial novel. Emphasis is placed on Margaret's inner progress at the seaside town Cromer.

Chapple, John, and Alan Shelston, editors. *Further Letters of Mrs Gaskell*. Manchester UP, 2000.

Chapple, J. A. V., and Anita Wilson, editors. *Private Voices: The Diaries of Elizabeth Gaskell and Sophia Holland*. Keele UP, 1996.

Chapple, J. A. V. and Arthur Pollard, editors. *The Letters of Mrs. Gaskell*. Manchester UP, l966.

Collection of Gaskell's surviving letters (many were destroyed in 1913 by one of her daughters according to her own wish), which show the novelist's power as a letter-writer and her wide range of correspondence with contemporary authors such as Charlotte Brontë, Elizabeth Browning, Charles Dickens, George Eliot, Charles Kingsley, W. M. Thackeray, and John Ruskin.

Clay, Charles Travis. "Notes on the Chronology of 'Wuthering Heights.'" *Brontë Society Publications: Transactions,* vol. 12, 1957, pp. 100-05.

Revision of C. P. Sanger's chronology and genealogical table.

Colby, Robin B. *"Some Appointed Work to Do": Women and Vocation in the Fiction of Elizabeth Gaskell*. Greenwood, 1995.

The title phrase of this book is taken from one of Gaskell's letters: "I do believe we have all some appointed work to do," where she acknowledges women's need for labour as well as their potential for it (12). The author reads Gaskell fiction as displaying the process of finding a woman's vocation as central to her life. For example, *North and South* is the story of asserting "women's right to participate in public life" (13). Margaret's recognition of her role as a mediator and the public and private meanings of some incidents are explained in the discussion of this novel.

Collin, Dorothy W. "The Composition of *North and South*." *Bulletin of the John Rylands University Library of Manchester*, vol. 54, 1971, pp. 67-93.

A detailed investigation into Dickens's editorship and Gaskell's response, and comparison between the *Household Words* text and the revised text of the book.

---, editor. *North and South*. By Elizabeth Gaskell, introduction by Martin Dodsworth, Penguin, 1970.

Colloms, Brenda. "'Tottie' Fox, Her Life and Background." *The Gaskell Society Journal*, vol. 5, 1991, pp. 16-26.

Cook, Chris and Brenda Keith. *British Historical Facts 1830-1900*. Macmillan, 1975.

Cooper, J. C. *An Illustrated Encyclopaedia of Traditional Symbols*. Thames and Hudson, 1979.

Craik, W. A. *Elizabeth Gaskell and the English Provincial Novel*. Methuen, 1975.

Detailed character analyses are carried out for *Ruth*.

Craik, Wendy. "Lore, Learning and Wisdom: Workers and Education in *Mary Barton* and *North and South*." *The Gaskell Society Journal*, vol. 2, 1988, pp. 13-33.

The author surveys the levels of education some main characters—chiefly workers—of both novels received, by whom themes and plots are propelled. She argues that the stress shift from workers to masters revealed in the two stories reflects the novelist's handling of characters' learning. For example, the evidence of working men's literacy becomes sparser in *North and South* than in *Mary Barton*, because the focus moves on to masters, and because the intellectual debate involves economic, social, even political concepts (30).

Crick, Brian. "The Implications of the Title Changes and Textual Revisions in Mrs Gaskell's *Mary Barton: A Tale of Manchester Life*." *Notes and Queries*, vol. 27, no. 6, 1980, pp. 514-19.

The author claims that *Mary Barton* should be read as a social-problem novel, stressing the centrality of John Barton. The change of the sub-title—from "A Manchester Love Story" to "A Tale of Manchester Life"—is the indication that "Mrs Gaskell did not see her book as a love story and she was unwilling to couple the heroine's name with that misleading label" (518).

Cunningham, Valentine. *Everywhere Spoken Against: Dissent in the Victorian Novel*. Clarendon Press, 1975.

Daley, A. Stuart. "The Moons and Almanacs of *Wuthering Heights*." *The Huntington Library Quarterly*, vol. 37, 1974, pp. 337-53.

Corrections of C. P. Sanger's chronology by referring to the moons and almanacs of 1826 and 1827.

---. "The Date of Heathcliff's Death: April, 1802." *Brontë Society Transactions*, vol. 17, 1976, pp. 15-19.

Based on his meticulous reading of the text and with the help of astronomical data, the author explains that the date of Heathcliff's death falls in April, 1802.

---. "A Revised Chronology of *Wuthering Heights*." *Brontë Society Transactions*, vol. 21, 1993, pp. 169-73.

Daly, Macdonald. Introduction. *Mary Barton: A Tale of Manchester Life*, by Elizabeth Gaskell, Penguin, 1996, pp. vii-xxx.

d'Albertis, Deirdre. *Dissembling Fictions: Elizabeth Gaskell and the Victorian Social Text*. St. Martin's Press, 1997.

The author reads Gaskell's fiction as both equivocal and dissembling. "Dissembling," remarks she, "is a technique for organizing equivocal attitudes or beliefs in Gaskell's fictional system" (3). She also sees her writing as experiments in genre: "The richness of Gaskell's work springs from the sophistication of her large-scale experiments in form, from her willingness to risk the failure of such hybrids, and from the enigmatic consciousness that informed those experiments" (16). In analysing *Ruth*, she examines "various modes, literary and non-literary production of a new genre, the penitential narrative, as foundational in the development of a feminist sexual politics from the 1860s on" (73-74).

---. "'Bookmaking Out of the Remains of the Dead': Elizabeth Gaskell's *The Life of Charlotte Brontë*." *Victorian Studies*, vol. 39, 1995, pp. 1-31.

David, Deirdre. *Fictions of Resolution in Three Victorian Novels: North and South, Our Mutual Friend, and Daniel Deronda*. Columbia UP, 1981.

In discussing the three Victorian novels, the author focuses on how each writer depicts political, social, and sexual conflicts, and resolves them in his/her fiction. In the examination of *North and South*, for example, David, inserting character analysis into her argument, clarifies the process of solution of the conflicts among the Hales, the Thorntons, and the Higginses as well as of sexual tension between Margaret Hale and John Thornton. Her concern is primarily on content rather than form, since, for her, the novels are "social products performing a social function" (xii).

Davidson, Elizabeth Livingston. "Toward an Integrated Chronology for *Tristram Shandy*." *English Language Notes*, vol. 29, 1992, pp. 48-56.

De Man, Paul. *Blindness and Insight: Essays in the Rhetoric of Contemporary Criticism*. 2nd ed. Minneapolis: U of Minnesota P, 1983.

Dodsworth, Martin. Introduction. *North and South*. By Elizabeth Gaskell, edited by Dorothy Collin, Penguin, 1970, pp. 7-26.

Against two orthodox readings of Gaskell—Lord David Cecil's "feminine" novelist and Raymond William's and John Lucas's "industrial" novelist, the author stresses her unconventional power of imagination and creativity. He asserts Margaret Hale is similar to Jane Eyre and Lucy Snowe in her "spiritual isolation," "integrity," and "toughness," and regards this book as her Bildungsroman.

Duthie, Enid L. *The Themes of Elizabeth Gaskell*. London: Macmillan, 1980.

The author analyses Gaskell's complete works from various perspectives, including nature, family, religion, and literary form. Rather than dedicating separate chapters to individual novels, this book offers a more integrated analysis. One of the author's most compelling arguments is that an important role is almost always given to a servant in Gaskell's works—for example, Dixon in *North and South*, Betty in *Cousin Phillis*, and Kester in *Sylvia's Lovers*.

Eagleton, Terry. "*Sylvia's Lovers* and Legality." *Essays in Criticism*, vol. 26, 1976, pp. 17-29.

---. *Literary Theory: An Introduction*. 2nd ed., Blackwell, 1996.

Easson, Angus. *Elizabeth Gaskell*. RKP, 1979.

---. "Explanatory Notes." *Wives and Daughters*, Oxford UP, pp. 689-90.

---, editor. *Elizabeth Gaskell: The Critical Heritage*. Routledge, 1991.

---. Introduction. *The Life of Charlotte Brontë*, by Elizabeth Gaskell. The World's Classics. Oxford: Oxford UP, 1996.

Ehrenpreis, Anne Henry. "Elizabeth Gaskell and Nathaniel Hawthorne." *The Nathaniel Hawthorne Journal*, 1973, pp. 89-119.

Eifrig, Gail Mcgrew. *Growing out of Motherhood: The Changing Role of the Narrator in the Works of Elizabeth Gaskell*. Diss. Bryn Mawr College, 1982, UMI, 1983.

Eliot, T. S. "A Dialogue on Dramatic Poetry." *Selected Essays*, 3rd ed, Faber, 1976, pp. 31-44.

Engels, Friedrich. *The Condition of the Working Class in England*. Penguin, 1987.

Eve, Jeanette. "A Misdated Gaskell Letter and the Background Story to *Ruth*." *Notes and Queries*, vol. 34, 1987, pp. 36-39.

Ewbank, Inga-Stina. "The Chronology of *Wuthering Heights*." *Wuthering Heights*. Edited by Emily Brontë, Clarendon, 1976, pp. 487-96.

After synthesizing chronologies by C. P. Sanger and A. S. Daley as well as offering her own minor corrections, the author presents the most reliable chronology of the novel.

Ffrench, Yvonne. *Mrs. Gaskell*. London: Home & Van Thal, 1949.

The sixth biography of Gaskell published after her death. The book takes an orthodox method of relating her life in chronological order, including the author's interpretations of Gaskell's works wherever appropriate.

Flint, Kate. *Elizabeth Gaskell*. Writers and Their Work, Northcote House, 1995.

A succinct survey of Gaskell's life, her major works, and her recent criticism. Especially insightful is the author's summary of critical works on Gaskell published in the 1950s and after. According to the author, it is Katherine Tillotson (*Novels of the Eighteen-Forties* (1954)) as well as the two Marxists Arnold Kettle ("The Early Victorian Social-Problem Novel" (1958)) and Raymond Williams (*Culture and Society* (1958)) that have been most influential in changing Gaskell's presumed status as a gentle feminine writer to an industrial novelist. While Joseph Kestner places her within a tradition of female writers dealing with public themes in *Protest and Reform* (1985), C. Gallagher (*The Industrial Reformation of English Fiction* (1985)) and Rosemarie Bodenheimer (*The Politics of Story in Victorian Social Fiction* (1988)) do not only continue to regard her as a social-problem writer but also stress the power Gaskell has assigned to her female characters. The greatest impetus in recent decades to reassessing Gaskell's fiction has been provided by feminist criticism, which attempts to examine language, narrative strategies, and patterns of rhetoric employed by novelists to authorize women's voice in their works. Most momentous among feminist studies is Patsy Stoneman's *Elizabeth Gaskell* (1987); she aims at finding woman's authentic voice in the novelist's work, and searching it out in woman's capacity for bonding with other women, rather than in her differentiation from a paternal character. Concern for narrative technique has also been increasing; the most elucidatory one among such studies is Robyn Warhol's *Gendered Interventions: Narrative Discourse in the Victorian Novel* (1989), which argues narrative intervention in Gaskell's early works and its disappearance in her later ones. What is impressive about Hilary Schor's *Scheherezade in the Marketplace* (1992) is "its willingness to [. . .] adopt the methodologies of other disciplines, in particular cultural anthropology and historiography" (65). Flint's comment of this being "the direction some of the most interesting criticism of Victorian literature is now taking" (65) reminds us of Megan Perigoe Stitt's use of philology and science as a framework for her discussion in *Metaphors of Change in the Language of Nineteenth-Century Fiction* (1998). After having briefly referred to Felicia Bonaparte's unique study of Gaskell's inner self (*The Gypsy-Bachelor of Manchester* (1992)) and Jenny Uglow's far-reaching biography of Elizabeth Gaskell (1993), Flint predicts that the directions Gaskell criticism may take in the future will be the construction of selfhood, the question of gender, and the connections between Gaskell and aesthetics.

Fraser, Rebecca. *The Brontës: Charlotte Brontë and Her Family*. Crown, 1988.

Fryckstedt, Monica Correa. *Elizabeth Gaskell's* Mary Barton *and* Ruth: *A Challenge to Christian England*. Almqvist & Wiksell International, 1982.

Detailed examinations of *Ruth*'s social background—prostitution and dressmakers in the Victorian England—and of its predecessors are attempted.

Gadamer, Hans-Georg. *Truth and Method*. 2nd ed. Trans. Joel Weinsheimer and G. Marshall. London: Continuum, 2006.

Gallagher, Catherine. *The Industrial Reformation of English Fiction: Social Discourse and Narrative Form 1832-1867*. U of Chicago P, 1985.

Through the analysis of its literary form, the author attempts to demonstrate the basic changes the English fiction underwent when it became the discourse over industrialism. According to her, the framework of the traditional realist fiction can no longer be applied to that of the industrial novel. Her analysis is deconstructive: she shows one solution and its contradiction as well. Focusing on the narratives of six condition-of-England novels, including *Mary Barton* and *North and South*, the author tries to show the variety of narrative forms each novelist employs to demonstrate his/her interpretation of social reality. For example, she explains the narrative of *North and South* by using the metaphor of Margaret Hale's "private" and "public" relations to people around her: the heroine tries "to advocate that the relations between classes become like the cooperative associations of family life" (148). Superb is her explanation about the hidden meanings of the two episodes: Margaret's public protection and her private lie for saving Frederick (172-77). Gallagher's achievement is that she examined social-problem novels as independent art, not as social or political affiliations as they have often been regarded (Bodenheimer 7).

Gallagher, Susan VanZanten, and M. D. Walhout, editors. *Literature and the Renewal of the Public Sphere*. Macmillan, 2000.

Ganz, Margaret. *Elizabeth Gaskell: The Artist in Conflict*. Twayne, 1969.

Points out *North and South* can be divided into two parts. In the first half, focus is placed on the industrial conflict, while in the latter it shifts onto the progress of romance.

Gaskell, Elizabeth. *Cousin Phillis and Other Tales*. Edited by Angus Easson, World's Classics, Oxford UP, 1981.

---. *Cranford*. Introduction by Frank Swinnerton. Everyman's Library. Dent, 1973.

---. *The Life of Charlotte Brontë*. Edited by Angus Easson. Oxford UP, 2001.

---. "Lois the Witch." *Cousin Phillis and Other Tales*, Oxford UP, 1981, pp. 105-93.

---. *Mary Barton: A Tale of Manchester Life*. Edited by Edgar Wright, introduction by Jenny Uglow, Everyman's Library, Random House, 1994.

---. *Mary Barton: A Tale of Manchester Life*. Edited by Edgar Wright, World's Classics, Oxford UP, 1998.

---. *North and South*. Ed. Angus Easson. Oxford: Oxford UP, 1982.

---. "Preface." *Mary Barton: A Tale of Manchester Life*, edited by Edgar Wright, Oxford UP, 1998, pp. xxxv-xxxvi.

---. *Ruth*. Ed. Alan Shelston. World's Classics. Oxford: Oxford UP, 1998.

---. *Sylvia's Lovers*. Edited by Andrew Sanders, World's Classics, Oxford UP, 1999.

---. *Wives and Daughters*. Edited by Angus Easson, World's Classics, Oxford UP, 2000.

Gerard, Bonnie. "Victorian Things, Victorian Words: Representation and Redemption in Gaskell's *North and South*." *The Victorian Newsletter*, vol. 92, 1997, pp. 21-24.

The author views the tension between John Thornton and Margaret Hale as the conflict between materialism and idealism, and, accordingly, the novel's resolution as a "compromise, in which Margaret's idealism is brought to bear on Thornton's materialism in the form of a powerful socioethical project" (22). A Neoplatonic reading.

Gérin, Winifred. *Charlotte Brontë: The Evolution of Genius*. Oxford UP, 1977.

---. *Elizabeth Gaskell: A Biography*. Oxford UP, 1977.

This is the eighth biography of Gaskell published after her death, and the first to use the Chapple and Pollard edition of her *Letters* (1966). The author describes Gaskell's life in chronological order, inserting her interpretations of the novelist's individual works in chapters corresponding to each stage of her life. The author's aim is to throw Gaskell's portrait into relief as objectively as possible; therefore, she reveals even her demerits. It is emphasized in this book that Manchester and Knutsford play significant roles in Gaskell's life, and that Gaskell was first and foremost a mother and wife, not a novelist. Gérin regards *Wives and Daughters* as Gaskell's masterpiece, since various characters are vividly depicted.

Gill, Stephen. Introduction. *Mary Barton: A Tale of Manchester Life*, by Elizabeth Gaskell, Penguin, 1976, pp. 9-28.

Goodridge, J. F. *Emily Brontë:* Wuthering Heights. London: Arnold, 1964.

A concise but comprehensive analysis of the novel. Especially interesting are his research into its time-structure (47-50) and topography (60-64).

Graham, Shawn, Scott Weingart, and Ian Milligan. "Getting Started with Topic Modeling and Mallet." *The Programming Historian 2.* Web. 19 July 2013.

Guy, Josephine M. *The Victorian Social-Problem Novel: The Market, the Individual and Communal Life*. New York: St. Martin's, 1996.

According to the author, the romance and political plots in *North and South* involve a paradox. While the former argues that the private ethics should inform the public of commerce, the latter shows the market is impervious to such moralising (172).

Haldane, Elizabeth. *Mrs. Gaskell and Her Friends*. London: Hodder and Stoughton, 1930.

The fourth biography of Gaskell published after her death. Her friendship with Florence Nightingale and Charlotte Brontë is narrated in detail.

Handley, Graham. "The Chronology of *Sylvia's Lovers*." *Notes and Queries*, vol. 12, 1965, pp. 302-03.

The author quotes historical data to point out errors in the novel's straight chronology.

---. *An Elizabeth Gaskell Chronology*. Palgrave Macmillan, 2005.

Harman, Barbara Leah. *The Feminine Political Novel in Victorian England*. UP of Virginia, 1998.

The author attempts "to identify the occasions, describe the condition, and chart the complications of women's emergence onto the public stage" (8) through what she calls "the feminine political novels" including *North and South*. By arguing that they all have "the struggle to provide a means for female public appearance" (178) as their central theme, she implies the existence of such a sub-genre in the tradition of English fiction. In discussing *North and South*, she reads Gaskell's positive view in the heroine's public protection of the mill-owner and her loss of moral purity.

Harsh, Constance D. *Subversive Heroines: Feminist Resolutions of Social Crisis in the Condition-of-England Novel*. Ann Arbor: U of Michigan P, 1994.

Henry, Nancy. Introduction. *Ruth*, by Elizabeth Gaskell, Dent, 2001, pp. xxiii-xxxvii.

The author focuses on the concurrent occurrence of "the typhus epidemic" and "the national triumph of army" to create her own chronology. By proving that this war refers to the Opium War, she points out that Gaskell uses the imagery of an opium-induced delusion to emphasise Ruth's unconsciousness of her actions, and thus defends her heroine.

Hirsch, E. D., Jr. *Validity in Interpretation*. Yale UP, 1967.

---. *The Aim of Interpretation*. Chicago: U of Chicago P, 1976.

Holmes, David I. "Vocabulary Richness and the Book of Mormon: A Stylometric Analysis of Mormon Scripture." Ross and Brink, pp. 18-31.

---. "Using Math to Decode History." *The College of New Jersey School of Science*, 1 Sept 2011. Web. 2 Jan. 2015.

Hopkins, Annette B. *Elizabeth Gaskell: Her Life and Work*. John Lehmann, 1952.

The seventh biography of Gaskell published after her death, and the second comprehensive one after E. H. Chadwick's. The aim of this book is to throw light upon the novelist's various sides of character by letting herself, her family, or her friends narrate what she is. She makes full use of the information obtained from many primary sources never used before by the previous biographers.

Ingham, Patricia. Introduction. *North and South*, by Elizabeth Gaskell, Penguin, 1995, pp. vii-xxiii.

Irwin, William. *Intentionalist Interpretation: A Philosophical Explanation and Defense*. Greenwood, 1999.

---, ed. *The Death and Resurrection of the Author?* Westport: Greenwood, 2002.

Iser, Wolfgang. *The Act of Reading: A Theory of Aesthetic Response*. Johns Hopkins UP, 1978.

---. *The Implied Reader: Patterns of Communication in Prose Fiction from Bunyan to Beckett*. Johns Hopkins UP, 1974.

Jenkins, Ruth Y. *Reclaiming Myths of Power: Women Writers and the Victorian Spiritual Crisis*. Associated UP, 1995.

The author argues that *Ruth* is the story of the victory of New Testament's value over the Old Testament's, and that Ruth's main plot is connected with Richard Bradshaw's subplot through Leonard.

Juhl, P. D. "The Appeal to the Text: What Are We Appealing to?". *Journal of Aesthetics and Art Criticism*, vol. 36, no. 3, 1978, pp. 277-87.

---. *Interpretation: An Essay in the Philosophy of Literary Criticism*. Princeton UP, 1986.

"Kaspar Hauser." *Wikipedia: The Free Encyclopedia*, 23 February 2006, http://en.wikipedia.org/wiki/Kaspar_Hauser.

Katayama, Haruo. "The Literature of Ayako Miura and Her Christianity." *Studium Christianitatis*, vol. 37, 2002, pp. 31-40.

Kenny, Anthony. *A Stylometric Study of the New Testament*. Clarendon, 1986.

Kestner, Joseph. *Protest & Reform: The British Social Narrative by Women 1827-1867*. London: Methuen, 1985.

In his analysis of *North and South*, the author pays attention to Gaskell's use of symbolism. For example, he explains that Margaret's process of recognition of the north is registered by the rose image and why Thornton defences Oliver Cromwell.

Kitchen, Martin. *Kaspar Hauser: Europe's Child*. Palgrave, 2001.

Kobler, J. F. "Confused Chronology in *The Sun Also Rises*." *Modern Fiction Studies*, vol. 13, 1967-68, pp. 517-21.

The author concludes Hemingway's errors in the novel's chronology are "not purposeful, but accidental" (520).

Koga, Hideo. *Chachisuto Undo* (Chartist Movement). Kyoikusha, 1986.

Kroeber, Karl. *Styles in Fictional Structure: The Art of Jane Austen, Charlotte Brontë, George Eliot*. Princeton UP, 1971.

Statistics is used to attempt an objective analysis of the underlying structures of fiction.

---. "Chapter 13: Computers and Research in Literary Analysis." *Computers in Humanistic Research: Readings and Perspectives*. Prentice Hall, 1986, pp. 135-42.

Kucich, John. *The Power of Lies: Transgression in Victorian Fiction*. Cornel UP, 1994.

Kuhlman, Mary H. "Education through Experience in *North and South*." *The Gaskell Society Journal*, vol. 10, 1996, pp. 14-26.

The paper explores the learning Margaret experiences through dramatic events (such as marriage proposals, the strike, and deaths), dialogues with John Thornton and the Higgins, and movement from place to place. The author emphasizes the educational influence railway travels exercise over the heroine, and thus regards the novel as a Bildungsroman fused with industrial elements.

Lane, Margaret. Introduction. *Ruth*, by Elizabeth Gaskell. Dent, 1967, pp. v-xi.

---. Introduction. *Mary Barton: A Tale of Manchester Life*, by Elizabeth Gaskell, Dent, 1977, pp. v-x.

Lansbury, Coral. *Elizabeth Gaskell: The Novel of Social Crisis*. London: Paul Elek, 1975.

Insightful readings of Gaskell's major works chiefly from the feminist perspective. In her analysis of *Ruth*, the author inserts her readings in accordance with the plot flow.

---. *Elizabeth Gaskell*. Twayne English Authors Series 371, Twayne, 1984.

In *North and South*, the author examines some of its chief problems, including romance and social plots. According to her feminist reading, Richard and Frederick Hale lack the masculine responsibility for their household.

Le Beau, Brian F. Foreword. Upham, *Salem Witchcraft*, pp. vii-xxix.

Lenard, Mary. *Preaching Pity: Dickens, Gaskell, and Sentimentalism in Victorian Culture*. Studies in Nineteenth-Century British Literature 11, Peter Lang, 1999.

Lerner, Laurence. Introduction. *Wives and Daughters*, by Elizabeth Gaskell, edited by Frank Glover Smith, Penguin, 1969, pp. 7-27.

Concise explanations about Gaskell's major works included.

Levin, David. *Cotton Mather: The Young Life of the Lord's Remembrancer, 1663-1703*. Harvard UP, 1978.

Lodge, David, ed. *Modern Criticism and Theory: A Reader*. Longman, 1988.

Logan, Deborah A. *Fallenness in Victorian Women's Writing: Marry, Stitch, Die, or Do Worse*. Columbia: U of Missouri P, 1998.

The author's comments on the long discussed topics about *Ruth*—why she refuses Bellingham's proposal and why she dies—are worthy of notice.

Lucas, John. *The Literature of Change*. Harvester Press, 1980.

Macherey, Pierre. *A Theory of Literary Production*. Translated by Geoffrey Wall, Special Indian Edition, Routledge, 2006.

Mahlberg, Michaela. "Digital Forum: Corpus Linguistics and the Study of Nineteenth-Century Fiction." *Journal of Victorian Culture*, vol. 15, no. 2, 2010, pp. 292-98.

---. *Corpus Stylistics and Dickens's Fiction*. London: Routledge, 2013.

Matus, Jill L. *Unstable Bodies: Victorian Representations of Sexuality and Maternity*. Manchester UP, 1995.

In discussing *Ruth*, the author views the central concern of the novel is the reactions of people around Ruth to her secrecy, and focuses on the meaning of secrecy and the raison d'être of Jemima.

McVeagh, John. *Elizabeth Gaskell*. Profiles in Literature. London: Routledge, 1970.

---. "Notes on Mrs Gaskell's Narrative Technique." *Essays in Criticism*, vol. 18, 1968, pp. 461-70.

The author claims that Gaskell's works are basically structureless and become best when the static narrative technique is taken. Accordingly, he regards *Cranford*, *Cousin Phillis* and *Wives and Daughters* better than other major novels; structurally *Cousin Phillis* is best.

Meckier, Jerome. "Dating the Action in *Great Expectations*: A New Chronology." *Dickens Studies Annual*, vol. 21, 1992, pp. 157-94.

Mews, Hazel. *Frail Vessels: Woman's Role in Woman's Novels from Fanny Burney to George Eliot*. Athlone, 1969.

Michie, Elsie B. *Outside the Pale: Cultural Exclusion, Gender Difference, and the Victorian Woman*

Writer. Cornell UP, 1993.

    The author interprets the two most significant scenes in *North and South*—Margaret's public protection of Thornton and her shielding her brother at the station—in terms of public woman and impropriety. She compares the Bradshaws (*Ruth*) and the Gradgrinds (*Hard Times*), seeing the master-man relation in the father-children relation.

Mitchell, Sally. *The Fallen Angel: Chastity, Class and Women's Reading, 1835-1880*. Bowling Green U Popular Press, 1981.

Miura, Ayako. "We Want to Meet That Person: Ayako Miura." *NHK Archives*, https://www2.nhk.or.jp/archives/articles/?id=D0009250093_00000.

Moore, Gene M. "Of Time and Its Mathematical Progression: Problems of Chronology in Faulkner's 'A Rose for Emily.'" *Studies in Short Fiction*, vol. 29, 1992, pp. 195-204.

Moretti, Franco. *Graphs, Maps, Trees: Abstract Models for a Literary History*. Verso, 2005.

Morgan, Susan. "Gaskell's Heroines and the Power of Time." *Pacific Coast Philology*, vol. 18, nos. 1-2, 1983, pp. 43-51.

    Discussions on *Cranford* and *Ruth*. The author examines the latter in relation to other "fallen women" novels, stressing the redemptive power of time.

Morse, Deborah Denenholz. "Stitching Repentance, Sewing Rebellion: Seamstresses and Fallen Women in Elizabeth Gaskell's Fiction." Edited by Vanessa D. Dickerson. *Keeping the Victorian House: A Collection of Essays*, Garland Publishing, 1995, pp. 27-73.

    The author treats Gaskell's four stories in which seamstresses are focused: "The Three Eras of Libbie Marsh," "Lizzie Leigh," *Mary Barton*, and *Ruth*. She considers Jemima as Ruth's alter-ego.

Murase, Tomoko. "Jane Austen's Authorial Intention in *Persuasion*." *Kumamoto Studies in English Language and Literature*, no. 50, 2007, pp. 105-27.

Myers, Ben. "Shusaku Endo: Christ and Japan." *Faith and Theology*. 14 March 2011. Web. 23 Nov. 2016.

Nehamas, Alexander. "What an Author Is." *The Journal of Philosophy*, no. 83, 1986, pp. 685-91.

Newton, Judith Lowder. *Women, Power, and Subversion: Social Strategies in British Fiction 1778-1860*. New York and London: Methuen, 1981.

    Feminist reading of *Evelina*, *Pride and Prejudice*, *Villette*, and *The Mill on the Floss*. Includes a brief analysis of *North and South*.

Nord, Deborah Epstein. *Walking the Victorian Streets: Women, Representation, and the City*. Cornell UP, 1995.

    "The subject of this book," declares the author, is "the role of the woman on the street in the creation of a literature of rambling and urban investigation" (15). Based on the assumption that the female spectator cannot but become the object of public exposure and of sexuality, Nord regards *Mary Barton*, *Ruth*, and *North and South* as stories of heroines' struggle to "assume authority in a sphere of masculine concerns" and of their "anxiety about the public exposure that attends such authority" (13, 145). She views "women's need to bear witness" and "the public disgrace that inevitably follows" (178) as the common theme of these three novels.

Ohno, Tatsuhiro. "'Waves' in *Sylvia's Lovers*." *Kyushu Studies in English Literature*, vol. 8, 1991, pp. 17-45.

---, translator. *Siruvia no koibitotachi* [Sylvia's Lovers]. Sairyusha, 1997.

    The first Japanese translation of the novel with Gaskell's detailed chronology and the translator's commentary included.

---. "*Mary Barton*'s Chronology." *Gaskell Studies*, vol. 9, 1999, pp. 37-48.

Creates an accurate chronology of *Mary Barton* based on time data scattered over the pages, and proves that the story opens in May 1834 and ends in late autumn of 1842 or 43.

---. "Is *Mary Barton* an Industrial Novel?". *The Gaskell Society Journal*, vol. 15, 2001, pp. 14-20.

---. "Textual Criticism of Elizabeth Gaskell's Thirty-Six Works." *Kumamoto Studies in English Language and Literature*, vol. 46, 2003, pp. 19-46.

---. "The Structure of *Ruth*: Is the Heroine's Martyrdom Inconsistent with the Plot?". *The Gaskell Society Journal*, vol.18, 2004, pp. 16-36.

---. "The Chronology of *North and South*." *Kumamoto Journal of Culture and Humanities*, vol. 87, 2005, pp. 21-31.

---. "Chronologies and Statistics: Objective Understanding of Authorial Meaning." *English Studies*, vol. 87, no. 3, 2006, pp. 327-56.

---. "Dramatic Irony in *Ruth*." *The Gaskell Society Journal*, vol. 21, 2007, pp. 86-90.

---. "Statistical Investigation into the Authorial Meaning in 'Lois the Witch.'" *Kumamoto Studies in English Language and Literature*, vol. 50, 2007, pp. 155-73.

---. "Statistical Analysis of the Structure of *North and South*: In the Quest for the Standard Interpretation." *The Gaskell Society Journal*, vol. 22, 2008, pp. 116-44.

---. "A Topic-Modelling Analysis of Christianity in *The Life of Charlotte Brontë*." *Kumamoto University Studies in Social and Cultural Sciences,* vol. 17, 2019, pp. 77-108.

"Our Eternal Life." Topics. *The Church of Jesus Christ Latter-Day Saints*. Web. 30 Dec. 2014. https://www.lds.org.

Parker, Pamela Corpron. "Constructing Female Public Identity: Gaskell on Brontë." Gallagher, S. V., pp. 68-82.

---. "From 'Ladies' Business' to 'Real Business': Elizabeth Gaskell's Capitalist Fantasy in *North and South*." *The Victorian Newsletter*, vol. 91, 1997, pp. 1-3.

In Margaret's offer of financial help to Thornton in the final scene, the author sees an example of "the private language of romantic courtship" being replaced by "the public discourse of 'Political Economy'" (1), as well as that of the interaction of the marriage plot and the industrial plot. "*North and South* advocates an integration of domestic and industrial economies, male and female spheres of influence, and public and private life" (1)—is the purport of her assertion.

Parkins, Wendy. "Women, Mobility and Modernity in Elizabeth Gaskell's *North and South*." *Women's Studies International Forum*, vol. 27, 2004, pp. 507-19.

The author addresses "some of the different aspects and accounts of modernity offered in *North and South*, giving special attention to the novel's treatment of nostalgia and travel, in order to show that it is not just an industrial novel, it is a narrative of modernity which places a bourgeois woman at the centre of modernity" (508).

Peck, John, and Martin Coyle. *Literary Terms and Criticism*. Macmillan, 1993.

"Perpetual Calendar." 14 March 2003, http://utopia.knoware.nl/users/eprebel/Calendar/Perpetual/.

Peterson, Linda H. "Elizabeth Gaskell's *The Life of Charlotte Brontë*." Matus, *Cambridge Companion*, pp. 59-74.

Pike, E. Holly. *Family and Society in the Works of Elizabeth Gaskell*. New York: Peter Lang, 1955.

The author reads Gaskell fiction as a study of "the role of the family within society" (1). Pointing out the change in her treatment of the family during her career as a novelist, she argues "Gaskell moves from using realist fiction as a vehicle for social reform to using it as a means to social and historical understanding" (1). Detailed analyses of Margaret's love for Thornton and vice versa are incorporated in her discussion of *North and South* to show each "has learned to appreciate the good points of the value system held by the other, and has discovered that they are not incompatible" (98).

Pollard, Arthur. *Mrs Gaskell: Novelist and Biographer*. Harvard UP, 1967.

Power, S. A. "The Chronology of 'Wuthering Heights.'" *Brontë Society Transactions,* vol. 16, no. 2, 1972, pp. 139-43.

Comparing Sanger's chronology and Clay's and pointing out their mistakes, the author gives his/her own dating to some controversial events. The article reveals Emily Brontë's miscalculations.

Pykett, Lyn. "Emily Brontë." Thormählen, ed. pp. 68-74.

Recchio, Thomas Edward. "The Problem of Form in Mrs. Gaskell's *Mary Barton*: A Study of Mythic Patterning in Realistic Fiction." *Studies in English Literature: English Number*, 1985, pp. 19-35.

Reddy, Maureen Teresa. *Elizabeth Gaskell's Short Fiction*. Diss. U of Minnesota, 1985, UMI, 1985. 8519340.

Richardson, Brian. "'Hours Dreadful and Things Strange': Inversions of Chronology and Causality in *Macbeth*." *Philological Quarterly*, vol. 68, 1989, pp. 283-94.

Ross, Don, and Dan Brink, eds. *Research in Humanities Computing 3: Selected Papers from the ALLC/ACH Conference, Tempe, Arizona, March 1991*. Clarendon, 1994.

Rubenius, Aina. *The Woman Question in Mrs. Gaskell's Life and Works*. Uppsala: A.-B. Lundequistska Bokhandeln, 1950.

In the analysis of *North and South*, the author attempts to identify the models of Margaret Hale, her father, and her brother, and to suggest the resemblance in plot between Henry Fothergill Chorley's *Pomfret* (1845) and *North and South*. Investigation into the social background is helpful in understanding *Ruth*.

Sanders, Andrew. "Appendix B: A Revised Chronology for *Sylvia's Lovers*." *Sylvia's Lovers*, by Elizabeth Gaskell, Oxford UP, 1999, pp. 508-09.

---. "A Crisis of Liberalism in *North and South*." *The Gaskell Society Journal*, vol. 10, 1996, pp. 42-52.

The author sees Gaskell's liberalism in Richard Hale's disposal of Anglicanism and Frederick Hale's mutiny against authoritative injustice. He also regards Margaret Hale as the icon of Gaskell's liberalism, because the upper-middle-class heroine finally comes to live in industrial Milton as the wife of a reforming manufacturer. He supports his assertion by using letters as well as historical records.

Sanders, Gerald Dewitt. *Elizabeth Gaskell*. 1929, Russell & Russell, 1971.

Sanders, Valerie. "Harriet Martineau and Elizabeth Gaskell." *The Gaskell Society Journal*, vol. 16, 2002, pp. 64-75.

Sanger, Charles Percy. "The Structure of *Wuthering Heights*." 1926. Rpt. in *Wuthering Heights*, by Emily Brontë, Norton Critical Edition, 2nd ed., Norton, 1972, pp. 286-98.

Discovers the symmetrical pedigrees of the family trees in *Wuthering Heights* by his close investigation of dating in the novel. The "classic demonstration of the careful time schemes of the novel" (Daley 337).

Saracino, Marilena. "Elizabeth Gaskell's *Lois the Witch*: Witchcraft and its Fictional Representation." Marroni and Shelston, pp. 199-221.

Schor, Hilary M. *Scheherezade in the Marketplace: Elizabeth Gaskell and the Victorian Novel*. Oxford UP, 1992.

The author makes an ambitious attempt to prove the significance of Gaskell in the history of the English novel by reassessing her through the investigation of her whole career. Her focus is primarily on the writer's struggle with literary conventions, female authorship in relation to the literary marketplace, fictional forms including narrative coherency, and the heroines in Gaskell's works. Schor's approach can be defined as "cultural feminism" [my term], for she aims at understanding the female plot in connection with cultural or social phenomena, which has been neglected in previous feminist criticism. For example, she explains the heroine Margaret Hale's growth in terms of her acquisition of Milton workers' language to demonstrate the complexity of *North and South*. "To be a heroine in Milton-Northern," observes the author, "is to learn a new sign system—and, by extension, then to be a different kind of heroine." Quoting Pierre Macherey's support for subjective interpretation, the author interprets Ruth's story in relation to its social context.

Sharps, John Geoffrey. *Mrs. Gaskell's Observation and Invention: A Study of Her Non-Biographic Works*. Linden, 1970.

Comprehensive and detailed analysis of Gaskell's complete fiction, including short stories. A brief comment on the origin of *The Life of Charlotte Brontë* is included in one of the Appendices. Based on comprehensive information on primary sources, his approach is principally historical and biographical; and sometimes impressionistic.

Shattock, Joanne, et al., editors. *The Works of Elizabeth Gaskell*. Vols. 1, 2, 3, 5, 7. Pickering & Chatto, 2005.

Shelston, Alan. Introduction. *The Life of Charlotte Brontë*, by Elizabeth Gaskell, Penguin, 1975, pp. 9-37.

---. Introduction. *Ruth*. The World's Classics. Oxford: Oxford UP, 1981. viii-xx.

The author argues that Gaskell makes her heroine almost faultless because of her over-consciousness of public hostility against her theme.

---. Introduction. *Mary Barton: A Tale of Manchester Life*, by Elizabeth Gaskell, Dent, 1996, pp. xix-xxviii.

Simons, N., editor. *The Statutes of the United Kingdom of Great Britain and Ireland*. Vol. 12, Eyre and Spottiswoode, 1832.

---, ed. *The Statutes of the United Kingdom of Great Britain and Ireland*. Vol. 17, Eyre and Spottiswoode, 1845.

---, ed. *The Statutes of the United Kingdom of Great Britain and Ireland*. Vol. 18, Eyre and Spottiswoode, 1847.

Skrine, Celia. "*Six Weeks in Heppenheim* as Seen from Heppenheim." *The Gaskell Society Journal*, vol. 12, 1998, pp. 55-58.

Smith, Margaret, editor. *The Letters of Charlotte Brontë: with a Selection of Letters by Family and Friends*: 1829-47. Vol. 1, Clarendon, 1995.

---, ed. *The Letters of Charlotte Brontë: with a Selection of Letters by Family and Friends*: 1848-51. Vol. 2, Clarendon, 2000.

---, ed. *The Letters of Charlotte Brontë: with a Selection of Letters by Family and Friends*: 1852-55. Vol. 3, Clarendon, 2004.

Smith, Walter E. *Elizabeth Gaskell: A Bibliographical Catalogue of First and Early Editions 1848-1866*. Heritage Book Shop, 1998.

Spear, Hilda D. and Huang Xiaoming. "The Chronology of *Maurice*." *Notes and Queries*, vol. 42, no. 2, 1995, pp. 217-18.

Spencer, Jane. *Elizabeth Gaskell*. Women Writers. London: Macmillan, 1993.

Margaret in the final scene of *North and South* is interpreted as a woman who "exchanges

economic power and an independent position for a spiritual and moral authority" (95).
Steyvers, Mark, and Tom Griffiths. "Probabilistic Topic Models." *Latent Semantic Analysis: A Road to Meaning*, edited by T. Landauer, et al. Erlbaum, 2007. PDF file. 24 July 2013.
Stone, Donald D. *The Romantic Impulse in Victorian Fiction*. Harvard UP, 1980.
Stoneman, Patsy. *Elizabeth Gaskell*. Harvester, 1987.
    The author reviews the history of Gaskell criticisms, including psychoanalytic and Marxist, before launching her feminist reading of her works. According to the author, feminist criticism is the only approach to help critics to find a theme common to the novelist's works. *Ruth* is discussed in terms of imagery and dreams to show repressed female sexuality. She argues that they are all about women. Past criticisms on Gaskell are surveyed in the first chapter.
Storey, Graham, et al., editors. *The Letters of Charles Dickens*. Vol. 6-10, The Pilgrim Edition, Clarendon, 1988-98.
Sutherland, John. *Is Heathcliff a Murderer?: Puzzles in 19th-Century Fiction*. Oxford UP, 1996.
---. *Can Jane Eyre Be Happy?: More Puzzles in Classic Fiction*. Oxford UP, 1997.
---. *Who Betrays Elizabeth Bennet?: Further Puzzles in Classic Fiction*. Oxford UP, 1999.
    Short chapters on Ruth's place of degradation (*Ruth*) and Richard Hale's religious doubts (*North and South*) are inserted.
Tanner, J. E. "The Chronology and the Enigmatic End of *Lord Jim*." *Nineteenth-Century Fiction*, vol. 21, 1967, pp. 369-80.
Taylor, Dennis. "The Chronology of *Jude the Obscure*." *Thomas Hardy Journal*, vol. 12, 1996, pp. 65-68.
Thomson, David. *England in the Nineteenth Century: 1815-1914*. The Pelican History of England, vol. 8, Penguin, 1978.
Thomson, Patricia. *The Victorian Heroine: A Changing Ideal 1837-1873*. Oxford UP, 1956.
Thormählen, Marianne. *The Brontës and Religion*. Cambridge UP, 1999.
Tillotson, Kathleen. *Novels of the Eighteen-Forties*. Oxford UP, 1962.
"Topic Modeling." *Mallet*. UMASS Amherst. Web. 8 Jan. 2015.
Towheed, Shafquat. "The Chronology of Charlotte Brontë's *Villette*." *Brontë Society Transactions*, vol. 23, 1998, pp. 186-87.
Trevelyan, G. M. *English Social History: A Survey of Six Centuries Chaucer to Queen Victoria*. Penguin, 1967.
Trudgill, Eric. *Madonnas and Magdalens: The Origins and Development of Victorian Sexual Attitudes*. Heinemann, 1976.
Uffelman, Larry K. "Elizabeth Gaskell's *North and South*: The Novel in Progress." *The Gaskell Society Journal*, vol. 14, 2000, pp. 73-84.
    Through thorough comparison between Gaskell's original *Household Words* text of *North and South* and its final version of published form, the author researches into her true intention of revision to conclude that this novel should be read as a Bildungsroman (the story of Margaret's development) rather than as a condition-of-England novel. He uses the fact of *Margaret Hale* being Gaskell's intended original title as evidence to support his assertion.
Uglow, Jenny. *Elizabeth Gaskell: A Habit of Stories*. Faber and Faber, 1993.
    The tenth and most comprehensive biography of Gaskell published after her death. Uglow reviews Gaskell's life in chronological order, incorporating her readings of her major fiction, which are generally subjective. Uglow forms her view of Gaskell's life through her extensive readings of primary sources.
---. Introduction. *The Life of Charlotte Brontë*, by Elizabeth Gaskell, Everyman's Library, Dent,

1992, pp. xi-xxi.
Unsworth, Anna. *Elizabeth Gaskell: An Independent Woman*. Minerva Press, 1996.
Upham, Charles W. *Lectures on Witchcraft: Comprising a History of the Delusion in Salem in 1692*. Carter, Hendee and Babcock, 1831.
---. *Salem Witchcraft: With an Account of Salem Village and a History of Opinions on Witchcraft and Kindred Subjects*, 1867, Dover, 2000.
Vickers, Brian. *Shakespeare, Co-Author: A Historical Study of Five Collaborative Plays*. Oxford UP, 2004.
Waller, Ross D., ed. *Letters Addressed to Mrs Gaskell by Celebrated Contemporaries: Now in the Possession of the John Rylands Library*. Manchester UP, 1935.
Walze, Florence L. "The Life Chronology of *Dubliners*." *James Joyce Quarterly*, vol. 14, 1977, pp. 408-15.
Ward, A. W. Biographical Introduction. *Mary Barton: A Tale of Manchester Life*, vol. 1 of *The Works of Mrs. Gaskell*, Knutsford Edition, AMS, 1972, pp. xv-l.
   A compact and helpful account of Gaskell's life and her major works. The author's point is to stress that Gaskell is equal to Charlotte Brontë and George Eliot in her capacity of "understanding and reproducing the varieties of human character" (l).
---. Introduction. *The Works of Mrs. Gaskell*, vol. 1, Knutsford Edition, AMS, pp. li-lxxxi.
---. Introduction. *Ruth*, *The Works of Mrs. Gaskell*, vol. 3, AMS, 1972, pp. ix-xxxii.
---. Introduction. *Cousin Phillis*. *The Works of Mrs. Gaskell*, vol. 7, AMS, 1972, pp. xiii-xliii.
Warhol, Robyn R. *Gendered Interventions: Narrative Discourse in the Victorian Novel*. New Brunswick: Rutgers UP, 1989.
"Waugh, Evelyn." *The Oxford Dictionary of National Biography*. https://www.oxforddnb.com/.
Weingart, Scott B. "Topic Modeling and Network Analysis." 15 Nov. 2011. Web. 21 June 2014.
Wheeler, Michael. "The Sinner as Heroine: A Study of Mrs. Gaskell's *Ruth* and the Bible." *The Durham University Journal*, vol. 68, 1976, pp. 148-61.
   Focusing on the use of biblical quotations and references, the author reads the novel as a fable of sin and forgiveness. "The aim of this study," remarks the author, "is to examine Mrs Gaskell's depiction of her heroine's spiritual development, relating her handling of the subject to her Unitarian background, and to discuss her use of biblical quotations and references in the novel" (148).
---. *The Art of Allusion in Victorian Fiction*. Macmillan, 1979.
   The aim of this book is to point out that "the use of literary and biblical allusion" is "an important convention in Victorian fiction" (ix). Having explained the functions of allusion in a literary text in the first two chapters, the author demonstrates his readings of eight Victorian novels—*Jane Eyre*, *Mary Barton*, *Hard Times*, *Middlemarch*, *The Egoist*, *Robert Elsmere*, *The Return of the Native*, and *Tess of the d'Urbervilles*. According to his interpretation of *Mary Barton*, the difference of education and outlook between Jem Wilson, a Manchester artisan, and Harry Carson, a master and his rival in winning Mary's heart, is underlined by Gaskell's contrastive references to Burns and Shakespeare (48); the piece of the valentine inscribed with Samuel Bamford's poem is the reply of John Barton, a leading Trade Unionist, to the other piece of paper on which Harry Carson scribbled a caricature from Shakespeare (50). In addition, Wheeler traces the different understandings of the Bible between John Barton and John Carson, Harry's father, to emphasise Gaskell's use of biblical references as a means of illuminating these contrasts. He concludes his assertion by stating "Elizabeth Gaskell does succeed in accommodating parable within her social realism through allusion, bringing the Condition

of England Question home to her readers as a crucial test case, Dives versus Lazarus, to which Christian ethics should be applied" (60).

Whitfield, A. Stanton. *Mrs. Gaskell: Her Life and Work*. George Routledge & Sons, 1929.

The second biography of Gaskell published after her death, following E. H. Chadwick's.

Williams, Raymond. *Culture and Society 1780-1950*. Penguin, 1979.

Six industrial novels—*Mary Barton*, *North and South*, *Hard Times*, *Sybil*, *Alton Locke*, and *Felix Holt*–are discussed in Chapter 5. The author's conclusion is that recognition of social evil is balanced by the fear of becoming involved, and that sympathy is transformed into withdrawal (119).

Wise, Thomas James, and John Alexander Symington, eds. *The Brontës: Their Lives, Friendships, and Correspondence*. 2 vols, 1933, Porcupine, 1980.

Wright, Edgar. *Mrs. Gaskell: The Basis for Reassessment*. Oxford UP, 1965.

He reads the theme of *North and South* not as a reconciliation between the two cultures but as a better understanding of the North.

---. Introduction. *Mary Barton: A Tale of Manchester Life*, by Elizabeth Gaskell, World's Classics, Oxford UP, 1987, pp. vii-xxiii.

Wright, Terence. *Elizabeth Gaskell 'We Are Not Angels': Realism, Gender, Values*. London: Macmillan, 1995.

Through "an expansive, open and comparatively unjudgemental" approach, the author attempts to show Gaskell's skilful treatment of "love, death and the meaning of life" (xiii). His subtitle "We are not angels" is taken from the words of the *Wives and Daughters*'s heroine Molly Gibson to imply imperfections of human beings and the novelist's concern with women. In Introduction, the author surveys Gaskell's features as a poetic realist, referring to her main characters as well as her own life, then, examines her major works, including short fiction, chiefly from biographical and historical perspective in the subsequent chapters, and finally summarizes "her values, her beliefs about women and her status as an artist" (203) in his Conclusion. One of the characteristics of his analysis is the suggestion of Wordsworth's influence on Gaskell, who describes common things and ordinary lives, believing the power of nature (203). He concludes his assertion by stating that "we have no need to apologise for ranking her with the foremost writers of her age" (212). Insightful comments are scattered everywhere in his discussion of *Ruth*, but fundamentally impressionistic.

Yamawaki, Yuriko. *Erizabesu Gyasukeru Kenkyu* (A Study of Elizabeth Gaskell). Hokuseido, 1976.

A pioneer study of Gaskell in Japan, including the survey of her life and analysis of her major works. Emphasis is placed on re-estimation of Gaskell and her fiction; therefore, critics' favourable comments are quoted often.

Yarrow, P. J. "The Chronology of *Cranford*." *The Gaskell Society Journal*, vol. 1, 1987, pp. 27-29.

In response to three critics' conflicting statements on *Cranford*'s chronology, the author offers his own.

Young, G. M., editor. *Early Victorian England 1830-1865*. 2 vols., 1934, Oxford UP, 1988.

INDEX

A

AntConc 147, 158, 160, 162, 185, 221

author construct 7, 14, 15, 17, 20, 30, 32, 34, 35, 36, 37, 48, 51, 72, 84, 98, 114, 128, 133, 135, 141, 144, 145, 147, 162, 167, 185, 221

authorial intention 16, 19, 21, 30, 32, 39, 40, 90

authorial meaning 14, 15, 16, 17, 18, 19, 20, 21, 22, 24, 25, 29, 30, 31, 33, 34, 36, 37, 39, 40, 41, 42, 43, 44, 45, 46, 47, 48, 49, 50, 58, 63, 72, 76, 85, 87, 90, 91, 113, 123, 135, 143, 144, 162, 187, 188, 198, 219, 221, 222, 223

B

Barthes, Roland 16, 21, 22, 23, 33, 48

Bayesian 150, 151

Bible 59, 77, 119, 130, 131, 132, 146, 163, 164, 178, 179, 185, 233, 248, 253

Booth, Wayne C. 35, 50, 319

Boyle, Nicholas 146

C

Catholic 146, 264, 319

Christ 59, 100, 104, 105, 146, 209, 233, 311

Christian 7, 20, 45, 59, 62, 72, 83, 84, 90, 99, 100, 103, 110, 128, 131, 132, 145, 146, 147, 153, 162, 163, 170, 172, 173, 179, 182, 183, 184, 185, 186, 187, 188, 192, 196, 198, 200, 201, 203, 204, 208, 209, 210, 212, 213, 216, 217, 218, 219, 220, 221, 222, 245, 270, 281, 290, 296, 302, 303, 307, 308, 310, 317

chronology 7, 16, 19, 21, 27, 37, 40, 41, 42, 43, 44, 49, 52, 53, 54, 55, 57, 58, 59, 89, 91, 92, 93, 94, 95, 96, 114, 115, 116, 187, 188, 211, 226, 235, 243, 257, 320, 321, 323, 325, 326, 328, 329, 330, 334

corpus 145, 146, 147, 150, 163, 173, 295

Cousin Phillis 7, 12, 14, 188, 223, 322, 324, 327

Cranford 7, 14, 44, 223, 327, 328

criticism 15, 16, 19, 20, 21, 22, 23, 24, 25, 26, 27, 29, 33, 34, 35, 38, 39, 40, 41, 43, 46, 48, 49, 74, 77, 90, 104, 110, 120, 129, 137, 154, 162, 196, 214, 229, 254, 308, 309, 310, 311, 323, 331, 332

E

Eagleton, Terry 16, 17, 21, 22, 23, 24, 25, 26, 27, 28, 31, 32, 33, 38, 39, 40, 44, 45, 46, 47, 48, 49, 50

Easson, Angus 40, 41, 51, 52, 53, 58, 59, 63, 66, 68, 80, 84, 85, 87, 89, 90, 91, 92, 93, 95, 100, 101, 102, 104, 105, 106, 109, 110, 111, 113, 114, 115, 118, 124, 135, 142, 143, 162, 163, 169, 170, 172, 191, 209

Eliot, T. S. 146

Endo, Shusaku 146

F

faith 39, 75, 100, 130, 132, 178, 179, 180, 182, 186, 198, 208, 216, 218, 219, 221, 281

form 33, 39, 42, 43, 46, 47, 49, 51, 52, 83, 90, 92, 103, 109, 111, 113, 130, 142, 153, 171, 217, 219, 284, 286, 312, 321, 322, 324, 331, 332

Frye, Northrop 49

G

Gadamer, Hans-Georg 27, 28, 29, 30

Gaskell construct 7, 17, 19, 20, 70, 83, 87, 113, 114, 120, 122, 124, 125, 128, 135, 139, 140, 143, 144, 147, 160, 162, 163, 170, 172, 173, 182, 184, 185, 186, 191, 192, 193, 194, 196, 198, 199, 201, 203, 204, 205, 207, 208, 209, 210, 211, 212, 215, 219, 220, 221, 222

God 16, 21, 23, 33, 59, 60, 61, 62, 68, 70, 73, 77, 81, 83, 102, 103, 104, 110, 117, 124, 130, 131, 132, 136, 146, 149, 164, 165, 167, 173, 179, 180, 183, 184, 186, 187, 195, 199, 201, 202, 203, 204, 212, 213, 217, 218, 219, 221, 222, 227, 239, 273, 274, 276, 277, 283, 290, 295, 296, 306, 310, 311, 313, 314, 315, 316, 317

H

Hirsch, E. D. Jr. 14, 16, 21, 22, 23, 24, 25, 26, 27, 28, 29, 30, 31, 32, 33, 34, 35, 36, 37, 38, 39, 40, 43, 45, 46, 47, 48, 49, 50, 85, 91, 144
hermeneutic 16, 19, 22, 24, 32, 37, 38, 39, 46
hermeneutist 7, 14, 22, 26, 34, 35, 48, 162, 185
humble 101, 119, 134, 140, 141, 144, 162, 188, 204, 214, 288, 289, 290, 303, 304, 313, 314, 316
humility 138, 196, 200, 217, 303, 307

I

intentional fallacy 39, 90
intentionalist 7, 14, 15, 16, 17, 19, 22, 30, 31, 33, 34, 84, 162, 185
interpretation 7, 8, 14, 15, 16, 18, 19, 20, 21, 22, 23, 24, 25, 26, 28, 29, 30, 31, 32, 33, 34, 35, 36, 37, 38, 39, 40, 43, 45, 46, 47, 48, 49, 50, 52, 82, 84, 91, 106, 111, 113, 137, 143, 144, 145, 147, 172, 173, 188, 205, 208, 220, 222, 316, 319, 320, 323, 324, 331, 333
Irwin, William 14, 15, 16, 17, 22, 23, 25, 27, 28, 29, 30, 32, 34, 35, 36, 37, 38, 222

K

Kroeber, Karl 15, 16, 19, 21, 33, 37, 40, 42, 43, 44, 45, 47, 48, 49, 50

M

MALLET 147, 150, 151, 154, 155, 158, 160, 162, 163, 185, 221
Mather, Cotton 196, 207, 217, 259, 260, 265, 282, 298, 307, 308, 309, 310, 311
Miura, Ayako 146
modest 75, 136, 154, 173, 191, 203, 309
moral 16, 19, 36, 50, 69, 70, 75, 90, 91, 100, 103, 104, 109, 110, 128, 130, 134, 138, 147, 165, 167, 168, 173, 174, 175, 176, 177, 178, 179, 181, 182, 184, 185, 186, 210, 219, 222, 235, 270, 276, 279, 288, 289, 307, 308, 312, 313, 325, 332

N

narrator 16, 18, 41, 44, 52, 53, 54, 55, 57, 58, 60, 62, 69, 72, 73, 74, 75, 76, 79, 82, 83, 85, 91, 92, 93, 94, 95, 97, 99, 102, 109, 115, 116, 130, 131, 135, 140, 142, 164, 165, 168, 169, 171, 172, 174, 175, 176, 177, 179, 185, 188, 192, 194, 199, 206, 208, 214, 219, 222, 226, 260
novella 187, 189, 190, 191, 194, 208

O

OED 205

P

perseverance 45, 172, 188

R

reader 7, 16, 17, 18, 21, 23, 28, 31, 32, 33, 34, 35, 39, 41, 42, 47, 48, 68, 73, 74, 76, 82, 86, 89, 90, 100, 103, 106, 107, 108, 109, 111, 113, 115, 120, 125, 139, 144, 146, 168, 171, 199, 200, 207, 209, 215, 334
religion 105, 108, 131, 145, 146, 147, 149, 165, 167, 168, 173, 174, 175, 176, 177, 178, 179, 181, 182, 184, 185, 186, 191, 274, 276, 288, 296, 310, 311, 312, 317, 322

S

Sanger, C. P. 15, 16, 19, 21, 22, 37, 40, 41, 42, 44, 45, 47, 48, 49, 321, 323, 330
scripture 24, 163, 202, 203, 316
Sharps, J. G. 12, 52, 59, 67, 85, 89, 91, 92, 101, 102, 103, 120, 124, 125, 191, 192, 214
Shelston, Alan 52, 64, 66, 67, 84, 89, 90, 91, 92, 93, 102, 103, 105, 110, 169, 170
sincerity 107, 109, 152, 155, 199, 203, 204, 283, 313
statistical 7, 14, 15, 16, 17, 18, 19, 20, 32, 37, 45, 47, 48, 49, 50, 51, 52, 58, 84, 85, 92, 113, 120, 143, 144, 145, 148, 149, 150, 162, 172, 185, 187, 188, 189, 210, 221, 223
statistics 16, 17, 19, 21, 27, 34, 37, 43, 47, 48,

49, 84, 151, 194, 326
structure 7, 14, 15, 16, 17, 18, 19, 20, 26, 27, 33, 35, 38, 39, 40, 41, 42, 44, 46, 47, 51, 52, 63, 79, 84, 85, 86, 90, 91, 98, 99, 102, 103, 110, 113, 114, 133, 143, 144, 145, 149, 150, 162, 185, 210, 211, 212, 219, 221, 222, 223, 325, 326, 327
stylistic 26, 44, 145, 146, 147, 173
stylometric 19
stylometry 48, 148
Sutherland, John 12, 41, 44
Sylvia's Lovers 7, 14, 73, 86, 87, 222, 223, 322

T

theme 16, 19, 21, 26, 40, 48, 52, 65, 86, 90, 91, 92, 97, 101, 113, 144, 145, 147, 149, 169, 173, 187, 188, 191, 212, 216, 221, 222, 321, 323, 325, 328, 331, 332, 334
theology 307, 313
Tillotson, Kathleen 35, 52, 53, 63, 64, 84, 323
topic model 147, 148, 149, 151, 164
topic-modelling 20, 145, 147, 148, 149, 150, 151, 155, 160, 162, 163, 165, 166, 168, 172, 173, 176, 178, 179, 181, 182, 184, 185, 186, 221

U

Uglow, Jenny 51, 52, 53, 59, 64, 66, 67, 82, 85, 89, 90, 92, 96, 100, 104, 106, 110, 113, 124, 125, 134, 136, 142, 143, 169, 170, 172, 187, 191, 205, 323, 332
Unitarian 102, 192, 333
Upham, Charles W. 12, 45, 187, 188, 189, 190, 191, 192, 193, 194, 195, 196, 198, 199, 200, 202, 203, 204, 205, 208, 209, 210, 219, 283, 284, 285, 290, 291, 292, 302, 303, 305, 307, 308, 309, 310, 311, 312, 313, 317, 318, 333
urauthor 7, 14, 32, 34, 35, 36, 37, 38, 52, 135, 169, 180, 189, 192, 193, 196, 198, 200, 201, 203, 205, 207, 210, 219, 221
urinterpretation 23, 25, 34, 35, 36, 37, 38, 114

V

validity 15, 19, 20, 22, 26, 29, 32, 35, 37, 47, 86, 89, 147, 158, 160, 212

W

Ward, A.W. 51, 52, 54, 58, 91, 100, 118, 120, 125, 187, 203, 220
Waugh, Evelyn 146
Wives and Daughters 7, 13, 14, 73, 86, 87, 222, 223, 325, 327, 334

著者紹介・略歴

About the Author

Tatsuhiro OHNO, Professor of English in the Faculty of Letters at Rissho University in Tokyo, Japan, has devoted over 40 years to the study of Elizabeth Gaskell (1810–65) and English literature, with previous teaching roles at Ehime University and Kumamoto University. From 2020 to 2024, he served as the 6th President of the Gaskell Society of Japan. Born in Kumamoto in 1958, he was educated at Kyushu University, the University of Bristol, and the University of Birmingham. His research interests centre on structural analysis in fiction, pursuing absolute interpretations, and scriptural analysis, exploring how characters' thoughts and actions reflect the divine Plan of Salvation. His notable publications include the first Japanese translation of *Sylvia's Lovers* by Elizabeth Gaskell (Sairyusha, 1997), *The Life of Elizabeth Gaskell in Photographs* (Osaka Kyoiku Tosho, 2012), and *Literature as Theology: The Parable of the Prodigal Son in the Fiction of Elizabeth Gaskell* (Sairyusha, 2020), along with monographs on the Brontë sisters, George Eliot, and Jane Austen. E-Mail: eph0429@hotmail.com.

立正大学文学部学術叢書10

LITERATURE AS SCIENCE:
A Statistical Analysis of the Structures of the Works of Elizabeth Gaskell in Quest of the Absolute Interpretations 1848-59

科学としての文学：統計的構造分析によるエリザベス・ギャスケル作品の絶対解釈探求 1848-59

2025年3月31日　初版発行

著　者	Tatsuhiro OHNO　大野龍浩（おおの たつひろ）
発行者	石川一郎
発　行	公益財団法人 角川文化振興財団 埼玉県所沢市東所沢和田 3-31-3　〒359-0023 ところざわサクラタウン角川武蔵野ミュージアム 電話 04-2003-8700 https://www.kadokawa-zaidan.or.jp/
発　売	株式会社KADOKAWA 東京都千代田区富士見2-13-3　〒102-8177 電話 0570-002-301（ナビダイヤル） 受付時間11時〜13時 / 14時〜17時（土日祝日を除く） https://www.kadokawa.co.jp/
印　刷	株式会社暁印刷
製　本	株式会社暁印刷
装　丁	可野佑佳
DTP組版	星島正明

本書の無断複製（コピー、スキャン、デジタル化等）並びに無断複製物の譲渡及び配信は、著作権法上での例外を除き禁じられています。
また、本書を代行業者などの第三者に依頼して複製する行為は、たとえ個人や家庭内での利用であっても一切認められておりません。
落丁・乱丁本は、送料小社負担にて、お取り替えいたします。
下記KADOKAWA購入窓口までご連絡ください。
（古書店で購入したものについては、お取り替えできません。）
電話 0570-002-008（土日祝日を除く 10時〜13時 / 14時〜17時）

© 学校法人立正大学学園、大野龍浩 2025 Printed in Japan
ISBN978-4-04-884643-1 C0397

刊行のことば

　立正大学文学部は1924（大正13）年に荏原郡大崎村谷山ヶ丘の地（現在の品川キャンパス）で産声をあげた。2014（平成26）年は、その創設から数えて90年目の年にあたる。本学文学部は日本の私立大学の中でも有数の輝かしい歴史と伝統を誇る学部なのだ。

　本学文学部は創設以来、幾多の時代の荒波に揉まれながらも着実な発展を遂げてきた。学術研究の領域においては人文科学系に関する諸事象や諸問題を深く掘り下げ、現実に確固たる軸足を置きつつも未来への眼差しに寄り添った観点から、それらを根源的かつ現実的に捉えた独創性に富む研究を展開し、さらに知的公共財としてその多様な成果の積極的な公表と普及に努め、もって学術文化の発展に寄与してきたのである。

　谷山ヶ丘での長い歴史の中で紡がれてきた伝統の重みを真摯に受け継ぎながらも、文学部は創設90周年という大きな節目を迎えたことを記念し、より広く学術の振興を図るとともに浩瀚な知の創成と継承に裨益することを目的として『立正大学文学部学術叢書』の刊行を開始した次第である。

　この叢書の刊行を契機に、文学部はその成果を単に激動のグローバル化時代を牽引する知的原動力にとどめるだけではなく、豊かな明日のサステナブルな社会の構築にも直結させることで教育および学術研究機関としてのひとつの使命を果たしてゆきたい。

　　2015年3月　　　　　　　　立正大学文学部長　　齊　藤　　昇